The Silent Land

David Dunham

Matador
9 Priory Business Park,
Wistow Road, Kibworth Beauchamp,
Leicestershire. LE8 0RX
Tel: (+44) 116 279 2299
Fax: (+44) 116 279 2277
Email: books@troubador.co.uk
Web: www.troubador.co.uk/matador

ISBN 978 1785892 547

British Library Cataloguing in Publication Data.
A catalogue record for this book is available from the British Library.

Printed and bound by CPI Group (UK) Ltd, Croydon, CR0 4YY
Typeset in 11pt Aldine by Troubador Publishing Ltd, Leicester, UK

Matador is an imprint of Troubador Publishing Ltd

FSC
www.fsc.org
MIX
Paper from responsible sources
FSC® C013604

For Melissa and Judith

ONE

31 December, 1903, Cambridgeshire, England

Rebecca Lawrence reached a count of sixty in her head and slid her finger into the back pages of her mother's diary. Mistaking the diary for a book granted her innocence the first time she'd opened it. She had no argument for innocence now. She checked her mother remained asleep and began to read.

November 29

I deceived my brother today. He'll receive the same lie that Emily did. Whatever pity they would have given me can be shared among others this Christmas. I have enough of my own. There are mornings I wake and for a moment I am free, and then the unhappy truths of life rise up and the time that had seemed endless is taken from me. I'll not allow this disease to reduce me to misery in Rebecca's presence, although I wish I had the courage to bring this trial to an end myself; to end her suffering which I fear is greater than mine. It seems, however, I have been stripped of courage also.

Rebecca turned the page. It was blank. She heard the front door close and her father ask Elsie to bring up a pot of tea. Rebecca put the diary back on the bed and sat still, waiting. Her mother opened her eyes.

'You haven't moved,' she said, smiling weakly.

Rebecca leaned forward. 'I didn't want to leave you. Not until Papa returned.'

'You'll need to leave me this evening, remember?'

'I'd prefer to be here with you.'

'No, you're attending the dance, just as we agreed. Poor Tilly will be lost without you and Mrs Pugh would have already prepared your room.'

Rebecca watched her mother wince as she pushed herself up on to the pillows and felt a rush of guilt for troubling her. She glanced at the bed, suddenly doubting she had returned the diary to its correct place.

There were footsteps on the stairs. Rebecca's mother put her diary under the quilt. She looked Rebecca in the eye and said, 'Everyone is allowed a secret. This is mine, and now it's also yours. Your father need not know about it. Agreed?'

The footsteps came closer. Rebecca's father stepped into the room and smiled.

'You'd be wise to rest a while, Rebecca,' he said, putting down his medicine bag. 'You've a long night of dancing ahead of you.'

'She's considering changing her mind,' said her mother.

'Then she will have to re-consider, won't she?'

Rebecca looked away from her parents and stared at the firelight, searching her mind for an excuse. She wondered if snow had begun to fall. The walk into the village would be too dangerous in snow.

'Come and sit by me for a moment.'

Rebecca did as her mother requested, perching herself on the edge of the bed. Her father sat down next to her.

'You'll disappoint George if you stay at home,' he said, taking Rebecca's hand.

'George?'

'Turner. I understand he's keen to dance with you.'

Rebecca thought of George Turner's fat hands touching her waist and turned to her mother for help. Nothing in her expression gave Rebecca any hope of being excused.

'Your father and I want you to be with your friends tonight,' she said. 'We want you to forget how I am, even for a few hours. Can you try? Please, for me.'

Rebecca nodded reluctantly.

'Perhaps we'll go for a ride in the morning.'

'You really think you're strong enough?'

'Just so long as you promise to forget about me tonight, then I promise I'll attempt riding tomorrow.'

Rebecca kissed her mother on the forehead and stood up. She wanted to draw out the truth about how her aunt and uncle had been deceived. But as she opened her mouth to speak, her mother's eyes began to close.

'Be kind to George, Rebecca,' she said. 'Don't give him false hope, though. That wouldn't be fair.'

Rebecca was escorted to the dance by her father. It was his duty as parish doctor, he said, to make an appearance.

'I'll stay an hour and leave discreetly,' he said. 'I expect most folk will have drunk too much ale to notice.'

The paralysing cold had been shut out of the village hall. The fireplaces were ablaze, and though there were no chairs, there were hay bales against the walls. It seemed to Rebecca that with the exception of her mother, she was in the company of every man and woman in Welney. The piano fallboard was raised and an accordion, drum, and fiddle set in place, but the musicians were yet to begin playing. They were gathered by a cart where Tilly's mother was ladling drink into mugs. She caught Rebecca's eye and winked.

'He's here.'

Rebecca turned. Tilly smiled at her, eager and sweet.

'Who's here?'

'Tom Guest,' said Tilly. 'He arrived home today. George said he plans to stay.'

'You've spoken to George Turner?'

Tilly nodded. 'Tom and he are friends. That means you *have* to dance with George. You will, won't you? Please say you will or Tom will never dance with me.'

Rebecca glanced towards the cart, pretending to ignore what Tilly had said. 'I should say hello to your mother.'

Tilly sighed. 'If you must. But we can't stand about too long. Tom and George are over there.' Rebecca resisted looking away and kept walking. Mrs Pugh opened her arms and embraced her.

'Is your mother here?' said Mrs Pugh. 'I'm desperate for her to try my mulled wine.'

'Mama's resting. She's been a little more tired than usual today.'

Mrs Pugh touched Rebecca's arm. 'I'll keep you a serving to take home. Your mother will soon have colour in her cheeks.'

'Tom glanced at me, Mama,' said Tilly. 'Ever so coy he was. Should I approach him?'

Mrs Pugh frowned. She filled two mugs and passed them to Rebecca and Tilly. 'If a man lacks the courage to approach a young lady then his character is flawed. When you wish to attract a man's attention, pay him no attention whatsoever. Strangely, they seem to thrive on this.'

'But what if Tom's attention is taken by someone else?'

'Tilly, dear, every other lady here is either years away from coming of age, or is married. Unless Tom Guest intends to anger a husband or father, there are only two ladies he can attempt to charm tonight. Rebecca, or you.'

'Then it must be me as George is in love with Rebecca.'

Rebecca raised her eyebrows. 'In love?'

'Of sorts. At least, he's talked of finding a wife. He wants to take her to America.'

'Why would he want to leave the village for America?'

'Excitement, fortune. I'd leave if Tom invited me.'

Mrs Pugh scoffed. 'You most certainly would not. Your home is here in the Fens, just as Rebecca's is.'

Tilly pulled a face. 'Don't say that to George, Rebecca, it might upset him. He might leave early and take Tom with him.'

The young men of the parish approached Rebecca one by one after her father departed. Whenever she was asked about her mother's health she excused herself from the conversation or pretended she could hear nothing above the music. Midnight approached and she had danced with every man, save for George. She caught sight of him running his finger round the inside of his collar as his friends found partners to share the turn of the year with. However uncomfortable she felt at giving false hope, she could not bear to allow George's discomfort to continue. She wove her way through the crowd and tapped his shoulder.

'We seem to be the only ones not dancing,' she said.

George's eyes widened. 'Yes, it seems that way.'

Rebecca said nothing. She braced herself for George's request for a dance.

'How is your mother?'

'I adore this one,' said Rebecca quickly. 'Shall we?'

No sooner had George led Rebecca once round the dancing circle, the music stopped. The fiddle player stared at his pocket watch and began to count down from ten. The count reached five and George's hands remained on Rebecca's hips.

'Four.'

Rebecca glanced down. George's boots, muddied and wide, moved closer to hers.

'Three, two, one!'

Rebecca looked up. George's lips parted.

'Happy New Year!' shouted everyone together.

Rebecca stared at George, waiting for him to find the courage to kiss her. He stared back, saying nothing. As the silence dragged, Rebecca went up on her tiptoes and kissing him on the cheek, said, 'Happy New Year, George.'

George's face lit up. 'And you, Miss Lawrence. Happy New Year.'

Rebecca woke to the familiar feeling of time pressing against her. She pulled back the quilt and got dressed. A note had been pushed under the door. It was from Mrs Pugh.

There's a tin of biscuits on the hall table. I made them extra thick for your father. Don't wait for us to appear.

Rebecca crept downstairs, picking up the tin before she left The Three Tuns by the back door. As she came round the front, a window above opened.

'Fancy your first kiss being with George,' said Tilly smiling. 'You *will* have to sail to America with him now.'

Rebecca frowned. 'That was not a kiss, not a real one, and I'm most definitely not sailing to America with George Turner, or anyone else for that matter.'

Tilly laughed. 'If you insist… Mrs Turner.'

'I am *not* marrying George Turner, Tilly Pugh.'

Tilly laughed again. 'I'm merely teasing. Anyhow, no man will take you away from Welney while I'm living here.'

'Even if you marry Tom?'

'Even *when* I'm married to Tom. He'll propose by the year's end, I'm convinced of it.'

'I think you're still feeling the effects of the wine.'

'Perhaps, or it could be love. You will be my bridesmaid, won't you?'

'Only if you stop talking about George.'

'Agreed.'

'Good, and call this afternoon. Mama will want to talk to you about last night. I'll leave the part about Tom for you to tell.'

'And I'll leave the part about George for you.'

Rebecca scowled. Tilly poked her tongue out at her, waved and closed the window.

The momentary relief of Tilly's good humour gave way and reality hit Rebecca hard. It seemed that while others were waking with hope at what the new year could bring, she could not see beyond her mother's illness. For the present she knew she had to prepare for an interrogation about her evening. Questions from her mother about Tilly and George were inevitable. She resolved to be as truthful as she could be, but reveal nothing of the kiss. It was, after all, not a real kiss.

She left the riverbank and turned down the path that led to River Cottage. At the garden gate she glanced up and wondered if Elsie had been given the morning off as there was no smoke rising from the chimney. She stepped into the hall expecting to find her father carrying a coal bucket. The house was only a little warmer than outside. Rebecca paused at the foot of the staircase, anticipating a sound. Even the grandfather clock was silent.

'Hello?' She waited for a reply. None came and she climbed the stairs. As she reached the landing, she heard the rocking chair by her parents' bed being pushed back. Her father had fallen asleep in it again, she thought. He opened the door halfway.

Rebecca cleared her throat. 'Good morning, Papa. I'm sorry I woke you.'

'Wait in your room, please.'

'Is Mama still asleep?'

'Please.'

'Are you unwell?'

'I'll be with you shortly.'

Rebecca stepped across the landing. The door began to close. 'Papa, what's the matter?'

'Give me a few minutes.'

Rebecca put her foot in the doorway. 'Papa, tell me.'

The door began to open again. Even in the dim light Rebecca could see that her father's eyes were red and swollen.

'Wait in your room.'

Rebecca's lip began to quiver. 'I want to see Mama.'

'Please.'

'Mama?'

'Rebecca, stop this.'

'Mama?'

'Rebecca, please! She's dead… your mother's dead.'

Rebecca dropped the tin. She pushed past her father, falling to her knees at the bedside. Her father's arms came round her. She turned and put her head against his chest, tightening her grip even as her own chest ached with the strain of weeping.

'She's at peace now, Rebecca. Her suffering is over.'

The coffin was placed in the morning-room. The clocks remained stopped, and the curtains stayed closed. The vicar came and said a prayer over Rebecca's mother, thanking God for taking her to heaven while she slept. He passed Tilly and Mrs Pugh on his return to the riverbank. Tilly struggled to talk as she hugged Rebecca, managing only to say she understood her grief. News of the death spread through the parish. Many of the church congregation called. They looked into the coffin, offered their condolences and went on their way. Rebecca sat with her mother throughout the procession of sympathy. On the third day of mourning her father encouraged her to leave the house. She rode for hours across the Fens, all the while fighting the thought of her mother being lowered into a hole and covered with earth. Snow began to fall. Rebecca felt mocked by its lateness. Had it fallen when she'd wanted it to she would have been at her mother's bedside as she faded, not in the hall, dancing and drinking. She turned for home. As she passed the church she saw two men with shovels enter the graveyard. They stopped and looked back to the far gate. Striding towards them was Rebecca's father. He shouted to them and pointed to a corner of the graveyard. Rebecca wondered if he had chosen the burial spot, or was acting upon instruction.

'…I hope you can take comfort in that.'

Rebecca looked down. 'Comfort in what?'

'In your mother's strength,' said Mrs Pugh. 'She was tremendously courageous. Just as you are.'

I wish I had the courage to bring this trial to an end myself.

The sound of shovels hitting the frozen ground carried across the graveyard. Rebecca stared at her father, certain her memory was playing a trick on her. It occurred to her the house was empty. She could search for the diary without being disturbed. Her father's attention shifted to a woman in black standing at the gate. Even from a distance Rebecca recognised her from a photograph.

He'll receive the same lie that Emily did.

'Do you know her?' asked Mrs Pugh.

'I know who she is, but I wouldn't say I know her.'

'Should I introduce myself?'

'No, not now. Leave them be for a while.'

'If you wish.'

'I should go. Mama's on her own.'

Rebecca stepped under the porch and hesitated. The diary was her mother's secret. To search for it would be a betrayal of trust.

I'll not allow this disease to reduce me to misery in Rebecca's presence.

Rebecca glanced behind her. There was no-one in sight. She breathed in, checked the riverbank again, and went inside.

TWO

Ten months later

Rebecca was promised the finest tea in England.

'It'll surpass anything you've had in Ely,' said her father. 'Your uncle will want to impress you on your first visit to London.'

A man in the corner of the compartment lowered his newspaper and glanced at Rebecca. She turned quickly to the window, wishing she had brought her own newspaper to hide behind, or that the man left at the next station, or her father suddenly changed his mind about moving and realised that living close to his sister would not be a cure for grief. A whistle was blown. Rebecca thought of the home she was being taken away from, and the flat lands of the Fens, and was certain she would burst into tears. A stranger would soon be in her room, admiring the garden, the weeping elm and the riverbank, claiming it all as their own.

'Don't cry,' she said to herself as they left the station behind. 'Not in front of Papa.'

The locomotive puffed through countryside and into London's belly of coal pyramids and dirty terraces. It was Monday, which meant wash day. Rebecca could see women working in backyards no larger than a stable. Some were removing clothes and grey sheets from short lines, others were carrying baskets. Even at forty miles per hour the square box houses did not change in size, each was as small as the next. Rebecca could not understand how a family managed to fit into such a cramped space. Her father closed his book and leaned towards her.

'Did you know, the approach lines to St Pancras were built on a graveyard?' he said.

Rebecca shook her head.

'I also read that underneath the station is a warehouse for a brewery. Imagine all that beer under the tracks.'

Rebecca did not trouble her imagination. She was certain Tilly could imagine a warehouse of beer, but then she had lived above The Three Tuns most of her life. Tilly would be at home now, she thought, waiting for the farm workers to make their way across the Fens for beer and card games by the fire.

The train began to slow on the graveyard lines. The landscape changed to one of wagons, sheds and railwaymen with blackened faces.

'We're about to pass under the largest single span arch in the country.'

'The largest?' said Rebecca, not really caring.

'That's what your uncle said in his letter, and there's very little he doesn't know.'

A tunnel of iron and glass had a roof as high as a cathedral nave. It seemed to Rebecca there would be no end to the station and it would continue into Piccadilly Circus or Leicester Square or one of the other famous places she had read about.

Passengers filled the corridor, shuffling their way outside. Rebecca turned back to the window and watched young boys weave luggage trolleys between mail carts and people. A guard put his pocket watch away and marched along the platform. As he passed by, Rebecca noticed a man staring at her. A pair of spectacles sat on the bridge of his nose and he was holding a cane. He lifted his hat and lowered it. His black, oiled hair was parted in the middle.

'Wave to your uncle, Rebecca.'

Rebecca raised her hand and followed her father off the train. Her uncle stepped forward. 'James, wonderful to see you,' he said.

'And you, Henry.'

'Hello, Rebecca. Welcome to London.'

'I didn't mean to ignore you just now,' she said. 'I was just a little dazed.'

'I'm no different after a long journey, and *that's* travelling in first-class.'

Rebecca's father cleared his throat. 'Yes, well, I didn't intend this to be so rushed.'

'Just so long as you rest before you resume work.'

'I'll try to.'

'Good. Well, shall we leave? I'm famished.'

Henry took the lead towards a line of carriages. His need for a cane, Rebecca decided, was to swing it back and forth at his side as he showed no sign of a limp. She moved closer, but still had to strain to hear him above the noise of doors slamming and locomotives coming and going.

'The hotel I've booked for tea is not too far away,' he said. 'Famous writers apparently hide in the corners, making notes on people's behaviour and creating plots.'

'Where to, sir?' asked a coachman, hunched up in his seat.

'The Langham. After you, Rebecca. Your brief tour of London is about to begin.'

The carriage joined the queue for a ramp. Something about entering a great city suddenly unsettled Rebecca and she gripped the edge of the seat. On the road below, she could see a carriage that moved without horses. It was more than double the length and height of theirs and had exposed seating on a second level reached by a spiral staircase.

'Look back to the station, Rebecca, and you'll see why it's the most striking in Europe.'

Rebecca wanted to ask instead how the magic carriage moved. She leaned across her father and saw a mass of red bricks decorated with turrets and spires, and with a clock tower that touched the clouds. Her father was correct. No railway station in Europe, or the entire world, could be as impressive as St Pancras was.

'The front of the station is actually a hotel,' said Henry. 'The Midland Grand Hotel. A railway company built it.'

Rebecca strained her neck a little more. 'It doesn't seem to end. It must have hundreds of rooms.'

'I'd say at least three hundred. Perhaps you'll stay there one day. What do you say, James?'

'One day, perhaps.'

The hotel passed out of sight. The carriage shuddered, causing Rebecca to fall back.

'Sorry, I should have warned you,' said Henry. 'You'll soon adjust.'

Rebecca sat up straight again. She held on to the seat until the carriage turned into a street that was broad and curved, and lined with shops. Most of the ladies on the pavement had companions, though some were alone and reading books as they walked.

'This is Regent Street,' said Henry. 'I could stroll up and down here for hours and not lose interest.' Henry pointed to a shop. 'That's Airey and Wheeler, the court tailor, and then down that arcade is where ladies go for their gloves from Paris. If we had more time I would have taken you to the Café Royal. It was one of Oscar Wilde's haunts.'

'Do you go there?' asked Rebecca.

'If I'm close by. I have a few places, including my club.'

Rebecca considered asking Henry what he meant by 'my club'. He said it so matter-of-factly, as if everyone had one, that she decided to remain silent and instead gazed out of the window, wondering if her mother had ever walked along Regent Street or been with Henry to the Café Royal, and if she had met Oscar Wilde.

'Only a few people know this,' said Henry, 'but a few months ago I happened to be in a shop at the top of Regent Street buying a gift when the King entered. I was leaving and had to step aside he was so large. He smiled and said thank you. I think I was too stunned to reply. I'd only been back on the street a minute when a man came after me and requested I speak nothing about the visit, and then asked for my address.'

'I take it you asked why?' said Rebecca.

'The man was with the King so I trusted he had good reason. One week later I received six bottles of champagne, a case of cigars and a note thanking me for keeping quiet. You mustn't tell anyone as I've smoked all the cigars and there's only one of the champagne bottles left. I still can't understand the need for secrecy, although one does hear stories about the King and his companions. It was a shop for ladies, after all.'

The carriage finally came to a stop under a stone arch. Rebecca followed her father and Henry up white steps and through a door held open by a man wearing a top hat. They entered a grand lobby with marble pillars, a mosaic-tiled floor and walls painted with murals of foreign scenes. Guests sitting in velvet-backed armchairs were watching other guests or reading, and no-one was talking above a whisper.

'This way,' said Henry. 'We're in Palm Court.'

Rebecca tried to remember what she had heard in the village about London hotels. She was certain someone had said waiters poured guests' tea, and that well-to-do ladies only ate a mouthful of their food. At White's in Ely her father poured and she would always choose a wedge of cake with icing on the top and a finger-thick filling. She glanced round the room. There were only a few men and they were busy eating, while the women were busy taking notice of each other, and caring little for the cakes on their plates. Across the walls were mirrors with exotic palms standing in front of them. It was only a minute past five but every table was taken. Rebecca stood aside as a young man wearing a white bow tie pulled out a chair for her.

'It always pays to reserve a table here, even on a Monday,' said Henry, lowering his voice. 'Some ladies are known to have weekly reservations for months on end. They come merely to be seen, or to attract a writer's attention. I haven't read it, but a Sherlock Holmes story is partly set in the Langham. Have you read Conan Doyle, Rebecca?'

'No, but then detective stories have never interested me.'

'Rebecca mostly reads Eliot and Dickens when she's not sitting at the piano,' said her father.

'I wasn't aware you played the piano,' said Henry.

'Mama taught me.'

'I expect she enjoyed doing so.'

Rebecca forced a smile. 'I expect so too.'

There was silence as the waiter positioned a tiered cake stand in the centre of the table. Next to it he placed a smaller stand holding scones, and alongside that two dishes, one with strawberry jam and the other with cream as thick as butter.

Rebecca watched Henry as he listed London's merits. The only physical resemblance she could find to her mother was his hazel eyes. His voice was soft like hers, but he spoke quickly, as if in a hurry. Rebecca wondered if he had been a kind older brother or if he had been cold hearted and a bully. She knew so very little about him she was unable to even make a guess. Her only memory of him was from the funeral when he introduced himself and said something about the shock of grief easing over time.

'Are you excited about seeing your new home?' asked Henry.

Rebecca, fearing she would cause offence by speaking the truth, felt compelled to ignore the question. 'It seems so far away at the moment. I expect we'll be excited once we're closer.'

'It's a beautiful part of the country. I'm confident you'll be happy there. Both of you.'

The longing Rebecca felt for her true home, to be near to what was familiar, began to overwhelm her. She stood up and said, 'If you'll excuse me.'

On her way to the cloakroom, Rebecca passed ladies whose hair was arranged in curls that touched their shoulders. They must be the ones, she thought, who wish to be seen. Some ladies, who were noticeably older, had their hair fully swept back like hers, and some wore hats with dark blue plumes. A young man, handsome and with a lady with red hair, smiled at her. She lowered her head and kept walking, certain she must have food on her chin.

The cloakroom was empty. Rebecca went straight to the mirror. Her blushes remained but her face was clean. She stood still and looked around her as her cheeks cooled. The cloakroom, with its vases of dried roses, polished brass handles and a chandelier, was like none she had ever been in. She thought of how excited Tilly would be if she was with her presently, and realised it would be months, or even a year, before she saw her again. The door opened. The lady with red hair ignored Rebecca and took her place in front of the mirror, tutting once.

As she returned to the table, Rebecca could see her father leaning towards Henry. His expression was one of anguish. She considered hesitating, but Henry glanced at her and she kept walking. There was an uncomfortable silence as she sat down. She took a sip of tea, paused, and sipped again. A new conversation began, with sentences built upon *since we saw you last* and *so much has happened this year*. To Rebecca it was as if there was an understanding her mother's death would not be spoken of in her presence.

When the second pot of tea was finished, Rebecca's father checked his watch and said it was time to leave. There was another train to catch. Cases, coats and hats were returned and the man in the top hat hailed two carriages. Darkness had fallen on London.

'I'm sorry I can't come with you to the station,' said Henry. 'Hopefully next time you'll stay a few days.'

Rebecca lacked the spirit to consider returning to London. All she could think of was the long journey that lay ahead.

'I'll say farewell then,' said Henry. 'Please pass on my regards to Emily, and tell her she's also welcome to visit.'

'I shall,' said Rebecca's father, shaking Henry's hand. 'Though you shouldn't expect her to. You know how difficult she can be about travelling.'

Weary, stiff and cold, Rebecca put down her case and looked out at the dim lights of a city at rest.

'Your aunt wouldn't have forgotten our arrival time, Rebecca. I hope she has something for us to eat.'

Rebecca was past hunger. She wanted to climb into a bed, and hopefully one with warm sheets. Her father pointed to a carriage approaching the station and said, 'This must be her.'

Rebecca stayed behind her father at the carriage door.

'Hello, Emily. It's wonderful to…'

Emily leaned forward from her seat. 'Don't loiter you two, I'm cold enough as it is.'

Rebecca's father sighed. 'As are we.'

'Then get inside. Sit opposite me, Rebecca. I'd rather look at you than my brother.'

Rebecca kept her head up as she was inspected. Emily had a slender neck and sharp cheekbones. She was wearing a fur coat and her hands were hidden in a muff.

'Your lips are blue, dear,' said Emily, removing a blanket from her lap. 'Take this.'

Rebecca raised her hand in resistance. 'You keep it, please.'

'Too late, it's on you now.'

'You're very kind.'

'And you're very tired. There's supper waiting for you, but you won't offend me if you wish to go straight to bed.'

'Supper would be lovely, thank you.'

'Breakfast will be served early though. Your father will be keen to get on the road to your new home, as I'm sure you will be.'

Rebecca dressed and drew a curtain to view Waterloo Square for the first time in daylight. On the other side of a narrow park was a row of white houses with spiked railings and deep front steps. Emily had said at supper she lived on the superior side of the square and that her home was superior to all. She received guests two afternoons a week and one Saturday evening a month, and she held a garden party every summer. Only people of importance were invited, and everyone accepted.

Rebecca turned away from the window and left the room, conscious she was wearing the same clothes as the day before. As she reached the landing, she heard her name being spoken downstairs. She stood still. The discussion between her father and Emily continued.

'She understood, I hope, the need to leave?' said Emily.

'For me she did.'

'But not for her?'

'She's only known the Fens.'

'Yes, well, she would have felt secure there, just like her mother did.'

In her mind, Rebecca could see her father with his head bowed. She fought her instinct to go to his side, curious as to what would be said next.

'You're doing what's best for her,' said Emily. 'Hiding in the Fens would only have prolonged her grief, and yours with it.'

'I've had times of doubt.'

'I'm certain it's what Elizabeth would have wanted. Not that she ever wrote of important matters in her letters, and neither did you, for that fact.'

'We're not arguing again about what I did. Not this morning, please.'

Emily sighed. 'Very well. What about marriage? Did Elizabeth ever speak of Rebecca finding a husband?'

'She held on to the hope of Rebecca marrying for quite some time. Love just never came Rebecca's way.'

'But she does *want* to marry?'

'She's never mentioned it.'

'Surely she would have had suitors?'

'There were very few men her age in Welney. When I suggested an introduction with a friend's son, she objected.'

Rebecca frowned, certain her father was referring to George Turner.

'Then might I suggest that I…'

Someone was coming. The maid paused in the hall and glanced up. Rebecca panicked and descended the staircase, smiling as best she could as she entered the dining-room. She stood close to the door, wondering if her eavesdropping had been suspected.

'Good morning, dear,' said Emily. 'Do come and join us.'

Rebecca kissed her father on the cheek and sat down opposite him.

'You certainly look fresher than you did last night,' said Emily. 'Why you two travelled all that way in one day is beyond me. You should have stayed with Henry and arrived at a respectable hour.'

Rebecca caught sight of her father rolling his eyes and said, 'I suppose it was quite a long journey.'

'And hopefully you won't have to do it again.'

'Oh, I'll be doing it again, just perhaps not for a while.'

There was a long silence. Rebecca had no intention to break it.

'I expect you've been thinking about your new home since you woke?' asked Emily finally.

Rebecca tried to smile. 'I have, yes.'

'If the house wasn't in a village I'd happily live in it. Takes too long to travel anywhere for my liking. You must be used to that though, coming from the Fens.'

Rebecca wanted to fight back and say she had already planned her journey home. Her attention was stolen by the pendant around Emily's neck. It bore the portrait of a girl with light hair. For a moment Rebecca thought she was looking at herself as a child. Emily touched the pendant, covering the girl's face. She took her hand away and unfolded a newspaper. Everything about her manner discouraged Rebecca from enquiring about the girl.

'Why did you buy the house if you didn't want to live in a village?' she said instead.

Emily raised her head slowly. 'My late husband believed that one day I might want to live away from a town. Rather foolish of him, really. Nevertheless, I'm pleased he bought it as it means you can travel here without any bother. A few journeys a week into town should be quite easy for you, wouldn't you say?'

Rebecca felt her chest tighten, as if winded by the expectation she was to visit regularly. 'I'm sure there are many things I'll discover about living here. Travelling into town from time to time will no doubt be one of them.'

Emily returned her gaze to the newspaper. Without glancing up she said, 'Yes, dear. No doubt it will.'

Two brothers, unmarried and childless, had been Emily's only tenants. When one of the brothers died the other moved on. The house had been empty for months.

'Did he die in the house?' asked Rebecca as they left Emily and Waterloo Square behind.

'My sister didn't mention it. She did make a point of saying there were plum and damson trees in the garden, and apple and pear too.'

'Does she know I bake?'

'She does, yes.'

'I hope she doesn't think it strange of me.'

'Even if she did, it shouldn't matter to you.'

The carriage went through the centre of the city of Worcester, across an old river bridge where distant hills came into sight, and on to a straight road heading west. About two miles past the city's boundary Rebecca's father looked out of the window and said they were approaching Hallow. At the entrance to the village was a church. It sat above the road and had a lychgate in which Rebecca could see a man with grey hair pinning a sheet of paper to a board. The carriage passed a graveyard, went round a bend and at the border of a green turned on to a lane. The horses slowed and came to a halt.

'This is the end of our journey, Rebecca.'

Rebecca knew her father had been planning this moment. She paused for a moment to compose herself and left her seat.

'This is Peachley Lane… and this is Croft House, our new home. What do you think?'

Rebecca bit her lip. Croft House was built of red brick, had three floors and was decorated at the front by a Virginia creeper that extended from a black door to a bedroom window.

'It's much larger than I expected,' said Rebecca.

'Yes, it is rather grand. Come, let's go inside.'

Rebecca made her way up a gravel path and passed between two white pillars. She stood back as her father used his weight to open the stiff door. 'After you,' he said.

The hall smelled of pipe smoke. Rebecca opened the first door on her right, half expecting to see the dead brother's ghost. Instead, she found pieces of furniture that had survived the journey from the Fens intact but looked lonely in a room that was long and wide.

'Rebecca... are you there?'

Rebecca retreated into what she presumed was the morning-room. Her father smiled at her.

'I told you not to worry,' he said.

Her piano was a fist's width from the wall as requested. She raised the fallboard and ran her finger along the keys. The temperature changes of the journey had altered the pitch, but otherwise the piano was as it should be.

'Would you like to see the bedrooms? There are six.'

Six bedrooms seemed unnecessary to Rebecca. The maid would have to work hard, she thought, though it was unlikely the four empty rooms would ever accommodate guests.

'Emily said she had to choose our rooms because of moving the beds. But if you want to change you must say so.'

After Rebecca had inspected the final room, which was up a second flight of stairs, she said Emily had chosen correctly. She was to have a room overlooking Peachley Lane.

'Are you quite certain?'

'I am. It's the one I would have picked,' said Rebecca.

'She chose well for me too. I'll enjoy being up here, as high as anyone in the village.' Rebecca's father stepped across the landing and into the room opposite his. The room was lined with bookshelves in front of which were crates filled with books.

'I'm confused as to why Emily decided this room should be my study. You won't mind climbing the stairs to find a book, will you?'

'Not at all,' said Rebecca, turning away to hide her tears. 'I should look at the kitchen.'

Rebecca paused on the first floor landing. The door to her new room was open. Through the window she could see the church spire, intimidating and sharp, like a giant needle. She thought of the church at home and wished she was there, tending to her mother's grave, or riding Darcy across the Fens, or in Mrs Pugh's parlour eating warm biscuits. Croft House was impressive and convenient, but it was too large, too quiet. It was a house for a family, not one for a widower and his daughter.

Rebecca woke early the following morning. She looked at her clothes hanging neatly in the wardrobe and wondered how to spend the coming hours. There was not a trunk in the house to be unpacked, or a speck of dust to be wiped away. The lamp reservoirs brimmed with oil and the pantry shelves were filled with packets and tins. Emily had even seen to it that the cobwebs in the cellar – for Rebecca was certain every cellar had them – had been cleared. She had given her new tenants the simple tasks of arranging books, eating the food she had left, and sleeping. She had also left a gift with a note attached. It read: *Dearest Rebecca, may this provide you with many evenings of entertainment. We shall purchase your first gramophone record together. With much affection, Emily.*

A fear came over Rebecca that each day of her new life would be identical to the one before it. She would wake, get dressed and go downstairs with little purpose. At home she would have taken Darcy for a ride or visited Tilly, or prepared for an early caller. At home she would have had choices. Before the move she had not anticipated boredom but now she was in dread of it, knowing that an unoccupied mind would sharpen her pining for the Fens. Anxious, and doubting the remains of the small loaf left by Emily would satisfy her father's appetite, she decided to walk into the village. The bitterness of the morning came as a shock to her. She had been told the west of England was warmer than the east and that people in some counties had never even seen snow. Part of her rather liked winter; the excitement it brought of her birthday, Christmas and skating on the frozen Wash with her friends. Presently it brought only discomfort and self-pity. She quickened her stride, her head lowered to the cold air, her back slightly bent. A thought came to her and she stopped suddenly, certain she would have to turn back. She patted her coat and smiled to herself. The change Mr Graves had given her three days before was still in her pocket.

'Morning.'

The voice came from Rebecca's side. A woman was approaching the gate of the first cottage on the lane. Rebecca took a hesitant step towards her, hoping not to be delayed by questions.

The woman introduced herself as Mrs Kitty Munn. She was big hipped, had swollen pink cheeks and was wearing an apron made from a feed sack. Her face contorted. She pulled a handkerchief from underneath her apron and sneezed into it. 'Don't worry, I'm not ill, I never get ill. Neither did my husband till the Boers shot him. Wasn't the bullet that killed him, it was the hospital. Never a sensible place to be if you're sick.'

Rebecca, uncertain how to respond, said, 'Can you tell me where the bakery is, please?'

'You'll find it between The Crown and the post office.'

'And where are they?'

'Turn right on the main road and you won't miss them. But don't go across the green, not in those nice boots. You might get stuck in the mud.'

Rebecca looked down. Her boots appeared old to her.

'And don't buy any eggs,' said Mrs Munn.

'Pardon?'

'Eggs. I've got plenty. I'll give you some when you return.'

Rebecca glanced at Mrs Munn's tired clothes and felt a moment of embarrassment at being offered food by a widow.

'You'd better get going. Mr Evans will be selling out of loaves soon.'

'Thank you. Goodbye.'

'I didn't catch your name, miss.'

Rebecca stopped. 'Sorry, I should have said. It's Rebecca, Rebecca Lawrence.'

Rebecca walked with her head down, believing that people were watching her from front windows, making guesses as to where she was from and why she had moved to the village. She avoided the green and found the bakery. The air close by smelled of stale ale and fresh bread. Rebecca was the only customer but the bread trays were nearly empty. Mr Evans, bearded and with greased hair, said the early morning rush had passed and he was preparing for deliveries.

'I'm sorry there's not much left,' he said. 'I'm sure I can find you a better loaf out the back. Wait here a moment.'

Mr Evans returned with a loaf as large as any Rebecca had seen. He wrapped it in thin paper and began a story of how Queen Elizabeth had once hunted in the village.

'She killed a buck,' he said. 'Not far from here it was. That's quite a feat, don't you think?'

Rebecca, in a hurry to return to the house, smiled politely and paid, deciding to enquire in the post office about a piano tuner another day. As she entered Peachley Lane, she heard a door creak open.

'Wait a moment,' said Mrs Munn, waddling down the path. She put down her bucket and reached into it, pulling out four eggs. 'Here, have these.'

Rebecca knew she had no choice. She held her basket over the gate and produced a coin from her pocket.

'No, no, I won't be taking any money,' said Mrs Munn,

beginning to turn. 'Good day to you, Miss Lawrence. And welcome to Hallow.'

The book was an early birthday gift, Emily told Rebecca. 'We can go shopping together for your real present,' she said. 'Might I suggest for a coat or skirt, or both. You seem to be in need of them.'

Rebecca resisted the temptation to look at her skirt and instead focussed on the book.

'*All in the Way of the Flesh* is such a gripping title, I just had to buy it,' said Emily. 'I'm uncertain if it's actually about flesh, but you can tell my friends all about it.'

Rebecca felt a twinge of anxiety. 'I'll start reading this evening then.'

'Good, because you'll be meeting them soon. They're all rather keen to see my beautiful niece. Now, let's eat. Your father has said great things about your baking.'

Emily was silent as she cut a scone into four equal pieces. She left her plate on the table and stared across the room. Rebecca had the sense her mood was being read. She looked to her father, hoping he would start a discussion. His plate was nearly empty and his mouth was full.

Emily smiled and said, 'Did you teach the piano in Welney?'

'I only played for Mama, or if a friend asked me to,' said Rebecca.

'Surely you wanted to teach?'

'I suppose I might have done, if I had the time.'

'But you'll have more time here. There are no horses to care for and your cook starts tomorrow, though I still find it rude of her employer to hold on to her.'

'I'm quite happy cooking, just as Mama was before she became unwell.'

Emily sighed. 'You really shouldn't be in the kitchen. A

man of your father's means doesn't require it of his daughter. And may I suggest you speak little, or nothing, of it to my friends. They can be rather quick to judge.'

Rebecca wanted to say she cared nothing for the opinions of Emily's friends. She swallowed the words and looked again to her father for help.

'Teaching would be good for you,' he said. 'It'll help you adjust to living here, help you to meet people.'

'I may not be suited to teaching.'

'Just remember how your mother taught you and you'll be more than competent.'

Emily cleared her throat. 'I have a friend, Mrs Austin, who wishes her daughter to learn. I could suggest you as a teacher.'

Rebecca suspected the suggestion had already been made. 'How old is the girl?'

'Seven, possibly eight.'

'I haven't had the piano tuned yet.'

Emily's eyes widened, as if an idea had come to her. 'You could teach her at my house. A baby grand would be better than an upright, would it not?'

'I wouldn't want to intrude.'

'It'll be no intrusion, I assure you.'

'It does seem a long way to travel for one lesson though.'

Emily picked up her plate. 'You can come to tea beforehand. My friends will enjoy listening to a younger person's opinion.'

Rebecca poured more tea into her cup, hoping to gain time to gather her thoughts. On what subjects, she wondered, was she to give her opinion to Emily's society friends? She took the smallest of sips and said, 'Would all of the lessons be at your home?'

'I hadn't given it much thought,' said Emily. 'But I see no reason why not. It would be convenient for them and I certainly wouldn't object.'

Rebecca's father cut a thick slice of Victoria sandwich.

'The lessons can be arranged on the days I work. I can call in at Emily's and we can travel home together.'

Rebecca swallowed. 'There'll be more than one lesson a week?'

'I would presume she'd need more than one a week to make progress?' said Emily.

'She would, yes.'

'How many, would you say?'

'It depends on how eager her mother is.'

'I assure you she's very eager, very eager indeed.'

Rebecca glanced away, searching for an excuse that hid her fear of inadequacy. She caught sight of Emily's eyebrows rising and said, 'Then I'll help her.'

Emily smiled. 'Splendid, I was certain you would. I can negotiate your fee, if you wish.'

'Fee?'

'You certainly won't be teaching for free, dear. You can visit me on Monday and meet Mrs Austin. I'm sure you'll get along.'

THREE

Voices carried down the hall as the morning-room door opened and Emily appeared. She tilted her head ever so slightly and stepped forward, saying nothing.

Rebecca looked down. She wanted to retreat out of sight, or better still, return to that morning when she could have dismissed the idea of styling her hair like the ladies at the Langham.

'Raise your chin, dear,' said Emily.

Rebecca did as she was told, desperate for the inspection to end.

'Have you had this style before?'

'No.'

'Did your mother use curling tongs?'

'When I was younger.'

'And are you satisfied with what you've done?'

'I'm a little uncertain.'

Emily hesitated and then said, 'There's no need to be. Curls suit you.'

'I was worried you'd be upset – that I'd embarrass you.'

'You won't, but you should revert to your old style when you're in the village.' Emily adjusted a brooch on Rebecca's blouse. 'Come, let's not keep my friends waiting any longer.'

Rebecca breathed in as Emily took her hand and led her into the room.

'Ladies,' said Emily, 'allow me to introduce my niece, Miss Rebecca Lawrence.'

Three women smiled at Rebecca.

'This is Mrs Austin,' said Emily.

Mrs Austin, pretty and closer to forty than thirty, said, 'I prefer Charlotte, and I'll call you Rebecca, unless you object. In front of my daughter you'll be Miss Lawrence.'

'Of course,' said Rebecca, wondering if she had already been approved of. She turned to the two ladies sitting rigidly on a sofa. Both appeared as old as her father.

One of the ladies smiled. 'I'm Mrs Adams.'

'And I'm Mrs Finch,' said the other lady, who was much broader round the waist.

Rebecca was directed to an empty chair. Four pairs of eyes were fixed on her. Mrs Finch glanced at the slices of cake within her reach.

'I'm intrigued, Miss Lawrence, to hear your opinion of our part of England,' said Mrs Adams.

'I've seen so little it would be unfair to say.'

'But I understand where you lived before was rather flat. It must be inspiring to be so close to hills?'

'Yes, I daresay it is.'

'And do you plan to walk on the Malverns?'

'I'd like to. They look so distant, though.'

'Oh, they're no more than eight miles away. Dickens walked them, and Darwin.'

Mrs Finch, looking smug as she raised her cup, said, 'Roosevelt took the waters in Malvern when he was ill as a child. He returned to America quite well.'

Emily coughed deliberately. 'Rebecca's uncle took her to the Langham.'

'We always stay at the Langham when we're in town,' said Mrs Adams, glancing at Mrs Finch. 'Did you see Palm Court, Miss Lawrence?'

Rebecca remembered the room of palm leaves and mirrors. 'We took tea there.'

'I do hope you were taken shopping. My favourite shop only sells items made in France. The gloves are divine.'

'I plan to take Rebecca out this week,' said Emily. 'I expect we'll find a pair of gloves here that are suitable. English-made, of course. I'd want them to last.'

Charlotte cleared her throat. 'Your aunt mentioned that your mother lived here.'

'She did,' said Rebecca, 'though she moved back to the Fens.'

'Elizabeth was my dearest friend,' said Emily. 'My brother stole her from me.'

The ladies laughed. Emily looked away from Rebecca.

'How do you find your new vicar?' asked Mrs Finch.

Rebecca saw in her mind the short and fat-nosed Reverend Harding standing at the lectern, making theatrical movements with his arms. 'He's more enthusiastic than I'm used to. The vicar at home is much older.'

'And what of the gentlemen in the village?' said Charlotte. 'How do you find them?'

Rebecca tried to remember the congregation. 'I'm not sure. They look pleasant enough.'

'No doubt you'll meet gentlemen at social engagements,' said Mrs Adams.

'I've been told there's a summer fete.'

'There'll be the hunt on Boxing Day,' said Mrs Finch.

'We'll be attending the races,' said Emily. 'It's glorious fun.'

'You would have had dances in your old village, I suppose?' said Charlotte.

'At Christmas, midsummer and harvest,' said Rebecca.

'And what other entertainment would you have had?'

Rebecca thought of the Saturday afternoons she spent singing with Tilly and Mrs Pugh in the lounge of The Three Tuns, and said, 'I'd play the piano if we had guests.'

'Well, *we* have recitals and music hall, and dinner parties.'

'I've never been to music hall.'

Charlotte pulled a face. 'That's awful. Then I'll invite you and insist you attend.'

The questions stopped and a discussion began of people Rebecca did not know. As she grew weary of mirroring the reactions of the others, the maid announced that three carriages were waiting outside.

The ladies filed out of the room. Emily told Rebecca to remain where she was. She heard Mrs Adams and Mrs Finch say goodbye in the hall. Enough time passed before the third farewell for her to wonder if Charlotte had had second thoughts about her as a teacher.

Emily returned to the room. She clapped once and said, 'Well done! You'll give your first lesson on Wednesday.'

Rebecca's heartbeat quickened. 'Mrs… Charlotte hasn't even heard me play.'

'She doesn't need to. You were taught by your mother, and your father says you play beautifully. I said that was acceptable to me.'

'And that was acceptable to her?'

'Of course.'

'But we didn't even discuss the piano.'

Emily waved her hand dismissively. 'She wouldn't have wanted to listen to you talk about the piano all afternoon.'

'She wouldn't?'

'No, she wouldn't.'

Rebecca tried to smile. 'I'll have to start preparing.'

'Her daughter is a beginner. So long as she makes progress you can teach her however you wish.'

Rebecca sat down. A comment Emily had made during tea came back to her. 'Would you mind explaining something?'

Emily picked up a silver cigarette case and flipped the cover. 'What would you like me to explain?'

'What you said about my father.'

'Remind me, dear. I've forgotten.'

'That he stole my mother from you.'

Emily looked quizzically at Rebecca. 'Oh, *that*. You shouldn't trouble yourself with it. No doubt your father has told you about the past.'

'He said he met Mama on her twentieth birthday.'

'That's correct. As I said, there's probably little you don't know.'

'I'd like to hear what you remember. It might be different. Please.'

'How they met was quite normal. I expect it's how many men meet their wives.'

'Through their sisters?'

Emily nodded. 'It was a long time ago. Are you certain you wish to hear?'

'I am.'

Emily sighed. 'Very well, as you're being so insistent.'

'Thank you.'

Emily drew on her cigarette and exhaled smoke. 'I remember that Elizabeth's mother, your grandmother, entered my mother's social circle.'

'How?'

'Most likely through fundraising for a good cause, they were both keen at it. Elizabeth used to accompany her mother to our house, and there'd always be at least two or three others there, not that we were ever in the room for very long. We were always asked to leave.'

'What did you do?'

'Nothing, they just didn't want us to hear their gossip. We caught some of it from time to time. My mother had a tremendously loud voice, it was impossible not to hear her, particularly when standing with your ear against the door.'

'You eavesdropped?'

Emily grinned. 'We did. It was great entertainment

listening to our mothers pull apart local society. Occasionally the door would open suddenly and we'd have to explain ourselves. Elizabeth always had an answer ready, not that it was ever believed.'

'I expect my father didn't believe you either.'

'He was away at university. He was soon besotted though after meeting your mother. She wouldn't admit it, but I could tell she felt the same. James could be working in the study and she'd find a reason to talk to him.'

'I always imagined her to be shy when she was younger.'

'Elizabeth was never timid around my brother, it was just how she was. The gap between James's visits shortened soon after he met her. He would write telling me he had little planned for his weekend at home. I knew, of course, this was his way of ensuring your mother called.'

Rebecca sat forward. She wanted to discover more about her mother's past, to hear her name spoken again, as if it brought her back to life.

'I should have chosen different words earlier,' said Emily. 'James didn't steal Elizabeth from me. They would have met somehow, just as you'll eventually meet your husband.'

'What was she like at my age?'

'Look in the mirror and you'll see for yourself.'

'I meant her character.'

Emily ground out her cigarette. 'She talked more than you do. Your father can be hopeless at conversation so it suited him.'

'I remember Mama saying she waited a long time for a proposal.'

'James proposed one year after they met. He'd asked Elizabeth's father for permission after six months.'

'That doesn't make sense.'

'Your grandfather said he'd give his consent once James had completed his studies. He kept his word, but James had to wait to find out if he would.'

'Did Mama know at the time?'

'She may never have known. James only told me after the wedding.'

'Why keep it secret?'

Emily looked away.

'I've no intention of talking with Papa about it, and my grandfather's been dead for years.'

Emily pursed her lips and said, 'I suppose no harm can come of it.'

Rebecca straightened her back. She felt she had won a small victory.

'James didn't give me an explanation, but then he's always kept his secrets to himself. He would have wanted to protect her, though. She would have been hurt had she known there was a condition placed upon his happiness.'

Emily rose and went to the drinks cabinet. She removed the stopper from a decanter and poured amber liquid into a glass. 'I can't imagine how difficult it was for him to wait. There were others who wanted to court Elizabeth. Men with status and wealth.'

'She must have asked why she'd been kept waiting?'

'All I know is that when James proposed he had an answer ready. He was convinced she believed him.'

Rebecca hesitated with her next question. She swallowed and said, 'Why didn't you visit us?'

Emily turned slowly. 'You lived too far away.'

'My parents visited you.'

'Yes, well, the Fens are so bleak, aren't they?'

'Not always.'

'Oh, please, Rebecca, they are very bleak. They're flat and cold and barely part of England.'

'My mother was happy there.'

'She was happier when she was here, as was your father. The Fens changed them. They should never have moved there.'

Rebecca clenched her hands in her lap. 'Surely you could have visited Mama when she was sick? No matter how much you dislike the Fens, surely you would have wanted to support her?'

'Why I never visited is between your father and me.'

'But I have a right to know.'

'I said, it is between your father and me.'

Rebecca heard her father greet the maid.

Emily drained her glass. 'It's best you don't mention what I've told you. Your father spends too much time in the past. He should think only of the future now.'

Rebecca stepped away from the piano, telling herself she had to appear self-assured, particularly if the girl was a reluctant pupil. The door opened and Emily came forward, followed by Charlotte and her daughter. Without saying a word, Emily went to the chaise longue by the window, leaving Rebecca in control. The girl, fair haired and wearing a yellow dress, held on to Charlotte's skirt.

'Elizabeth's a little nervous,' said Charlotte. 'She's been talking about your lesson all afternoon, haven't you, darling?'

Elizabeth, her head bowed and her feet turned inwards, said nothing.

Rebecca moved a little closer. 'You have a beautiful name. It's the same as my mother's.'

Elizabeth raised her head a little.

'She can be shy with strangers,' said Charlotte.

'Perhaps if she comes with me to the piano she'll feel better.'

Elizabeth was nudged forward. Rebecca escorted her across the room.

'There's space on here for both of us,' said Rebecca, sitting down.

Elizabeth perched on the edge of the seat. Her knees were touching.

'Sit up straight, please, and place your feet flat on the footstool... you'll need your fingers.'

Elizabeth pulled her hands out from under her legs.

'Place your fingers apart as mine are on the keys... a little more of a gap. Try to shape your hand like a bridge... good. Now, imagine you're holding a ball... there, that's it. Well done!'

Rebecca inspected Elizabeth from head to waist. She did it slowly so that it was noticed by the girl. 'It's clear you have the posture of a piano player.'

Elizabeth bit her lip.

'Oh yes, you're quite elegant.'

'Thank you, Miss Lawrence,' said Elizabeth quietly.

'You're welcome. Let's continue.'

Elizabeth obediently followed every instruction and when the lesson finished asked if she could return.

'That will be for your mother to decide,' said Rebecca.

Charlotte stood up from her seat. 'I'm happy for you to teach her whenever you wish. She'll want to improve quickly.'

Rebecca looked down at Elizabeth. 'Would two days be enough time for you to practise?'

Elizabeth nodded.

'She'll practise at every spare moment,' said Charlotte.

Elizabeth pulled the back of Charlotte's skirt.

'I think she's keen to leave,' said Rebecca.

'Our Christmas tree was delivered earlier. I promised she could help decorate it.'

Rebecca smiled. 'I was no different at her age.'

Charlotte's skirt was tugged again.

'Elizabeth!'

The girl dropped her chin to her chest.

'We should be going,' said Charlotte. 'Thank you, Miss Lawrence.'

Emily showed Charlotte and Elizabeth into the hall. Rebecca felt a moment of triumph as she returned to the piano. The thrill passed and she dropped the fallboard, conscious that soon more would be expected of Elizabeth, and of her.

FOUR

Rebecca placed her gift under the tree and went in search of her father. She found him in the kitchen, pouring coffee into cups.

'Merry Christmas,' he said, kissing her on the cheek.

'And you, Papa.'

'Sleep well?'

Rebecca yawned and nodded at the same time, and took a seat at the table. She dropped a sugar cube into her coffee and began to stir. Steam rose from the darkness.

'Stay where you are.'

Rebecca knew what was coming. Her father whistled to and from the morning-room. 'Close your eyes,' he said.

Rebecca heard her cup being moved.

'You can open them now.'

A brown parcel, the size of a pillow and tied with a gold ribbon, sat in front of Rebecca.

'As you can tell, I didn't wrap it.'

Rebecca moved the parcel closer. She untied the ribbon, peeled the paper away and smiled. 'It's wonderful… thank you.'

'Emily helped. She said the colour suited you.'

Rebecca put her coat on. It was emerald and stopped just below the knee. 'It's perfect, I adore it. Thank you, thank you very much.'

'You can wear it this morning. Everyone will notice you.'

The church pews appeared to be full. Rebecca resisted the impulse to look down as she walked towards the altar, even though she had the sense of being scrutinised because of her Langham curls and her expensive coat.

'Miss Lawrence!'

Rebecca and her father turned. Mrs Munn patted the spaces either side of her.

'We're not taking anyone's place, are we?' asked Rebecca.

'No, you're just fine,' said Mrs Munn. 'Mr Crump usually sits where I am but he's unwell. His wife always sat where you are.'

'Always?'

'She died two months ago… tuberculosis. She was the cook at Hallow Park, not that she ever had to cook much as the owner was always abroad. Mr Crump's the gardener.'

The hum of soft chatter petered out as Reverend Harding made his way to the pulpit. His service had fewer Bible passages than Rebecca was accustomed to at Christmas, and the choir sang with less vigour than Welney's. Within an hour the service came to an end and the congregation started their slow march out. Rebecca waited in the dead cook's seat until the pews had emptied. She hoped for no further delay, but in the porch the vicar stopped her father to resume a conversation they'd had days before about Fen wildlife.

Rebecca's concentration began to drift. Her feeling of being watched returned, though she resisted looking around her.

'Sorry to interrupt, vicar,' said the verger. 'But Mrs Harding requires you in the crypt.'

'I'll be there in a few minutes.'

The verger remained where he was. 'I think she'd prefer it if you came at once. It's Mrs Ramsay… she's become emotional again.'

The vicar nodded. 'Please excuse me, Dr Lawrence. Merry Christmas to you both.'

Rebecca shivered as she left the porch. She moved closer to her father and put her arm through his.

'You'll soon warm up at Emily's,' he said. 'I doubt she's given her servants the day off as we have.'

Rebecca's thoughts of a fire were fleeting. Standing by the lychgate was a young man. He was neatly dressed like the men Rebecca had seen on Regent Street, and he was staring at her. Another man, just as tall but slightly older, tapped him on the shoulder and said something. His words failed to steal his companion's attention.

Rebecca kept her gaze, but just a few steps from the lychgate her courage deserted her and she looked away.

'Merry Christmas.'

Rebecca turned her head. The young man smiled at her.

'Merry Christmas to you too,' said her father.

Rebecca said nothing. She passed through the lychgate, counted to ten and glanced behind her. The man was now standing on the road, alone and watching her.

'Rebecca?'

'Sorry, Papa, what did you say?'

'I asked if you were excited about seeing your cousin Edward.'

'Yes, of course.'

'Emily's keen for you to spend some time with him.'

'She talks about him as if we're friends. I think she forgets we haven't seen each other since childhood.'

'That's my fault. I should have brought you here when I visited.'

'Or they could have visited us?'

'From what I know of Edward he'd be terribly bored in the Fens, and Emily can't abide travelling.'

Rebecca hesitated and then said, 'Is that why she didn't visit Mama when she was ill?'

There was a long silence. Rebecca began to regret her question.

'Distance wasn't the reason. And you shouldn't blame Emily for not visiting.'

Rebecca wanted to ask something else, but the note of reluctance in her father's voice stopped her. She thought about the young man again, wondering if it was her he had been staring at, or if she had imagined it.

'I'm ever so relieved you're happy with your coat.'

Rebecca smiled back at her father. 'And you're certain I gave you the right books?'

'Very much so. They'll keep me occupied for weeks, months even.'

Rebecca stole another glance over her shoulder. Her heart sank a little. The man was walking away, a young lady now at his side.

Rebecca hesitated in the doorway, wondering if she should wait for her father to appear. Edward turned suddenly and she froze.

'Come on in, cousin,' he said. 'It's just us at the moment.'

Rebecca sat down at the table. Edward, still standing and with one hand on the back of a chair, lit a cigarette. His thick hair had yet to be combed, and his silk dressing gown was untied, revealing light blue pyjamas underneath. With cheeks as red as his hair, and smoke coming from his lips, he appeared to Rebecca to be overheating.

'Cigarette?' he said, reaching for a case.

'No, thank you.'

'How about champagne?'

Rebecca stared at Edward, convinced she had misheard. 'Pardon?'

'Would you care for a glass? It's part of our Boxing Day

tradition. Mother will have two glasses before we leave for the races, I have every intention of having four.'

'I think I might have coffee.'

'Do you not like champagne?'

'I've never tried it.'

Edward frowned. 'Never tried it? Oh you poor thing. Well, this could be your last chance until next Boxing Day so I insist you join me.'

Rebecca glanced at the door, expecting her father to appear. 'All right, then.'

'Bravo! You know it's perfectly sensible to drink champagne in the morning, and should be compulsory when you have a day of leisure ahead.' Edward removed a bottle from a silver bucket and began to pour. 'À votre santé, cousin,' he said, passing a glass across the table.

Rebecca took the smallest of sips, paused as the bubbles fizzed in her mouth, and swallowed.

'It's delicious, don't you think?'

Rebecca nodded and took a longer sip. The bubbles found new life in her chest. She put her hand to her mouth, but failed to muffle the noise in time.

Edward laughed. 'Really, please, don't be embarrassed, that was quite tame. You should hear the chaps at Oxford, they make a sport of belching.'

'Now you're teasing me.'

'I'm most certainly not. Some of them are phenomenally loud.'

Edward topped up his glass and ran his hand through his hair. He flicked ash from his shoulder and began to drink.

'I'm sorry I didn't know the music you asked for last night,' said Rebecca.

'Don't be. What you played was divine, and you managed to make my mother smile. Normally she's a bore on Christmas Day.'

'She doesn't enjoy it?'

'Finds it awful. She can't see the sense in getting excited when it's just the two of us. Apart from this year the decorations have always been for show. It was rather exciting to learn we were having guests.'

'You really don't have to say that on my account.'

'I know I don't, but my mother bangs on about you so much in her letters I was sure you'd improve the day. She also told me I had to entertain you while I was here.'

'I'm quite happily entertained as it is.'

'But I want to. You're my only cousin and you've been hiding from me in the wilderness for years. Besides, we have so much in common.'

'I was worried you wouldn't think so.'

'You needn't have done. We're about the same age and neither of us has brothers or sisters. That seems more than adequate to me.'

'I meant with you being at university.'

'Oh, I see. Well, I suppose it isn't all champagne and belching. I do have to study from time to time, not that I care to do so.'

'You don't want to be a lawyer?'

Edward pulled a face. 'Sitting in a court is ever so dreary. I'd much rather stumble from country to country for a few years.'

'Have you told your mother that?'

'Good Lord, no. She'd tell me I was a fool and that I'd never find my way back to England.'

'And that would stop you from going?'

Edward began to pour again. As he went to speak, Emily appeared at the door.

'Yes, please, Teddy. And don't forget Rebecca.'

'I've had a glass, thank you.'

Emily turned her cheek so that Edward could kiss it. 'Time

for a second then. Your father won't mind; it's only once a year.'

'Perhaps just half a glass.'

'Probably for the best. Someone will need to stop Teddy from putting all of his money on a long shot.'

'I'm afraid I don't know much about racehorses,' said Rebecca.

'Neither does Teddy, do you, darling?'

Edward chuckled. 'She's right, I'm utterly hopeless. But I've every expectation you won't be.'

'I wouldn't want to lose any money,' said Rebecca.

Emily raised her glass. 'Oh, you ought not to worry about that, dear. It's my money you'll be losing.'

Rebecca picked out her father in the grandstand. He was squeezed between Emily and Charlotte and was being talked across.

'Being up there is dull,' said Edward, leaning back against a barrier. 'It's far more exciting to be down here when the horses pass by.'

Rebecca, lowering her binoculars, thought of the view the grandstand offered and the comfort of a seat.

'One also has freedom when standing,' said Edward. 'People down here explode like a jack-in-the-box when they win. People up there just clap.'

'What do you do?'

'I never get the chance. I shall today though. I'm sure of it.'

'Are you always so confident?'

Edward nodded. 'An inheritance from my mother.'

'Can I ask what you inherited from your father?'

'His hair. Bloody unfortunate, I say. His ability to make money would have served me better. It must have passed to his first child as my pockets always seem to be empty.'

'You had a brother?'

'A sister. I was only five when she died so my memory of her is vague. Mama never talks about it, so you shouldn't bother asking her.'

There was a moment's hush. Edward, folding his arms high, turned to face the course. Rebecca followed.

'It would be rude,' said Edward, 'if I failed to ask about your inheritance.'

'I wouldn't believe it to be rude.'

'You'd prefer not to be asked?'

'I'd prefer not to bore you by talking about myself.'

'Dear cousin, a person with either brains or beauty should never be shy.'

'And what if a person has neither?'

'Then they should say little, or mix with people who are just as unappealing.'

'Dare I ask how I should act?'

Edward leaned towards Rebecca and said, 'With much less modesty, cousin.'

Rebecca smiled. 'You don't have to be kind because we're related.'

Edward sprang back. 'No, but I shall be honest and it's clear you have both a brain and beauty.'

Rebecca's smile widened. 'You'll make me blush if you don't stop.'

'Then I'll stop. Though if I wished to make you blush I would belch and when people looked over I'd point at you.'

'You wouldn't be so cruel.'

'Wouldn't I? Let's try, shall we?'

In a panic Rebecca moved her hand to Edward's mouth. Edward began to laugh. 'Don't worry,' he said, still grinning. 'I wouldn't be so cruel to you. Well, not quite yet.'

Large Scotch in the 1.40 and *Miss Tangle* in the 2.20 ensured Rebecca and Edward broke even from the five races.

'Our luck was miserable,' said Emily. 'Not one in the top three. Rebecca can sit with us next time, Teddy. Evidently, she carries good fortune.'

Edward's attention was elsewhere. 'Sorry, back in a tick, don't move.'

He ran between bodies, calling out 'Rupert'. Rebecca watched him come to a stop ahead of a set of steps. A man turned and after a moment's adjustment beamed. Rebecca felt her heartbeat quicken. Edward's friend was the man who had stared at her after church. Three other young men, one of whom had also been by the lychgate, gathered in front of Edward. He moved on to a step and raised his hand. The friends turned towards Rebecca. She looked away, as if she had not seen the summons.

'The handsome one is Rupert Salisbury,' said Emily. 'Next to him is his older brother, Alfred. Let's go over and you can meet them.'

Rebecca, linking arms with her father, met no-one's eyes as she approached the group. Edward stepped down and began the introductions.

'You all know my mother, of course,' he said. 'This is her brother, Dr James Lawrence, and his daughter Rebecca, who is far better at picking winners than I am.'

The men smiled at Rebecca. Rupert's chestnut-brown hair was a little longer than the others', and his skin was without blemish and impossibly smooth, as if he had yet to start shaving. He held his gaze at Rebecca, breaking it as Emily enquired about his studies. He said he continued to be inspired at Cambridge and that his father was presently at the hunt. Alfred, who with thin cheeks and dark shadows under his eyes appeared underfed and tired, said his work in London was 'rather exacting', though he gave no hint of what his occupation was. Nothing was asked of the other companions and any questions the brothers might have had were stifled by

Emily announcing her need to return to warmth. Her final comment was an instruction to Rupert.

'You must call before you return to Cambridge,' she said. 'Edward may well disappear on a jaunt with little notice so it would be best if you came soon, though Rebecca and I can entertain you if he's away. Do bear it in mind, won't you?'

There was a knock at the front door of Croft House. Rebecca and her father lowered their books.

'I bet you it's the vicar's wife,' said Rebecca. 'She's been threatening to stop by.'

'I say it's Mrs Munn. We should place the crumpets out of sight or there'll be none left for us.'

The maid appeared. 'Mr Salisbury is here.'

'Rupert?' said Rebecca.

'No, his brother. He asked to speak to you, Dr Lawrence. He said he preferred to wait outside.'

Rebecca stood by the door as her father talked to Alfred. She listened hard, but caught nothing of what was said. She hurried back to her chair as her father returned to the room.

'We've been invited to dinner,' he said.

'By Alfred?'

'No, by his father, Charles. Alfred is just the messenger. He's on his way into town.'

'Will you accept?'

'I see no reason to decline.'

'But…'

'You wish to go?'

Rebecca nodded.

'Good, then I'll say we're both looking forward to it. I hear Ashgrove is rather grand. No doubt the dinner will also be.'

Later that morning, a second caller came to Croft House. Rebecca, passing through the hall, answered the knock, certain it was the vicar's wife. 'Edward, what a lovely surprise, come on in.'

'Sorry, can't dilly-dally, you must come with me.'

'This very moment?'

'Mama said she'd be offended if I returned without you.'

'Whatever's the matter?'

'Charles Salisbury's dinner. Alfred called with an invitation and said he'd also been here. The moment the door closed, Mama said I had to dress and fetch you. She said time was short and I should stop asking questions.'

'Oh.'

'She did say something, although I can't remember what. It was terribly early.'

'And you're certain I have no choice in the matter?'

Edward raised his eyebrows.

'I understand. I'll let my father know. Wait a moment.'

FIVE

Rebecca paused in Ashgrove's hall as her coat was taken. She suddenly felt exposed and wished she had told Emily the gown's neckline was cut too low, the bare back was daring and she preferred pale blue to cream.

Charles Salisbury, flushed in the cheeks and with a trimmed moustache, was waiting by a staircase that went round three sides of a marble hall decorated with tapestries, the mounted heads of horned animals, and paintings of men with dogs and horses. The other guests had arrived, said Charles, ushering Rebecca and her father into a room. Rebecca recognised every face before her. Emily was sitting opposite the vicar and his wife, Kate; Edward was standing with Alfred, and Rupert was placing a record on a gramophone. Rebecca wondered if she should step forward, but as the music started Alfred began to approach her. He welcomed her to Ashgrove and then returned to Edward, allowing Rupert to take his place. Rebecca was welcomed again. She expected Rupert to move away as his brother had. He remained at arm's length, silent and staring at her.

'How did you find…' they both said.

Rupert smiled. 'Please, after you.'

Rebecca blushed a little. 'I meant only to ask if you enjoyed the races.'

'I think I would have enjoyed them more had any of my horses come in. Edward took some pleasure in saying how successful you both were.'

'I merely picked the ones with the names I liked.'

'Then perhaps I should join you next time. The horses with the names I liked seemed to have no interest in winning.'

A gong sounded. Charles took command, asking the guests to follow him to the dining room. Rebecca was placed between the vicar and Edward. Her father was the first to talk, his questions prompting Charles to say he was a retired colonel with business interests in a vinegar works, a railway company, and the neglected malthouse that bordered the village green.

'Will you restore it?' asked the vicar.

'No, I shall raze it and build cottages in its place,' said Charles.

'And will they be for lease?'

'Of course. Villages such as Hallow should take advantage of the expansion of towns and cities. I'm confident I'll find tenants before the cottages are even built.'

The discussion of village affairs continued as courses came and went. Kate predicted that hop pickers from as far away as London would be 'booking their beds soon' in readiness for the season, her husband shared his fear of a disease outbreak closing the elementary school, and Charles declared his loathing of the poachers operating in Hallow Park's hunting grove. Rebecca shared only nods and smiles and had yet to speak at the table. Her father and Charles began to dissect a war between Russia and Japan, while at the other end of the table Alfred was championing the motor car to the vicar. Unaware of the war, and noticing that Rupert's head was turned towards his brother, Rebecca focussed on Alfred.

'Improvements in speed and capacity are inevitable,' he said. 'By the end of the decade there will be tens of thousands of motor cars on our roads.'

'And you regard that as progress for the country?' said the vicar.

'Without question. Britain needs a new industry and new jobs for the working classes.'

'And how do you expect all of these motor cars to be accommodated? The roads in towns are congested as it is.'

'Then more will have to be built. As my father said, cities are expanding. The migrating population will need better roads.'

The vicar shuffled in his chair. 'I have no fear of progress, but I do fear the erosion of our way of life. Roads busy with motor cars taking people from village to town will have that effect. Would you agree with me, Miss Lawrence?'

The question caught Rebecca by surprise. The vicar and Alfred had such a grip of their arguments she felt pulled towards neither. She swallowed and said, 'I would fear a restraint on society's progress as much as I would fear village life being eroded.'

The vicar pursed his lips. 'And what of living standards? Do you believe a motor car can lead a person to a better life?'

'I believe that living standards will improve if new jobs are created. It could be that the people employed in production will want to stay in towns. It's convenient… it's all they know.'

The war analysis stopped abruptly. Rebecca began to fear she had said something witless. Desperate for help, she glanced at Rupert.

'I believe you're correct, Miss Lawrence,' he said. 'It *is* natural for a person to be close to what they know.'

Rebecca felt flushed with relief and smiled at Rupert.

'It is also natural,' said Charles, holding the stem of a full glass, 'for a man to be close to what he aspires to know, hence the value of travel. I studied Ancient Rome for a term when one day in the Colosseum would have served me equally as well.'

'The principle of your argument, therefore,' said Kate, 'is that familiar surroundings can impede development.'

'How can that be?' said Rupert.

Kate looked at Rebecca. 'If I may use Miss Lawrence as an example?'

Rebecca wanted to object. 'If you wish,' she said, hoping for only a brief scrutiny.

'Every day for twenty years Miss Lawrence woke to the same landscape. However, by leaving that one perspective of the world she had no choice but to adapt, and consequently she's grown in experience. Now, had she remained cushioned by familiarity she might never have taught, met new people or considered the opportunity I'll discuss with her later.'

'Is there not a risk of severing one's heritage by migrating?' said Rupert.

'What I believe, and my husband agrees with me, is that roots can't be cut by a generation, no matter the circumstances.'

'And what of a man's occupation?' said Emily. 'A reputation of note cannot be gained by flitting from place to place like a gypsy.'

Kate smiled smugly. 'History would show us that those with the greatest minds have feet that are restless from time to time.'

'Then I hope that's why my sons' visits are so brief,' said Charles.

Rupert and Alfred glanced at each other and then returned to their food.

'Edward is no different,' said Emily. 'He feels compelled to leave by his third or fourth night at home, don't you, Teddy?'

Edward shrugged and reached for his glass.

'Perhaps young men now feel expected to move from one place to another,' said Kate.

'If they do then the motor car will become indispensable,' said Alfred.

Charles leaned forward and addressing Rupert, said, 'You should not expect, my dear boy, that I shall buy a motor car to assist such wanderings at university.'

'I've no use for one,' said Rupert. 'A bicycle is adequate in Cambridge and a horse is adequate in Hallow.'

'Glad to hear it,' said Charles.

'I presume you ride, Miss Lawrence?' asked Rupert.

'A bicycle?'

'Sorry, I meant a horse.'

Rebecca felt warmth come to her cheeks. 'I do ride, yes, though I plan to wait a while before buying a horse here.'

The vicar turned to Rebecca. 'I hope you had no objection to my recruitment of your father?'

Rebecca's father cleared his throat. 'I've yet to tell her.'

'Oh, I am sorry. I shouldn't have mentioned it.'

'It's quite all right, Rebecca's used to me being in a choir.'

The vicar turned again to Rebecca. 'I couldn't resist asking him, you see. One of our baritones died last autumn and it's been a struggle to replace him.'

'They're rather impressive for a village choir,' said Charles. 'I'd join if I had a voice anyone wished to hear.'

'Perhaps Rupert will consider joining us when he finishes university?' said Rebecca's father.

'I expect to train as an officer after Cambridge,' said Rupert.

Charles drained his glass. 'A man with an education and a few years in the army can make a good life for himself if he wishes to. Unless he's a dunce that is, which thankfully neither of my sons are.'

'Did the army not appeal to you, Alfred?' asked Kate.

'My eyesight was not up to scratch.'

'Probably for the best,' said Charles. 'He's doing rather well in London. At least, that's what my spies tell me.'

Kate waited until after dinner to reveal her opportunity to Rebecca.

'Our church has a wonderful Sunday school, everyone in the parish says so,' she said. 'However, my assistant, Mrs Ramsay, is expecting her first child and I'll soon be on my own. What I wish is for you to be my new assistant. What do you say?'

'I... I...'

'Of course, there are others I could ask, and there are a few who would want to be asked, but *my* school requires one to mix well with all types.'

'I really don't know what to say.'

'Your role will be to help the children and play the piano. I plan the activities and take the lessons, though you shouldn't hold back on any ideas you have. I'm confident you'll have many.'

'What if your husband has someone else in mind?'

'He doesn't. Unless her baby arrives early Mrs Ramsay will be helping me for the next two Sundays, so there's no hurry. I do hope you'll accept, you're perfect for the position, you really are.'

Rebecca promised an answer within days. Back at Croft House, drinking cocoa in the kitchen, Rebecca concluded Kate's request to be a blessing. She could quell her anxieties about settling in the village, and being busy on a Sunday might numb the memories of her mother being too weak to attend church. She suspected Kate had been influenced, and that her father had used joining the choir as leverage. As he began to speak of his enthusiasm for singing, it struck Rebecca that motherhood might be her only excuse for stepping down. Her obligation to Kate, and to her father, could last years.

Rebecca closed her diary and turned away from her desk. 'Come in, Papa.'

'Mr Salisbury is outside.'

'Alfred?'

'No, Rupert.'

Rebecca went to the window. Rupert was on the lane.

He was holding the reins of two horses; both chestnut and immaculately groomed.

'He's invited you riding. He said he felt sorry for you being without a horse at present.'

'But I've received no notice from him,' said Rebecca.

'I can't see why you would need any.'

Rebecca turned back to the window. Rupert glanced up at her.

'I said you'd be down once you were dressed suitably.'

Rebecca was in the hall within minutes. Her father passed her a scarf.

'It'll rain by the afternoon,' he said.

'He won't plan to be out that long, will he?'

'I expect not, though he might be offended if he's kept waiting any longer.'

Rebecca kissed her father on the cheek and left the house, focussing on the path until she reached the gate.

'I hope you don't mind me calling,' said Rupert.

'Not at all. It's very kind of you to consider me.'

'My brother would have joined us, only my father has him tied up with some business matter. I was given leave, thankfully.'

Rebecca smiled. 'Then I'm very grateful to your father.'

Rupert held the reins of Rebecca's horse as she mounted. 'Have you been along the river, Miss Lawrence?'

'Only towards the city.'

'Then we'll ride upstream, past the Camp Inn. You're on my late mother's saddle so you should be comfortable.'

Rupert took the lead to the riverbank. The Severn had burst into the meadows opposite.

'I haven't known a winter when the river hasn't flooded,' said Rupert, keeping to a walk. 'It's beautiful in the summer though. We often came down here during the school holidays. Edward roped me into all manner of trouble.'

'He does seem to have a sense of fun.'

'Always has had. My mother adored him. Whenever we played hide and seek in the garden she would give him a green cap to cover his hair.'

'I suppose it would have been easy to find him otherwise.'

'He remained hopeless. He could never stay still long enough to win.'

Rupert slowed and leaned down to open a gate. Rebecca would have jumped it had she been alone.

'I hope you weren't uncomfortable last night,' said Rupert. 'Mrs Harding can be a little forward. She seemed to command the table at times.'

'I wouldn't disagree.'

'Neither would her husband.'

'I suspect he may not be allowed to.'

Rupert laughed.

'I shouldn't say such a thing,' said Rebecca. 'Kate's been very welcoming.'

'I've no doubt she has. I laughed because you said what I was thinking. My father said something similar at breakfast. He'll probably repeat it next time you visit.'

Rupert kicked on. Rebecca followed, wondering if she would be invited to Ashgrove before Rupert returned to university. She hoped he would say more as she rode by his side, but he was silent until they reached the path that led to the inn.

'I'm not quite ready to return yet,' he said. 'Shall we keep going?'

Rebecca glanced at the clouds. They were dark and threatening. 'Perhaps just a little longer.'

Rain soon began to fall, intensifying as Rebecca and Rupert crossed a field. Rebecca looked for shelter. Suddenly, the landscape seemed to be stripped of trees.

'We should turn back,' said Rupert. 'If we ride fast we can make the Camp Inn before it worsens.'

The horses galloped side by side through fierce rain. Rebecca found the ride exhilarating and could not help smiling. She wanted to pass Rupert, but she kept level instead, conscious it would be foolish to compete when she had not ridden for months.

Opposite the inn was a stable. As she dismounted, Rebecca felt raindrops trickle down her spine and she shivered.

'You're drenched,' said Rupert. 'I must get you warm. Follow me.'

Rebecca ran with Rupert across wet cobbles to the inn. They entered a dim room with low beams and stools upturned on tables.

'Hello,' called Rupert, leaning over the bar. 'Hello.'

The sound of heavy footsteps came from above. They continued down a staircase and a door opened. A woman as round as a barrel and with grey, curly hair stepped forward.

'Sorry I kept you,' she said. 'Don't normally open till twelve. Must have forgotten to lock the door last night.'

'We were hoping we might start a fire. And buy a drink, of course,' said Rupert.

'Be my guest. There's plenty of newspaper and wood over there in the basket, and I've got some matches round here somewhere. Now, what would you like to drink, sir?'

'Miss Lawrence?'

'Do you have ginger beer?'

'I do.'

'Two then,' said Rupert. 'In fact, I'll have a brandy in mine.'

'Do you want a brandy too, miss?' said the woman.

'You'd better not,' said Rupert. 'It'll thin your blood.'

Rebecca moved to the fireplace and attempted to remove her sodden coat. Her numb fingers wouldn't do what she wanted them to and she gave up.

'Let me help you,' said Rupert.

Rebecca held her breath as Rupert released the buttons.

He wrapped the coat round the back of a chair and began to start a fire. Rebecca glanced down. Her boots and skirt were splattered with mud.

'Your lips are blue,' said Rupert, staring at Rebecca. 'I'll ask the woman for a blanket.'

'I'll be fine. I promise.'

'Then sit as close as you can to the fire. It'll catch hold soon.'

Rebecca did as she was told. Rupert placed a chair opposite her and sat down. His attention remained on the fire.

'Have you always wished to join the army?' asked Rebecca.

Rupert turned his head. 'Not always, though my father has never concealed his expectation I should join.'

'Do you have a choice?'

'I wouldn't dare disappoint him, particularly as Alfred missed out.'

'So what would you do if you did have a choice?'

Rupert shrugged his shoulders. 'I really don't know. My father said he was the same at university. He said the army gave him time to organise his mind.'

'Perhaps time will help you too.'

'Perhaps. I would certainly cherish the clarity that Alfred has. For a man with poor eyesight he sees the world very clearly. You'll never see him troubled.'

'Is that why he's doing so well in London?'

'Probably, not that he ever talks about his work. He says a man would need to appreciate advanced mathematics to understand it. I don't, and have no care to, hence we never discuss it.'

Rupert began to ask Rebecca questions, all of which she had become accustomed to answering. She said she found the villagers friendly, her teaching rewarding and in time would regard Croft House as her home. She told Rupert about Kate's Sunday School request, though held back from saying if she had accepted.

'It doesn't surprise me you've come to her attention,' said Rupert. 'Did she tell you her children's governess will also be leaving soon?'

Rebecca swallowed. 'No, she didn't.'

There was a long silence. Rupert broke it by explaining the history of the inn's name as he stoked the base of the fire. Rebecca looked to the window. The rain had started to ease.

'Will you be at your aunt's on New Year's Eve?' said Rupert.

'No, we'll be in the village.'

'Do you have any plans?'

Rebecca shook her head, hoping Rupert would not ask why.

'Edward's invited me to London. He said I'd need a strong stomach and a costume.'

'Which will be?'

'I'll have no need for one. Much to Edward's annoyance I had to decline his offer. My father had already accepted an invitation to the Earl of Dudley's ball at Witley Court. It's a grand place, makes Ashgrove appear tiny. Alfred managed to squirm his way out of attending. He finds parties terribly dull. To him the conversation is too polite to ever be interesting.'

'I hope he didn't find last night dull.'

'To the contrary, he said he found it stimulating.'

The landlady cleared her throat. 'Will you be wanting any more drinks? I've got a new brew of cider in if you fancy something different?'

Rebecca declined, as did Rupert. They left the warmth of the fireside for light rain and a headwind. Close to a gate, Rupert shouted, 'Shall we jump it?'

Rebecca kicked on, making the jump without hesitation. There was no sound of Rupert's horse following her. She slowed and looked behind her. Rupert was unlocking the gate.

'I blame the horse,' said Rupert as he caught up. 'Clearly the rain has affected her confidence.'

Rebecca went to speak, but Rupert pressed forward, remaining in front until they arrived at Croft House.

'I should apologise to your father about the state of your clothes,' said Rupert, taking the reins of Rebecca's horse.

'There's really no need to. I've been in far worse weather in the Fens. He'll expect me to be like this.'

'Very well, but please get dry and warm. I shan't forgive myself if you fall ill. Goodbye, Miss Lawrence.'

'Goodbye, Mr Salisbury.'

Rupert made his way up the lane. Rebecca stood still, wondering if he would glance back. The front door of Croft House opened and she was called inside. Her thoughts changed to a bath, a pot of tea and Charles Salisbury. She would write to him and make him an offer for his horse. She was certain Rupert would persuade him to sell.

A boy cycled past Rebecca on Peachley Lane and came to a stop. 'Are you Miss Lawrence, Miss?'

'I am.'

'This is for you then,' said the boy, passing Rebecca an envelope. 'Afternoon, Miss.'

Rebecca put the letter in her pocket, deciding to read it in private, free from her father's questions. He stepped into the doorway of the drawing room as she made for the staircase.

'How was Mrs Munn?' he said.

'She was grateful for my concern, and the cake.'

'Do you think I should visit? I suspect she hasn't seen Dr Wheeler, not unless he accepts eggs as payment.'

Rebecca started to move upstairs. 'Perhaps you could call tomorrow.'

'If you think that's best. Keep warm up there. I don't want you getting cold again.'

Rebecca closed her bedroom door and opened the letter. It was from Rupert.

Ashgrove
30 December, 1904

Dear Miss Lawrence,

I hope you do not mind, but I made a comment to my father at lunch regarding your situation for New Year's Eve. We shared the opinion it would be quite awful if you did not celebrate the arrival of the New Year. To that end, I request that with your father's consent you accompany me to the Earl of Dudley's ball at Witley Court.

I await your reply with anticipation.

R.J Salisbury

Rebecca glanced behind her to check the door was closed. She read the letter a second time and began to panic. New Year's Eve was only a day away which meant a reply was required by the morning at the latest. She thought of what her father would say. He would insist she accepted, leaving him alone on the first anniversary of her mother's death.

The invitation would have to be declined using the lie of sickness, Rebecca decided. If she was fortunate neither her father nor Emily would learn of it and Rupert's estimation of her, whatever it was, would remain intact.

SIX

Rebecca's guilt about lying in her letter to Rupert started to fade the following morning when a sudden weariness came over her on her way home from the post office. As she returned inside, she passed her father in the hall. He placed his hands on her cheeks and asked how she felt. She lacked the strength to reassure him she was well and was ordered to rest. Staring at her bedroom ceiling, shivering despite extra blankets, Rebecca thought of how falling ill had become a blessing. With the cook and maid also suffering from a fever, her father was too busy making soup, tea and keeping fires alive to grieve, and when those tasks had been completed he was given a further distraction. The library, Rebecca told him, required order. The bookshelves on one side should hold non-fiction in categories of history, geography and science, and opposite should be novels arranged alphabetically by author. Late in the evening, Rebecca was startled by the thud of hurried footsteps.

'I have to tell you what I've just read,' said her father, cradling a book.

Rebecca sat up.

'I started to read about the Civil War and found this passage that says after a battle near here, the defeated Royalists passed through Hallow and camped on the riverbank about a mile away. That's quite remarkable, don't you think?'

Rebecca nodded. In her mind, she saw Rupert stoking the fire in the Camp Inn as he talked of the area's history.

'I'll leave you alone again. Call out if you need me.'

Rebecca glanced at the clock: the ball had begun. The dances would have been unfamiliar to her, she thought, and Rupert would have found partners who knew the steps, leaving her waiting to be spoken to. The evening would have been draining, though in the morning she would have told her father otherwise. As she turned down the lamp, it struck Rebecca she had thought more about the invitation than she had the anniversary of her mother's death. Exhausted, and still cold, she turned on her side and fell asleep.

One routine of 1904 passed into 1905 with Rebecca taking tea before Elizabeth's lesson.

'How terribly cruel it was for you to be unwell on New Year's Eve,' said Mrs Finch. 'Judging by the gowns I saw at Witley Court, it clearly has become the most important evening of the year for young ladies.'

Rebecca suddenly felt tense. 'You attended the Earl's ball?'

'We did. The Earl was very keen for us to be there.' Mrs Finch looked at Emily and said, 'We spent much of the ball talking with a friend of your husband's.'

'Is that so?' said Emily. 'And his name?'

'Charles Salisbury. A humorous man, though he did have quite a thirst. His son was ever so popular with the Earl's daughter. Few of the other gentlemen got to dance with her.'

'Was it the youngest daughter?'

Mrs Finch nodded. 'Correct. She's recently returned from Europe, I believe. Charles said they'd been invited to her birthday celebration. He seemed very pleased with himself about it.'

Rebecca heard Charlotte's voice in the hall and went straight to her teaching room, instructing Elizabeth to begin playing at once. The talk of Charles Salisbury and the Earl's daughter was too much to endure and she resolved that next year she would hide in Croft House until all discussion of New Year's Eve had passed.

Elizabeth pulled her hands back to her lap and dropped her head.

'Wonderful!' said Rebecca. 'I'm impressed. Now, start again please.'

After the lesson, Charlotte insisted Rebecca and Emily join her at the theatre that evening.

'The top act is fabulous,' said Charlotte. 'She's become quite famous. I'm amazed you haven't heard of her.'

Rebecca left her father at home. A book, he explained, gave him greater entertainment than music hall ever could. Rebecca knew this to be the truth, though as applause filled the Alhambra – Charlotte said it was Spanish for palace – she wished her father had joined them. Even Emily seemed to lose herself in laughter at the actress's impersonation of a man.

As soon as the curtain came down Emily stood up, saying she had no wish to wait for a carriage. She cut her way through the chatter on the stairs and in the foyer, but outside there was a queue and heavy rain. Charlotte was nowhere to be seen.

Emily huffed. 'I'm certainly not waiting. Somebody will have to surrender their carriage for us. Come on, Rebecca.'

Emily made for the head of the queue, ignoring the comments about rudeness.

'Miss Lawrence!'

Emily tugged Rebecca's arm, turning her attention to a carriage close by. Stepping out of it was Rupert. He held the door open and pointed inside.

'Splendid,' said Emily. 'We're in luck.'

Rupert sat opposite Rebecca in the carriage. Emily led the conversation throughout the short journey to Waterloo Square, asking Rupert for his opinion of the performance, details of his studies, his father's health and Alfred's endeavours in London. Rebecca was not given the chance to speak, which suited her as she was considering what to say during the return to Hallow. As she said goodnight to Emily, it occurred to her she had been left with no questions to ask.

'I trust you've recovered from your illness?' said Rupert.

'I have, thank you. I hope I didn't inconvenience you in any way.'

'Not at all, I was disappointed for you. I'm certain you would have loved the ball, although it wouldn't have been wise for anyone unwell to attend. I was exhausted by midnight. I think I danced with every lady there. Even when I wanted a rest my father ordered me away.'

Rebecca remembered what Mrs Finch had said: *Few of the other gentlemen got to dance with the Earl's daughter*. She wanted to repeat the comment aloud, to draw a response for comparison, but kept quiet and a silence fell.

Rupert finally turned his face from the little window and said, 'I understand you accepted the Sunday School position?'

'I start this week. Did Kate Harding tell you?'

'No, I overheard two ladies in the shop. Well, it was impossible not to hear them.'

'Oh, I see.'

'I'm sure Mrs Harding will tell me great things about you when I'm here again.'

'You're leaving?'

'For university, the day after tomorrow, though I get the sense my father would be happy for me to extend my stay. Alfred's visits seem to be increasingly brief and irregular. I suppose that's what happens when you live for your work.'

'Then I hope the army doesn't do that to you.'

There was another silence, just as intimidating as the one before it.

'When will you return?' asked Rebecca hurriedly.

'At Easter. Edward's threatening to kidnap me and take me to Paris.'

'Paris? He told my aunt he was going to Venice.'

'Then who knows where he'll end up? Edward is wonderful company, but I'd be exhausted after a few evenings with him. I'll stay here, for self-preservation's sake if nothing else.'

Rebecca smiled. 'Then I hope Edward changes his mind and stays at home.'

'I shouldn't count on it.'

'No, I suppose not.'

Rupert hesitated and then said, 'Would you care to take the horses for another hack?'

Rebecca felt her heartbeat quicken. 'Very much so. I certainly don't expect to be abroad at Easter.'

'I meant tomorrow. I'm busy in the morning, but I'll be free by the afternoon.'

Not for the first time Rebecca regretted having to take tea with Mrs Finch and Mrs Adams. Forget about the ladies and Emily, she told herself, accept Rupert's invitation. Instead, she found herself saying, 'I'm afraid I have to be at my aunt's in the afternoon. I couldn't disappoint her.'

'Then I insist we go out at Easter, presuming I'm not kidnapped.'

'I'm confident my aunt will talk Edward out of going anywhere. He'll have to amuse himself at home.'

'So long as there's champagne close by he'll amuse himself anywhere.'

They reached Croft House. Even in the carriage's dim lamp light Rebecca could see Rupert's eyes widen.

'We should stay out for longer at Easter,' he said. 'I promise you won't get as wet as before.'

'We'll just have to make for the Camp Inn if we do.'

'I'd like that. Until Easter it is. Good night.'

Rebecca went straight to her room and opened her diary. Sitting on the edge of her bed, she counted the weeks until

Easter. The weeks became months and she gave up. Rupert, she thought, would have forgotten the invitation by his return, or he would have forgotten her. He could even be tempted abroad.

Rebecca felt anger rising over her obligation to help Emily entertain Mrs Finch and Mrs Adams. She closed her diary with a heavy sigh and fell back. Easter was too far away.

Rebecca spoke nothing of Rupert's invitation at breakfast, though all she could think of was how the afternoon ahead could have been filled. She decided to call at the vicarage, despite having no pressing need to. Little instruction for the assistant's duties was required, Kate had told her, but she should say if uncertain, which she was not.

She arrived at the vicarage just as Kate emerged from the church path.

'I've been helping my husband prepare for a funeral,' said Kate. 'You wouldn't have known the man. He was from outside the village.'

'I can return later.'

'No, no, you're welcome company. Preparing for a funeral can be a glum business. I'll be glad to talk of other matters.'

Kate looked over Rebecca's shoulder. The sound of horses' hooves on the lane became louder. Rebecca heard a familiar laugh and turned. Rupert touched the rim of his hat and smiled. His companion, a young woman wearing a scarlet coat that covered the saddle, ignored Rebecca as she rode by.

'I'm surprised to see her out,' said Kate. 'I would have thought she'd be conserving her energy for this evening. Everyone will want to wish her a happy birthday.'

Rebecca said nothing. A numbness came over her as she realised Rupert's companion was the Earl's daughter. She was the reason he had not suggested a morning ride.

'Of course, we've been invited to the celebration,' said

Kate, 'though I can't say I care much for attending. I'm perfectly happy at home on a winter's evening.'

Rebecca held her gaze of Rupert. He looked at the Earl's daughter and said something that made her laugh.

'Come, let's escape the cold and talk about your duties,' said Kate. 'I can tell you're excited about being my assistant.'

Rebecca put down her book as her father returned to the morning room. She noticed a letter in his hand and said, 'Who's written to you?'

'Henry.'

'What does he say?'

'I don't know yet. I'll read this while you speak to Jack.'

'Who?'

'Jack Clarke, the postmaster. He's at the front door with his son. You shouldn't keep them waiting.'

The son, no older than seven and staring at the ground, was attached to Jack's leg. Rebecca recognised him from Sunday School.

'Sorry if we've disturbed you, Miss Lawrence,' said Jack. 'It's just my lad wants to ask you something.'

'Please, ask away.'

The boy raised his head slightly.

'Go on, Harry,' said Jack. 'You know what to say.'

Harry shifted his feet a little. 'I want to play the piano, Miss.'

'Keep going, lad.'

'Can I have lessons, Miss?'

Jack nudged Harry. 'Please!'

'Please, Miss.'

Rebecca put her hand on Harry's shoulder. 'Why do you want lessons, Harry?'

'He says he wants to play like you do,' said Jack. 'Don't you, lad?'

Harry, running his cap through his fingers, nodded.

'That's very sweet of you,' said Rebecca. 'But you should know it takes many years to play as I do. You'll need to be patient and be disciplined.'

'I'll see to it that he practises every day,' said Jack.

Rebecca looked at Harry. She could see hope in his eyes. 'You'll have your lessons here. I expect you to be on time and show enthusiasm.'

'He will. He'll never miss a lesson,' said Jack.

Harry began to turn. Jack stopped him with his arms and said, 'I was wondering, just so I know what to put aside each week, what the lessons would cost?'

Rebecca thought of how much Charlotte paid her. She noticed the collar of Harry's coat was frayed and could not bring herself to say the fee. 'It'll only be a small amount. He'll have to come here twice a week if he hopes of playing as I do. If that's what you want, Harry?'

The boy nodded. Jack released his hand. 'His uncle gave him some money earlier. I said he could spend it in the shop once we'd been to see you.'

'Then I'm already impressed by your patience, Harry. Just ensure you never lose it.'

Rebecca returned inside. Her father was moving a second chair closer to the fire.

'Come and get warm and tell me what Jack wanted,' he said.

Rebecca repeated the request for lessons. As she spoke of her agreement, she could see her father's expression change.

'I'm pleased you're helping the boy, but remember you already give three lessons a week. You should be mindful of tiredness.'

'I couldn't say no to him. Mama wouldn't have.'

Rebecca watched her father switch his attention to the fire and wished she had not mentioned her mother. She looked at the letter and said, 'How's Uncle Henry?'

'He's troubled.'

'Why? What's happened?'

'His wife has to leave London on a family emergency. He doesn't explain further, only that it concerns her sister. He's requested we visit him.' Rebecca's father put on his reading glasses and raised the letter. 'He writes that his daughter refuses to leave London and he's too occupied with his work to keep a watch on her. Apparently, you'll be great company for each other.'

'Keep a watch? Whatever's wrong with her?'

'He doesn't say. I do find it odd he calls her his daughter. He's only been married to the girl's mother for two years. I doubt she's forgotten who her real father is.'

'And when does he want us to visit?'

'Preferably the twentieth, or earlier if possible.'

'The twentieth is next week. I teach Elizabeth on that day.'

'She can miss a lesson, can't she? I wouldn't expect her mother to have any objection.'

'I suppose. Will your partner manage without you?'

Rebecca's father folded the letter and placed it on the chair arm. He leaned forward and locked his fingers. 'My partner is away next week. I couldn't close the surgery for two days. It wouldn't be fair on our patients.'

'So you'll tell Henry we can't visit?'

'No, I plan to tell him that you'll visit.'

Rebecca's heart beat a little faster. 'On my own? But I don't know London. I'll get lost.'

'Not a chance. Henry will take care of you.'

'But he's busy. He said so himself.'

'Then his daughter will be with you when he's at his office.'

'We may not get along. She could abandon me.'

'She won't abandon you and you will get along. Henry wouldn't have asked you to visit otherwise.'

‘I couldn’t leave you. You’ll be on your own, it’ll be awful for you.’

‘It’s just for a few days. I’ll visit Emily if I get lonely.’

Rebecca’s father passed her the letter.

‘Your mother would have wanted you to support your uncle. Give it some thought. Please.’

Rebecca was left alone. She sat still on the edge of the chair, unable to shake off the thought she was being sent away. As much as she knew her mother’s wishes had been spoken of with deliberate impact, she knew her father was correct: her mother would have wanted her to help Henry.

A door upstairs creaked open. Rebecca placed the letter in her pocket. At the foot of the staircase she paused and held her breath. A railway platform, so crowded there was no room to move, came to her mind. Nausea rose from her stomach and she exhaled hard. She gripped the banister for support and began to climb.

It seemed to Rebecca that everyone had advice to give her about London, even Kate who had never visited the city. The fog, Rebecca was assured, was so thick in winter that by dusk one could see only the length of one’s arm.

‘Not that you should be in the street at that time of day,’ said Kate. ‘It’s far too dangerous. There are thieves and drunkards on every corner.’

Emily too was cautionary. Her warning was of male flattery. ‘A shy young man is rare in London,’ she said. ‘If you do encounter one he’s likely to be a visitor, in which case he might be foreign and should be avoided, most definitely so if he’s French. They’re the worst type if a pretty lady is close by. My advice is you speak only to English gentlemen, though not if they have the look of the north about them. Viking blood remains in their veins.’

Rebecca’s father had only a few words to say at the station.

'I don't want you worrying about what awaits you,' he said as the locomotive pulled in. 'Can you promise me that?'

Anxiety about her father being alone spared Rebecca from breaking her promise until the city had been left far behind. She thought of distracting herself by reading, though it occurred to her she would have to bring down her case. The man sitting opposite her would look at it and think she was in the wrong compartment.

'Let the porter take it,' Emily had said on the platform. 'A lady travelling in first-class should never carry her case onto a train, even if it's more fitting for third.'

The man tutted. 'We're late,' he said to the woman at his side. 'The standards of this railway company are falling, and my shares are falling with them.'

Rebecca resisted looking his way, even as he tutted again. At Oxford, the next station, the man rose with a huff and hurried his companion into the corridor, threatening to lodge a complaint.

It seemed strange to Rebecca that Edward was nearby. He could be in a lecture, she thought, or with friends, or quite possibly still be asleep. She wished he came and joined her for the remainder of the journey. Passengers were entering only the third-class carriages, which she was certain Edward would never travel in. Emily would not allow it, just as she had insisted on paying for a first-class ticket that morning.

Rebecca sat forward on the seat. A whistle sounded and she stood at once, relieved she was alone and could remove her book from her case above. The compartment door opened and she froze.

'Allow me,' said a man, bringing down the case from the rack.

'Thank you.'

Rebecca opened her book and glanced over the top. The man was tall, close to Edward's age and out of breath. He began to adjust his tie while looking out of the window. Whatever he could see absorbed his concentration as he made a knot and started to tug at it.

'Damn lucky I'm here,' he said, turning his attention to Rebecca. 'If it hadn't have been for my friend's singing I'd still be asleep. The fool believes he has a voice. Anyone who has heard it will argue the opposite. He's quite awful.'

Rebecca smiled and raised her book again.

'It was the home brew that did it,' said the man. 'I would have been up with the lark had it been kept out of sight. My friend warned me it had a kick. I just didn't anticipate the kick to be so hard.'

Rebecca smiled. Surely, she thought, she was not expected to comment.

The man began to add to the details of his evening, explaining that another friend had knocked himself out when he came off his bicycle. A slap to the face had brought him round.

'He got straight back on the saddle,' said the man, 'and came straight off again. Didn't bleed a drop, just had a bump on his forehead that made him look rather careless.'

The man laughed and started a new anecdote which again involved a friend, liquor and a mishap. Rebecca maintained the charade of taking an interest, all the while hoping the man would leave her be. Suddenly, he cut a sentence short and said, 'Will you lunch with me? It's depressing eating alone on a train.'

'I expect it is.'

'I'm glad you agree. We should go now. I arrived late in a dining carriage once and they'd run out of what I wanted. I had to order again. Can you imagine it?'

Over luncheon Rebecca learned the man's name was Ralph Schapell. They shared no common interest. Mr Schapell cared nothing for literature or the country, but not once did silence fall upon the table and even back in the compartment his conversation remained alive.

'Which show do you intend to see in London?' he said, as Paddington's engine sheds came into sight.

'My uncle hasn't told me of his plans. He may not have time to take me.'

'Oh, you must attend a show, even if you'd prefer to avoid it, there's little reason for visiting London otherwise.'

Mr Schapell produced a card from his pocket and wrote on it. 'The name of my hotel is on the back. I'd be quite happy to escort you to a show if your uncle is occupied.'

Rebecca glanced at the bodies on the platform, hoping to see Henry. The locomotive came to a halt.

'You can share my carriage if you wish,' said Mr Schapell.

'I'll be all right, thank you.'

'Very well. Goodbye, Miss Lawrence. Perhaps we'll meet again.'

Rebecca waited a moment to compose herself and stepped on to the platform, anticipating a greeting.

'Can I help you with your case, Miss?' asked a porter.

'No, thank you. I'm being met by someone.'

Rebecca wondered if the details of her arrival had not reached Henry. She saw Mr Schapell in the distance and decided to hurry after him.

'Cousin Rebecca?'

Rebecca turned. A young woman, little older than eighteen and with dark ringlets touching her cheeks, smiled at her.

'I'm your cousin Alice.'

'Alice… hello.'

'Papa was waylaid at the newsstand by a friend. He sent me to greet you.'

Rebecca looked to where Alice was pointing. Henry was striding towards her.

'I'm ever so excited to meet you,' said Alice, as they began to walk. 'It's been tremendously dull in the house with Mama away. I promise you won't have a moment's boredom when you're here. I have it all planned.'

Henry kissed Rebecca on the cheek. 'Welcome back.'

'Thank you.'

'Alice has worn me out asking questions about you. For days she seems to have talked about nothing other than your visit.'

Alice touched Rebecca's arm. 'Papa has promised to buy us each a new hat.'

'Only if Rebecca finds one to her taste.'

'I'll pick for her if she doesn't,' said Alice. 'And then we'll take tea and you can tell me everything about you that Papa hasn't.'

'Rebecca may be tired,' said Henry.

'Oh please say you're not tired, please!'

'I'm not,' said Rebecca.

'Then we should hurry. I've seen the hat I want. It would be horrible if it was sold and there were none left.'

Claridge's was chosen for tea. They were early, which suited Alice as she wanted to watch people arrive. Henry had an appointment and excused himself.

'Papa has been asked to stand for Parliament,' said Alice. 'I can't remember for where, but apparently the current man is too old and fresh blood is needed, or something like that. I think Papa will be a splendid MP, don't you?'

'Yes, I do. Sorry, for which party?'

'The Conservatives, of course. He knows all the right people through his business and often has to dine at his club because he works so late. Dear Mama will always stay up for him.'

Alice began to comment about the clothes worn by the ladies entering the room (some were in fashion, others were dull). Rebecca listened, trying to remember what she had been told about her cousin. Alice was an only child and her mother, long bereaved, was the sister of Henry's business partner, the architect of the union. The courtship had been brief and the wedding invitation sent to the Fens gave so very little notice that acceptance, Rebecca could recall, was discouraged. Nevertheless, her mother attended, though she returned after just one night away. London's heavy air had made her feel unwell.

'How many children do you want?' asked Alice.

Rebecca thought she had misheard. 'I can't say I've considered it greatly.'

'Have you not? I certainly have. I hope for three, or four if I marry early, which is quite possible. Mama doesn't want me to be left behind.'

'No, I suppose not.'

'Will you marry soon?'

'It's difficult to say.'

'Well, if I marry first you can be my bridesmaid. But of course you *will* be first, and then I can be your bridesmaid. What do you say? Please say yes.'

Rebecca took a long sip of tea to give her time to think. 'I daresay any bride without a sister would instinctively think of a cousin as a bridesmaid.'

'Yes, they would, wouldn't they? Oh I do love having a cousin, you're all that Papa promised.'

Alice began to tell Rebecca what the hours ahead offered. As she reached a description of her home she leaned forward and said, 'There's a man who's been looking at you for a minute or more. He's not being at all discreet about it.'

Rebecca started to turn.

'Stop! You don't want to flatter him,' said Alice.

'Are you certain it's me he's looking at?'

'Quite certain. He's with an older couple, and he's terribly handsome.'

Rebecca put her napkin on the table. 'I think we should leave.'

'Wait, he's standing. He's coming over.'

'He must be confused. You can talk to him, I really don't have a care for…'

A man cleared his throat.

Rebecca turned her head. 'Mr Schapell… hello. I thought you were staying elsewhere.'

'Apparently my hotel will not do for tea. Hence we came here.'

'Then we're glad you did,' said Alice. 'I'm her cousin, Miss Alice Gray.'

Mr Schapell took Alice's hand and shook it gently. 'Delighted to meet you, Miss Gray.'

'And I'm delighted to meet you, Mr Schapell.'

Rebecca, watching Alice slide her hand slowly away, said, 'I wouldn't want to keep you from your companions.'

'They're my parents.'

'Even more so.'

'Quite. Well, I hope London is kind to you during your stay.'

'It has been so far.'

'I'm pleased to hear it. Good afternoon Miss Lawrence… Miss Gray.'

As soon as Mr Schapell was out of earshot, Alice began to ask questions. Rebecca lowered her voice and supplied all that she could remember of their time together, from his help with her case until his carriage offer at Paddington. She even mentioned the friend's bicycle fall. The details were unsatisfactory as Alice's intrigue returned over dinner. Rebecca repeated what she had said at Claridge's, adding Mr Schapell's instruction to see a show.

'Did he say what type of show?' said Alice hurriedly. 'Was it music hall? Oh please let it be so and we see him at the Hippodrome.'

Henry frowned. 'I've yet to decide about tomorrow night.'

'But this has made the decision for us, don't you agree?'

'Not necessarily.'

'You really are a tease, Papa. I know you already have the tickets. Rebecca agrees with me that we should go, don't you, cousin?'

The following morning, Henry asked Rebecca how she wished to spend her day.

'There's really not much to discuss,' said Alice quickly. 'There's an exquisite glove shop on Regent Street that I know Rebecca will adore, and then afterwards we can visit her friend Mr Schapell at his hotel.'

'That's a little forward,' said Henry.

'I'm sure he won't mind. He did invite you, didn't he?'

Rebecca, glancing at Alice, said, 'I'm not certain it was an invitation as such.'

'But he appeared rather happy to see you yesterday, and me. I'd say he'd be pleased if we happened to meet again.'

'I'm too busy to accompany you, and Rebecca is our guest,' said Henry. 'She should have first say on what she wishes to do.'

'I don't wish to be any trouble. I'd be happy to visit this shop,' said Rebecca.

'I was going to suggest the National History Museum, or as it's such a fine day, a walk in Hyde Park. I understand the circus is on. That's always entertaining.'

'I've never been to a circus,' said Rebecca.

'Have you not? Then the circus it is.'

'We don't have to if Alice prefers something different.'

'No, no, Alice will be delighted to take you, won't you?'

Alice smiled. 'Of course. But we must go to the Hippodrome tonight, we must!'

'Yes, I agree. You'll adore it, Rebecca. It's the finest music hall in London.'

The tightrope walker was Rebecca's favourite circus act. At the finale, after the little man had dropped the balancing beam and kept his arms by his side as he wobbled back along the wire to his perch, she joined others in a standing ovation. Alice remained in her seat. She said the best act – the knife thrower – was still to come. Rebecca closed her eyes as a drum roll began, convinced the pretty girl bound by rope to a target would be struck in the chest. Even at the sound of applause she kept her eyes closed. Alice gave her a nudge and said the show had come to an end.

As they left the giant tent, Alice congratulated Rebecca on her choice. 'And it didn't drag on as long as I expected which means we'll have more time to try on gloves. Mama has an account at the shop. She'll want me to use it as you're here.'

The shop was on the ground floor of an arcade that had a glass roof, polished tiles, and a fountain set in a round pool, the bottom of which was layered with coins. Hanging outside the shop was a sign with a foreign name. Rebecca could see a woman closing a cabinet.

'That's the owner, Madame de Lausanne,' said Alice. 'She's ever so elegant. Come, let me introduce you.'

A little bell rang as Alice opened the door. Madame de Lausanne looked up.

'Mademoiselle Gray,' she said. 'What a delight to see you.'

'Bonjour, Madame.'

Madame de Lausanne, silver haired and dressed in blue velvet, came forward. She kissed Alice on one cheek, and then the other.

Alice, at ease with the greeting, said, 'Mama's away, but I've brought my cousin, Miss Rebecca Lawrence.'

'Bonjour,' said Madame de Lausanne, offering her hand.

'Good afternoon, Madame.'

'Your cousin is très belle, Mademoiselle Gray.'

Alice smiled. 'Yes, she most certainly is.'

Madame de Lausanne took Rebecca's hand again. 'But her gloves do not match her beauty. This must change.'

Alice and Rebecca sat down as a selection of gloves was laid out on the table in front of them. Rebecca counted a dozen pairs arranged in colour by Madame de Lausanne who explained they were the latest designs from Paris and had arrived that morning.

Alice made her selection. Rebecca stared at the display, wondering which pair was the least expensive.

'Let me help,' said Alice. 'I know the colour to suit you.'

'No need, I've made my decision.' Rebecca touched a pair as scarlet as the riding coat worn by the Earl's daughter.

'An excellent choice,' said Madame de Lausanne. 'Please, look in the mirror.'

Alice stood at Rebecca's side. The mirror was wide enough for both reflections. The little bell rang and Madame de Lausanne excused herself.

'Papa says you remind him of your mother when she was your age,' said Alice.

Rebecca turned. 'He speaks of my mother?'

'When asked about his childhood. I don't care much for remembering my own, but Papa always seems to perk up when he recalls his.'

'Does he talk of more recent times?'

'Very little. He didn't speak a word for days when he learned of your mother's death. The surprise of it all caught him off guard.'

'Surprise? I don't understand.'

'May I help you further, ladies?' said Madame de Lausanne.

Alice replied in French and gave Madame de Lausanne her gloves to wrap. Back in the arcade, Alice said she would wear her new gloves to the Hippodrome that evening. 'Every lady will desire them. They'll think the same of yours, of course. You wouldn't have brought a gown to match them so you can wear one of mine.'

As they passed the fountain, Alice stopped and said, 'We should make a wish.'

'I don't hold much belief in making wishes.'

'Do you not? I do, so does Mama. It can't do any harm, and we can wish at the same time.'

Rebecca accepted the offered coin. On a count of three, and with her eyes closed, she released the coin into the water.

'You see, quite harmless,' said Alice. 'What did you wish for?'

'I thought it was bad luck to say?'

'Nonsense. Where's the fun if you can't share what you wished for?'

'I suppose.'

Alice linked arms with Rebecca and resumed walking. 'Well, *I* wished that you return soon. It makes me sad to think you're leaving tomorrow. We've only just started to get to know one another, and there's so much I want to share with you.'

'Then I'll return.'

'Soon?'

'Yes, soon.'

'Wonderful! Now, tell me what you wished for.'

SEVEN

Rebecca, standing in the Hippodrome foyer after the show, was told her wish had come true.

'It was the most entertaining night of my year too,' said Alice. 'Wasn't the woman marvellous? I expect you've never laughed so much.'

'No, I daresay I haven't.' The lie made Rebecca uncomfortable. Her laughter during the performance had been sincere, though the impressionist was not as amusing as she had been at the Alhambra.

'Can you see him?' asked Alice.

'Who?'

'Mr Schapell. If he loves the theatre so much he'd be here.'

'Perhaps he's at another show.'

'But it's opening night. A gentleman of any worth should be here. Are you certain of what he said? Some men like to play tricks.'

'He seemed pleasant. I can't see why he'd want to trick me.'

'Well, he wouldn't dare trick me if we were to meet again. Mama wouldn't allow it.'

Rebecca awoke the following morning to find Alice sitting next to her in bed.

'It's not fair you're leaving,' said Alice.

Rebecca sat up. 'You're welcome to visit me.'

'To your village?'

'Yes.'

'But what would we do there?'

'Umm... we could take tea with my aunt's friends, walk along the riverbank, and you could help me at Sunday School if you wished to. I'm sure the children would adore you.'

Alice frowned. 'I think it would be easier if you came here again first, and I don't expect Mama would allow me to travel without her, particularly when I tell her about Mr Schapell and how he preyed upon you on the train. There could be others of his type.'

Rebecca was left to dress and was the last down for breakfast. Alice was standing at Henry's shoulder, looking down at a letter.

'Rebecca! Something incredible has happened. Your...'

'Alice, sit down and allow Rebecca to do the same,' said Henry. 'Good morning, Rebecca.'

'Good morning, uncle.'

'There, she's sitting now so you can read it to her,' said Alice.

Henry sighed. 'Very well. Your Aunt Emily has written to me.'

'And she says...'

'Alice! Please.'

'Sorry.'

Henry raised the letter. 'Emily has written that your cousin Edward is in town. She suggests we join him this evening for dinner.'

'But I'm leaving in an hour,' said Rebecca. 'My father will be expecting me at the station.'

'Emily recommends you wire him with notice you'll be arriving a day later at the same time. She writes: "I shall forewarn him, and ask him to stay."'

'When did my aunt write this letter?'

'The afternoon you left, according to the date. I must say, it's very decisive of her.'

'Yes, she can be that way.'

'This means you simply must stay another night,' said Alice. 'Your aunt insists, and so does Papa, don't you?'

Henry returned to the letter. 'Apparently, your cousin can be found at the Park Royal and is likely to be with a friend.'

'The Park Royal is ever so popular, Papa. You'll need to make a reservation at once,' said Alice.

'There's no need. I'll contact Edward and invite him here, and his friend. A table of young people will be good for the house.'

'And we get to spend another day together, Rebecca. Isn't that wonderful?'

Rebecca smiled as best she could. 'Yes, it is.'

Henry opened his newspaper and began to read aloud reports of parliamentary affairs. Rebecca tried to appear interested, though all she could think of was her father and how an extra day's separation risked bringing a depression upon him. Instead of sitting by the fire in Croft House, asking questions about London from arrival to departure, he would be dining at Emily's, listening to an account of what Mrs Finch and Mrs Adams had said that afternoon.

'Do you agree with them, Rebecca?'

Rebecca stared at Henry, wondering if she should ask him to repeat himself. She cleared her throat and said, 'Yes, I think I do.'

'Glad to hear it, so do I. It certainly is high time a woman was allowed to vote. Only those of a certain credibility and age, mind you. One has to maintain standards.'

The grandest of the four guest bedrooms in Henry's home was on the third floor and at the back of the house. It was sheltered from the noise of the street and the comings and goings in the hall, and at the time of going down for dinner Rebecca was uncertain whether Edward had arrived. As she reached the top of the lower staircase, she found Alice standing with her hand on the banister.

Alice put her finger to her lips. 'They're here,' she whispered. 'Papa's having drinks with them. The maid said your cousin's friends are rather handsome.'

'Friends? I thought Edward was bringing just one guest?'

'There are two. And you should know that your cousin has a bump on his forehead.'

'A bump?'

Alice nodded. 'I'm glad I was told. I would have stared at it otherwise.'

Rebecca kept alongside Alice until the drawing room. A thought about Edward's bump came to her and she hesitated. Alice pulled her forward.

Edward and his friends were standing with their backs to the door, listening to Henry.

Rebecca swallowed. 'Rupert?'

Rupert turned and smiled. 'Good evening, Rebecca.'

'Mr Schapell?' said Alice.

'Good evening to you, Miss Gray,' he said. 'And to you, Miss Lawrence.'

Edward looked at Mr Schapell and then Rebecca. 'Do I not get a greeting, cousin?'

Rebecca came forward, kissing Edward on the cheek.

'I hope you're not too surprised by my choice of companions,' said Edward.

'A little. I wasn't aware you and Mr Schapell were friends.'

'We're in the same college. He's studying something rather tiresome and needs distracting from time to time.'

Rebecca glanced at Edward's bump. 'As do you, cousin.'

'Do you enjoy the theatre, Mr Schapell?' said Alice.

'Please, I prefer Ralph. I had hoped to catch a show last night. Unfortunately, I was waylaid.'

'Well, *we* saw Vesta Tilley at the Hippodrome. She's awfully funny.'

Rupert turned to Rebecca. 'Was she as entertaining as when we saw her at the Alhambra?'

'She was, yes.'

'You'd seen her before?' said Alice.

The gong sounded, allowing Rebecca to ignore Alice's question.

'Follow me, gentlemen,' said Henry.

Rupert sat next to Rebecca at the dining table. Alice placed herself next to Ralph.

'Has London charmed you enough to make you want to return, Miss Lawrence?' asked Ralph.

'I hope to return in the summer. I expect there are many places I should visit here.'

'There are,' said Alice. 'But I insist you come with us to Brighton.'

'Perhaps our paths will cross there,' said Ralph. 'We always take rooms at the Royal.'

'How remarkable,' said Alice. 'That's where we stayed last year. I expect we'll be there again this summer. Will you be?'

Henry cleared his throat deliberately. 'I haven't given any thought to our hotel, Alice. Your mother may desire a change.'

'She won't, I know it. She found the Royal to be charming. You'll think the same, Rebecca.'

'I wouldn't want to intrude.'

'Not at all, you're very welcome,' said Henry. 'Your father may even wish to join us.'

'He's often talked about taking me to the seaside.'

'You've never been?' said Rupert.

'No, our holidays have always been spent close to home.'

'Is Schapell a German name?' asked Alice.

Ralph smiled. 'It is. My grandfather was German. He met

my English grandmother when she was on a tour in Italy. He followed her to England and never lived in Germany again.'

Alice's eyes widened. 'I suppose that's the effect love can have.'

'Yes, I suppose it is.'

'And you speak German?' said Rupert.

'I struggle to speak a word. I can't say I've been interested in the language.'

'Papa's teaching me French,' said Alice. 'You speak it perfectly, don't you?'

'Almost. My father tutored me as a boy.'

'Did my mother have tuition?' said Rebecca.

'Possibly, though your mother's focus was on her music. I expect staring at a blackboard would have been a little dull for her.'

'That I can understand,' said Edward. 'I'm forever closing my eyes in a lecture, however hard I fight it.'

'It could be, that what is being said is the reason for your fatigue,' said Rupert. 'I can't say I know of any man at Cambridge with such a complaint.'

'Perhaps that's because every man at Cambridge, present company excluded, is a bore.'

Henry looked at Alice and smiled. 'Did I not say that having young people here would be good for the house? Please, gentlemen, don't hold back on my account.'

'There's no need to, Mr Gray,' said Edward. 'Rupert has greater intelligence than I to realise I am correct.'

Rupert, Ralph and Edward laughed. Rebecca waited until the noise died down and said, 'What brought you to London, Rupert?'

'Edward. He wired me this morning telling me I had to come to his hotel at once. I presumed he was in some sort of bother.'

'I most certainly was,' said Edward. 'The chap who was

meant to come down cancelled on me. Rescuing Rupert from a library to keep me company seemed the decent thing to do.'

'I'm glad you did,' said Henry.

'My mother's also to blame,' said Edward. 'She suggested I invited you down.'

'Aunt Emily said Rupert should visit?' said Rebecca.

Edward nodded. 'A little complicated, is it not?'

'I'm sure it was very clear to your mother.'

'And then by chance I came across Ralph this afternoon. He was loitering in my hotel's foyer with a glum look about him. I told him he was to cancel his plans for the evening and join us. I don't believe I've ever seen a chap's mood change so quickly.'

'Were your plans ghastly?' said Alice.

'They were certainly not of my choosing,' said Ralph.

'And what a coincidence it is that we'd already met.'

'I always prefer to say fate rather than coincidence.'

Alice's eyes widened again. 'Do you really? Then so shall I.'

'And what do you believe in, Rupert?' said Henry. 'Fate or coincidence?'

'I prefer to believe the life I lead is one of my design and any coincidence or fate is merely good fortune.'

'In which case, it is our good fortune you're here.'

Rupert glanced at Rebecca and said, 'And mine.'

When the time came for the guests to leave Alice did her best to delay Ralph by interrogating him about his life in Oxford. Rebecca stepped away as the questions dragged. Rupert followed her.

'I hope you don't find Hallow too quiet when you return,' he said.

'I don't expect to, although I'll miss Alice's company. I seem to only spend time with ladies my father's age or with children.'

'I'll be there soon, if you wish to speak to someone closer to your age, that is. And Edward will be home for at least part of Easter, unless he's tempted abroad.'

'We could threaten to punish him if leaves the country.'

'And what would you have in mind?'

'Tickling. Aunt Emily says that after champagne it's his greatest weakness.'

'Is it really? I never knew. I wish I had. It would have been rather useful when we were younger.'

'I believe he's still young enough to be teased.'

Rupert smiled. 'Well said. So do I.'

Rebecca was met off the London train by her father and Emily. During lunch she narrated her time away, but spoke nothing of Rupert until Emily asked whether Edward had been accompanied to dinner.

'Schapell?' said Emily. 'I can't recall Edward ever mentioning him. Is he foreign? I expect he is. They seem to prefer Oxford to Cambridge. For some peculiar reason they believe it's warmer.'

'There's nothing peculiar about it,' said Rebecca's father. 'It's the truth.'

'He said he had German heritage,' said Rebecca.

'Perhaps Oxford took him for its eights crew,' said Emily. 'Germans are rather good rowers. A very powerful race.'

'He did say his parents live in Hertfordshire and he's studying economics.'

'Economics? Oh, how very German of him. Well, I hope he can influence Edward to be a little more careful with money. He exceeds his allowance every term and swears his friends suffer the same predicament. Did Edward speak of money to you?'

'No.'

'And he appeared healthy?'

Rebecca thought of Edward's bump. 'He seemed very happy.'

'A man of his age should be. And is this Mr Schapell a person of means? Gentlemen who study economics either have a desire to create wealth or avoid losing it.'

'He said his father had a knighthood.'

Emily raised her eyebrows. 'A German with a knighthood? Then he must have money. Your uncle would be wise to get one if he's serious about politics. No doubt someone in his party will help him.'

'Perhaps Edward will invite Mr Schapell to visit,' said Rebecca's father. 'I'm eager to brush up on my German.'

'He can only speak a few words,' said Rebecca.

Emily frowned. 'He can't speak his mother tongue? How odd, though some may regard it as a blessing. German is such a coarse language to listen to.'

Rebecca's father sighed. 'And was Rupert impressed by him?'

'I couldn't say. We talked only briefly.'

'I'll ask Edward to invite him,' said Emily. 'I expect you to be there too, James. Should Mr Schapell suddenly decide he can speak German we'll need an interpreter.'

After every question Rebecca sought to ask her father one of her own. Fear of damaging his mood kept the words in her mind. By the evening, when weariness from the journey had set in, she could sense her patience begin to break.

'I think I'll read in bed,' said her father, making for the door. 'Good night.'

'Papa, Alice made a comment I couldn't understand. At least, it sounded strange to me.'

'Did she? What was it concerning?'

'Henry… and Mama.'

'In what respect?'

Rebecca swallowed. 'How he reacted to news of her death.'

'What did Alice say?'

'She said Henry was in shock because it came as a surprise to him.'

Rebecca's father stared at the fire in silence. His face hardened. 'Your mother wouldn't have wanted me to lie to you, even more so with Henry and Emily in your life now.'

'Emily?'

'Yes. You see, your mother's death came as a surprise to them both.'

'How can that be?'

'Because neither of them knew your mother had cancer.'

'What?'

'They didn't know she had cancer.'

'But she would have told Henry in a letter, and you would have told Emily.'

'She didn't want them to know, and I gave up trying to change her mind.'

'Not even towards the end?'

Rebecca's father sat down. He remained staring at the fire. 'Your mother couldn't bear them seeing what cancer had done to her. She didn't want them to see her in bed, weak and in pain. She didn't want you to either.' Rebecca's father paused. He swallowed and said, 'When your mother was at her very worst she wanted you to stay with Emily.'

'She spoke nothing of it to me.'

'I said I wouldn't allow you to leave. I said you had the strength to cope… that I needed you.'

'I wouldn't have gone.'

'I know.'

Rebecca felt a surge of love for her mother. She began to cry.

'Come here.'

Rebecca went to her father's side. She closed her eyes as an arm came round her. In her mind, she could see her mother lying in her bed, the bones in her face too easily seen.

'We can't live in the past, Rebecca. We can't change it, however much we want to.'

EIGHT

Rebecca placed two envelopes side by side on the table. She reached for the one with the handwriting she recognised, put it down, and opened the other letter, curious as to who had sent it.

Dearest cousin,

I write urgently as Ralph demands it. He's returning to London (without me) and wishes to know what response he should expect if he was to write to your uncle with a request that Alice accompany him to dinner. He has no desire to appear a fool and receive a polite rejection, although the fool mentions your cousin's name more often than is healthy so a rejection may not be such a terrible thing. I have news of my own, but I shall keep my powder dry until Easter when I may well disappear. Until I do I wish to see much of you. Please forgive me for ending abruptly – the professor keeps looking my way.

Rebecca opened the second letter. As she finished reading it, her father appeared.

'You're rather popular this morning,' he said.

'Edward's written to me.'

'I'm pleased to hear it. And the other letter?'

'From Rupert. He requested I speak to you.'

'Oh. Concerning?'

'Seeking your permission for me to walk with him on the Malvern Hills at Easter.'

Rebecca's father raised his eyebrows.

'Edward will also be there, and it would be on a day I wasn't teaching,' said Rebecca.

'I think it's a fine idea. Your mother and I walked on the Malverns many times, often with Henry. She even insisted walking on them when she was pregnant.'

'With me?'

Rebecca's father looked down. 'No, not with you.'

'Sorry, I should have thought before asking.'

'Write to Rupert today. You should stress in your reply to Edward we expect him to visit us at Easter. Any means of keeping him from disappearing will make Emily happy.'

Rupert made all the arrangements for the walk. During the journey to the station, he told Rebecca that on a clear day Wales could be seen from the top of the Malverns.

'There's a bluff, seventy miles or more away, that's just on the other side of the Welsh border,' he said. 'Cloud often hides it. Hopefully we'll be in luck today.'

When it seemed there was nothing more to say about the hills, Rupert spoke about London and how after dinner at Henry's, Edward had taken him to a public house.

'Dear Edward drank far too much,' said Rupert. 'As did Ralph.'

'What do you make of him?'

'Ralph? I suppose he's charming enough. Edward says he's impossibly clever, though he mentioned nothing of his studies when we were in the pub. He spent most of the night talking about your cousin Alice.'

'Oh dear. Poor Alice.'

'I hope my presence at your uncle's wasn't an unwelcome surprise. I was a little fearful what your reaction might be.'

'You had nothing to fear. I was pleased to see you.'

'You were?'

'Very much so.'

When they reached the station, Edward was waiting on the platform. He was holding a walking stick the height of his chest. 'Are you ready to conquer the mountain?' he said.

'I thought it was just a hill?' said Rebecca.

'Mountain sounds far more adventurous and the peak is not far off from it qualifying as one.'

'It's about sixty feet shy,' said Rupert.

'There you have it. Just ten more of Rupert and you have a mountain.'

Edward kept a grip of his walking stick on the train, ignoring the suggestion it would be better placed on the luggage rack.

'I'm amazed you still have it,' said Rupert.

'It's been in the corner of my room for years. I thought it was high time it was put to use.'

'Perhaps you could explain to Rebecca how your walking stick came into being.'

'There's not really a tale to tell.'

'Come now, Edward. Don't deceive your cousin.'

'No doubt your mother would reveal its history if I asked?' said Rebecca.

'Some of its history,' said Rupert. 'She's unaware of the whole truth, is she not, Edward?'

'That may be true.'

'Now I'm intrigued even more,' said Rebecca.

'Promise me you won't say a word to my mother.'

'I promise.'

Edward sighed. 'Then I suppose I have no choice, do I?'

'No, you don't,' said Rupert.

'Mmm... Where shall I begin?'

'How about with Oscar?' said Rupert.

'Oh yes, Oscar, my father's best friend.'

'Oscar was a Labrador, Rebecca.'

'And a very handsome one,' said Edward. 'He and my father were inseparable. Anyhow, when the poor chap died Papa was devastated and buried him in the garden, and planted an oak tree by his grave. Mama said she would often catch him standing by it, talking to Oscar as if he was still with us. He cared for this tree so dearly he even put a little fence around it to stop the neighbour's dog from going to the toilet on it. Unfortunately, it was the only young tree in the garden. Every other tree was old and with trunks that were impossible for a seven-year-old to climb.'

'I should point out that we did try,' said Rupert.

'We tried very hard. We attempted every trunk until there was only one remaining.'

'Oscar's?' asked Rebecca.

'Correct,' said Edward. 'However, it was not as strong as we anticipated.'

'Please tell me you didn't bring down the tree.'

'No, not the tree, just a branch, only with me sitting on it. I fell on to the grave.'

'Your mother was outside in a shot,' said Rupert.

'It was impossible to avoid a whimper. It jolly well hurt.'

'I recall a scream.'

'Either way, Mama was furious.'

'As was your father.'

'He was, although I recall you were not there to find out.'

Rupert crossed his arms. 'I wish I had been.'

'My arm was in a sling.'

'As a precaution, not necessity. What Edward omitted, Rebecca, is that the blame for climbing the tree was placed entirely upon my shoulders.'

'Edward!'

Edward bowed his head. 'I know, I know, it was shameful.'

‘Apparently, I had forced him to climb the tree as I was older and bigger,’ said Rupert.

Edward looked up. ‘Quite a clever explanation, I thought. Certainly took the sting out of my father’s voice.’

Rebecca turned to Rupert. ‘Surely you pleaded your innocence?’

‘I could have done, but I felt so sorry for Edward with his bruised arm, and even more so for his father and his tree, that I remained quiet.’

‘For which I am forever grateful,’ said Edward.

‘You might have absorbed my share of the punishment.’

Edward frowned. ‘And have you miss out on learning how to make a staff from a tree branch? I could never do such a thing to you. Now, if you say flattering things about me I’ll let you borrow it on the mountain. But not on the steep parts, I’m feeling a little delicate today.’

A trail of carriages occupied by daytrippers began at Malvern station, continued through the little town and went up a winding road to the starting point of the walk. At a gate was an open cart with two shire horses. Nearly all the spaces on the benches were taken.

‘I’ve no intention of sitting next to a stranger on such a thing,’ said Edward.

‘And I have no intention of being idle,’ said Rupert. ‘Sorry, unless you wish to take it, Rebecca?’

‘Not in the slightest. I’m here to walk, not sit down.’

Edward became distracted. ‘Don’t move you two,’ he said, handing Rupert his walking stick. He marched across the road to a cottage, re-emerging within minutes with a green kite the shape of a diamond.

‘I couldn’t resist,’ he said, grinning as he returned. ‘The man said it was a new design, and it was the only one in my favourite colour.’

'So there are other kites?' said Rupert.

'There's a room full of them. A boy nearly got his hands on this one before I did. Don't worry, though. I'll let you fly it.'

'I shall fly my own, thank you. Rebecca, would you care to help me?'

The room of kites was filled with young children, all with their hands clasped behind their backs.

'We must choose one that's more impressive than Edward's,' said Rupert. 'If his kite embarrasses ours we'll hear his boasts all the way home. It would be unbearable.'

On display higher than any other was a yellow kite, smaller than Edward's but with a blue ribbon attached to the tail. Rebecca stepped closer to get a better look.

'Pretty, isn't it?' said the shopkeeper.

'But is it quick?' asked Rupert.

'As quick as a hawk, sir.'

'Then we'll take it. Agreed, Rebecca?'

Rebecca held the walking stick as Rupert paid. At the head of the stick was the rough inscription of three names: Edward... Rupert... Jane.

'Who is...?'

'Edward won't stand a chance,' said Rupert. 'Sorry, what were you about to ask?'

'It's nothing. I do hope Edward doesn't sulk when he's defeated.'

'Well, if he does we'll have to take him to a pub. No doubt his spirits will rise with a glass in his hand.'

There were two paths to the top of the Malverns. Edward insisted on taking the narrow one as it avoided the slow procession of carts. From time to time he swept aside brambles, paused as if he had heard something, and then pressed on.

Walking single file suited Rebecca, as did the privacy

of being at the back. She felt free of the need to make conversation, although every five minutes or so Rupert looked over his shoulder and smiled. Rebecca thought of her parents, convincing herself she was walking in their footsteps and that they had viewed what she was presently viewing: fields that stretched forever, little lanes and workers' cottages, perhaps while talking of their unborn child, and later, when bereaved, of returning to the Fens to live. For a moment Rebecca wished her father was with her, and then felt relieved he was not. It would be cruel, she thought, to return him to a time in his life when he knew only joy and was unaware of the agony that awaited him.

'Perfect spot to test our kites,' said Rupert, as the wind picked up.

'Patience,' said Edward. 'Once we've reached the very top we can have our fun.'

The highest point on the Malverns was marked by a slab of stone little more than a metre in height. Walkers touched it, made comments about the majesty of the view and then dispersed.

Edward put down his staff and attempted to light a pipe while cradling his kite under his arm. Every match was blown out before it reached the tobacco.

'Which way is Wales?' asked Rebecca, raising her voice because of the wind.

Rupert pointed. 'It's over there, although there's too much cloud to see it. We'll have to return on a clearer day.'

Edward gave up on his pipe. 'I'm bored. Time to let my kite embarrass yours, Rupert. Be a darling, Rebecca, and bring my staff.'

Edward, skipping more than walking, led the way to the other side of the hill. Out of a pocket he produced a hip flask and took two swigs from it. 'I feel as if I could jump off here and float to the bottom on a current. Care for a drop?'

Rupert took a sip and passed the flask to Rebecca.

'It's a twenty-year-old malt,' said Edward. 'Your body will be glad of the warmth.'

Rebecca glanced around to see if there was anyone watching.

'Just have a little,' said Rupert. 'You might get a shock otherwise.'

Rebecca put the flask to her lips and tilted it. The liquid burned the back of her throat. She resisted the urge to spit it out and gripping the staff, swallowed.

'Good show!' said Edward. 'Now that we're all warmed up we can begin.'

Rebecca sat with her back to a rock, sharing her attention between Edward and Rupert and the fields below. At times she glanced at passers-by, certain that no-one, unless they were from a landscape as flat as the Fens, was as in awe of the view as she was.

'Rebecca...would you care to take over?'

Rebecca went and stood at Rupert's shoulder.

'Come and stand in front of me,' he said.

Rebecca ducked under the kite string. She sensed Rupert move closer and looked down. His boots were nearly touching hers.

'Put your hands just below mine,' he said. 'That's it. In a moment I'll release my grip and you'll be in control. Are you ready?'

'I hope so.'

The kite lost height as Rupert moved his hands along the string. They touched Rebecca's and stopped.

'Hurry up, cousin,' said Edward. 'My kite's getting lonely up there.'

Rebecca glanced down again as Rupert released his grip. His boots were no longer by hers.

The wider path was chosen for the return to the bottom. There was space for Edward, Rupert and Rebecca to walk side by side.

'Damn! Nearly empty,' said Edward, tilting the hip flask. 'Probably for the best. I know a chap who tumbled down a hill when he was tight. Silly bugger broke his arm.'

'Perhaps you should have your staff for balance then,' said Rebecca.

'No, no, you look quite suited with it. Don't you agree, Rupert?'

'Very much so. It's rare to find a young woman with the confidence to carry such a thing.'

'Then perhaps you should visit the Fens,' said Rebecca. 'You'll find most young women are quite different to the ones you know.'

Edward slowed. He placed his pipe in his mouth, lit the tobacco and began to puff.

'You'll need to call early tonight, Rupert, and help me prepare. How I, of all people, can argue the case for temperance is beyond me. You're sober more often than I am, so I'll need your help.'

'I'm afraid you'll have to prepare alone. I'm not attending the debate.'

'Not attending? It's the annual old boys' debate, Rupert, it's compulsory you attend. Death and madness are the only excuses not to show up, and you are neither dead nor mad.'

'No, but I do have a father who says I must help him entertain the Earl of Dudley at dinner.'

'Why the devil does he need your help? Surely he has plenty of friends who can hold a conversation.'

'None the age of the Earl's daughter.'

Edward pulled a face. 'Well, I can't hide my displeasure. It's damned inconsiderate of the Earl to drag his daughter along. I thought she was meant to be abroad again.'

'Abroad wasn't to her taste.'

Edward sighed. 'If your evening fails to pass off successfully I'll be mightily irritated.'

'Then I'm afraid you will be as I have no interest in being anything other than polite.'

Rebecca, remembering how the Earl's daughter had made Rupert laugh, searched for a distraction. Ahead she could see a man and woman resting on a bench. She presumed they were husband and wife as the man was rolling a perambulator backwards and forwards. As the woman stood and leaned over the baby, Rebecca felt a sudden desire for the scene to play out in her own life.

'What do you say, Rebecca?'

She turned to Rupert.

'Are you keen to stand on that?' he said.

Jutting out from the hillside was a rock. Rebecca imagined it giving way under the weight of three people.

'It's said that Dickens stood there,' said Edward. 'Apparently, he was struggling with one of his stories and didn't move until he'd worked it out.'

'Then we must stand on it,' said Rupert. 'Follow me, you two.'

There was no marked path down to the rock. Rupert and Edward went slowly, staying low and holding on to tufts of grass. Rebecca considered saying she would stay back and watch, but then found herself following along, her eyes fixed to the ground with each hesitant step.

'Be careful,' said Rupert.

Rebecca glanced up and lost her balance, rolling her left ankle. The agony was too much and she fell back on to the hillside, groaning.

'Don't move!' said Edward. 'Stay very still.'

Rupert reached Rebecca first. 'Do you think it's broken?' he said.

'It could be just a sprain. I've done it before.'

'We need to be on the path when the cart passes,' said Edward.

Rebecca looked over her shoulder. The climb up the hillside seemed impossible. 'I might need some help.'

'You could hold on to my shoulder and hop up,' said Edward.

'No, you'll risk putting weight on your ankle,' said Rupert. 'I'll carry you up.'

'Are you certain you can?' said Rebecca.

'Just so long as you hold on. And Edward will be behind me, won't you?'

'Every step.'

Rupert moved to Rebecca's side. 'Keep your ankle still. Now, put one arm round my neck… good. Hold on to it with your other hand and keep your fingers locked… that's it.' Rupert put one arm under Rebecca's knees, and the other round her back. 'On the count of three I'm going to stand. Don't let go when I do.'

Rebecca winced in pain.

'One, two, three!' Rupert wobbled as he stood. 'Don't worry. Just close your eyes.'

Rebecca could hear Rupert's breathing become heavier as he climbed the hill again.

'Nearly there,' he said. 'Final step, hold on… and we're up.'

Edward looked into the distance. 'I can't see a cart.'

'I could try walking,' said Rebecca.

'Not a chance,' said Rupert. 'We could be at the bottom in twenty minutes. I say we continue.'

'You could strain your back.'

'Never mind me, I want to hear a doctor say your ankle isn't broken.'

'We'd waste time trying to find one in the town,' said Edward. 'It would make sense to go to your father's practice.'

Rupert adjusted his grip. 'I'd prefer not to trouble him, but I agree. Can you hold on, Rebecca?'

'Yes.'

'Put your head on my shoulder otherwise your neck will hurt. Good, then let's begin.'

The pace was slow. At one point Rebecca looked up and caught sight of the strain on Rupert's face. He smiled when he realised the attention.

'I could try walking again,' said Rebecca.

'Sorry, can't allow it. I shouldn't have led you down the hillside.'

'You're not at fault, I was careless. And I would have heard a crack if I'd broken my ankle. I'm sure in a few days I could be back up here, flying a kite and...'

Edward stepped in front of Rupert. 'The kites! We left them behind. They would have blown away!'

Edward began to run up the path. As Rupert turned, Rebecca's hat came down over her eyes.

'One moment,' said Rupert. 'Keep your hold.'

Rupert lowered Rebecca to the grass bank and released his grip. He re-positioned the hat and swept back a strand of Rebecca's hair that had come free. He moved closer, putting his arms under Rebecca's body. 'I really am very sorry for what's happened,' he said. 'I feel as though I've ruined your day.'

'Don't be sorry. You haven't ruined anything.'

Rebecca opened her diary and read the few sentences she had written the night before. It was her timidity, she decided, that had stopped her from writing of the thrill of being held by Rupert, of her body touching his. Looking at her ankle, bandaged and resting on a pillow, she wondered if Rupert had been proud to carry her. He had been quick to decline Edward's offer of help, and even at the station, when all she required was the support of a shoulder to hobble the few metres across the platform, he had refused to put her down.

There was a cough. Rebecca instinctively closed her diary.

'Sorry, did I disturb you?' said her father, standing at the door.

'No, not at all. I was just thinking of what to write.'

'I can help you upstairs if you'd prefer to be in your room.'

'I'm fine, thank you.'

'I still believe you should cancel your lesson, and tomorrow's.'

'And I believe you should be at your surgery instead of staying here.'

'You sound very much like your mother.'

'Does that mean you won't try and argue your point any longer?'

'I suppose not. I'll leave you be.'

Rebecca picked up her pen and returned to her diary.

Papa treats me as one of his patients. A true patient is unwell, or at the very least has a broken bone. I have merely a sprained ankle, and which I am tired of already. Papa has written to Rupert, apologising for his want of appreciation yesterday. His gratitude will no doubt be met by Rupert's guilt, even though there is no cause for self-reproach. I am to blame.

Rebecca held her pen still. A motor car's engine became louder and then faded outside Croft House. Rebecca hobbled to the window and put her crutches to one side. Out of the car climbed Rupert. He straightened his cap and jacket, and approached Rebecca's father on the path. As they talked, Rupert glanced at the window. Rebecca quickly drew back.

Her father returned to the morning-room. He looked at the crutches still resting against a chair and said, 'As you can see, Rupert is here.'

'It was difficult not to hear him.'

'Indeed. He wishes to take you for a drive.'

'Is it safe?'

'I can't see why it wouldn't be, and he has instructions you're not to put any weight on your ankle.'

'You've accepted for me?'

'Would you have declined?'

Rebecca shook her head.

'It won't be for long. Rupert needs to be at the station by one o'clock.'

'He's leaving?'

'Edward's persuaded him to go to London. No doubt your cousin is restless and needs company.'

Rebecca was given her crutches and helped outside.

'You appear to be mastering those,' said Rupert, standing on the path.

'I hope I don't become too much of an expert. With luck I shan't require them within a few days.'

'I'm glad to hear it. I really am truly sorry.'

'You've apologised enough. I was at fault, no-one else. Agreed?'

Rupert smiled and moved aside as Rebecca passed through the gate.

'I wasn't aware you knew how to operate a motor car,' she said.

'Alfred has given me two lessons. He said the hardest part is ensuring your cap is not blown off in the wind. I've still got mine so we should be all right.'

Rupert helped Rebecca into the passenger seat. He leaned down and removed a metal object by her feet.

'Would you mind helping with the hand crank, Dr Salisbury? I'll need to be in the driver's seat while you turn it.'

'Happy to. Although I've never used one.'

Rupert slotted the crank into the front of the car. 'The

trick is to think of this as a key to a clock,' he said. 'All you're doing is winding up the engine. Alfred did warn me not to grip with the thumb. Oh, and be prepared to pull your hand away when the engine starts.'

Rupert took his seat. 'You can begin,' he said, pulling a lever.

'Righto!'

The engine came to life. Rebecca passed her crutches to her father.

'Remember, no walking,' he said.

It took some effort for Rupert to manoeuvre in the lane. At the final turn the car lurched forward and began to pick up speed. Rebecca gripped the sides of the seat. 'I thought your father cared little for having a car?' she said.

'He didn't until he caught word his closest friend had bought one.'

'It's very kind of him to allow you to take me out in it.'

'I suppose it would be kind if he'd suggested it.'

'He does know you've borrowed it?'

Rupert glanced at Rebecca and smiled.

'You took it without permission?'

'My father's in town and I've no intention of crashing it so he may never find out. Now, where do you wish to go?'

A fear came over Rebecca of being caught by Rupert's father. 'Somewhere quiet where we won't be seen.'

Rupert took the road to the city. At the village boundary he started to brake and turned on to a lane lined with trees.

'Are we allowed along here?' said Rebecca.

'Possibly not.'

'What will you say if we're stopped?'

'Don't worry, we won't be.'

The lane road curved. Into view came a house that was built of light stone, had tall pillars and was larger than Ashgrove. The shutters were closed, and a fountain at the front was dry. There was no-one to be seen.

'Welcome to Hallow Park,' said Rupert. 'We have the estate to ourselves.'

'Is the house empty?'

'The owner's been in America for months. When he left he let all the staff go except for the gardener and the gamekeeper. Both their sons served under my father in South Africa so I know neither of them will bother us.'

Rupert steered on to a drive that ran along the side of the house, and brought the car to a halt. Rebecca anticipated the gamekeeper appearing before them with a shotgun over his arm. Instead, she saw a lawn that sloped to a lake, in the centre of which was a little island, beyond which ran the river. Higher up, by the house, was a terrace and steps bordered by flower beds.

'Does your father come here?' said Rebecca.

'I doubt it.'

'Is the owner unfriendly?'

'Apparently he's good company. The reason my father would not come here is because it would be too painful for him to remember.'

'Remember what?'

'My mother.'

'Sorry, I shouldn't have asked.'

'No, I'm glad you did. I want you to know.' Rupert turned the engine off, but kept his hands on the wheel. 'My father was friends with the previous owner. We often came here in the summer holidays and swam in the lake. Edward came too. Can you see the jetty?'

'It doesn't look safe.'

'Never has done. It used to have a rowing boat tied to it, a terribly old thing, I always expected it to sink. It's strange how even now I can look at the jetty and think only of Edward.'

'He did something silly, didn't he?'

'One could say that, although Alfred and I are to blame for teasing him so much about his red hair.'

'Poor Edward.'

'I disagree. You see, one summer we were allowed to camp on the island, just the three of us. I remember waking to Alfred being in a rage. Dear Edward was so unimpressed by our teasing he sought retribution by rising early… and leaving us.'

'In the rowing boat?'

Rupert nodded. 'He was on the other side of the lake pulling faces at us. The rowing boat was attached to the jetty. Alfred was furious.'

'But you weren't?'

'I was when Edward refused to return. Alfred made me swim to the jetty and row back. The water was freezing and I caught a chill. To this day Edward has never apologised, and he's thwarted every attempt I've made at revenge. Perhaps you could help me?'

'I wish I could, but family loyalty rules me out.'

'Damn! Then I'll have to be more cunning.'

Rebecca looked out at the vast lawn. In the distance she could see a narrowboat on the river. 'I can understand why your father doesn't visit here. Memories are hard to bear for some people.'

There was a long silence. Rebecca began to regret what she had said.

'I wouldn't dare ask him, but I'm confident my father had the happiest moment of his life here.'

There was another silence. Rebecca waited for Rupert to break it.

'Can you see the bench next to the oak tree?' he said.

'Yes.'

'That's where my father proposed to my mother.'

'You should go down there.'

'It would be rude to leave you.'

'Well, if you don't go I'll be cruel and say you're to blame for my ankle sprain, and then you'll feel rotten.'

Rupert smiled. 'Then I have no argument.'

Rebecca watched Rupert as he walked away. Suddenly, he turned round and approached her. 'I'd like it if you came with me.'

'But I don't have my crutches.'

'I'll carry you. I promise your ankle won't touch the ground.'

Rebecca rested her head on Rupert's shoulder as she was carried down the lawn, finding pleasure again in her body being against his, of his arms under her legs. Rupert lowered her on to the bench and caught his breath.

'Would you think it odd of me if I said I talk to my mother when I sit here?' he said.

'Speaking from experience, no.'

'What would you think?'

'I would think that you should speak to her.'

'While you were here?'

'Now that would be odd.'

'Agreed.'

'What would you have said had I not been here?'

'What do you talk to your mother about?'

Rebecca hesitated for a moment. 'I suppose if I was in the Fens I'd tell her about friends of hers, or any news in the village, my father, of course, perhaps a little about myself.'

'That seems similar to what I would say.'

'Which today would be?'

'You can be quite persistent.'

'I'm sorry. Don't feel obliged to say.'

'No, I'm quite happy to. Let me think… I would probably talk about our walk yesterday and about the hills. I might mention how relieved I was when your father said your ankle wasn't broken.'

'You would truly say that?'

'I can't see why I wouldn't. It was the most memorable day of my holiday.'

'I would have preferred it to have been your happiest.'

'Oh, it was that too. Until your fall, that is. As I said, I really am…'

'Don't you dare apologise again.'

Rupert looked towards the terrace.

'Is it time we left?' said Rebecca.

'It just occurred to me I might struggle to start the engine on my own.'

'But you're not on your own.'

'I couldn't ask you to help.'

'There must be something I can do.'

'There is, but I fear what your father might think.'

'Don't worry, I shan't tell him.'

Rupert raised his eyebrows. 'Do you promise you won't put any pressure on your ankle?'

Rebecca held out her hand for Rupert to shake.

'We should leave then,' said Rupert. 'Alfred made a point of telling me I mustn't be late returning. He can be quite a tyrant about keeping to a timetable.'

Rebecca was carried back to the car where she was helped into the driver's seat and told to remain still. She looked at the large wheel and the pedals by her feet, and felt her confidence begin to abandon her.

'Your part is very simple,' said Rupert. 'First, you need to pull out that thing there. It's called the choke.'

'What's its purpose?'

'It reduces the air supply to the engine. Now, move that stick on your left from side to side… is it loose?'

'It feels so.'

'That means the gear is in neutral.'

'What does this do?'

'That's the hand brake. Please don't touch it when I'm at the front.'

'What would happen if I did?'

'It's possible the motor car will jump forward and hit me.'

'Oh.'

'What you need to do is push that button. That's the ignition. Good. Now, when I say, you need to lightly press the throttle.'

Rebecca looked around her.

'It's the pedal by your right foot. Don't use your left, it might hurt. Are you ready?'

Rebecca glanced at the hand brake and put her hands on her lap. 'I'm ready.'

Rupert took the hand crank to the front. He inserted it into the engine and turned it. The engine resisted. 'This time!' The engine started. 'Now!'

Rebecca pressed the throttle. The engine responded with noise.

'Well done!' said Rupert, returning to the driver's side. 'You're a natural.'

'You don't expect me to drive, do you?'

'Not today. I could give you a lesson when I'm home next.'

'Would you father know?'

'Not if we return here. With a bit of luck the owner will still be away during the summer.'

Rebecca manoeuvred herself out of the seat with Rupert's help. For a moment he held her and moved closer. The engine began to fade.

'Excuse me,' said Rupert, jumping into the driver's seat. He brought the engine back to life and looked up. 'I'll carry you round.'

'I'll manage. You need to stay where you are.'

Rebecca noticed a change in Rupert's mood during the return to Peachley Lane. His grip of the wheel seemed tighter than necessary, and his attention did not stray from the road. The silence continued outside Croft House. Rebecca waited for Rupert to open his door, but he remained seated.

Rebecca started to move. 'I should go. I wouldn't want your brother to be annoyed.'

'I'd very much like to write to you. If you wish me to, that is.'

'Hello!' said Rebecca's father, approaching down the path. In his hands were the crutches.

'Will you reply if I write?' asked Rupert.

'Immediately.'

Rebecca waited at the gate as Rupert turned the motor car. As he passed by, he said something. All Rebecca heard above the noise of the engine was 'write soon'.

'That reminds me,' said Rebecca's father. 'A letter came for you earlier.'

Rupert squeezed the motor horn and waved. He reached the green and faded from view.

'I should have wished him good luck. I trust you did.'

'Good luck for what?' said Rebecca.

'For his final term. I hardly spoke a word to anyone when I did mine. All I had time for was books and sleeping.'

'I barely thanked him for taking me out. He'll think I was rude.'

'He won't give it a moment's thought, trust me. Come, I want to check if the swelling on your ankle has gone down.'

Rebecca's anxiety lingered as her bandage was removed. She felt compelled to write to Rupert with encouragement for his final term, though it occurred to her that to ask Edward or Charles for his address would risk interference from Emily.

'Rebecca...'

'Yes?'

'Don't forget your letter.'

Rebecca picked up the envelope beside her and opened it.

'The swelling is down, but you'll need the bandage on for another day or two. You must use your crutches until then. Is that understood?'

Rebecca did not respond.

'Is that understood?'

Rebecca glanced up. 'Sorry, I was reading.'

'It must be compelling not to have heard me.'

'It's more troubling than compelling.'

'Who's it from?'

Rebecca looked down at the letter. 'It's from Tilly. I have to return home.'

Nine

Rebecca was assured by her father there was no reason to worry about Mrs Pugh.

'Her doctor's competent,' he said. 'But I can understand your desire to support Tilly. I know she'd come to your side if you asked for help.'

Rebecca had no time to meet Henry or Alice in London, though in the carriage between stations she searched for their faces among the masses. What she did see was the arcade that housed the glove shop. She was decisive in her choice of gloves for Tilly and with some encouragement from Madame de Lausanne she bought a pair for herself. As she passed the fountain, she stopped and made a wish for Mrs Pugh's fever to pass quickly. She removed another coin from her purse, checked no-one was watching, and dropped the coin into the water.

Her conviction about what might occur in Cambridge began to wane as the city came into view, and then left her completely as she stood on the platform, indecisive and lonely. Only a fool, she thought, would have spent money wishing for a chance encounter with Rupert. She could not help but think of him though, and how he was close by, staring at a book or listening to a professor, or perhaps thinking of the letter he had intended to write to her.

'Can I help you, Miss?'

Rebecca looked to her side. 'I'm quite all right, thank you.'

The guard nodded and turned away.

'Wait! How long till the next train to Welney?'

'Another hour, Miss.'

'Is there a tearoom close by?'

'Simpson's is popular. Turn right at the front of the station and walk for about a quarter of a mile. You can't miss it, there's always an old man playing an accordion outside.'

Rebecca remembered her father's warning about straining her ankle and took a cab. Simpson's was an ancient building of oak beams with a roof that sagged in the centre. According to the inscription above the door it had been Cambridge's finest teahouse for one hundred years. The accordion player appeared to be just as old.

Rebecca could sense the glare of customers as she stepped inside. Although most of the tables were taken there was a peculiar silence about the room, as if only whispering was allowed. Even the young man who guided Rebecca to a table by the window spoke quietly. No-one else was alone as she was. She gave her order and stared out of the window, watching the smartly dressed scholars laughing as they passed by.

'Is that all?' said the waiter, clearing his serving tray.

Someone knocked over a cup. Rebecca glanced towards the table by the fireplace. A woman was using a napkin to soak up spilt tea. The man opposite her had his head turned away and was doing nothing to help. As Rebecca watched the woman fluster, she was struck by the sense she had been in Simpson's many years before. She began to look around her, at the square tables, the counter, the narrow staircase, and then back to the fireplace, certain she had sat by it as a child. Her mother was travelling somewhere… was it to London? She could remember saying goodbye on the platform and crying after being told to stay with her father.

She turned back to the window. A queue was forming at a newspaper stand across the street. A man stepped away and raised his head, and Rebecca froze. It's him, she thought. It's Rupert. She hurriedly placed some coins on the table and left Simpson's without saying a word. She searched the street for Rupert and saw him on the footpath, walking away from her. Ignoring the faint stabs of pain from her ankle, Rebecca quickened her stride, wondering what she would say. Surely, she thought, Rupert would believe fate was at play. He slowed. Rebecca willed him to turn, but instead he opened his arms. A woman approaching him did the same and they embraced. Rebecca stood still, staring at Rupert as he released the woman from his embrace. The woman touched Rupert's hand and put her arm through his. Rebecca walked towards them again, her attention fixed on Rupert's reaction to what the woman was saying.

'Miss… hello.'

Rebecca looked behind her.

'You forgot this,' said the waiter from Simpson's.

Rebecca took her case from him.

'Thanks very much for the tip. It's the first I've 'ad.'

Rebecca said nothing and turned. The woman was leading Rupert away.

'Rebecca… Rebecca.'

The voice, faint but familiar, stirred Rebecca.

'You came,' said Mrs Pugh. 'Tilly said you would. I knew you would.'

Rebecca sat up straight. A book fell from her lap to the floorboards. 'I should have come earlier. I'm sorry.'

'Don't be. You're here now.'

Rebecca pulled away her blanket and rose from the rocking chair. She sat down on the edge of the bed. 'Tilly said the doctor believes the worst has passed.'

'It feels so. He's not as thorough as your father though.'

Rebecca smiled. 'Few doctors are.'

'Where's Tilly?'

'She's in her room.'

'I'm glad. She's barely left my side for days.'

'It took some persuasion to get her to sleep in her own room. I threatened to leave if she didn't agree.'

Mrs Pugh pushed herself up on the pillows. 'We've missed you. Tilly was very upset after you left.'

'You have only to write and I'll visit.'

'With your father?'

'Just me, I expect. Papa may never want to return to Welney.'

Mrs Pugh squeezed Rebecca's hand. 'I understand.'

There was a long silence. Rebecca wondered what she could say about her new life in Hallow.

'I'm afraid Tilly won't be her normal self while you're here,' said Mrs Pugh.

'I wasn't my normal self while my mother was ill. Tilly always found a way of helping, often by making me smile.'

'I hope you can do the same for her.'

'I'll certainly try to.'

Mrs Pugh's eyes began to close. 'I remember seeing you sit by your mother's bedside,' she said. 'I'm sorry you've been called to be at mine.'

Rebecca remained still as Mrs Pugh fell asleep. A sadness anchored deep in the past came over her. All she could do was hold Mrs Pugh's hand, or cool her forehead, or pour her a glass of water. She felt as helpless as she had when her mother was sick.

'Is she sleeping?'

Mrs Pugh's eyes twitched at the whisper. Rebecca took Tilly on to the landing, closing the door behind her.

'She's fine,' said Rebecca. 'Have *you* slept?'

'I couldn't. I kept wanting to check on her.'

'She needs rest, as do you.'

'I want to be next to her.'

Rebecca sighed. 'Promise me you'll try to sleep.'

Tilly nodded.

'You have to take care of yourself. Your mother needs you to be well.'

The bread in Mrs Pugh's pantry was stale and the egg basket empty. Tilly said she had meant to place a delivery order, but had feared leaving her mother alone. Apart from the doctor, Rebecca was the first visitor in five days. The Three Tuns had not been open during that time as both barmen had also fallen ill, as had the maid. Rebecca cursed herself as she walked into the village. If she had not been so careless on the Malverns she could have travelled immediately to Tilly's side instead of having to delay her journey until her ankle's swelling had reduced.

Her uncertainty about whether she should still regard Welney as her home also bothered her. She found comfort in the sight of the morning mist clinging to the Old Bedford River and the limitless horizons of the Fens, but even in the familiarity of The Three Tuns she had the sense of being a visitor. What was it, she thought, that she had pined for? The landscape? Tilly's friendship? Or was it for the life she once had?

Mr Graves was nowhere to be seen in his shop. Rebecca gave her delivery order and left, relieved a stranger had served her. At the turning to The Three Tuns she stopped and looked the other way, telling herself not to be scared of what lay ahead. She pressed on, her head lowered and the ache from her ankle growing with each step. Her heart beat faster as she took the path off the riverbank. The gate at the end was closed. Rebecca reached to open it.

'Can I help you?'

Rebecca turned sharply. A man carrying a doctor's bag stepped a little closer.

'I didn't mean to startle you,' he said.

'You didn't… I should leave.'

'You're Dr Lawrence's daughter, aren't you? We met when I came to look at the house. You were playing the piano.'

An upstairs window opened. A girl stared at Rebecca.

'That's Anna, my eldest daughter,' said the man. 'I believe she's in your old room.'

'That was my parents' room. Mine was at the back of the house.'

'Oh, then my other daughter is in your room. Would you care to meet them?'

Rebecca looked up again. Anna remained at the window. 'I must go… goodbye.'

Later that night Rebecca and Tilly sat by the fire in the empty lounge of The Three Tuns, sipping cocoa and playing bridge. Mrs Pugh remained in bed. She had managed to stay awake for the best part of the day and her temperature had cooled.

'You can disagree,' said Tilly, 'but I wouldn't be surprised if you become engaged before I do.'

Rebecca laughed. 'What an odd thing to say.'

'It was Mama who made me think so.'

'Then your dear mother is mistaken, though I blame the fever for affecting her judgement.'

'She seemed convinced.'

'That I was soon to be engaged?'

'No, that was my prediction.'

'So what was your mother convinced of?'

'That you're in love.'

Rebecca raised her eyebrows. 'Why would she think that?'

'Will you deny it?'

'Of course.'

'Are you certain?'

'Very much so.'

'Oh, then I'm sorry to hear it. It's not fair you've never been in love.'

'I'm only twenty-one.'

'Which means it's high time you thought about marriage.'

'You sound like my aunt.'

'Then your aunt is a wise woman. Surely she can introduce you to someone?'

There was a knock on the front door of The Three Tuns.

'Allow me,' said Rebecca, relieved to evade Tilly's question.

Sheltering under the porch was Mr Graves, soaked from rain and holding a walking stick. 'I saw the light and thought you were open again. I would have gone to the Black Swan but my hip's playing up.'

Rebecca felt a rush of pity. She invited Mr Graves in and guided him to her chair.

'I won't be keeping you,' he said. 'Just need to warm up a bit.'

Tilly poured Mr Graves a whiskey. She was generous in her measure and told him to put his money away. 'I do expect you to play bridge with me, however,' she said.

'Happy to oblige, though you should prepare to lose. The last person to beat me was my wife. I didn't have the heart to win. We were on our honeymoon, after all.'

The following morning Mrs Pugh left her room for the first time in a week and sat at the table for breakfast. Tilly still refused to leave the house, though this suited Rebecca as she wished to be alone for a while. She found enough daffodils in the garden to make a bunch, tying the stems together with a piece of yellow ribbon Tilly had found.

The graveyard was empty except for those at rest. Rebecca stopped for a moment at the entrance to compose herself. The plot next to her mother's had been filled. Dorothy Graves, beloved wife of Albert, had died four months before, just days from turning seventy.

Rebecca moved along. She stared at the headstone inscription, swallowing hard as she read 'adoring mother of Rebecca'. She placed her flowers on the grave and stepped back.

'The flowers are from Tilly's garden. The poor thing's been in a terrible way with worry. I can't bear saying goodbye again.' Rebecca looked around her, checking she was alone. 'People still ask why we moved to the village…I expect some know the true reason.' Rebecca paused again, wondering what her mother would want to hear. 'There's a girl in your room now. Her name is Anna. I could have met her. This sounds cowardly, but I was too scared to go inside.'

Rebecca suddenly remembered a room of people dressed in black. She stared into the distance, allowing a tear to slide down her cheek. Past the church she could see her house and her bedroom window. The memory began to fade.

'I feel lost, Mama. I've been made a fool of. I thought someone…'

Rebecca sensed she was being watched. As she turned, she caught sight of a woman walking away from the graveyard. Her head was lowered and a hat concealed the colour of her hair. Rebecca felt a twist of anxiety. She wanted to be inside, out of sight and close to Tilly.

'I have to leave now. I love you, Mama. I'll return. I promise.'

The Three Tuns remained closed. Mr Graves called, drawn again by the light from the lounge. Rebecca let him in and poured his whiskey as he settled by the fire.

'Will you play chess with me?' he said.

'I don't know how to. I expect Tilly does. She'll be down shortly.'

'I can teach you if you wish. I'd be happy to.'

Rebecca could see loneliness in Mr Graves's eyes. She pulled out a chair and agreed to the lesson.

'I told my wife that if she could master chess then our marriage would be better than most folk have,' said Mr Graves. 'You have to be patient, calm, and able to anticipate what might happen next. My wife soon picked it up.'

'Chess, or marriage?'

Mr Graves smiled. 'Both, bless her.'

As Mr Graves arranged the chess pieces, it occurred to Rebecca that never in Hallow could she play chess in a pub with a man as Emily would never allow it.

Tilly brought two glasses of brandy to the table and topped up Mr Graves's whiskey. 'Mama wants me to call on our staff in the morning. We could be open again tomorrow.'

'A toast to your mother,' said Mr Graves. 'And to you both.'

Glasses were chinked over the chess board. Rebecca felt flushed with a sense of belonging and wanted to pledge her swift return. She thought of Rupert and how cruel false hope can be and said nothing. Whispered instructions from Tilly kept her in the chess match, though Mr Graves was kind with his moves and even kinder following each sip of whiskey.

There was a knock at the front door. Tilly stood up, leaving Rebecca to decide what move to make.

'There's someone here to see you,' said Tilly, as she returned to the lounge.

'For me?'

'It's one of the girls who moved into your house. The eldest one, Anna.'

'What does she want?'

'She didn't say. Said she preferred to wait in the porch.'

Mr Graves reached for his glass. 'Perhaps she thinks this is a place of sin. A woman tried to get me to sign a pledge card the other week. I said I'd think about it while I was in here.'

'Take my place, Tilly. Don't wait for me if you know what to do.'

Anna, dark haired and with her hands behind her back, looked up as Rebecca opened the door.

'I hope I haven't interrupted you,' said Anna.

'Not at all. Won't you come in?'

'I can't. My father will be back soon.'

'Oh.'

'I meant to speak to you this morning.'

Rebecca studied Anna's hat and coat. 'That was you watching me in the graveyard?'

'It didn't seem right to disturb you.'

'So you've waited until now?'

'I saw you come in here earlier.'

'You followed me?'

Anna nodded.

'What is it you want to talk to me about, Anna?'

'Was your mother's name Elizabeth?'

Rebecca crossed her arms. 'Why do you ask?'

Anna brought her hands to her front. She held out a leather-bound book wrapped in a dark blue ribbon. 'This is your mother's. It's her diary.'

'What did you say?'

Anna raised the book. 'This is her diary.'

'Where did you find it?'

'In my bedroom. I was searching for an earring and noticed there was part of a floorboard missing. When I lifted it, I found this.'

Rebecca's heartbeat quickened. A memory of sitting next to her mother flashed at her.

'There's a photograph inside. It's of a girl and a woman. The girl looks like you.'

Rebecca said nothing.

Anna presented the diary again. 'I don't want it in my room. Take it… please.'

For a moment Rebecca wished the knock had been

ignored; that she was still inside playing chess. She uncrossed her arms and took the diary. 'Have you read it?'

'Not a word. The moment I realised what it was I put it back under the floorboard. It's been there for months. I'd forgotten about it until yesterday when my father said who you were.'

'Who have you told about it?'

'No-one. Not even my father.'

Rebecca stared at Anna.

'I haven't told a soul. Please believe me.'

'Have you found anything else?'

Anna shook her head. 'Will you come to the house? I'd like it if you did. My sister would too.'

'I don't think I can. Goodnight, Anna.'

Rebecca looked away from Tilly as she crossed the lounge. She kept the diary at her side, hoping it went unnoticed.

'You'll be pleased to know you haven't lost yet,' said Tilly.

Rebecca kept walking.

'Rebecca?'

'Keep playing. I'll be back in a moment.'

Rebecca closed the bedroom door behind her, conscious it would be best to hide the diary and return to the lounge immediately. She found herself sitting down in an armchair.

A delay, she thought, could do no harm. She pulled the ribbon free and removed the photograph. Staring back at her, smiling and with an arm round her waist, was herself. Her mother was by her side, untouched by cancer and holding a bouquet of flowers. It was the evening of the midsummer ball, three or four years ago.

'Is something the matter?' said Tilly, from the landing.

'No, I'll be right there.' Rebecca slid the photograph back into the pages. She ran her hand over the black leather and placed the diary under a cardigan in her case, deciding to leave it there until she was alone in Croft House.

Moving from one side of her bed to the other, Rebecca gave up hope of falling back to sleep. She lit her bedside lamp and sat up. The temptation of opening the diary, of reading just one page before hiding it permanently, remained as strong as it had been at The Three Tuns. Her sense of guilt at not telling her father about the diary, the photograph that by rights was his, lingered.

In her mind Rebecca could see the diary, wrapped in her cardigan which was still in her case. She tiptoed to the wardrobe, pulled out her case and opened it. What harm, she wondered, could come of reading one page? She placed the diary on her bed and kneeled as if in prayer. Her mother's Christian name was at the top, the space below blank except for the manufacturer's name of Hawthorne & Hartley of London. Rebecca pinched the edge of the first page and turned it, running her finger down the spine. She knew she had to close the diary. Instead, she began to read.

January 10, 1903

'Hope abandoned me today. It fled as I looked the doctor in the eye and then I saw it leave James as the diagnosis was given. I have as little as six months until cancer kills me. Rebecca will have to be told tomorrow. If I could wait then I would, but I can deceive her no longer. Our explanation for visiting London shall remain a lie, as it will for Henry, though my deception of my darling brother shall be the greatest of all. He will remember me as I was last evening: sitting at his piano, playing the songs our mother loved. The memories about to burden Rebecca will be heavy. No child should witness a parent's slow death as she will. A quick passing without affirmation of one's love would be less harsh. I fear the temptation of giving her hope will overcome James and I tomorrow. It is a parent's right to give their child comfort, as it is their duty to speak the truth. Tomorrow Rebecca's world of today will be no more. I have failed her. May God bless her with courage in the darkness that is to come.'

Rebecca pressed her wrist hard against her mouth, fearing her sobs would wake her father. She wiped her cheeks with her nightgown sleeve and stared at the diary. Floorboards upstairs creaked. Rebecca looked for a better hiding place. In a trunk, among childhood books and old clothes, she found a scarf she had no use for. She wrapped the diary in it and closed the trunk lid, turning the key for the first time since the move from the Fens. Floorboards creaked again. Rebecca removed her own diary from her desk and slid the trunk key into the sleeve. Her old diary! It had also been made by Hawthorne & Hartley. She could remember receiving it the night her parents returned from visiting Henry. She had stayed a night at Tilly's while they were absent; her plea to go to London having been dismissed because Henry was unwell. It had all been a lie. A realisation came over Rebecca that her mother's suffering had begun weeks or possibly months before she knew of it. She put her hand to her mouth again. A shiver went through her and she climbed back into bed. As she went to turn down the lamp, she caught sight of the ribbon on the floor and reached for it. Another creak came from above. Rebecca pushed her face down into the pillow to muffle her weeping. Clasping the ribbon she whispered, 'Help me, Mama… please.'

Rebecca had worried about the diary since waking. It was quite possible, she decided, her father knew of its existence. He might have searched for it after the funeral and then asked the new owner of their home to look for it. Anna might have lied about not telling anyone. Rebecca questioned what she should say if her father received a letter from Anna; whether it was best to deny she had the diary or speak the truth.

She stared at the river, desperate for the stillness of the water to bring her peace. Harry came to her mind. If she made him swear not to tell a soul he could find Anna's letter in the post office before his father delivered it. The diary would remain secret.

Rebecca resumed walking. She stopped suddenly, turning one way then the other, reducing screams of frustration to a sigh. 'I won't do it! I won't ask Harry to deceive his father,' she said to herself. She continued on until she reached the jetty. She stepped along planks still wet with morning dew and sat down on the jetty's edge, remembering how she would stand with her mother on the banks of the Old Bedford, skimming flat stones across the surface when it was calm, willing her stone to hit the water one more time until it disappeared. The key! She could throw the trunk key in the water and temptation with it. The diary would remain unread, just as her mother had intended it to be.

'It's very peaceful that spot, wouldn't you agree?'

Rebecca turned. The Earl's daughter, standing on the riverbank, stared back at her.

'I would, yes,' said Rebecca.

'I've sat there many times, mostly as a child though. We used to sail little boats when the current was strong. It was tremendous fun.'

'I always found the making of the boat to be the most fun part.'

'Oh, I never made my boat. Rupert always did.'

'Your brother?'

'No. Rupert Salisbury.'

Rebecca said nothing.

'We've been friends for years. My father thinks the world of him. As do I, of course.'

Rebecca swallowed. 'Of course.'

'I should leave you alone, I've interrupted your solitude long enough. Good day to you, Miss Lawrence.'

Later that day, at Waterloo Square, Emily announced she had terrible news about Edward.

'The silly boy says he's in love.'

Rebecca glanced at the ladies, wondering who would react first.

'I don't understand,' said Mrs Finch. 'Why is that terrible news?'

'Because he's in his final term. His mind won't cope with thoughts of a young lady. The only saving grace is that the girl is Rupert's cousin. He introduced her to him last week in Cambridge. She lives there apparently.'

'I'd be rather relieved if my son said he was in love,' said Mrs Adams. 'Occupying oneself with nothing but study can only lead to poor health.'

'What does she look like?' asked Rebecca.

'Who, dear?' said Emily.

'Rupert's cousin.'

'I've never met her.'

'Has Edward not described her?'

'Only in so much that he believes her to be the most beautiful young lady he's ever seen.'

Rebecca was unsatisfied. 'When *do* you expect to meet her?'

'I don't expect I ever shall. Edward has been infatuated with half a dozen or more young ladies in the past and will soon forget Rupert's cousin. One can only hope the poor girl will soon forget him.'

Rebecca left the trunk key in Croft House the next time she walked along the riverbank, and soon found herself in a routine after her father went to bed. Sitting cross-legged on the rug by the fire, she read page after page of her mother's diary until weariness or emotion overcame her. She had buried her grief as deep as she could, but now it was resurrected she feared she would never be free of it. Nevertheless, she read on. Some entries, when there were accounts of the hunt ball, Easter gala, and rowing on the Old Bedford River, seemed untouched by darkness, as if the cancer did not exist.

Rebecca looked at her father at breakfast every day, debating whether she should be honest with him. His claim to the diary was equal to hers, or more so given it had been hidden in his room. There were entries when her name was not even written; when the emphasis was on her father's suffering and how he blamed himself for failing to make an early diagnosis. It was after reading these pages that Rebecca thought it best to withhold the truth. One morning her father lowered his newspaper and asked why she looked sad and tired. She gave the explanation she had rehearsed: that she missed Tilly and had lost sleep worrying about her.

Afternoons in Waterloo Square passed by without further talk of Edward's infatuation with Rupert's cousin. His new interest was to become an officer in the British Army.

'He's under the misapprehension that all he would do is gad about in a foreign land and from time to time parade in front of a colonel,' said Emily. 'When he realises he'll be shot at by natives he'll discover a new plan for when he leaves Oxford, which will be unfortunate. Army discipline could be the making of him.'

Edward wrote to Rebecca in early June, demanding her company before his officer training commenced.

'I shall be rising late and retiring when it suits me. I expect your attention in the hours I'm awake, and request you remember every smile, laugh and misdemeanour as I shall soon be cleansed of all three. Cousin Teddy of Waterloo Square is to be polished into Second Lieutenant Edward Warwick of Norton Barracks, Worcester. You may curtsey if you wish when you see me in my officer's uniform, but I shan't think any less of you if

you don't (though I beg of you to make a fuss if there are young ladies present). Oh, I very nearly forgot. Rupert said he would write to you. Much love, Edward.'

Rupert's letter swiftly followed Edward's. He opened with an apology for failing to write sooner. Recompense would come in the form of the loan of his horse, and a lesson in how to drive a motor car. Rebecca read his final sentence over and over.

'It is my fervent hope that the weeks of summer ahead are as happy for you, Edward and me as any that have come before.'

For all of their eagerness to pass time with her, neither Edward nor Rupert told Rebecca the date of their return home. Emily too was none the wiser.

'I'll let you know the moment Edward appears,' she said, 'though don't be too expectant. He's long threatened to travel to Paris for a holiday when he leaves Oxford.'

The diary and preparations for the midsummer dance distracted Rebecca from thinking too much about Rupert. Sitting on a bench in her garden, she stared at the blank sheet of paper in her hands, wishing she had spoken up when Kate had asked her to write a list of dances. She knew the names of many dances, but feared each belonged to the Fens and her suggestions would be frowned upon. The heat of the day was working against her. The maid approached her as she stood up.

'Your cousin Edward is here,' said the girl.

'Wonderful, thank you.'

'He's with his friend, Mr Salisbury.'

Rebecca drew in a breath. 'Are they at the front door?'

'In the hall, miss.'

'Then I'd better not keep them waiting.'

The maid turned away.

'Stop! Ask them to come out here. We'll sit under the tree. Please bring some tea and cake.'

Rebecca checked her dress for any marks. The tip of her finger was blue with ink. It occurred to her she had just swept her hair with that hand. Her face was possibly marked with ink.

'Cousin!'

Edward strode up the path. He opened his arms and hugged Rebecca. Rupert stepped forward and kissed her on the cheek.

'Welcome home,' said Rebecca.

'Thank you,' said Rupert. 'It's lovely to see…'

'I'm famished,' said Edward, picking up the pen and paper to sit down. 'I hope you have something sweet for me.'

'Of course, though if I'd known you were calling I would have made arrangements,' said Rebecca.

'Not my fault, blame Rupert. I should be in London, but he wired me to say he was coming back a couple of days early so I thought I'd also return to the nest.'

'You chose to visit your mother over London?'

'It sounds terrible, doesn't it? Where I really wish to be is Paris. Mama wouldn't give me any more money, hence I'm still in England.'

'Then I'm pleased Aunt Emily was so strict.'

Edward yawned. 'Sorry. I arrived late last night and Mama had me hard at work all morning.'

'Now, now, Edward,' said Rupert. 'Be honest.'

'I am. It was damned hard work, I promise you, Rebecca.'

Rupert scoffed. 'Putting up bunting for a party at an orphanage is not hard work.'

'It is when the bunting's all tangled. And I also had to move hay bales for the coconut shy. My back feels as though it's been trampled on.'

'I'm certain the children are grateful,' said Rebecca.

Edward pulled a face.

'I would have gladly helped you. I'm surprised your mother didn't mention it yesterday.'

'Apparently, you're occupied enough with a dance.'

Rebecca pointed to the blank piece of paper and confessed her struggle. 'I wish some other task had been asked of me. I'll never complete it.'

'Nonsense,' said Rupert. 'We'll help you. I've lived here long enough to know what people will expect.'

Rupert and Edward started to list the names of dances. Some were familiar to Rebecca, although after one that sounded foreign, Rupert added that it was his favourite.

'And as such, I request you be my partner,' he said. 'It's quite simple. You'll pick it up quickly.'

When the list was completed, Edward turned to Rebecca and said, 'I hear you dashed back to the Fens to help a friend? That's very Florence Nightingale of you.'

'She needed my help.'

'Of course, I now expect the same devotion should I ever require a nurse.'

'Without question, cousin.'

'I take it you passed through Cambridge?' said Rupert.

'I did.'

'I wish I'd known, I could have met you. Railway stations can be lonely if you're waiting on your own.'

For a moment Rebecca could see Rupert not in front of her but standing instead on a Cambridge street, embracing the young woman. She held her eye contact and said, 'There wasn't really much time between trains. But yes, I can understand how people can feel lonely.'

Edward yawned again. He put his elbow on the bench arm and let his head fall on to his palm. Rebecca poked him.

'Sorry,' he said, sitting up. 'I normally have a sleep about now. It's my body's fault; likes to have a routine. Exercise or champagne usually tricks it. Do you have any?'

'I doubt it.'

'Oh, pity. Exercise it is then. We should go for a walk, right away, by the river. What do you say?'

Rebecca agreed, as did Rupert, who smiled as Edward turned his back. He pointed to his cheek and then to Edward and the pen. He put his finger to his lips and winked.

They took the long way to the riverbank so Rebecca could deliver the list to the vicarage. Soon after, as they made for the path to the Severn, someone from behind called out 'hold up!' The village thatcher approached. He had a bloated stomach and was carrying a scythe.

Edward took a step closer to Rupert. 'Do you think he's mad? He certainly looks it.'

'He's all right. Just brace yourself for his smell.'

The thatcher kept his distance. 'You'll have bother getting down there, folks.'

'Why?'

'Stingers, Mr Salisbury. Right across the path they are. I'm on my way to clear them.'

'And we can't get through?' said Rebecca.

'Not unless you want to get stung, Miss. Haven't seen 'em this thick in years. My advice is you take the other path.'

'Have you any more of those?' asked Rupert, pointing to the scythe.

'Reckon I might have a couple. Not as sharp as this one though.'

'Well, go and get them anyway. My friend is keen for some exercise, aren't you, Edward?'

The thatcher, who had an odour of sweat and alcohol, left his scythe with Edward and fetched two more. He strode into the stinging nettles first, grunting as he cut them down. Rupert and Edward pursued, clearing the ones that had been missed. The path was cleared within half an hour. Rupert and Edward grinned as they returned to Rebecca. They passed the scythes to the thatcher and were told to wait outside his cottage.

'It's well known he's got a cider press,' said Rupert. 'I've heard he only sells his cider if he's really hard up. Some say he even drinks it at breakfast.'

'Sounds reasonable to me,' said Edward. 'I can't see any difference between having a drink at breakfast and having one at lunch.'

The thatcher emerged from a side gate with a small barrel under his arm. He placed it on top of an old cask and pulled out the bung. Glasses were filled with a cloudy liquid and passed to Rupert and Edward.

'Do I not get to try it?' said Rebecca.

'It's probably not a drink for a lady,' said the thatcher.

'Then just give me a little. You'll soon find out if I dislike it.'

'All right, be my pleasure, Miss.'

Rebecca glanced behind her to see if Kate was at the window. She winced at her first sip. The cider was lemon sharp with a ginger kick and sultanas. As Rebecca sipped again, the thatcher and Edward started their second glass.

'Good, isn't it?' said the thatcher, coming up for air. 'I'm proud of this one. Don't expect it'll last.'

Rebecca suddenly felt light-headed. It was certainly no drink for a lady, she thought. Even the men in The Three Tuns would struggle past a pint.

'I think it's time we let the man be,' said Rupert.

Edward put his hand on the barrel. 'He doesn't look like a man who wants to be let be. Do you want to be? I don't believe that you do.'

Rupert tugged Edward's arm. 'The Severn awaits us. It was your idea, remember?'

Edward sighed. He thanked the thatcher and said he'd return to buy a barrel of cider for his breakfast. As he stepped on to the cleared path, he began to skip. Rupert remained close to Rebecca, walking slowly in front of her.

'Don't be a bore, Salisbury,' said Edward. 'I'm lonely down here.'

Rupert chased after Edward. They skipped side by side on the riverbank, both whistling and with their hands in their pockets. Edward tried to unbalance Rupert by charging him with his shoulder. The execution was clumsy and expected as Rupert stopped at the last moment and Edward went into a hedge. Rebecca laughed, as did Rupert who taunted Edward by making beckoning gestures as he ran backwards.

Edward and Rupert were on the edge of the jetty when Rebecca caught up with them. Edward was red faced and threatening to jump into the water.

'I'm either going to cool off in there or with a drink,' he said. 'I can't quite make up my mind.'

'I don't want to pull you out of the river so we'll go to the Camp,' said Rupert. 'Only if you're happy to walk, Rebecca?'

'It's really not that far for me.'

'Well it is for me,' said Edward. He looked down at a rowing boat tied to the jetty. 'I say we go in that.'

'We're not stealing someone's boat,' said Rupert.

'It'll only be for a short while. No harm will come of it. Come on.'

Edward stepped awkwardly into the boat and took hold of the oars. 'Hurry up, I'm thirsty. The Camp may close soon.'

Rupert turned to Rebecca. 'We can't leave him. He'll either lose the oars or crash into a barge.'

Edward sang a sea shanty as he rowed. He insisted Rebecca and Rupert learn the chorus.

'It's ever so simple, it's about a drunken sailor,' he said.

'How appropriate,' said Rebecca, gripping the sides of the boat. She could see a barge in the distance.

'Pay attention, cousin. You'll need to compensate for Rupert's voice as it's ghastly.'

Rupert sighed.

'So, the chorus goes, *Way-hay up she rises, way-hay up she rises, way-hay up she rises, early in the morning*. Do you need me to repeat it?'

Rebecca and Rupert shook their heads.

'Good. I'll start you off. *Way-hay up she rises, way-hay up she rises...*'

Edward, still unaware of the ink on his face, was too tired to sing on the return from the Camp. About halfway back to the jetty, Rupert began to row towards the riverbank.

'I hope you don't expect me to take over,' said Edward. 'I was only jesting about your technique. It's far better than mine.'

'Don't worry, I know you've done your turn. I thought you might enjoy a spot of fun before you went home.'

Edward looked over Rupert's shoulder and smiled. 'Bravo! We should have a contest, like when we were boys, only I shan't let you win this time.'

Rupert laughed. 'You never did. I always beat you fair and square.'

'Well, you won't today. Just you wait and see.'

The contest, Rupert explained to Rebecca, was to discover who could swing the farthest over the river on the rope tied to a tree branch. Edward said Rupert should be the one to test the rope as he weighed less and his suit was older.

Rupert cheered as he swung over the water and cheered louder as he pushed off the riverbank for a second swing. 'There you are, Edward,' he said, holding out the rope.

Edward dug his hands into his pockets. 'Oh, I couldn't possibly go before Rebecca. Please, after you, cousin.'

Rupert looked at Rebecca. 'You don't have to. I know Edward is keen to have his attempt at beating me.'

'And I'm equally keen to beat you both,' said Rebecca, wondering how deep the water was.

'That's the spirit. Clearly you have a greater appetite for competition than Edward does.'

'I doubt it,' said Edward. 'I just don't want either of you to mimic my style.'

Rebecca held a knot in the rope as tight as she could and stepped back.

'On my count,' said Rupert. 'One, two… three!'

Rebecca ran forward and, closing her eyes at the last moment, jumped from the riverbank. As she swung back in, she realised she was facing the wrong way. She tried to turn, but an arm came round her waist.

'I've got you,' said Rupert.

Rebecca kept still as she caught her breath. She wanted to be pressed against Rupert's body for just a little longer.

'Rather impressive for a beginner,' said Edward, taking the rope. 'Now, if you step aside I'll demonstrate how a master does it.'

Edward returned to the riverbank disappointed.

'Not quite far enough,' said Rupert. 'I think I'll declare myself the winner with Rebecca as second.'

Edward huffed. 'I'm certain there was a disadvantage in going last. It's only proper I have another swing.'

'Sorry, you know the rules.'

'Please, just today, never again. I'll be in a terrible funk if you don't let me. And I promise I'll row back.'

'The rope's looking a little tired,' said Rebecca.

'Nonsense, it could hold all three of us.'

'Very well, if you insist,' said Rupert. 'You still won't beat me. And if you change your mind about rowing I'll throw you overboard.'

Edward took the rope back as far as he could. He breathed out hard and sprinted towards the river. A cry of triumph came within seconds, followed by the snap of the rope and the splash of Edward's body hitting the water.

'Oh hell!' said Rupert, removing his jacket. 'He's a terrible swimmer. I'm going in.'

Edward popped up. He swept his hair away from his eyes and smiled. 'I won!' he said, raising his fist. 'I won!'

TEN

Rebecca had seen nothing of Rupert for days. Every time she had heard the gate open she had gone to the nearest window, only for her heart to sink at the sight of someone other than him. On the evening of the fifth day her desperation to see Rupert became too much to bear and she guided a conversation with Edward towards his name. Rupert, he said, was in Cambridge for a ball.

Rebecca went over and over in her mind every word Rupert had said at their parting. He had made no mention of a ball or Cambridge or when they would spend time together again. Even at the piano with Elizabeth and Harry, Rebecca questioned everything Rupert had said to her, for any evidence of insincerity. Her only time of respite was while reading the diary. She began to consume weeks at a time, becoming more daring with where she read it and when. Concealing it behind a larger book, she sat in the morning room, garden, or in her bedroom, reading every entry twice, often aloud if there was no-one close by. The reality of life fading ran through her mother's reflections. A birthday gift had been given to a friend for a final time, the final longest day had been observed, a last christening attended. Her mother had written of days when she knew only weakness and pain, and when the basics of life – of eating, washing, even talking – seemed worthless. And then there were other days when food and words were savoured, and the view across the Fens was appreciated as if she had taken it in for the first time. Rebecca could remember those days because she had been told to. 'This is who I am,' her mother had said. 'Forget how I was yesterday, or how I am tomorrow. Today is how you will remember me.'

Rebecca sat down on the riverbank and opened the diary where she had left off. The entry was shorter than normal. Her mother had written that her dosage of morphine was inadequate; it neither satisfied her craving nor numbed her pain and she wished she had never demanded it. Rebecca kept reading, reaching her father's birthday in late autumn. Her mother had managed just one sentence: *I want to die.*

'Good morning!'

Rebecca stared at her mother's words. The letters were twice the normal size and the ink was heavy, as though the nib had been pressed hard against the paper.

'Hello!'

Rebecca glanced up. Sitting at the rear of a rowing boat was Rupert. The man rowing gave Rebecca a courteous nod and smiled. A woman at Rupert's side leaned forward and leaned back again. Rebecca recognised her at once. She appeared even prettier than she did in Cambridge.

Rebecca pretended to read. She could not hear what was being said in the boat and despite the voices fading she kept her head lowered. Finally, when she was satisfied her solitude had been restored, she stood up and made for the path to the vicarage. In the distance she heard a man laugh. It was Rupert.

The midsummer dance was about to begin. Rebecca looked around her, searching.

'I'm astonished Edward isn't here,' said her father.

'As am I,' said Emily. 'He clearly lied to me about needing an early night. He hasn't had one since he was a baby.'

There was a cough. Rebecca turned. Rupert stepped closer, as did the woman and the man from the rowing boat.

‘Dr Lawrence, Mrs Warwick… Rebecca, good evening,’ said Rupert. ‘Allow me to introduce my cousin, Victoria.’

Victoria offered her hand to Rebecca. ‘I’m delighted to finally meet you.’

‘And you.’

‘And this is Toby,’ said Rupert. ‘Victoria’s fiancé. He’s recently completed his medicine studies and is hoping to work in London.’

Toby and Rebecca’s father began to discuss their profession. Victoria stepped away a little, taking Rebecca with her. ‘We’re planning to climb the Malverns tomorrow,’ she said. ‘Will you come? It’ll be great fun.’

Rebecca sensed Rupert turning his head towards her.

‘Thank you. I’d be delighted to join you.’

‘Splendid. And I promise you won’t end the day on crutches. Rupert said he was reckless the last time you walked on the hills.’

Later in the evening, Rebecca’s father said he suddenly felt very tired.

‘We should leave,’ said Rebecca.

‘I’ll leave, but you must stay. Rupert will escort you home. Besides, I understand you’ve promised to be his partner for his favourite dance.’

Rupert’s favourite dance was not as popular as the one that had come before it. Half the couples returned to their tables as it was announced, leaving Rebecca feeling unsure of herself. She remembered how she had practised with Charlotte, and took her first steps. Soon she was struck by how calm she felt at being close to Rupert, even as he leaned in and his cheek touched hers. She had listened to the music so many times on her gramophone she knew when the dance was reaching its end. The musicians stopped playing and everyone clapped. Someone called three cheers for the band and also for Kate. People began to leave.

Rebecca looked at Victoria and Toby holding hands as they walked into the night and laughed quietly to herself.

'I hope you're not laughing at my expense,' said Rupert.

For a moment Rebecca considered speaking the truth, but smiled instead. 'I was just thinking of Edward falling in the river. I can't understand why he's not here.'

'I think I can. As soon as I mentioned Toby had accompanied Victoria he said he had something important he must attend to.'

'That's not the reason my aunt gave. She said he preferred to stay at home.'

'Then he's most likely sitting in a pub sulking. You ought not to worry about him. He'll soon forget about my cousin.'

Rebecca and Rupert left the village hall, arm in arm as husbands and wives were doing. As they passed others, Rebecca became conscious of her pride at being escorted home by Rupert. She was certain the attention would lead to garden gate talk of impropriety. If gossip was born out of envy then so be it, she thought.

They walked slowly, almost deliberately so. When Croft House was finally reached they stood facing each other.

'Tell me you won't have a change of heart about tomorrow,' said Rupert.

'I won't have a change of heart about tomorrow.'

Rupert stepped forward. He was as close to Rebecca as he had been during the dance.

'Goodnight,' he said, kissing Rebecca on the cheek.

Rupert headed into the darkness. Rebecca willed his footsteps to grow louder, for him to return, to allow her to say something that he would remember as he went to sleep. She held her breath, listening.

'Are you there, Rebecca?'

Rebecca restrained a sigh. 'Yes, Papa. I'm coming.'

Rebecca looked out towards the Welsh border, hoping Edward was no longer sulking.

'Do you think you could come?' asked Victoria.

'Sorry, where to?'

'To our wedding in Cambridge. You can be Rupert's guest – can't she, Rupert? I know you don't have one. You would have told me if you did.'

Rupert cleared his throat. 'Yes, I suppose I would have done.'

'So that means you can ask Rebecca, can't you?'

'Please, you don't have to,' said Rebecca.

'As I'm his cousin I believe he does,' said Victoria. 'And as I'm the bride, I expect you to accept.'

Rupert turned to Rebecca. 'Then I don't believe we have a choice, do we?'

'No, I don't believe we do.'

Victoria clapped. 'Wonderful! And with you there, Rupert won't be pestered by my friends. Now, shall we make our return? I'm likely to fall asleep if I stay sitting here any longer.'

As they passed Dickens's rock, Rupert stopped to tie up his shoelace, taking a little longer than was needed. Victoria and Toby kept walking. Rebecca held back.

'Are you certain you wish to come to the wedding?' said Rupert. 'My cousin was a little forthright earlier, and it's still months away.'

'Would you prefer it if I wasn't your guest?'

'Not in the slightest, I would be honoured to have your company. Having met Toby's brothers, however, I expect to spend much of the day answering questions about you.'

'About me? I don't understand.'

'Well, there are three brothers and from what I can tell each is desperate not to be the last to marry. The eldest will sail for Egypt at the end of the year to seek his fortune, but says he can't bear to leave England without a wife.'

'Poor man. He really shouldn't be so hurried.'

'What should I say if he enquires about you?'

'Me? Er…Please say I'm a terrible traveller, and can't abide hot climates.'

'And what about the other two?'

'Tell them whatever you wish. Nothing too repulsive, just enough to ward off any urge to propose.'

Rupert took a different road home. It was longer and in some places uneven. Rebecca gripped her seat as the motor car skidded, bounced and groaned its way around the Malverns and back on to the road to the city. As they finally reached Hallow, the car slowed and then came to a stop. The petrol tank, Rupert said, was empty.

'You should walk Rebecca home,' said Toby. 'I'll find fuel at Ashgrove. Come on, Victoria.'

Rupert offered his arm when they reached the riverbank. 'You could visit your old home after the wedding,' he said.

'I suppose it would make sense to.'

'Would you mind if I came with you?'

'To my village?'

'Say no if you'd prefer otherwise.'

'No, I'd like you to come. It's very quiet though. You ought not to expect much.'

Rupert began to ask Rebecca questions about Welney. She answered the best she could, all the while wondering what Rupert would think of the little railway station, The Three Tuns, and playing cards by the fire with the farm workers. His intrigue continued as they stood outside Croft House. Rebecca sensed Rupert was edging closer to asking about her mother's illness. Part of her wanted his questions to continue so that he would remain standing in front of her, just one step away from intimacy.

The church bells chimed five o'clock. 'I should check Toby has returned the car safely,' said Rupert. 'I'll be in trouble if he hasn't.'

Rebecca kept still as Rupert kissed her on the cheek. She was suddenly overwhelmed by the urge to look into his eyes. A gate opened and closed, and Rupert stepped back, looking up the lane. Mrs Munn waved.

'Time for me to leave,' said Rupert. 'Goodbye, Rebecca.'

That Sunday Rebecca went to church alone as her father was feeling unwell. As the vicar moved to the pulpit, she decided her place was at Croft House and she should leave. She picked up her scarf and hat, and stood still. Making his way along the pew was Rupert. He smiled and sat down next to her. There was no opportunity to speak as the vicar had commenced his welcome. Rebecca willed him to finish, for the first hymn to begin so she could tell Rupert how relieved she was to have his company. He leaned towards her and whispered, 'You look beautiful today.'

Rebecca's cheeks burned. She stood with the congregation, wondering if she had heard Rupert correctly. He said nothing more until the service came to an end and he enquired about her father.

Kate turned sharply. 'I'll need your assistance now, Miss Lawrence. Good day to you, Mr Salisbury.'

Rebecca became distracted again with worry about her father. She spoke to the children, but said little to Kate and spent much of the Sunday School hour glancing at the clock. She remained silent as the final child left, waiting for Kate to start her routine of making admiring comments about her husband's sermon, and listing those who had missed it. Kate began to rearrange the slate boards and books kept in a cupboard by a desk. She tutted as she went about her task, as though offended by the stacking of Bibles on the wrong shelf. Rebecca wondered if she had upset Kate with her silence.

'I heard someone say the midsummer dance was better than any before it,' she said, hoping to draw Kate's attention.

'Everyone seemed to have a wonderful evening. I certainly did.'

Kate continued her tidying. She kept her back turned. 'Yes, I noticed you looked happy. I believe others thought likewise when you left with Rupert Salisbury.'

'It was kind of him to escort me home. My father was very grateful.'

Kate paused in her task. A Bible remained in her hands. 'And is your father grateful that Rupert has escorted you on other occasions since?'

'I expect so.'

'So he knows about your little walks along the riverbank?'

Rebecca suddenly felt ill at ease. 'I've probably mentioned it.'

'And would you have mentioned how affectionate Rupert is to you?'

'What do you mean by affectionate?'

Kate put the Bible away. 'Oh, I'm sorry, I must have misunderstood what I was told.'

'And what exactly have you been told?'

'Nothing, Rebecca.'

Rebecca moved closer to Kate. 'Evidently it's not nothing as you wouldn't have said it. And you wouldn't have your back to me either.'

Kate sighed. She turned and said, 'It has been said to me that you have kissed Rupert in public, even near the church for all to see.'

'Who said that? Was it your husband?'

'People, Rebecca.'

'And what does it matter if I have? If Rupert wants to kiss me then it is no-one's concern but mine.'

'It matters because you are not engaged to be married and you are associated with the church. You've even taken it upon yourself to sit by him during the service so he can whisper compliments to you. What will you do next week? Hold his hand down the aisle? Allow him to kiss you in church too?'

Rebecca crossed her arms. 'If he chooses to, then yes, I will.'

Kate banged the desk with her fist. 'You're a Sunday School teacher in my husband's church, not a showgirl in a cabaret! I expect you to set an example. I'll not allow you to embarrass my husband any further.'

Rebecca stepped back. Tears began to form in her eyes.

'I hadn't intended to say anything, but I had to for your sake. People are talking about you.'

Rebecca sensed anger rise within her. She ran up the crypt steps and out of the church, making for the riverbank. Her breathing slowed as she stood on the jetty, turning over and over in her mind what Kate had said. The emotion of it all became too much and she screamed. She felt insulted by the constraints of Hallow. The village had again become a place to which she did not belong, but had to endure.

Rebecca kept Kate's attack to herself. She tried to put it out of her mind during the days that followed, and was grateful for Edward's insistence on keeping her company. One morning he called in Charles Salisbury's motor car. Rupert was behind the wheel, and in the back seat was a picnic basket and the kites.

The car strained its way up the road to the Malverns and rapidly picked up speed as it came down the other side. After three miles or so Rupert braked and brought the car to a stop. He got out and read a sign hanging on an iron gate.

'Sorry you two,' he said turning. 'The castle's closed to the public today.'

Edward huffed. 'Bloody rude of them to close it when we visit. I say we go in and if we're stopped we can say we're guests.'

'Not if it's the owner who stops us,' said Rupert.

'He'll be none the wiser. He's most probably old and forgetful. Check if the gate's locked.'

'I'll do no such thing. Not being allowed in gives us more time at the obelisk. And if you don't complain, I'll allow you to fly my kite. Yours looks in a terrible state.'

Rupert and Edward carried the picnic basket up a hill to the obelisk. Once lunch was finished they lay down and dozed with their hats tipped over their foreheads. Rebecca leaned back as quietly as she could, hoping not to disturb Rupert. She could sense him move closer to her. His hand brushed against hers.

'I'm bored,' said Edward, sitting up. 'There's a stream nearby with a little bridge over it. I say we sit on it and cool our feet.'

'I'm perfectly happy resting here,' said Rupert.

'That's not very British Army of you, Rupert. You've been lazing around long enough, and you cousin, come on!'

Edward persisted with talk of the military all the way to the bridge, continuing until they returned to the motor car. Rebecca felt a sadness come over her as Edward spoke of bayonet drill, target practice and shouting orders. It occurred to her that when they were reunited in weeks or months Edward would be sensible and rigid, while Rupert's softness of speech would have been hardened. Walks by the side of the River Severn, on the Malverns and stick races under the stream's little bridge would be dull to them, as would the village. Their visits home would become shorter and the gaps between letters longer. She would eventually be as lonely as she was when she arrived in Hallow.

The following day Rupert called again at Croft House, though he was alone.

'It's our first vintage so I insist you try it with me,' he said to Rebecca, producing a bottle from behind his back.

They sat in the shade of a pear tree, one glass of elderberry wine swiftly progressing to two. When Rupert said he had to leave, Rebecca followed him down the path. She kept at his side on the lane, walking slowly towards the green, ignoring the reality they were soon to part.

As they passed the church, Rebecca remembered what Kate had said about her being a showgirl, and instinctively put her arm through Rupert's. There was a moment's silence and then Rupert began to talk as though strolling arm in arm was a normal thing to do for them. Rebecca wondered if he had also been spoken to. She could not help but smile as she thought of how they were defying Kate.

'Have I said something humorous?' said Rupert, pausing his childhood story.

'No, no, I'm just happy to be listening to you. Please, continue.'

Later that afternoon the vicar delivered a letter. He handed it to the maid and turned away, saying he was in a hurry. Rebecca read the letter in the hall. There were only a few sentences.

'You're frowning,' said her father. 'What's the matter?'

Rebecca looked up. 'Pardon?'

'Is everything all right?'

'Yes, it's fine. It's nothing.'

Rebecca went to her bedroom and sat down at her desk, winded by what Kate had written. She read the letter again.

I have spoken to Mrs Ramsay and she is eager to resume her position as my assistant. I've asked her to return tomorrow which means I shall not require any further help from you.

I encourage you to use your time to yourself wisely.

Rage came upon Rebecca. She tore the letter up and threw the pieces on to the hearth.

It was obvious she had been seen walking arm in arm with

Rupert and as punishment, as an attempt to humiliate her, Kate had stripped her of her position in the village.

She left the house without an explanation and walked in a daze until she reached the swing. Staring at the rope, Rebecca knew she had to tell her father about Sunday School. If Kate revealed her accusations to him then so be it, she thought. He would pay no attention to her.

'People can talk as much as they wish,' he would say. 'You have nothing to hide. Walk proudly with Rupert.'

Rebecca's conviction about informing her father faded with each day in which Rupert was not mentioned. But when Sunday arrived, she knew her secret had to be shared. Sitting in a front pew, she thought of what was to come. Instead of waiting at the crypt door to take the children downstairs, she would join the congregation in filing past the vicar. There would be whispers as to why she was not assisting Kate. Her father would hear them and ask questions.

She heard a voice behind her. Rupert was a few pews back. Rebecca stared at him, willing him to make eye contact, only he bowed his head, as if in prayer, and failed to look up. Rebecca began to plan what she would say to him, deciding to tell him about the letter and that she cared nothing for the thoughts of others. The service dragged. It finally came to an end and Rebecca turned round at once. Rupert was already walking out. Rebecca apologised as she weaved between the dawdlers in the aisle, but said nothing to the vicar when she reached the porch. In the distance she could make out two figures heading towards Ashgrove. One was the butler and the other the stable boy. Rupert was nowhere to be seen.

Eleven

Rebecca spent the hours after church going over and over in her mind what had happened. As hard as she tried to believe otherwise, she feared Rupert had been advised to avoid her. She became convinced of it when Edward called later in the day, uncertain where Rupert was and eager to talk about his upcoming departure for Paris. There was such verve to his description of the city, of the cafes and theatres, architecture and parties, that Rebecca wondered if a cure for her suffering would be found in escaping the village for a while. Paris was too distant from her father, but London was not, and there she could laugh with Alice and care nothing for what others thought of her.

Her determination to leave Hallow was strengthened the following day as she listened to Mrs Finch and Mrs Adams gossip about people she had never heard of. She sensed that Emily too was tired of the tittle-tattle as she changed the subject to Edward and his trip abroad.

'And is Rupert Salisbury joining your cousin in Paris?' Mrs Finch asked Rebecca.

Rebecca felt inclined to ignore the question. She smiled and said, 'I wouldn't know.'

Mrs Finch raised her eyebrows. 'Oh, have you not seen him in the village recently?'

'Not of late, but if I do I'll pass on your interest as to his whereabouts.'

'No, no, dear, there's really no need to. I'm sure your aunt will inform us of any matters regarding Edward and your friend.'

Rebecca travelled home alone, her father having spent his day making local calls. As she stepped down outside Croft House she instinctively looked towards the green. Standing at the top of Peachley Lane was Rupert. He remained still for a moment and then turned away. Rebecca walked towards him, quickening her pace as he faded from view.

'Something the matter?'

Rebecca stopped walking and looked to her side. Mrs Munn smiled back at her. In her hand was a trowel.

'No, nothing's the matter,' said Rebecca.

'That's a relief, only I thought Mr Salisbury had left something.'

'Left something?'

'At your house. I only know because I've been out here most of the afternoon. Your father said gardening would be good for me.'

Rebecca wondered if Rupert was waiting for her.

'I reckon he could do with a bit of gardening himself,' said Mrs Munn.

'Who?'

'Your father. He was looking terribly pale when he saw me earlier.'

'I expect he's just tired. He insisted on walking to all of his patients today.'

'Just so long as he's well. Can't have our doctor falling ill, can we? I'd better let you go. You looked as if you were in a hurry.'

Rebecca glanced up the lane again. 'I was. But I'm not any longer. Good afternoon.'

Rebecca found her father at his desk. He was leaning back with his legs outstretched and his eyes closed. A blank sheet of paper was in front of him. Rebecca thought of leaving him alone. Her impatience got the better of her and she coughed. Her father flinched.

'Sorry, I didn't mean to wake you,' said Rebecca.

'It's fine. All of that walking must have taken its toll.'

'Mrs Munn said you were looking pale.'

'She's probably irritated I told her to lose weight.'

'She also said that Rupert had been here.'

'He called to speak to you. He didn't say what about, and I didn't ask.'

Rebecca crossed her arms. 'But he knows I'm always at Emily's on Thursdays.'

'He must have forgotten.'

'Mrs Munn said he was here for a while.'

'I suppose he was. He's a bright young man. I enjoyed talking with him.'

'What did you discuss?'

'Many different things.'

'Was I discussed?'

'Most probably.' Rebecca's father picked up his pen. 'I really should get back to my work now. You can tell me about your afternoon later.'

Rebecca drew the conclusion that Rupert had not called for her, but had been summoned. Stern words had been said, hence his avoidance of her on Peachley Lane. She spoke nothing of him at dinner, deciding to wait until afterwards when brandy and a pipe would put her father at his greatest ease. When the moment came he complained of weariness. Rebecca held her tongue, and did so again at breakfast the next day. She resolved instead to confront Rupert, to force him to confirm what she suspected. As she stood still on Ashgrove's steps, she began to lose her nerve. She listened for voices, but heard none. The wide door opened and she froze.

'Good morning, Miss Lawrence.'

Rebecca glanced past the butler's shoulder, expecting to see Rupert appear.

'How may I help you?'

Rebecca swallowed. 'I'm here to see Mr Salisbury… Rupert.'

'I'm afraid he's in Worcester. I presume he asked you to call at this time?'

Rebecca hesitated, wondering what to say. 'I thought he did. I… I suppose I could have misheard.'

'Perhaps the appointment is for another day. Mr Salisbury made no mention of expecting you.'

Rebecca felt her cheeks burn. 'Then I must be mistaken. Sorry for disturbing you.'

She turned quickly. A thought came to her and she stopped. She turned on the spot and said, 'Would you mind not telling him I called? It's a little embarrassing to have made an error.'

'If you wish, Miss Lawrence.'

Rebecca hurried down Ashgrove's steps, feeling a fool for believing she could confront Rupert. She kept up her quick pace on the drive, convinced that Rupert would learn of her visit.

The noise of a motor car became louder. Rebecca dashed to the nearest tree and pushed her back against it. The car, much grander than Charles Salisbury's, continued along the drive. Rebecca wondered if it was the Earl's and inside was his daughter, beautiful and confident, and early for an appointment with Rupert. She made for a stile across a corn field, caring nothing that her boots and the hem of her skirt were being covered in dirt. As she looked around her, certain she would be spotted, she lost her footing and fell to her side. She lay still on the ground, looking up at the corn, waiting for the first stab of pain from her ankle. None came and she stood up, brushing as much dirt as she could from her clothes.

She glanced both ways before climbing the stile. The road was clear. Rebecca began to think of the afternoon ahead, of having to face the ladies and what lie she would give when asked how her morning had passed. The slow approach behind of another car interrupted her concentration. She lowered her head as the car passed her, only the engine noise did not fade. The car had stopped. Rebecca looked up just as the driver's door opened.

'Hello,' said Rupert, stepping forward.

Rebecca glanced at her boots and skirt.

'Is everything all right?'

'It is, yes.'

'I'm glad to hear it.' Rupert moved a little closer. 'Would you care to walk with me in Hallow Park?'

Rebecca hesitated and said, 'I suppose I could. I have to teach this afternoon though.'

'Then we'll go now, unless you wish to go home first, that is?'

'I'm fine as I am, thank you.'

Rupert stopped on Hallow Park's terrace. The estate, he said, was all theirs. They walked in silence on the perimeter of the garden until they came back up the lawn and Rupert suggested they rest for a moment.

Rebecca sat down on the bench and stared at the little island, willing herself to ask Rupert why he had avoided her.

'Finishing university is a peculiar thing,' said Rupert. 'Suddenly one has time to consider the years ahead more than at any point in the past. Some of my friends have become confused… some less so.'

'What's happened to you?'

'Everything has become much clearer.'

'I hope it has for Edward too.'

'You see, what I've realised in recent days is that I haven't been as sincere with you as I should have been. I haven't lied to you, it's more that I've concealed something and I can't sit alongside you now and conceal it any longer.'

Rebecca noticed Rupert swallow. He took hold of the edge of the bench and turned to her.

'What I want to say, what I've been desperate to say, is that the time I spend alone with you, on the riverbank, or here, or wherever, is precious to me. When we're apart I seem to think only of being with you.'

Rebecca also gripped the edge of the seat. 'I'm confused. How can you think only of me and yet be so distant?'

Rupert sighed. 'I know I have, but please believe me when I say it's been for good reason.'

'I can't see what good reason you can have for ignoring me.'

'What I can tell you… what I want to tell you… even if you think I'm a fool.' Rupert swallowed again. His words seemed to be stuck in his throat.

'What is it you want to tell me, Rupert?'

He looked Rebecca in the eye. 'That I love you.'

Rebecca raised her eyebrows.

'I've been in love with you for months.'

'What?'

'I've been in love with you for months.'

'You love me?'

Rupert nodded. He stood and began to bend at the knee. One knee touched the ground. 'Rebecca, will you be my wife?'

Rebecca stared at Rupert, questioning if she had misheard him. He reached into his jacket pocket and unfurled his fingers. In his palm was a box. He opened it, revealing a ring of yellow gold with a solitaire diamond.

'You don't have to answer now.'

Rebecca's hands were shaking. 'You want to marry me?'

Rupert smiled. 'I do. I want to marry you.'

'I… I must speak to my father.'

'I've asked him for his consent.'

'When?'

'Yesterday, when you were at your aunt's.'

'What was his answer?'

'He gave me his blessing.'

Rebecca felt her chest tighten.

'I do beg of you, you must only accept if you love me. I would rather the pain of rejection than you accepting for any reason other than love for me. Can you promise me that?'

Rebecca nodded. She glanced at the ring, imagining it being slid down her engagement finger.

'I'm sorry if I've shocked you,' said Rupert.

'Don't be.'

'I've been in a terrible way trying to decide what I should say. I feared you would reject me at once.'

'I couldn't do that. What I mean is, I couldn't give you my answer at once. It wouldn't be proper without talking to my father.'

'I know.'

'It's just so unexpected that you want to marry me.'

'Well, I do. You don't have to answer this question if you don't wish to, but I must ask it.'

'Then ask it.'

'Whether you care for me?'

Rebecca noticed a tremor in Rupert's voice. She looked to her side. Rupert took the hint and sat down next to her. She held his hand and said, 'I do care for you. I can promise you that.'

Rupert smiled.

'I'm still confused,' she said. 'I thought you were leaving the village and I'd never have contact with you again, and now you've asked me to marry you. Part of me thinks I'm going mad. You did just ask me to marry you?'

'I did. I can propose again, if you wish?'

'Once for today is enough.'

Rupert smiled.

'We should leave. I need to find my father.'

Not a word was spoken in the car until they reached Croft House and Rebecca pledged to give her answer the following day. She made for the back garden, weaving between the trees and flower beds, pounding her fist against her palm as though it helped her think. The shock of what Rupert had said lingered. He was in love with her and had been so for months. On the eve of his departure from the village he had pledged himself to her and she had just a few hours to know that her will for marriage was as strong as his.

Rebecca spoke nothing of Rupert to Emily later that afternoon and apologised at the end of Elizabeth's lesson for being distracted. She guided the conversation away from herself at dinner and then went to her bedroom afterwards, still wondering if she had imagined the proposal. The grandfather clock struck nine and she stood up: time was running out. She climbed the stairs, breathed in and knocked on the study door.

'Come in.'

Rebecca stepped forward.

'Do you need something to read?'

Rebecca shook her head.

'Something else, then? Perhaps to talk?'

'I saw Rupert today.'

'I'm pleased to hear it.'

'You are?'

'Of course. His friendship is important to you.'

'What do you make of his character?'

Rebecca's father closed his book. 'He seems to be honourable and pleasant. I've no doubt he has other qualities. Why do you ask?'

'I ask because earlier today he took me to Hallow Park... '

Rebecca hesitated. She stared at the photograph of her mother on the wall.

'Yes?'

'While we there, he… he asked me to marry him.'

Rebecca's father leaned back. 'And what was your answer?'

'That I'd speak to you. He said you gave him your blessing.'

'I did. But that doesn't mean you should accept.'

'I said I'd give him my answer tomorrow.'

'Good. Any longer would be cruel.'

'What should I say?'

Rebecca's father reached for her hands. 'Do not question if you want to spend the rest of your life with Rupert. Ask yourself instead whether you can imagine your life without him in it. That's how you'll find your answer.'

Rebecca opened her mother's diary, paused, and closed it, knowing she would find only grief in the pages, not the reassurance she wanted. She placed a sheet of paper in front of her, picked up her pen and began to write.

Dear Rupert,

Please meet me at the bench at six o'clock.

Rebecca

TWELVE

Rebecca did not need a mirror to know she appeared tired. Emily's opening words to her in Waterloo Square were that she looked as if she had been awake all night. Rebecca feared that her father thought likewise. He spared her from saying so, just as he spared her from the question that was responsible for her sleepless night; the question she was presently considering as the carriage slowed on the return home.

'Why on earth are we stopping?'

'I asked him to,' said Rebecca.

'Do you wish to walk home?'

'I'm meeting Rupert at Hallow Park.'

'Oh, you've made your decision then?'

'I have.'

'And you're certain of it?'

'I am.'

'I'm relieved. Do you wish to tell me what your answer is?'

'I'd prefer to tell Rupert first.'

'I understand.'

'I should go.'

'Wait a moment.'

Rebecca paused at the carriage door.

'Soon after I met your mother, she made me promise that I would never offer her false hope, even if I believed it to be kind. If you have any doubts about being truthful with Rupert, now is the time to listen to them.'

Rebecca nodded. 'Thank you, Papa.'

'You best go. He'll be worried he's scared you away if you're late.'

Rebecca's anxiety grew as she stepped closer to the house. She repeated her answer until she reached the terrace and looked down the lawn. Rupert was nowhere to be seen. Rebecca made for the bench, telling herself she was early, though it occurred to her that her letter may have been mislaid and that Rupert was at home, watching the clock, doubting he would receive the answer he had been promised by the day's end. She listened for the distant approach of an engine. The silence was menacing. Rebecca began to walk back and forth, fearing she would have to give her answer at Ashgrove where the risk of stumbling would be much greater than at Hallow Park.

'Master Salisbury.'

Rebecca turned sharply. The gardener was pushing a wheelbarrow across the terrace.

Rupert dismounted from his horse and shook hands with the man. Rebecca sat down, turning her answer over and over in her mind. The words that had earlier been ordered suddenly became jumbled. She glanced up. Rupert was only a few yards away.

'I hope I haven't kept you waiting,' he said. 'I couldn't get the motor car to start.'

'No need to worry. Please, sit with me.'

Rupert positioned himself a little farther away from Rebecca than normal. He moved his hands from his lap to underneath the bench.

'I haven't been able to concentrate since I received your letter,' he said. 'I must have walked the estate half a dozen times or more. My father probably thinks I've gone mad.'

'Does he know you're here?'

'He does. But if you need more time you must say so.'

'I don't. I made my decision last night after speaking to my father.'

Rupert edged forward on the bench. 'What did he say?'

'That I should consider only whether I could imagine my life without you.'

Rupert's attention moved to his feet.

'The truth is, I can't imagine my life without you… I want to share my life with you.'

Rupert turned his head. 'You accept?'

'I do.'

'You truly want to marry me?'

Rebecca smiled. 'Very much so.'

Rupert moved closer to Rebecca. She could feel his breath on her cheeks.

'I thought you might say no,' he said.

'I couldn't. I want to be your wife.'

Rupert leaned in and kissed Rebecca on the lips. She wanted his arms to remain round her waist, for the comfort of being close to his body to continue. He released her, but kept his hand on the side of her face, his finger stroking her cheek.

'I love you,' he said. 'I promise I'll be the very best husband I can be.'

As they returned to the village, Rebecca yearned to be seen, for passers-by to be stopped and told of the engagement. Everyone would soon know there was a legitimacy to her being alone with Rupert, or sitting next to him in church. An engagement notice would be placed in *The Times*. Henry and Alice would read it, as would the ladies and Kate, and Emily would mention it to all of her acquaintances.

Outside Croft House Rupert surveyed the windows and the lane, and then kissed Rebecca. She could feel his chest expand against her own. A new impulse came upon her and she moved her hand down Rupert's back.

'We might be seen, Rebecca.'

'I don't mind.'

'Your father might.'

Rebecca moved her hand back up Rupert's jacket. 'Point noted.'

'I can come in with you if you wish.'

'I should talk to him alone.'

'I understand. And I should talk to my father too. I expect he'll be eager to make arrangements.'

'Not as much as my aunt will be.'

Rupert laughed. 'Yes, I agree. Most certainly not as much as your aunt.'

Word of the engagement soon reached Emily. She led Rebecca into her garden and announced her as the 'future Mrs Rupert Salisbury'. Mrs Finch and Mrs Adams clapped but remained stuck in their chairs, while Charlotte stepped forward with opened arms, saying how delighted she was. Even the maid said something fitting.

The congratulations gave way to interrogation. Rebecca stumbled with the month she wanted the wedding to be held in, and whether it would be in the morning or afternoon. When she said she was uncertain whether she would marry in Hallow or Welney, Emily scowled and said there was no choice to be made as the Fens were too far away. Rebecca did her best to show interest in the suggestions for how she should plan her day. Every caller to Croft House or villager she met on the street had advice to give. April was a beautiful month for a wedding in one person's opinion, whereas in another's it was unreliable and only August could be trusted, and while a honeymoon abroad was in fashion, Rebecca was assured an untravelled person such as herself would struggle with foreign food and she should remain in England. She became accustomed to smiling, nodding and giving thanks, but knew her tolerance for being told what to do was weakening and she soon yearned for no-one to mention the wedding. She sensed that Rupert's patience for what others had to say was also being tested as he spoke nothing of the decisions that had to be made. He was swift to kiss her the moment they became alone. Warmth no longer came to Rebecca's cheeks. She became less conscious too of framing her sentences before she spoke and as her desire to open her heart to Rupert grew, she felt rushes of happiness. During their private walks, or while riding, or sitting outside the Camp Inn, she hoped Rupert would tell her that he loved her so she could say it back.

One morning, Emily called without notice.

'I couldn't wait until tomorrow to tell you about Edward,' she said.

'Has something happened to him?' asked Rebecca.

'It may have done, not that he said. I wrote to him about your engagement and he wired back.'

'Saying?'

Emily produced the telegram. 'He wired "Must organise ball in their honour". It's a splendid idea, don't you agree?'

'I... think...'

'Of course you agree, why wouldn't you? You can leave all the arrangements to me. You won't have to lift a finger.'

It seemed to Rebecca that Emily had already planned much of the ball. It would be held at Ashgrove because it had a ballroom, and the date would be soon due to Rupert and Edward's departure for officer training.

'If Charles doesn't argue with me I'm confident the guests will be impressed,' said Emily. 'After all, it'll be your first public engagement as Rupert's fiancée. Everyone will be looking at you.'

Emily's determination to arrange the ball continued over luncheon. As she read out the names of guests that had to be invited, Rebecca wondered if she should contribute names, or if the only expectation of her was to tell strangers how pleased she was to meet them. A fear came over her that one day soon a wedding guest list would be presented to her, while a dress selected for her hung in a wardrobe, ready to be worn in a church that was another's preference and on a day she had not chosen.

'Those flowers are past their best,' said Emily, looking at the vase on the table.

'Harry gave them to me after he'd heard my news. I haven't the heart to throw them away.'

'Yes, well, you shouldn't be too soft when you tell the boy you can't teach him any longer. A little disappointment at an early age will strengthen him.'

'What gave you the impression my lessons will stop?'

'Nothing, dear, but you can't expect your life to stay as it is now when you're married. You can teach Elizabeth, but that's different. Her parents are connected and the girl has talent.'

'Harry has talent and with extra lessons he'd be Elizabeth's equal.'

Emily put down her knife and fork. 'I do hope you haven't offered him extra lessons. His father doesn't have the means to pay.'

'I shan't ask him to. I'd happily teach Harry for free.'

Emily's face hardened. 'For free! Have you lost your mind?'

'Not in the slightest. I'll teach Harry for as long as he's committed to learning.'

'And what if your husband objects? What will you do then? Put the boy first?'

'Rupert wouldn't object. I know he wouldn't.'

'When you're the mother of his children he will. And I can't say I'd disagree with him.'

Rebecca considered saying that a strong wife would not allow herself to be restrained. She waited, prolonging the silence across the table.

'I know you want to protect this pastime,' said Emily, 'but you must understand there'll be parts of your life that will have to change. Rupert will also need to make sacrifices.'

'I don't want him to and I'll never ask him to.'

'That may be, but he'll make them because he wants you to be happy. You'll be required to do the same for him. It's a wife's duty.'

Rebecca felt compelled to leave the room. Emily stood and came round the table, sitting down next to her.

'In marriage, you become someone different,' she said, taking Rebecca's hand. 'You do wish to marry Rupert, don't you?'

'Of course I do.'

'Then you shouldn't think twice about reducing your teaching if asked to.'

Rebecca swallowed. Against her instinct she nodded.

Emily smiled. 'Splendid. I can see that you'll be very happy together.'

After church that Sunday, Kate sought out Rebecca.

'Do you think your aunt would be happy if I called on her?' she said. 'I rather enjoyed her company the other day.'

'Emily visited you?'

'She was on her way to your home and stopped at the vicarage on the chance I was in. Fortunately, my husband was also there. He would have been ever so disappointed had he missed your aunt, and Charles.'

'Charles Salisbury was with her?'

'No, he just happened to call soon after your aunt arrived. It was a splendid coincidence, what with your families to be joined by marriage, don't you think?'

Rebecca was certain it was no coincidence 'What did you talk about?'

'The ball mostly, and also your wedding.'

'My wedding?'

'Yes, and please don't hesitate to come to the vicarage if you need advice. I'm quite used to having brides knock on my door with their troubles. They all leave a little more reassured about what to do. I expect you'll be no different.'

Rebecca had to wait until the following day to learn when her wedding would be. Although a spring afternoon was presented as a suggestion, Emily's swift mention of Charles's support and that Rebecca's parents had married in late April made it sound decided. Sitting at her desk that night, Rebecca opened her diary to the calendar for 1906. Her parents' anniversary date was to fall on a Saturday: the perfect day for a wedding. Rebecca circled the date, stared at it as if no other day in the year mattered, and closed her diary. She had just six months to wait until she became Mrs Rupert Salisbury.

THIRTEEN

Each guest Rebecca was introduced to asked to see her engagement ring. By the start of the first dance her arm was tired from raising her left hand and she had spoken of the wedding details more than she had ever thought of them. She glanced around the room as she moved with Rupert to the music, catching sight of her father and Emily smiling, Charlotte guiding Alfred with his steps and Edward attempting to make eye contact with the prettier of the young ladies. She remembered how anxious she had been on her first visit to Ashgrove and even more so when she had called to confront Rupert, and how at those times it would have been inconceivable for her to be where she was presently: at her engagement ball in the house she had once fled from by crossing a field.

The musicians stopped playing. Waiters holding trays of champagne glasses came forward and began to weave between couples. Charles stepped on to the shallow stage and tapped his glass with a spoon. The room fell silent.

'A ballroom should never be without music if there are people in it, so I shall keep this interruption short,' said Charles.

'Bravo!' said Edward.

'Quite. Now, we may be here to dance, but we're also here to celebrate the engagement of my youngest son, Rupert, to the daughter of Dr Lawrence, Rebecca.'

The guests nearest Rebecca smiled at her.

'If anyone doubted God's will in uniting two people then they need only look at my son and Rebecca to witness something magnificent at work in them both, and that, my friends, is love.'

'Well said!'

'Thank you again, Edward. So may I invite you all to join me in raising a glass for a toast… to Rupert and Rebecca.'

'To Rupert and Rebecca!' said everyone together.

Rupert took Rebecca's hand and squeezed it a little. The music resumed and people began to dance again. Rebecca's father gestured for her to step away with him.

'Charles would like to speak to you both,' he said.

Rebecca, Rupert and Emily were led to the library. Charles had a glass in one hand and a champagne bottle in the other. 'I promise this is my final interruption this evening,' he said. 'It seemed fitting that I spoke to you now as we're all here.'

'That sounds rather ominous,' said Rupert. 'Should we be concerned?'

'Not in the slightest, you should be happy. At least, I hope you will be.'

'I'm intrigued. We all are.'

'Both James and Emily know what I'm about to say.'

Rebecca glanced at her father and said, 'Then I'm intrigued even more.'

'Where do you expect to live when you're married?' asked Charles, emptying the bottle into his glass.

'We haven't discussed it,' said Rupert. 'I expect we will soon enough, though.'

'There's no need to, my boy.'

'I don't understand.'

'The lease for one of my properties expires early next year. I've decided to tell the tenants they can't renew it and instead I'll allow you to take it, for no cost.'

'You're giving us a house?'

'I am. At least, the free use of one.'

'Thank you, thank you very much,' said Rupert, shaking his father's hand.

'I would do the same for your brother if he ever found a wife. And I'd rather you live in one of my properties for free than pay a lease to someone I dislike.'

'All the same, it's terribly generous, isn't it, Rebecca?'

'Very much so, thank you. May I ask where in the village the house is?'

'Oh, it's not in Hallow,' said Charles. 'It's in Waterloo Square.'

'You'll be directly opposite me,' said Emily, smiling smugly. 'No more carriage journeys in the cold and dark. And if either of us is ever lonely or bored we need only walk across the square to keep the other company. Your father thinks it's a splendid idea, don't you, James?'

'It's very kind of Charles. I'm certain you'll both be contented there.'

'And with my help you'll soon adapt to living in a city,' said Emily. 'The ladies are ever so excited about calling.'

'So they should be,' said Charles. 'It's the finest house in the square.'

Emily raised her eyebrows.

'Or should I say, one of the finest.'

The thought of leaving the village depressed Rebecca. Emily had pulled her away from the Fens and now she was pulling her away from Hallow and her father. She knew she had to accept what was to come: that she was to live in Waterloo Square, exposed every day to callers prying into her marriage and dropping hints about motherhood. For the present, advice about how she should prepare for a wedding was replaced with advice of how to cope while Rupert was away. Emily suggested she join a charitable society, Charlotte recommended more evenings at music hall, Kate said she was welcome to return to Sunday school, and Mrs Finch advised her to take up needlework. Rupert's advice was that she ride his horse whenever she wished, and visit him in Surrey should he be granted a day's leave from the military academy.

'How I'll cope remains to be seen,' he said, as he rowed upstream to the Camp Inn.

'I expect you'll be too occupied to need to cope,' said Rebecca.

'It'll still be agony being apart from you. It's agony even now when we're apart for only a few hours. Do you know, I thought of you during an entire exam, and that was *before* we were engaged? All I could think of was returning to Hallow.'

'That I don't believe. Even Edward would concentrate properly in an exam.'

'It's the truth. I was so distracted I almost didn't finish the question.'

'Then I beg you not to be distracted when you're holding a rifle. I don't want to be responsible for you missing a target, particularly if Edward is wandering close by.'

Rupert laughed. 'I give you my word I won't shoot Edward, or anyone else for that matter.'

'I'm glad to hear it.'

'And will you give me your word you won't take up needlework?'

'You most certainly do have my word.'

'Then our time apart will whizz by, I promise.'

For all of Rupert's confidence, Rebecca knew time would be unsympathetic to the emptiness that was to come. Emily said she should wean herself of Rupert's presence. Instead, she filled her days with more and more of him. Rupert began to call at breakfast so they could eat together before spending the remainder of the morning walking or riding. He found new places to rest, and at each he carved their names into a tree, saying nature should be marked with their love.

'And when our children are born,' he said, putting his arms round Rebecca's waist, 'I'll return and carve their names on every tree.'

Rebecca cleared her throat, conscious that Rupert had given more thought to parenthood than she had. 'How many children do you expect we'll have?'

'Three. Two boys and a girl.'

'And what if nature has other intentions? Will you be disappointed?'

Rupert brought Rebecca a little tighter to his body. 'No, but I don't believe I'll have any cause for disappointment. I wished that we were to be engaged and it came true, just as my wish for two boys and a girl will. Unless you wish for something different, that is?'

Rebecca smiled. 'No. I think two boys and a girl sounds perfect.'

On the day before his departure, Rupert said he should dine with his father. Rebecca said she understood, but privately felt aggrieved she was being separated from him. As the afternoon passed into evening, restlessness began to take hold of her and she called out that she needed fresh air.

'I was about to suggest the same thing,' said her father, appearing at the top of the stairs. 'We haven't walked together for some time.'

'You shouldn't expect much conversation from me.'

'I understand. You can be silent if you wish.'

Rebecca turned at the gate towards the riverbank path.

'How about we go the other way, Rebecca? I thought we'd walk through Hallow Park and return along the riverbank.'

Rebecca's desire to turn back grew with each step. Hallow Park was a place she wanted to associate with Rupert only.

To stroll down the lawn, past the bench and the little island without him might weaken her memories of his proposal and her acceptance. She wondered if her father had sensed her reluctance as he began to quicken his pace.

The shutters across the windows were closed as normal. Rebecca thought the house appeared abandoned and lonely.

'I'll leave you here, Rebecca.'

'Why?'

'You'll understand soon. Just keep going. Trust me.'

Rebecca watched her father walk away. He made a gesture for her to move, and then made it again as he entered the avenue. Rebecca kept her head lowered until she reached the terrace. In front of her, shining in the evening sun, was Charles's motor car. She touched it, as if she needed convincing her eyes were not playing a trick on her. There were no gloves, scarf or hat to be seen. There was no evidence that *he* had driven it. Rebecca moved across the terrace and the grounds came into full view. Sitting on the bench with his arms spread out was Rupert. Rebecca went to shout, but held back, hoping to surprise him. She could feel her nose begin to tingle as she stepped down the lawn. The irritation of the cut grass intensified and she sneezed. Rupert turned sharply and stood up. In front of the bench was a tartan blanket, upon which was a picnic basket and a champagne bucket containing an unopened bottle. A candelabra was on the edge of the blanket, and on the bench was a gramophone player with records leant against it. Rebecca felt a rush of happiness at the effort Rupert had made.

'Your father's timing is perfect,' he said.

Rebecca glanced at the champagne bucket. The ice had yet to melt. 'And what if his timing had been rotten and you were alone as it became dark?'

'Then I'm afraid the champagne cork would have been popped and that bacon pie eaten. I'm famished, and thirsty. Shall we?'

Rebecca and Rupert lay side by side as they worked their way through the food. Rupert lit the candles as dusk began to fall. He put his arm round Rebecca's shoulder and shared a childhood memory of making a bonfire with Alfred on a Cornish beach at night.

'My mother used to say it was bad luck to put out a fire on a beach, but we'd have good luck if we waited until it went out by itself,' he said. 'It was past midnight when we returned to the hotel.'

'I can't say I've ever been excited by the thought of sitting on a beach.'

'Have you not? Well, that will all change on our honeymoon.'

'And may I ask where we'll spend our honeymoon?'

'Cornwall, of course.'

Rupert spoke of the coastal walks they would take and the fishing villages with steep streets they would pass through. If they were fortunate with the weather they could charter a boat to a bay that was accessible only from the sea. Rebecca kept her head on Rupert's shoulder, revelling in the comfort of being loved by a man that she loved, of her body touching his, of being together on the bench, staring at candles becoming brighter in the creeping darkness.

Rupert wound up the gramophone and taking Rebecca's hand asked her to dance.

As the final record played, it occurred to Rebecca that the following evening she would be in her room, lonely and pining for Rupert. She could sense herself become tense with resentment at how Rupert's future had been chosen for him. The stiffening of her body did not go unnoticed.

'I've kept you out late enough,' said Rupert. 'Your father will be worried about you.'

In the car outside Croft House, Rupert spoke briefly of the morning, saying it would be best if they met at the station as he had tasks to attend to in town. He forewarned Rebecca that he was poor at farewells and she should not think any less of his love for her should his words fail him. A silence fell. Rebecca expected Rupert to lean forward. Instead he guided her hand to his lips and kissed her engagement ring.

'I can't wait to marry you, Rebecca.'

'I can't wait either.'

'You won't change your mind, will you?'

'Not a chance.'

Rebecca wanted only Rupert to be at the station and to farewell Edward at another time. To say goodbye to them both, to share herself between them, particularly in front of her father and Emily, felt unfair. As they reached the old bridge across the river, the carriage suddenly came to a halt. Rebecca looked out of the window. Wooden crates had fallen off the back of a cart and were blocking the road. Three men were clearing the obstacle, though to Rebecca they seemed to be making slow progress. She opened the door.

'Where are you going?' said her father.

'To help.'

'They're almost finished. You'll only slow them down.'

Rebecca pulled a face.

'Come back inside… please.'

Rebecca sighed and returned to her seat. She thought that if the day was to show her any kindness the train would be delayed, but coming up the ramp to the station she could see smoke above the platform.

'It's due to leave in four minutes,' said her father.

Nausea rose from Rebecca's stomach. She rushed past the ticket office and ran up the footbridge stairs, weaving her way between people she met on their way down. At the bottom of the staircase on the other side was Emily.

'I'd almost given up on you,' she said.

Rebecca said nothing. She saw Rupert and strode towards him.

'I'm so sorry,' she said, struggling for breath. 'The man was late and then this accident happened on the bridge and...'

Rupert placed his hands on Rebecca's shoulders. 'You're here. That's all I care about.'

'I know, but I so wanted to...'

Rupert put a finger to his lips. 'Please, no apology is needed.'

'Write to me.'

'The first moment I can.'

Over Rupert's shoulder Rebecca could see Edward leaning out of a carriage window.

'Hurry up, Salisbury,' he shouted. 'You'll be in hot water if you're left behind.'

'I have to go.'

Rebecca nodded. Nausea rose again from her stomach.

'I love you,' said Rupert.

The guard blew on his whistle and Rupert stepped on to the train. Edward squeezed his way to Rupert's side at the window and began to wave. Rebecca locked her eyes with Rupert's as the locomotive pulled away.

'Take this, dear,' said Emily, passing Rebecca a handkerchief. 'He'll be back soon enough.'

'As will Edward.'

'I'm afraid there can be no knowing when Edward will reappear. Rupert, however, will return the moment he's allowed.'

'I hope so.'

'I very much know so. He's in love with you, just as your father was when he met your mother. But you shouldn't agonise too much over these matters. Your poor mother certainly did and it became tiresome.'

Rebecca wiped more tears away. 'I can't imagine Mama being so anxious.'

'She wasn't at all until she met your father. I suppose that's what love can do to a person. Her mind was calmed when she married, as yours will be.'

Rebecca gave Elizabeth and Harry additional lessons in the days that followed Rupert's departure, and called at Kate's to confirm her return to Sunday School. She spoke nothing of Rupert to her father, asking instead about the surgery and any subject that would distract her thoughts. One morning, as she emerged from the riverbank path on to Peachley Lane, she could see Jack Clarke approaching Croft House. He waited outside, his head bowed and his hands behind his back.

'I'm a little embarrassed, Miss Lawrence,' he said. 'Somehow I delivered a letter of yours to the wrong person. They brought it back. Here.'

Rebecca took the envelope. The handwriting on the front was Rupert's.

'As I said, I'm embarrassed, and very sorry.'

Rebecca could not help smiling. 'Don't be embarrassed, or sorry. Thank you.' Rebecca closed the gate. Something occurred to her and she said, 'Mr Clarke, who *did* you deliver this to?'

'To the vicarage. Mrs Harding assured me she didn't open it.'

Rebecca hurried inside and went straight to her bedroom. She sat on the edge of her bed, paused to enjoy a moment's relief, and began to read.

My Darling Rebecca,

I write to you in fear my words cannot bridge the separation of distance, or bring peace to our aching hearts. Every spare thought of mine has been of you. The day I left was one of exquisite pain. The agony of being taken farther and farther from you was followed by the most depressing rumour that we should not expect a day's leave until Christmas. There was much complaining, most of which was from Edward, and threats (Edward, again) of escaping without permission, until a chap asked a Major about the business. Apparently, the Major laughed at our naivety and said that other rumours would follow so we should have our wits about us. I have no intention of falling for such a devilish trick again, though I do have every intention of meeting you during my leave, which was confirmed this morning. We have two days in late October (details to follow) and I plead that you meet me in London. Edward may well be with me, but I expect his appetite for distraction will lead him astray. Please write today with a promise you accept my request. I don't think I could endure waiting past October to see you.

With all my love,
Rupert

Rebecca wrote to Henry at once. He replied swiftly, insisting that Rupert stay a night as his guest. At the bottom of his reply was a postscript from Alice. It read:

Dearest cousin, I've made it known that your wedding gown is to be made in London. Should you have an alternative arrangement it would cause me great embarrassment so please cancel it at once. You'll need at least four days here, and another in the future for the fitting. We should also discuss my gown, and I shall require all of your attention for the most exciting of developments regarding Ralph Schapell. Please hurry, Alice.

'Are you truly convinced?' said Alice. 'You might change your mind.'

Rebecca studied the design again. It was just as Emily had suggested her wedding gown should be. 'I'm convinced.'

'Then so am I. You'll look beautiful.'

Rebecca returned to Henry's to find a telegram waiting for her. It was plain, so she read it aloud.

'Rupert says we should meet him under the clock at Waterloo Station at midday tomorrow. Edward will also be with him.'

Alice clapped. 'We must tell Ralph, Papa. He'd be offended if he learned that Edward had dined here. Edward *will* be dining here, won't he, Rebecca?'

'I couldn't say what Edward has planned.'

'Oh, he must dine here. You haven't seen him for such a long time, and neither has Ralph.'

Henry sighed quietly. 'Edward may indeed have other plans. I wouldn't want him to feel obliged to come here.'

Alice looked at Rebecca. 'He wouldn't feel obliged, would he?'

'I really can't speak for him.'

'But you will ask him, right away at the station before he has a chance to change his plans? Please say you will.'

'I'll do my best.'

Alice smiled. 'I know you will. And I know that Edward will accept, as will Ralph. Mama will miss them again, but it doesn't matter. Ralph will want to return, I just know it.'

Rebecca's subtle hints that she would prefer to be alone at the station to meet Rupert and Edward were ignored.

'As your cousin I have a duty to accompany you until Rupert arrives,' said Alice as they left the house. 'I could never forgive myself if you were approached by a man without a conscience, preying on the vulnerable.'

Rebecca gave no time to thoughts of being preyed upon. All she could think of was how Rupert would greet her, whether he would embrace her or stand nervously, and what her opening words would be. If they were alone she might say what was on her heart, but in public she knew caution could overcome her.

At the station there were others near the clock. Rebecca cast her eyes over those waiting. None appeared to be the type that Edward would know and she was certain Rupert would not have arranged to meet anyone other than herself. She took her position and began to survey the platforms.

'Will they be in uniform?' asked Alice. 'Everyone will be filled with envy if they're in uniform when they greet us.'

Rebecca suddenly felt unsettled. It had not occurred to her that Rupert would be in uniform. A uniform was rigid and disciplined and could change how he acted around her. Alice tugged her arm.

'I can see them,' she said, pointing.

Rebecca found them among the passengers striding up the centre platform. Rupert, wearing the suit he had left in, appeared broader. Edward had lost the length of his fringe.

'Remember to ask your cousin about dinner,' said Alice.

Rebecca could feel her heartbeat quicken as she stepped towards the platform. Rupert saw her and smiled. He stopped as he came within touching distance.

'Hello,' he said.

'Hello.'

'I was worried you wouldn't be here.'

Edward came forward and clamped Rebecca by the shoulders. 'You look radiant, cousin. Wouldn't you agree, Rupert?'

'Very much so.'

Alice coughed for attention.

'As do you, Miss Gray,' said Edward, offering his hand. 'What a marvellous surprise you came.'

'I daren't miss it, Lieutenant Warwick.'

Edward smiled. 'Not quite lieutenant yet, though I expect Rupert will beat me to it. He's quite the act to follow, Rebecca.'

'I'm certain Rebecca and Alice don't wish to be bored with army talk, Edward,' said Rupert. 'Shall we leave?'

In the carriage, Alice was quick to insist that Edward attend dinner that evening. Edward accepted at once and agreed to contact Ralph. He shared his attention between Alice and the sights outside the cab, while Rupert's attention fell only upon Rebecca. She answered each of his questions with enthusiasm, yet she could not ignore the sadness growing within her. In their letters they had preserved the joy of their love, but presently it was as if their connection had been worn by distance and the hustle and bustle of the station.

Once Edward had left them for his hotel, Alice moved closer to Rupert and revealed what Rebecca had intended to tell him when they were alone: that a gown design had been chosen and Henry's wedding gift was to fund their honeymoon. Alice was relentless in her chatter and at lunch dominated the table. When she suggested they occupy their afternoon together, Rupert apologised, explaining that he felt obliged to call upon his cousin Victoria.

'The poor thing has been terribly unwell,' he said. 'I know it would raise her spirits if you accompanied me, Rebecca. She's ever so fond of you, and I happened to mention you were in town.'

'I wish I'd known about her condition. I would have written to her.'

'Sorry, I should have said, but it's been quite sudden and I didn't want to trouble you.'

'I wasn't aware you had a cousin in London,' said Alice. 'I should come with you. After all, we'll be related once you're married.'

Rupert sat up a little straighter in his chair. 'That's very kind of you, but I wouldn't want to overwhelm her with visitors. And Victoria would want to be at her best when she meets you.'

Alice sighed. 'I understand. I suppose I'll just have to find another distraction for my afternoon. Do you know if Edward has any plans?'

'I expect he has, but you should wire him. He may surprise us all and be at a loose end.'

Soon after they left the house, Rebecca suggested they buy Victoria a gift.

'That's quite unnecessary,' said Rupert.

'Why? My mother used to say that chocolates or flowers can restore health as swiftly as any medicine.'

'I agree, but to the best of my knowledge Victoria is perfectly healthy and is in Hertfordshire. I know this as my father has gone down for a shoot.'

'But you told Alice we were visiting her.'

Rupert grinned. 'I'm afraid I lied. I couldn't bear to share you with someone else for any longer. I want you all to myself.'

Rebecca smiled. 'You rascal!'

'You're not cross with me, are you?'

'No, I'm not cross with you. I'm relieved… very relieved.' Rebecca put her arm through Rupert's and said she wanted to spend their afternoon laughing together. 'All I seem to have done since you left is frown, and I'm tired of it.'

'Then I know the very place for a cure.'

The female impersonator Rebecca had seen at the Alhambra had returned from America and was performing a season at the Coliseum. Rupert said she had become world famous, which is why the theatre was full even though it was a matinee. Rebecca, sitting in the front row of the circle, looked down to the seats below. Her attention was caught by a hat decorated with ostrich feathers. The owner leaned closer to her male companion.

Rebecca pulled Rupert forward. 'About five rows from the stage, on the left aisle, who do you see?'

Rupert looked over the balcony. 'No wonder Edward was keen to go his own way this afternoon. And there was I believing that friends didn't have secrets.'

'Do you recognise her?'

'Vaguely, although Edward keeps so many lady friends it can be hard to tell the difference from one to another. We should introduce ourselves afterwards. I want to see Edward's face when we surprise him.'

'But *we're* meant to be at Victoria's. *She's* meant to be unwell.'

'Oh yes, I forgot. We could swear Edward to secrecy.'

'And what if his friend knows Alice? We can't ask her to do the same.'

'We'll just have to be cunning and avoid him. What do you say?'

Rebecca touched Rupert's hand. 'I say it sounds like fun.'

The following morning, Alice said she wished to go to the Coliseum.

'Vesta Tilley is performing there,' she said. 'You should invite Edward to come with us.'

'We'll be on the train by then,' said Rupert.

'Can't you wire someone and say you'll return tomorrow?'

'I'm afraid that's not how the army functions.'

Alice pulled a face. 'Poor Edward. It's unfair he's missed out on a show because he had to visit his friend yesterday. Do you think the man's caught the same illness as Victoria?'

Rebecca swallowed. 'I doubt it.'

'Well I hope we're free of whatever this illness is. I'm quite feeble when I'm unwell, am I not, Papa?'

Henry unfolded *The Times*. 'You can be, how can I put it, rather unhappy.'

'I'm confident Edward kept his distance from his friend,' said Rupert. 'Wouldn't you agree, Rebecca?'

Rebecca, thinking of the woman with the hat, struggled not to laugh. 'I quite agree. Remind me please of his friend's name.'

'His name? Er... it's suddenly escaped me. Probably a chap he knows from Oxford. They all tend to fall ill easily.'

The maid stepped forward with a telegram. 'This has just come for you, Miss Lawrence.'

'It'll be from Edward,' said Alice. 'He's had second thoughts about leaving and wants to take us to the theatre with Ralph and...'

Henry raised a hand to Alice. 'Rebecca, what's the matter?'

Rebecca lowered the telegram. 'It's from Emily. I have to leave... my father's collapsed.'

FOURTEEN

Rebecca glanced at the clock. Thirty minutes seemed excessive for a doctor to be with a patient.

'Are you certain you won't have a gin?' said Emily.

'I'm certain.'

'Well, I'm having one. I wouldn't have got through the morning without it.'

Rebecca checked the clock again.

'Pacing up and down won't help,' said Emily. 'It's what men do when they're feeling lost.'

'I spent four hours sitting on the train so I'll stand if you don't mind.'

There was silence. Emily returned to her chair.

Rebecca sighed. 'What's taking him so long?'

'Doctor Campbell is your father's partner. It's understandable he's being thorough, just as he was earlier.'

'I shouldn't have left Papa. He struggles by himself.'

'Your absence had nothing to do with it. Your father would have collapsed whether you were here or not.'

A door upstairs creaked open. Voices on the landing followed, continuing down the staircase. Doctor Campbell, thin, tall and grey, appeared.

'This is my brother's daughter, Rebecca,' said Emily.

Doctor Campbell shook Rebecca's hand. 'I'm sorry it's only now that we've met.'

'How is he?'

'He's weak. The attack was mild, but many do not survive them nevertheless.'

'What does that mean?'

'It means your father has a stronger heart than most. I've instructed the maid on what he can eat and drink, and I'll return tomorrow.'

'Can I see him?'

'You can, although he's sleeping now. Please be mindful he'll want to get out of bed sooner than he should. Until I say so he's not allowed to, even if he does believe he knows best.'

Rebecca pulled the curtains a fraction apart and looked across Waterloo Square to the house she would make her life with Rupert in. The sound of her father's shallow breathing made her think she should remain in Hallow, close by should he need her.

'Did you find a gown?'

Rebecca turned. 'Papa.'

'Hello.'

'I was hoping you'd stay asleep for a little longer.'

'I need to get up and walk.'

'You've been told to stay where you are.'

'My colleague is too strict.'

Rebecca sat down on the edge of the bed. 'I shouldn't have left you.'

'Nonsense. How are you?'

'I'm scared.'

'There's no need to be.'

'I wish there wasn't, but there is.'

'I'll be fine. You shouldn't worry.'

'You had a heart attack.'

'Barely even a mild one.'

'It was still a heart attack. I could have lost you.'

'You won't be losing me for some time.'

'Only if you rest.'

'You know very well I'm terrible at resting.'

'Then you'll have to do better.' Rebecca reached for her father's hand. 'I keep thinking of Mama when she was sick.'

'So do I.'

Rebecca wiped her father's cheeks with her sleeve. 'You must stop working so hard. I beg you… please.'

Later in the evening Emily brought Rebecca a glass of whiskey and hot milk. 'You'll be asleep within minutes, I promise you,' she said.

'I want to stay in here.'

'You won't sleep well in that chair, and tomorrow you'll have a sore back and sore eyes, and be of no use to your father.'

Rebecca knew Emily was right. She kissed her father goodnight and said they would eat breakfast together. She climbed into bed expecting the strain of the day's events to catch up with her, but minutes passed by and she remained awake. She lit the lamp and opened her case, confident that reading would send her to sleep. Underneath her book was her scarf, still wrapped around her mother's diary. She put her book to one side and found the date in the diary where she had left off weeks before.

There are moments when I forget my life is being ended by something I cannot see: when I wake and find James staring back at me, and when Rebecca and Tilly sing together downstairs as they did today. I fear sweet Tilly may never sing in this house again while I am alive. I fear so much I have found myself wishing it ends now. My darling daughter and husband have carried me for too long.

Kate and Charles called with sympathy, as did Jack and Harry Clarke, both dressed in their Sunday best and uncomfortable about entering Emily's home. Rebecca spoke to them all and then excused herself, knowing familiar voices would tempt her father to rise from his bed. Every two hours or so Emily relieved her from her vigil and she returned to her bedroom and the diary. On the third night in Waterloo Square she finished the entries for November. She knew it would be better to try and sleep, but she turned the page nonetheless.

December 1, 1903

I've pleaded all I can. I pray that James is protected from shame if he agrees, and Rebecca lives in ignorance, free to grieve without the bitterness that honesty would bring. I'll fail her with this lie, but spare her the worst that could come. My brother and Emily will remain protected until truth cuts them. I can only hope they read my final letters knowing the torment I have endured in excluding them from what was left of my life. Tomorrow, I'll learn my fate.

Rebecca pinched the top of the page and listened for voices. The silence gave her permission to continue reading.

I shall no longer be a burden. James has agreed to release me from this slow death. The date will be my choice. May God bless James with the strength needed to support our daughter.

Rebecca went to retch. Nothing came up from her stomach. She closed the diary, wrapped it in her scarf and returned it to her case. Her body began to tremble as her mother's words repeated in her mind: *James has agreed to release me from this slow death.*

Rebecca collapsed on to a chair, unable to escape the sentence and what it meant: her father had killed her mother and endured his shame in secret.

At breakfast Emily wasted no time in telling Rebecca she should have risen late.

'It won't help your father to see you so drawn. If he asks, say thoughts of the wedding kept you awake. He needs something to look forward to.'

Rebecca found her father sitting up, holding a piece of toast and looking down at a newspaper. He was clean shaven for the first time in days.

'Your uncle has had a letter published in *The Times*,' he said. 'He's making a point about trade with foreigners, although I can't understand what it is.'

Rebecca said nothing. All she could think of was that she had been denied the right to say goodbye to her mother.

'Henry isn't normally so confusing. He must be preparing for Parliament.'

'Perhaps I'll make a suggestion in my next letter to him,' said Rebecca coldly.

'Oh, I wouldn't do that; he's terrible at dealing with criticism. Your mother soon gave up saying anything other than kind things to him.'

There was a knock on the door. Doctor Campbell stepped forward.

'I'll leave you alone,' said Rebecca.

In private, after the consultation, Rebecca was told her father could travel home within a day or so.

'We can't allow him to work as hard as he did,' said Doctor Campbell. 'You'll need to remind him of his collapse if he becomes ambitious.'

When lunch was brought in, Rebecca's father pulled back the quilt and said he would take it downstairs. His colleague, apparently, had given him permission.

'A doctor never lies so you have to believe me,' he said. 'A few stairs can't hurt, and I promise not to exert myself any further.'

Lunch passed by as if the heart attack had never occurred. As she sat with her father during the afternoon, Rebecca felt her resistance to asking about the past weaken. When her father suggested she leave him for a while she decided her chance had come.

‘I prefer to stay here,’ she said. ‘If I left you I’d be worried about history repeating itself.’

‘What do you mean?’

Rebecca swallowed. ‘Mama was in better spirits when I left her. She said I should spend New Year’s Eve with friends. When I returned home she was dead.’

‘Knowing you were able to be with your friends would have consoled her. It should console you also.’

Rebecca hesitated, wondering if it would be wise to continue. ‘I can’t understand how she could have deteriorated so rapidly. I was only away for a few hours.’

‘We’ve talked about this, remember?’

Rebecca said nothing.

‘Just as the human body can heal itself without medicine, it can also break unexpectedly.’

‘I thought I’d be there when she died and I wasn’t. I should have been there.’

‘I know.’

There was a knock at the door. ‘You have a caller, Miss Lawrence,’ said the maid.

Rebecca sighed. ‘Can we resume talking when I return?’

‘If that’s what you wish.’

Rebecca wanted to make the caller wait. Her instinct told her it was Mrs Adams or Mrs Finch coming to pry. As she reached the hall she could hear Emily talking. Rupert’s voice followed. Rebecca stopped in front of the mirror, wondering if she had time to change her clothes. The maid opened the door for her.

Rupert came forward. ‘I’ve been sick with worry. How are you?’

‘I’m confused. You said you didn’t have leave for a while.’

‘I have two days, courtesy of my father’s friendship with a colonel.’

‘I thought for a moment something had happened to Edward.’

'Edward is fine. My father said he was worried about you and I should visit. How could I argue?'

'You couldn't,' said Emily. 'Such a considerate gesture of Charles to write to his friend. I'm surprised I didn't suggest it myself.'

Rebecca sat down next to Rupert, desperate to be alone with him. His questions about her father were answered by Emily and soon the conversation changed to the academy and Edward. Rebecca listened to every word, but could not stop her concentration from drifting to what her father had said about the body breaking unexpectedly. In her mind she could see him as she had left him: staring at the window, his heart heavy with pain from what he had done. It was not until Emily left the room that she found her voice. She began to talk of the house across the square and how she had stared at it day after day, imagining living there as husband and wife. Fleeting thoughts of how they might arrange the house were presented as well-laid plans, and as Rupert moved closer, Rebecca spoke of the need for a nursery. She smiled as she stopped talking. The joy of being next to Rupert had caught up with her.

'The wedding seems so far away,' said Rupert. 'I want to marry you now.'

'Perhaps we should elope?'

Emily reappeared. She had failed to knock. 'Sorry, did I interrupt?'

Rebecca restrained a sigh. 'No. We were just talking about my father.'

'My interruption is timely then. He's asked to speak to Rupert. He's looking very tired again so you shouldn't keep him waiting. Coming down earlier seems to have taken its toll.'

The bedroom door was open. Rebecca stood in silence for a moment, watching her father. He was standing at the writing bureau, with his back turned.

'Something important, Papa?'

'Not particularly. I was hoping to find some writing paper.'

Rebecca moved closer. 'I can find you some.'

'There's no need. It's probably best I avoid writing for a day or so.'

'Yes, it is.'

'I see we have a visitor, and a handsome one too. Wonderful to see you, Rupert.'

'And you, Dr Lawrence.'

'I hope you haven't come on my account.'

Rupert glanced at Rebecca. 'I was worried about both of you.'

'That's kind, although you shouldn't worry about me, and Rebecca is in good hands. I wouldn't want you to lose concentration on the parade ground.'

'I'll try not to.'

'As a matter of fact, there is something you can do for me. Rebecca hasn't left the house in days. It would ease my mind if she had some fresh air.'

'I'm quite all right,' said Rebecca.

'Even so, you should have some time alone. You can't count on it with Emily in the house, and it's not as if I'm going anywhere.'

Rebecca cared nothing for an argument. She kissed her father on the cheek and said she would return with a gift.

'I'd prefer it if you returned with a smile,' he said. 'It hurts me to see your eyes so sad. It's not how someone engaged should be.'

December's bite came as a shock to Rebecca, but as they reached the long street of shops she had adjusted to the cold and felt relief at being outside for the first time in days.

'I expect you've been in the cathedral?' said Rupert.

'Papa's long promised to take me. He says it's the most beautiful cathedral in England.'

'I wouldn't disagree.'

'It would make him happy if I went with you, I know it would.'

The cathedral, dominating the east bank of the river, seemed to be empty. Candles were lit, though no-one was to be seen.

'Would you care to see King John's tomb?' said Rupert.

'King John's tomb is here?'

'It is, and has been for quite a few centuries. Follow me.'

A man carrying a set of keys approached them as they read the tomb's inscription.

'Should we be leaving?' said Rupert.

'No, I was just wondering if you'd be wanting to climb the tower?' said the man. 'Most visitors normally do, only much earlier. For what it's worth, I reckon the view is best just before dusk.'

Rupert turned to Rebecca. 'You might find it tiring. There are quite a few steps.'

'Two hundred and thirty-five,' said the man.

'I'm sure I can manage,' said Rebecca. 'And if now's the best time then it makes sense to go up.'

The man led Rebecca and Rupert to an ancient door and unlocked it. 'There's only one rule to follow,' he said, 'and that's not to return in the dark. I wouldn't want you falling down the steps.'

The spiral staircase was narrow and without a handrail. The exertion after days of sitting in a chair brought an ache to Rebecca's legs. As she reached the roof, she paused and caught her breath. Suddenly, a gust of wind lifted her hat off her head, taking it over the side of the tower.

'That was a gift from my aunt. I've barely had it a month.'

'I'm afraid it'll soon be in the river or a field. I'm sure Emily will understand.'

Rebecca raised her eyebrows.

'Perhaps not. Were you fond of it?'

Rebecca put her hand to her mouth, but could not stop her laughter. 'I really didn't like it.'

Rupert laughed back. 'Neither did I.'

'You didn't?'

'I thought it was ghastly.'

'Me too. I'll have to buy another though. If I tell Emily the truth she'll say I was careless.'

Back on the street, Rebecca feared word would reach Emily if she went into the millinery shop. She sent Rupert inside instead, promising him a kiss should he succeed.

'And what if I don't?' he said.

'Then I'll tell my aunt you're to blame for my hat being blown away.'

'Then I'd better not fail. Your aunt would make many a man nervous, including me. It's no wonder Edward spends so much time away from home.'

Rebecca sat down on a bench close by. As she began to consider whether telling Emily the truth would make more sense, Rupert emerged from the shop carrying a box. Rebecca removed the blue and white striped hat and put it on. It was a perfect fit.

'Please say I picked the correct one.'

Rebecca said nothing.

'It looks like it is.'

Rebecca held her silence.

'Please tell me it is.'

Rebecca smiled. 'That's because it is.'

'That was cruel of you.'

Rebecca's smile grew. 'Only slightly.'

'Cruel nevertheless. I think I'll claim my reward now.' Rupert leaned in to Rebecca. At the very last moment she kissed him not on the lips, but on the cheek.

'That's teasing,' said Rupert.

'I said your prize would be a kiss. If you want a kiss on the lips you'll have to earn it.'

'Is that so?'

'It is.'

'And what, may I ask, must I do?'

'I haven't decided yet. Don't worry though, it won't be too demanding. I wouldn't want you to fail.'

Rebecca took Rupert's hand and led him across Waterloo Square to the gate of their future home.

'It may appear a little predatory if the tenants see us,' said Rupert.

'I just wanted to know how it would feel to stand here with you.'

'And how does it feel?'

Rebecca faced Rupert, pulling him closer. 'Like I want to live here now.'

'So do I. Somehow we'll have to be patient.'

'Yes, somehow.'

Rupert shivered. 'I think we've stood here long enough. We should save your father from your aunt.'

'We didn't buy him a gift.'

'He asked for a smile, didn't he? I think you have one of those.'

'I do, and if that's not enough I could tell him about the hat. That'll certainly make him laugh.'

As they crossed the square, the quick footsteps of a man grew louder. The man passed under a street lamp and his face became visible. It was Doctor Campbell. Rebecca ran towards Emily's house, shouting, 'Doctor Campbell! Doctor Campbell!'

He turned on the doorstep.

'What's happened?' said Rebecca hurriedly.

'It's your father. He's had another collapse.'

Rebecca went first up the steps. The door was open, but there was no-one in the hall. Rebecca hitched up her skirt and took two stairs at a time. 'Aunt Emily! Doctor Campbell's here. Aunt Emily!'

Emily met Rebecca on the landing.

'Is he all right?'

Emily said nothing.

'Is he all right? Tell me!'

Still Emily said nothing.

'I want to see him.'

'Let Doctor Campbell in first.'

'No! I want to see him.'

Emily grabbed Rebecca's wrist. 'Stop!'

'Let me go!'

'Stop, please!'

'No! I want to see my father.'

Rebecca struggled her way free. The bedroom was lit by a single lamp. The bed was empty and the pillows had been stacked on one side. A hand touched Rebecca's shoulder and she flinched.

'It's me,' said Rupert. 'I'm staying with you.'

Rebecca stepped forward, holding on to the bed frame. She reached the end and looked down. Her father was lying flat on the rug, his body covered with a bedsheet. Rebecca's legs gave way. Rupert's arms came round her waist, holding her up. She fought Rupert's grip and collapsed at her father's side. She pulled the bedsheet back and grief hit her. Clamping her head with her hands, she began to rock on her knees, unable to speak through her tears. Rupert tried to turn her towards him but she resisted, and touched her father's forehead. There was still warmth in his skin. Another wave of grief hit Rebecca. Rupert pulled her closer towards him. She had no will to resist and clung to him, pressing her head against his chest. Doctor

Campbell moved past them. Rebecca watched him take her father's wrist.

'I'm sorry,' he said.

Fresh tears filled Rebecca's eyes.

'Shall I cover his body?'

Rebecca shook her head. She held Rupert's hand and was pulled up. Everything went black.

'Just sit for a moment,' said Rupert, guiding Rebecca to the bed.

Rebecca waited until her dizziness faded. She bent down and took the sheet, extending it over her father's head. 'I love you, Papa… I love you.'

Emily came closer and embraced Rebecca. After a while she pulled back and wiped tears from Rebecca's cheeks.

'There's nothing I could have done. I tried… I couldn't save him.'

FIFTEEN

Four months later

'My niece would appreciate this being completed swiftly, Mr Phipps,' said Emily.

'I understand, Mrs Warwick. Your brother's will was brief so I expect this to only take a few minutes.'

'I'm relieved to hear it.'

'Shall I begin?'

'Are you ready, Rebecca?'

Rebecca nodded.

Mr Phipps picked up the will. He glanced at Rebecca and Emily, and cleared his throat.

'I, James Edward Lawrence, of Croft House, Hallow, in the county of Worcestershire, hereby declare this to be my last Will and Testament. I give the sum of my real and personal estate to my daughter Rebecca Hannah Lawrence. I give to her the property of Croft House, Peachley Lane, Hallow, and declare my blessing upon her decision whether she reside there or proceed to sale. I give to her…'

Rebecca raised her hand. 'You've made a mistake. My father didn't own Croft House. My aunt does.'

'The ownership changed,' said Emily.

'When?'

'Some time ago.'

'When precisely?'

‘I can check the transfer of title, if you wish,’ said Mr Phipps. ‘I have the papers here.’

‘There’s no need to,’ said Emily. ‘My niece and I can discuss this afterwards.’

‘No, I’d like the answer now,’ said Rebecca.

Emily frowned. ‘Very well. Please tell her, Mr Phipps. I can’t remember the date.’

Mr Phipps put the will to one side, replacing it with another document. ‘The ownership changed in September 1904.’

Rebecca turned to Emily. ‘That was close to when we moved.’

‘Quite possibly.’

‘I’m surprised my father had the means to buy it.’

‘He might have done. But I gave it to him, as a gift.’

‘So we were never tenants as I was told?’

‘No, although I can’t recall ever saying that you were a tenant.’

‘And would you have given the house to him had we stayed in the Fens?’

‘I’m sure Mr Phipps doesn’t wish to hear this.’

Mr Phipps said nothing.

‘Would you have given Croft House to my father had we stayed in the Fens?’

Emily sighed. ‘Of course not. It would have remained in my name and eventually passed on to Edward.’

‘So you used it to lure him here? To take me from my home?’

Emily looked Rebecca in the eye. ‘He’s my brother and he was floundering in grief. You haven’t lost a spouse so you have no appreciation of what it’s like to be surrounded by memories of them. I gave the house to James because I loved him. Your father’s roots are here, he belonged here, so don’t you dare think less of him for wanting to move. I didn’t lure him, Rebecca, I helped him, and you with it. Now this business is painful enough so if you don't mind I'd appreciate it being finished. Any other questions you have can wait until later.'

Rebecca gripped the chair arm. 'Continue, Mr Phipps.'

'Very well. I shall resume: "I give to my daughter my private papers, personal effects, books, prints and her mother's jewellery. I direct that I be buried in the grounds of St Philip and St James Church, Hallow, and commit my soul to the mercy of God, seeking forgiveness from our Lord Jesus Christ, and my daughter, for all of the sins and failures of my life.'

Rebecca wiped her cheek.

'Well, I didn't expect it to be *that* brief,' said Emily.

'There was a codicil,' said Mr Phipps.

'Declared when?'

'November 4, last year.'

'That was only a month before my brother died.'

'Correct.'

'And what does it say?'

Mr Phipps looked down. 'It says, "I, James Edward Lawrence, declare this to be a codicil to my very last Will and Testament. I give to my daughter the property of River Cottage, Welney, in the county of Cambridgeshire, and declare my blessing upon her decision whether she reside there, proceed to sale or collect the tenancy sums as presently arranged with the appointed agent.'

Rebecca sat forward. 'My father sold our house. I was with him when it happened.'

'He did sell it, yes,' said Mr Phipps. 'And he also bought it again.'

'Why?'

'I can't answer that. All I know is the owner wished to sell and your father had an agreement the house be offered to him first. There have been tenants since the sale.'

'Can I see those documents?'

'Of course.'

Rebecca was passed the will and deeds to Croft House and River Cottage.

'So what are you to choose?' said Emily. 'It's clear your father wanted you to.'

'What do you mean?'

'You've inherited two properties. Your father wanted you to choose between living in Hallow, near me, or for you to return to your home, as you call it. Quite why he thought it wise for you to linger in the past I don't know. But then he often ignored what I said, just as he ignored me in his will.'

'He would have thought of you.'

'Evidently not as there is no mention of my name.'

Mr Phipps stood up. 'I should give you some privacy.'

'No, no,' said Emily, 'there's nothing more for me to hear. I suggest you walk back to Waterloo Square, Rebecca. You've much to think about. Good day, Mr Phipps.'

Nine years later

SIXTEEN

July 1914, St Ives, Cornwall

'Happy Birthday, dear James, Happy Birthday to you. Hip-hip hooray! Hip-hip hooray! Hip-hip hooray!'

Everyone fell silent as a waiter placed a cake in front of James.

'Sebastian, only your brother can blow out the candles,' said Rupert.

Sebastian sat back in his chair. His attention remained on the cake.

'Remember to make a wish,' said Rebecca. 'On the count of three. One, two, three!'

James exhaled hard, blowing out the eight candles in one breath. Rebecca began to cut the cake into slices, passing the first to James.

'Slightly larger than that for me,' said Edward.

'There's a surprise.'

'Now, now, a soldier needs his strength.'

James ran his tongue over his lips. 'I love chocolate cake. I could eat it every day.'

'You're just like your grandfather,' said Rebecca. 'He once rode five miles to the nearest teashop just because he had a craving.'

'Sounds reasonable to me,' said Edward. 'What do you say, Sebastian?'

Sebastian nodded. His mouth, with icing around the edge, was full. He swallowed and said, 'I want to have my birthday here too.'

'Your birthday is in winter,' said Rebecca. 'Cornwall is probably very cold then.'

'I'll wear a scarf.'

'Can we go to the beach after this?' asked James.

Rupert glanced at Rebecca. 'Is it too late?'

'It's never too late,' said Edward. 'I'll take them and we'll make a fire.'

James and Sebastian both grinned.

'Just don't wear them out,' said Rebecca. 'Remember we're walking to Zennor tomorrow.'

'And don't take them into the Sloop Inn,' said Rupert.

'On an evening as glorious as this? I wouldn't dream of it. We'll sit outside instead and keep a watch for pirates. Come on you two.'

Rebecca and Rupert were left alone at their table. Hotel guests continued to file into the restaurant.

'I'm sure James was conceived in this hotel,' whispered Rebecca.

'It wouldn't surprise me. We were on our honeymoon, after all.'

'Why don't we go upstairs and discover if we're blessed here again?'

The waiter cleared his throat. 'Would you care for another brandy, sir?'

'No, we're leaving now,' said Rupert.

'I can have the cake delivered to your room, if you wish.'

'Er… no, we'll take it with us. Thank you.'

Up in their room, Rebecca went straight to the window and closed the curtains. She kept her back turned, wanting to tempt Rupert to come closer, to awaken his desire. He came up behind her, took the pins out of her hair, and began to kiss her neck from side to side. Rebecca remained rigid, but as Rupert drew back she turned round and kissed him on the mouth, slowly edging him backwards. They fell on to the bed, with Rebecca resting on her knees, leaning over Rupert, her lips still on his. She could feel her blouse being tugged and sat up to take it off, before slowly unbuttoning his shirt.

'This isn't too soon after what happened?' he said.

'No.'

'You must say if you're in pain.'

'I shan't be.'

Rupert turned Rebecca on to her back, sliding down her undergarments and then his own. Rebecca reached for Rupert's excitement, stimulating growth with each stroke until he was fully hard in her hand. She parted her legs, inviting Rupert to penetrate her. As he hesitated, Rebecca pulled him closer. She gasped, but with her hands on Rupert's buttocks pushed him further into her. She could feel him expand as they moved together, the throb of his flesh intensifying against hers.

'Are you sure you're not in pain?'

Rebecca said nothing. Instead, she put her arms round Rupert, turning him so that she was on top again. She held down his shoulders as she moved her hips gently back and forth, keeping to a slow pace to delay Rupert's release. He took her breasts in his hands and slid his finger down to the place where the greatest pleasure was found. Rebecca could not stop herself from moaning as a thrill was released in her. She abandoned her control and gripped the bedframe as she quickened the movement of her hips, desperate for Rupert's patience not to break.

'Wait,' he said. 'Slow down.'

Rupert put Rebecca on her back again, pausing before he entered her. As his pace reached its peak, he climaxed and all movement in his body suddenly stopped. Rebecca kept her hands on Rupert, wanting him to remain inside her for just a little while longer. He kissed her on the forehead, smiled and slowly withdrew.

Edward was standing in the lobby as Rebecca, Rupert and the boys came down for breakfast the following morning.

'Austria's declared war,' he said, glancing up from his newspaper.

'On who?' said Rebecca.

'On Servia.'

'Whatever for?'

'Because they're bullies. They wouldn't be going to all this bother if the Servian nationalist had missed that Archduke.'

Rupert reached for another copy of *The Times*. 'Or perhaps if Austria hadn't annexed Servia the nationalist would have grown up with more peaceful intentions for his life.'

'Where's Austria?' said Sebastian.

'It's far away enough for you not to worry,' said Rebecca. 'Why don't you and your brother find the best table for us.'

James led Sebastian into the restaurant. Rebecca heard James say he wanted to join the army when he was older.

'Austria-Hungary is hell-bent on revenge,' said Rupert. 'I wouldn't be concerned if Russia wasn't so protective of the Servians. They're spoiling for a fight too.'

'And I'm spoiling for a plate of bacon,' said Edward. 'And two boiled eggs and a rack of toast. Lord knows what we'll eat for lunch. You do know there's little to see at Zennor? One pub and a maypole is what a man at the Sloop told me last night.'

'I read that in the churchyard people often see the ghost of a mermaid,' said Rebecca.

'A mermaid? Now that's more like it. I hope she shows up when we're there. I've always wanted to see a mermaid. Do you know her name?'

'No.'

'Never mind, I'll introduce myself. Just don't say that I get seasick. It may scare her off.'

There was no mention of the war during the walk to Zennor. For five miles they crossed fields on a path that had moorland on one side and sea on the other, until they arrived at the village. There was no-one in sight. Even the inn, the Tinners Arms, was closed.

'I did warn you about this place,' said Edward, peering through the inn's windows. 'Where we should have gone was…'

There was a loud cheer, and then another, only much louder.

'It came from behind the church,' said Rupert, pointing up a hill.

'Maybe the mermaid is making an appearance,' said Edward. 'We should find out. What do you think, boys?'

Sebastian pulled a face. 'I'm tired.'

'I'll give you a piggyback,' said Rupert. 'Edward, you can carry James.'

'He's eight now. That's old enough to walk.'

Rupert crouched, allowing Sebastian to clamber on to him. 'My back hurts, which in my mind makes it a fair contest. First to the lychgate wins a bottle of champagne.'

'Right, you're on! James, come here. We're about to embarrass your father.'

Rebecca went ahead. Edward held the lead until the final yards when Rupert accelerated.

'I declare a draw,' said Rebecca. 'You can share the prize at the hotel.'

'We should have brought a bottle with us,' said Edward, red-faced and out of breath. 'I'm gasping for a drink.'

There was another cheer.

'We're missing the fun,' said Rupert. 'Follow me.'

Behind the church was a field in which a ring was lined

with men, women and children. Edward climbed a stile. 'So this is how tin miners occupy themselves on a Saturday… by wrestling. It doesn't surprise me. They're a violent breed these tinners.'

'Then try not to appear too much like a foreigner,' said Rupert. 'Lowering your voice would be a start.'

A man standing at the ringside turned and stared. He made a beckoning gesture with his hand.

'I'm not getting in there,' said Edward. 'Those men are huge.'

'I believe he's inviting us to watch, not participate,' said Rupert.

'Oh, that I can do. I hope someone's taking bets.'

The man ushered along those beside him, giving Rebecca and the others a view of the contest. Two wrestlers, both without shirts, left their corners and collided in the centre of the ring. The villagers began to shout the names of their favourite. One was called Sid, the other Davy. Sid soon fell. His shoulders were pinned and the umpire raised Davy's arm, prompting another cheer and the exchange of money between spectators. The ring was dismantled and a long piece of rope was laid out on the grass.

'What's happening, Papa?' said Sebastian.

'It appears a tug-of-war is about to start.'

'What's that?'

'Well, there'll be men on opposing sides and they'll be trying to pull each other past the winning mark.'

The man returned. 'You two gents want to join in?' he said, looking at Rupert and Edward. 'We like to get visitors involved.'

'I, er, couldn't possibly compete in these shoes,' said Edward. 'I'd slip and be of no use.'

The man bent down and removed his boots. 'You look about my size. Have these.'

The boots were a perfect fit for Edward. Another pair were passed to Rupert.

'Davy!' shouted the man. 'Which of these two do you want?'

Davy pointed at Rupert. Sid called Edward over to his side. Both men at the back of the teams tied the rope round their waists and smashed their heels into the ground.

'Take the strain,' said the umpire.

Now every man dug their heels in, pulling the rope as tight as it could be.

'On my whistle,' said the umpire. 'Get ready!' The umpire blew hard. Neither team moved, their strength being equal.

'Heave!' roared Edward, as his team gained the advantage.

Rupert and his men dug their heels in again, but their resistance broke and they were now being dragged along the grass. The umpire outstretched his arm towards their opponents and shouted, 'winners!'

Half of the crowd cheered, the other half sighed, while the winning team surrounded Edward, patting him on the back.

'Don't you dare say you lost because your back hurt,' said Edward, as he accepted Rupert's handshake.

'Not a chance of it, although your boots do appear to have superior grip to mine.'

'The boots! I must return them to that man. Where is he?'

The man was nowhere to be seen among the spectators walking away from the field.

'He'll be on his way to the pub,' said Edward, putting his shoes back on. 'Hurry up everyone. The man needs his boots and I need to celebrate.'

They found the man in the Tinners Arms, sitting with Sid and Davy. Rupert and Edward were fetched pints of beer and soon another, and then a third, with a fourth being halted by Rebecca's reminder that the hotel was two hours' walk away and Sebastian would want to be carried. It was late afternoon when they reached St Ives. Tea was being served on the hotel terrace.

'I think I'll have a lie down instead,' said Rupert.

Edward scoffed. 'No you won't! You'll share our prize with me. A few glasses of champagne will soon perk you up. You should join us, Rebecca. Let the old people take tea.'

The concierge coughed politely. 'Excuse me, Captain Salisbury, but this came for you earlier.'

Rupert was given a telegram.

'And there's one for you, Captain Warwick.'

'Mine will be from my mother,' said Edward, turning the card. 'Or unfortunately not.'

Rupert stepped closer to Edward. They looked at each other's telegram.

'Our leave's been cancelled,' said Rupert. 'We've been ordered to return to barracks.'

Rebecca put her arm round Sebastian's shoulders. 'Why? What's happened?'

'It doesn't say.'

'It's the Austrians' fault,' said Edward. 'Their declaration of war would have put the wind up our generals. They'll be worried our rifle drill is rusty.'

'That's no reason for our holiday to be affected,' said Rebecca. 'You should wire the regiment and say you'll return when you're meant to.'

'I can't do that,' said Rupert.

'Edward?'

Edward shook his head. 'Sorry, we really do need to return.'

'When?'

Rupert glanced at James and Sebastian, and then at Rebecca. 'The first train in the morning.'

Rebecca sighed loudly. 'Damn those Austrians!'

A guest tutted.

'We should pack,' said Rupert.

'We most certainly shall not!' said Rebecca. 'If this is going to be the last night of our holiday then I refuse to spend it folding clothes.'

Edward clapped. 'Bravo!'

The guest tutted again.

'Oh stop that,' said Rebecca, raising her voice. 'Come on, boys, we're going to the beach. Rupert, you bring the champagne. In fact, bring two bottles. I'm thirsty, as well as annoyed. Blasted Austrians. I hope they're taught a lesson in manners, and your generals too!'

SEVENTEEN

2 August, 1914

Dearest Alice,

Evidently we share the same irritation as I too have been delayed by your father's position on the Austria crisis. This morning it was my father-in-law who wished to discuss his speech in Parliament, and as with the vicar's wife yesterday, I was addressed as if I was my uncle himself. Conveniently I share his view that Britain should remain neutral on the invasion of Servia, and that if we did seek involvement it would be to appeal to Russia to resist coming to Servia's aid. Of course, I care for the Servians' plight, but I do not think it selfish of me to want the war to remain where it is so that Rupert can return home. The boys are desperate to visit him. His father offered to take us to the barracks, and we could reach them within half an hour, but I fear we'd arrive to find Rupert absent on a drill or a march, or whatever he's been required to do because of Austria's bloodied nose. I hope Ralph's work has not been inconvenienced by all of this aggression. He doesn't mix with Austrians, does he? I don't know a single one, and am relieved so. The premature ending of our holiday by these stupid…

Rebecca put down her pen and went to the window. Emily stepped out of a car, stared at it for a moment, and pushed open the gate.

'What do you think?' she said, as she met Rebecca on the path. 'It's elegant, don't you agree?'

'Yes, and clearly expensive.'

'Charles was terribly jealous. He said he wanted to buy this one, but now I've beaten him to it he'll have to choose again.'

'You've seen Charles today?'

'We've not long finished lunch together.'

'That's odd, he didn't mention he was expecting you for lunch when I spoke to him at church.'

'Nothing odd about it, Charles wasn't expecting me. I rang up this morning and told his butler I'd call and Charles would want me to lunch with him. You have the children so I didn't include you.'

James and Sebastian ran down the hall. 'Aunt Emily!'

'Hello, darlings. Did you enjoy your holiday?'

'Papa lost the tug-of-war to Uncle Teddy, and a man in a pub taught me how to juggle,' said James.

'You went in a pub?'

'Only the garden,' said Rebecca.

'Can you take us for a drive?' said James.

'Once I've talked with your mother.'

'Will you talk for long?'

Emily raised her eyebrows.

'Sorry.'

'Apology accepted. Now if you don't disturb us I may allow you to sit in the front seat. Off you go.'

Emily poured herself a brandy in the morning–room and, without asking, gave Rebecca a glass.

'Don't feel guilty,' she said. 'Your husband's away so you're entitled to a drink late in the afternoon.'

'It's three o'clock.'

'Which allows you to have another when it's five o'clock. I know I shall after what Charles said about the Germans.'

'Which was?'

'That they've declared war on Russia and invaded Luxembourg. At least, that's the rumour.'

Rebecca sat down. 'Those poor people.'

'Who?'

'In Luxembourg.'

'Never mind them. What about France?'

'France?'

'Charles said the French have a pact with Russia to defend each other.'

'Which means?'

'France will declare war on Germany.'

Rebecca sipped her brandy, and then again. 'Do we have a pact with France?'

'One of honour, according to Charles.'

'I don't understand.'

'It means that if France goes to war Britain will find it impossible to remain a spectator like your uncle believes we should.'

'We can't declare war on Germany, it's impossible. The King and the Kaiser are cousins. And what would Alice do? Her in-laws are German.'

'She'll have to cut ties with them and revert to her maiden name. Schapell is far too German to say in public.'

Rebecca finished her brandy and poured another.

'They're just rumours,' said Emily. 'And you should never dwell upon rumours, whether they be of war or infidelity.'

'Infidelity?'

'Many a marriage has floundered because of whispers of mistresses. This rumour about the Germans should be treated with equal suspicion.'

Sebastian burst into the room. In his hand was an apple. 'I won!'

'Only because you were closer,' said James, stepping forward.

'I won!'

'Won what exactly?' said Emily.

'A coconut.'

'But that's an apple.'

Rebecca stroked Sebastian's hair. 'They're practising for tomorrow.'

'Oh, I see. The coconut shy.'

'We haven't got any coconuts, hence the apple.'

'I wondered why a man was delivering coconuts to Charles's home. They looked very big. I'd be surprised if a boy could knock one off.'

'I will,' said James.

'And me,' said Sebastian.

'Perhaps your father can help you.'

'He can't leave the barracks,' said Rebecca. 'Even for the village fete.'

'He can if his father has influence. He has a day pass, Charles told me earlier, although Rupert may have wished to surprise you and now I've spoiled it for him.'

Rebecca smiled. 'I don't mind. That's wonderful news, isn't it boys? Your father's coming home.'

'Can we go in the car now?' said James.

Emily sighed. 'I suppose so, and I expect your mother needs the air.'

'I do, so we'll head to the Camp Inn.'

'A pub? I've never been in one. Is it safe?'

'Perfectly.'

'I think I'll leave my purse here, nevertheless. I've heard only poachers and drunks go in pubs.'

'Edward often frequents them.'

'Yes, well, he's not far off qualifying for one of those categories.'

Rebecca frowned.

'Come on then, let's go to the Camp Inn. If we're robbed, children, you can blame your mother.'

Rebecca picked up the dead flowers on the grave and replaced them with a bunch she had cut from her garden. She stared at her father's headstone, considering all that had happened since her previous visit. She knew she should speak of Cornwall, the war and preparations for the fete, but her dominant thought was being ready for Rupert's arrival.

'Mama! Look at me!'

Rebecca turned. Sebastian, sitting on Rupert's shoulders, waved. Ahead of him on the path was James. He was wearing Rupert's officer cap, although it was too big and covered his forehead.

'Time's up, Sebastian,' said Rupert, bending at the knee.

'I want to stay up here.'

'And I want to kiss your mother, so you're getting down.'

Rupert removed Sebastian from his shoulders and moved closer to Rebecca, kissing her once on the lips.

'I think four days' separation is worth another kiss,' said Rebecca.

'Later, when we're alone.'

'Papa came on a horse,' said Sebastian.

'A horse? I was expecting you to have been driven here,' said Rebecca.

'So was I, but everyone was in such a flap this morning about the Germans I feared I'd lose my pass if I made a fuss.'

'What about the Germans?'

'They've declared war on Russia.'

'And invaded Luxembourg?'

'Correct. Edward's furious. He's long been talking about attending a Bavarian spa for his next holiday.'

'Captain Salisbury! Hello!'

Rupert sighed quietly and whispered, 'I knew we wouldn't get any privacy.'

'I'm so thrilled you're here,' said the vicar, striding towards them.

'As am I.'

The vicar came between Rebecca and Rupert. 'I was wondering if I might ask for your help? Well, it's not quite help, it's more, well…'

'Yes?' said Rupert.

'Your father mentioned to me yesterday that you would be here, and so I had this idea.'

There was a long pause.

'And my wife shares the same opinion…'

'Which is?' said Rupert.

'That you should be the one who opens the fete.'

'But it's always you who does it.'

'I know, but I'd be delighted if you did, particularly as you're so smart in your uniform. We're all so proud of you. My wife says all the ladies in the village talk about you.'

Rebecca cleared her throat.

'Only in a very appreciative way, I mean.'

'They're too kind,' said Rupert.

'So you accept?'

Rupert glanced at the boys and Rebecca. 'I'd be honoured to.'

'Splendid. Now there are a few people you'll need to thank, so I've made a list. My wife is at home and can go over it with you. I should forewarn you, Mrs Salisbury, that she may well ask for your help.'

'With?'

'Tomorrow's outing to the castle. Mrs Archer withdrew yesterday, and Mrs Gibbs is too poorly to travel, leaving my wife on her own with a dozen children. The poor things will devastated if she has to cancel.'

Rebecca remembered the children playing with wooden swords on the green. 'There's no need to cancel. I can help.'

'Excellent! I told Kate we could rely on you. I should let you get on, and don't forget the list!'

By midday the road through Hallow was blocked with the cars, carts and carriages of people from the city, neighbouring villages and hop pickers permitted an afternoon off. Every part of the green was occupied. The church brass band played as girls with buttercup chains in their hair danced round the maypole, picking up their pace with the rhythmical clapping of the audience and the whistles of boys weaving their way through the crowd. Food, drink and crafts were sold from tables lining the green's perimeter, with the queue for the thatcher's cider stretching to the queue for the carousel operated by the travellers who had arrived that morning as they had done every August Bank Holiday for years. There were lines too for Charles's rhubarb wine, the swinging boats, the fortune teller, and for Mrs Munn's apples dipped in toffee. However, nobody was waiting at the coconut shy, allowing James and Sebastian time to perfect their aim. Despite the heat and little shade, everyone was dressed in their Sunday best, apart from Rupert and Harry Clarke. Harry too had been granted a day's leave, his first he told Rebecca since joining the Worcesters that spring. Rebecca found it strange to see him salute Rupert, though he appeared to take pride in doing so and he walked the green with a confidence that was absent in others his age. For all of the laughter she heard, Rebecca noticed that people seemed to be obsessed with Germany's declaration of war upon Russia and speculation of what was to come. No-one mentioned Luxembourg or Servia, or the bullying Austro-Hungarians, only France and what might happen to Belgium. Rebecca resisted asking Rupert for the truth as his attention was on the boys. She was also conscious of his leave approaching its end. Not for the first time she felt resentment towards the army and also to Charles for coercing Rupert into a profession in which he was absent from Croft House as much as he was present. It angered her that Rupert required permission to be at home and that he could give no assurance of when he would return next. It angered her even more that the sense of being rushed, of being cheated, was all because of a foreign war that should have no consequence for England or Hallow, or separate Rupert from her and their children. War had interrupted her holiday and now it was tainting her enjoyment of the village fete. Damn those Austrians, she thought, and the Servian nationalist, and the Germans with it.

'Thank goodness I've found you,' said Emily, appearing suddenly at Rebecca's side. 'Are you aware your village has been taken over by people from London?'

'They're here hop picking,' said Rebecca. 'They come every year.'

'Not to the village fete they don't. They should be hard at work. How else will they pull themselves out of the slums? The language I've heard is repugnant, and it doesn't look as though any of them has had a wash in weeks.'

'I won a coconut,' said Sebastian.

'Then I suggest you keep a tight hold of it. Not that I expect a hop picker would know what to do with a coconut should they steal it from you.'

Rebecca sighed. She wanted to correct Emily, but held her tongue.

'Would you mind caring for the boys?' asked Rupert. 'I'd like to walk with Rebecca before I return to the barracks.'

'We can't miss the race,' said James.

'It's the 100-yard dash,' said Rupert. 'I'm afraid I can't stay to watch.'

'What a pity,' said Emily. 'Although at least you've had

leave. Quite why Edward's request was denied is beyond me. I'm sure the regiment would have coped in his absence. And I gave your father plenty of notice to exert his influence. Clearly it must be waning.'

'Yes, well, I'm sure Edward will be home in the coming days.'

'I doubt it, not with the Germans acting as they are. The sooner their wings are clipped the better, not that the Russians will manage it. From what I've read, they can barely feed themselves, let alone hold a rifle. I suppose we'll just have to hope the French are up to the fight and don't give in as they did last time.'

Rebecca held her tongue again. She put her arms round the boys' shoulders and said, 'Your father has to go now.'

'Can we come and see you?' said James.

'Of course. Just not for a little while.'

'When?'

'The moment everything is back to normal.'

'When will that be?'

'I hope very soon. We all do.'

Rupert hugged James and Sebastian and kissed them both on the forehead.

'Come on boys,' said Emily. 'We need to find the best place to watch the race. The one who picks the winner gets a prize.'

'Can it be a toffee apple?' said Sebastian.

'No, your teeth won't cope. Goodbye, Rupert, and ask Edward to try harder with his leave requests in future. He'll have to bribe someone, or blackmail them, whichever is the more effective with your superiors these days.'

Rebecca went with Rupert to Ashgrove's stables. As they returned to the road, she prepared to say the parting words she had been repeating in her mind: 'Leave the army. I can't bear this separation… prioritise me, your family.' She anticipated

Rupert would stop, but he kept walking, leading his horse towards the city.

'We should part here. I don't want you to be punished for being late,' said Rebecca.

'Don't worry. I've plenty of time.'

'You only have an hour. It will take you that long to reach the barracks.'

'I managed to extend my leave by an hour… without my father's influence.'

'Or his knowledge?'

'I had to ensure I had some time alone with you.'

'By lying to your father?'

Rupert nodded. He kissed Rebecca on the lips.

'Then I'm glad you're a competent liar,' said Rebecca.

'And because I am we have the next hour to ourselves.'

'But we can't be seen. Your father knows everyone, and I'll be left to answer his questions.'

'I know, which is why I'll take you somewhere out of sight.'

Rebecca knew where she was being led to. She would have chosen the place, even though it saddened her to see a home left to decay. The hole in Hallow Park's roof had widened since she had stood months before with other curious villagers, staring at the house as it smouldered and creaked after a great fire. Soon, she thought, the remaining timber would collapse, taking with it what was left of the roof.

Rupert tied his horse to a balustrade on the terrace and took Rebecca's hand. He held it as they sat on the bench, looking down at the little island and the river in the distance. Rebecca caught a glimpse of Rupert's watch. They had barely a few minutes to be still in each other's presence, and she had questions she wanted answers to.

'What do you think the Government will do?' she asked.

'About what?'

'All the wars in Europe.'

'Oh, those. I'm confident Britain will remain an observer if the fighting remains in the east.'

'But what if it spreads to the west?'

'Are you sure you want to talk about this?'

'I need to hear it from you. All the speculation is confusing.'

'Then don't listen to it.'

'Tell me what you think then. I don't know when we'll be back together again.'

Rupert turned to face Rebecca. 'I understand. Well, if Germany declares war on France, then Belgium will be caught in the middle. And if that happens, Britain will find it impossible to avoid military intervention.'

'Why?'

'Because we're bound by treaty to protect Belgium. Most of our politicians probably regret it was ever signed. Only a cowardly Prime Minister, however, would carry on in ignorance should Belgian territory be violated.'

'My uncle says Asquith is a fool.'

'Perhaps, but he's no coward.'

'Would you be mobilised if we're brought into this?'

'Let's not think about that.'

'But would you be?'

'Yes.'

'And Edward?'

'Without question.'

'I'm scared.'

'Don't be. We can still be kept out of a war. And your uncle's speeches in Parliament will make a difference.'

'They'd make more of a difference if his party wasn't in opposition. He should never have joined the Conservatives.'

'And you shouldn't worry. And neither should the boys.'

Rebecca put her head on Rupert's shoulder. There was a long silence. 'I haven't stopped believing,' she said.

'I know.'

'It just feels so unfair.'

'We need to be patient.'

'Some days I find it impossible to be. I look at the boys and feel as if I've failed you.'

'You should never feel that. Ever.'

'I do though. You want a daughter… you've a right to want one.'

'As do you.'

'But all this talk of war, it just seems so threatening, and now you can't be at home, and if what happened means I can't conceive again and then…'

Rupert squeezed Rebecca's hand. 'We said we'd keep trying and we shall. And you must forget about the war. There's every hope for peace.'

'Please leave the army. Please.'

'Once this business is done with in Europe, we'll talk about the future and a life without the army.'

'You promise?'

'I promise.'

'And you want to keep trying for a girl.'

Rupert smiled. 'One day we'll have another child. Whether it's a boy or girl won't matter to me.'

'Then we'll keep trying.'

The exploration of the castle's dungeon, keep, banquet hall and turrets, from where imaginary arrows were fired down upon an imaginary enemy, was followed by a game of cricket in the grounds and slices of Victoria sandwich. There was more cake for the children on their way home as they took tea at Ashgrove, though it came after a treasure hunt arranged by Charles who insisted everyone participate, which meant more running around, and so when the evening came, Sebastian went to bed without the need for a story, and Rebecca fell asleep while it was still light.

The following morning, she was woken by Emily calling out her name. There was a knock on the door, but no pause for a response.

'I expected you to be up by now,' said Emily, stepping into the room.

Rebecca pushed herself up on the pillows. 'Sorry, I must have forgotten you were coming.'

'You didn't. I'm not supposed to be here.'

'Oh. Then why *are* you here?'

Emily opened the newspaper she was carrying. 'Because of this.'

WAR DECLARED
BETWEEN BRITAIN AND GERMANY
ARMY MOBILISED

Rebecca reached for the newspaper and began to read aloud the report on the front page. 'The strained relations between Great Britain and Germany, concerning the neutrality of Belgium, consequent upon the projected war between France and Germany, reached a climax last evening when war between this country and Germany was declared.'

Rebecca paused. Instead of reading on she stared again at the headline, concentrating on the final two words: ARMY MOBILISED.

'Those vile Germans just couldn't resist invading Belgium,' said Emily. 'They want to dominate us, that's what this is about. They're the most brutish of Europe's races. I hope Edward and Rupert shoot as many of them as they can.'

'I'd prefer it if they didn't shoot anyone, and no-one shot at them.'

'Well, some German upstart will try to.'

'But Rupert and Edward may stay here. It's not certain their regiment will be sent.'

'Oh, don't be naive, Rebecca. They could be on their way to France already. That's why I've come. We have to say goodbye before they sail.'

James stepped into the doorway. He was still wearing his pyjamas. 'Are we going somewhere?'

'I'm taking your mother to the barracks, and don't ask to come with us because you can't.'

James frowned.

'It's never a place for children, particularly so today.'

'Why not?'

'Because we're at war, James. Now hurry up and write your father a note while your mother gets up. Tell him that you love him and you'll write to him again soon. Can you do that for him?'

'Yes.'

'Good, and get your brother to sign it. Wake him up if he's still asleep. The Germans won't sleep in, so neither will you.'

Rebecca dressed quickly, gave instructions to the maid on how to occupy the boys, and hurried outside.

'Where's your driver?' she said, looking at Emily's car.

'I've no need for one so I let him go.'

'I wasn't aware you knew how to drive.'

'I've observed enough people over the years to get an idea. There's really not much to it.'

'But you've had instruction?'

'Of course, I'm not a fool. I had a lesson yesterday while you were off playing in a castle.'

Rebecca stepped back. 'Just one lesson?'

'Yes, just one. Now, do you want to see your husband?'

Rebecca nodded.

'Then stop doubting me and get in. Best you hold on to the seat. I don't dawdle as others do.'

Emily accelerated past every obstacle on the road out of Hallow, though when she reached the city she had to slow down. Posters with the words SOLD OUT were on the Journal stands on the main street. People were turning away and making for the closest person with a newspaper, reading over their shoulder the news that Britain was at war. Some men were smiling, as if they were pleased by the declaration, others had their arms crossed or were frowning, while most of the women in sight were looking through the windows of grocery stores as they queued outside, waiting their turn to enter.

'Are the queues normally that length?' said Rebecca.

'People are panicking about supplies running out. I sent my girl to Shoulton's first thing. There won't be a sugar cube left for sale by this afternoon, or tea for that matter.'

'It didn't occur to me that war would make people stock up.'

'I know, which is why I made an order for you. Keep it secret. You'll have all types of people inviting themselves in if they hear your pantry is full.'

Once out of the city, Emily put the car to work again, reaching its speed limit and sounding the horn to warn motorists and pedestrians of her approach. She only slowed as the barracks came into view, and then braked again 100 yards or so from the gatehouse when two soldiers, both holding rifles, stepped on to the road and raised their palms, signalling her to stop. One of the soldiers was Harry.

'I'm sorry, Mrs Salisbury,' he said. 'Only military personnel can go past this point.'

'But I've visited the barracks before.'

'I'm afraid no civilians are allowed in from today.'

'For what reason?'

'There's word there could be German spies operating round here.'

'I'm certainly not a spy, Harry.'

Emily leaned across Rebecca. 'And neither am I, young

man. Now if you don't move I'll drive through you and you'll be forced to shoot at us, which would be a waste of a good bullet as we haven't the slightest drop of German blood in us.'

Harry turned to the soldier. 'Go and fetch Captain Salisbury.'

'And Captain Warwick,' said Emily.

The soldier stood rigid. 'I'm going nowhere, Harry. We were told not to move until relieved of our post.'

Harry looked down, as if embarrassed.

'I understand, Harry,' said Rebecca.

Emily huffed. 'Well I don't. I wish to see my son. I know what a loyal man your father is Harry, so I know what he'd do.'

Harry glanced at Rebecca and turned again to the soldier. 'Wait here, and don't tell a soul about this, all right?'

The soldier sighed. 'Just don't get caught then.'

Rebecca watched Harry march towards the barracks. He went to the side of the gatehouse, climbed a wall and disappeared. When he re-emerged on the road he was two steps behind Rupert.

'Where's Edward?' asked Emily.

'He's in a briefing,' said Rupert.

'Can't he be removed from it?'

'No, he can't. I shouldn't be here either.'

'It's not Harry's fault,' said Rebecca. 'I told him to find you.'

'Don't worry, this will remain a secret. Agreed, Private?'

'Yes, sir,' said the soldier.

Rupert led Rebecca away from the others. She reached for his hand, but he put it behind his back.

'This isn't the time for public affection,' he said.

'But I'm your wife.'

'And I'm an officer. I must show restraint and discipline around those I command.'

'And for how long do you intend to be restrained?'

Rupert frowned. 'Until the war is over and we can return to normal.'

'Which will be when?'

'Some are predicting by the end of the year.'

'You'll be away all that time?'

'Most likely. Perhaps for longer.'

'What do you mean?'

Rupert stepped closer. 'The British army is well trained, but the German army is immense. Their number of soldiers crushes ours.'

'Are you saying the Germans could defeat us?'

'Keep your voice down. The men can't have any doubts.'

'But it is what you're saying?'

'I'm saying a little more caution would help brace people for what is to come.'

Rebecca's stomach turned. 'Don't leave. Have your father speak to someone, persuade them you're needed here by the boys… by me. Please, Rupert. Call your father right away, or I can visit him on the way home.'

Rupert looked towards the barracks. He took Rebecca's hands into his. 'We're joining up with the rest of the second battalion. As is Harry.'

'When?'

'In two days. The battalion will travel from Aldershot. We'll then march into the city and leave for Southampton.'

'And then where?'

'We sail for France the following day.'

'You're going straight to fight?'

'Wherever the French need support.'

Rebecca sucked in her breath. 'I didn't think you'd leave. I've been praying you'd be spared.'

'Bring the boys to the station on Friday. You must tell them not to worry.'

Rebecca nodded.

'And you mustn't worry either.'

'How can I not? You're going to war against an army that you say is vast.'

'I'm coming home, and so are Edward and Harry, and they'll be heroes and all of this will be forgotten.'

'Captain Salisbury,' said the soldier. 'I can see a patrol coming.'

'I have to go,' said Rupert.

'Until the station then.'

'You must find me. I can't leave without a goodbye.'

Rebecca's hands were released. 'I'll find you. And I'll be in the same place when you return. The boys too.'

'You can't worry. I want my parting memory to be a smile, not tears.'

Rebecca wiped her cheeks. 'I'll try.'

EIGHTEEN

'Can you see them?' asked Emily.

Rebecca went on her tiptoes. 'No, I can't, which is why I wanted to leave before lunch.'

'I wasn't to know every man and his wife would be here, and being at war is no excuse for missing lunch, even if I am saying farewell to my son.'

Sebastian tugged Rebecca's arm. 'Where's Papa?'

Rebecca went on her tiptoes again. 'He'll be at the front with the other officers.'

'I say we push forward then,' said Emily.

'Me too,' said James.

Rebecca thought the idea foolish. She looked behind her, expecting to see a bench to stand on, only the crowd now stretched back ten yards or more. Everyone was straining their necks to catch a glimpse of the soldiers on parade. A band began to play Rule Britannia.

'We'll miss the inspection and the salutes,' said Emily.

Rebecca, still with her back to Emily, glanced up. 'Perhaps not. Follow me.' Rebecca wove her way through the crowd and stepped into a linen shop.

'Hello?' she called out. 'Hello?'

There was no response.

Emily huffed. 'We're certainly not going to see Edward and Rupert from in here.'

'We shall from upstairs though. There must be a staircase at the back.'

'I'm not a burglar, Rebecca.'

'Do you wish to watch Edward on parade?'

'At least wait until someone appears.'

'I haven't the time to wait.'

The shop was long and narrow with the counter running down one side. Rebecca went to the end and found the staircase. 'It's here.' She paused on the bottom step and shouted, 'Is anyone up there?'

There was still no answer.

'A sign that we should return to the street,' announced Emily.

'Nonsense. I'm going up.'

Rebecca climbed the staircase. She stepped across a store room, expecting the shopkeeper to emerge from the rows of shelving. The two windows at the end of the room were open. Rebecca went to one and the boys to the other.

'Make room for me, Rebecca,' said Emily.

'There's Papa!' said James. 'He's talking to the man in the silly hat.'

Emily pushed the window up further. 'That's the mayor, dear.'

Rebecca found the mayor thanks to the feathers in his hat. He moved on from Rupert and made his way down the front row of the men, taking their salute and nodding in approval as he walked. He reached the end and looked towards the regiment's padre. The padre stepped on to a box and cleared his throat. The crowd fell silent.

'Eternal God, our maker and redeemer, we commend our cause to you, trusting in thy everlasting strength in the trials that lay ahead for your servants that stand before you today. In the face of danger and adversity, grant them the valour of those who have died before them for their King and country, grant them peace in the depths of suffering, and grant them the hope that is built upon our devotion to Jesus Christ, your son, our Lord. Amen.'

'Two hundred!'

Emily turned to James. 'Two hundred what?'

'I've counted at least two hundred soldiers.'

'I do hope there's a few more of them or the Germans will be spending Christmas in London.'

Rebecca nudged Emily. 'Don't worry them.'

'I was merely making light humour. Besides, the Germans would never dare cross the English Channel. Everyone knows they're terrible sailors. They may not be scared of the Belgians or French, but threaten them with seasickness and the cowards will run away.'

A command boomed across the street. The men turned to their right, remaining in three lines, all with their chins up and their backs straight as could be. The band moved to the front of the parade and arranged themselves again.

'They're about to march,' said Emily. 'Time we left too.'

Emily led the way down the staircase and back on to the shop floor. Suddenly, she stopped. Standing behind the counter was a man.

'Are you lost?' he asked. Emily went to speak, but no words came from her mouth.

'We were,' said Rebecca, stepping forward. 'And you're to blame as the shop was empty and we had to search high and low for help.'

'I'm sorry. I'm here now.'

'Well, now is too late as we are late. Come on boys... Emily.'

The band started to move, playing as they walked, followed by the soldiers.

'We need to be closer,' said Rebecca.

'We should get the tram,' said Emily. 'We'll never keep up otherwise.'

Rebecca looked at the queue for the tram. It was too long for her patience to endure.

'Hold my hands, boys. We're going to march with them.'

Rebecca elbowed her way through the crowd, ignoring the mutterings of those she knocked.

'Rebecca!'

The shout came from Emily. Rebecca pressed on, wondering if she could maintain her pace for the mile or so to the station. People on the street cheered as the soldiers passed by and many offered them cigarette packets. The men looked so strong and handsome with their moustaches neatly trimmed and hair cut short, that Rebecca found it difficult to believe they would soon be in a field pointing their rifles at other young men equally loved and proud.

'I'm tired, Mama,' said Sebastian.

'We're almost there,' said Rebecca. 'We need to reach the front to catch your father's attention.'

The only civilians now keeping up were on bicycles or those patient enough to wait for a tram. Rebecca sighed and abandoned her chase. When they reached the station the soldiers were lined up on the platform. The train had not arrived, yet the best viewing places on the bridge were already taken.

'We're going to have to push in somewhere,' said Rebecca, still holding the boys' hands.

They joined the queue to cross the bridge. Both sides of the steps were lined with people.

'Mrs Salisbury! Quick, come here!'

Jack Clarke stepped out from his place and gestured for Rebecca to take it. His wife stepped away too.

'You don't mind?' asked Rebecca.

'We'll find space elsewhere to see Harry,' said Jack. 'If you were wondering where your husband is, he's right there.'

Rebecca looked to where Jack pointed. Rupert was halfway

down the platform, standing next to Edward, unaffected by the shuffling of well-wishers into the station. There was a loud command, followed by another and the men were released from their positions.

'He's seen me!' said James.

'Then wave!' said Rebecca.

Rupert waved back and began to move through the crowd. Rebecca met him at the bottom of the bridge. He kissed her on the cheek and then bent down and hugged the boys.

'Can I hold your revolver?' asked James, touching Rupert's holster.

'Are you an officer in the British Army?'

'I want to be.'

'Oh, so you no longer wish to become a scientist?'

'Going to war is more exciting.'

'The going part, yes. The doing part, however, is very different.'

'What's that?' said Sebastian, pointing at a soldier holding a dagger-like blade.

'That's a bayonet. It's fitted to the end of a rifle.'

'What's it for?'

Rupert glanced at Rebecca and then back to Sebastian. 'It's for… protection. To keep us safe.'

'Boys! Hello!'

James and Sebastian raised their heads. Edward ruffled their hair.

'You look very smart,' said Rebecca.

'I feel ghastly. Had a terrible reaction to the typhoid inoculation. My arm aches and I've barely slept a wink since I had it. I'll never trust a doctor again.'

Emily appeared at Edward's shoulder. 'Finally, I've found you. Are you all right, Edward? You look worn out.'

'I think I'm well, was up all night though with the excitement of leaving.'

Emily raised her eyebrows. 'Well, try and get some rest before you arrive in France. The French all sleep on straw like peasants, and you won't find a decent bed outside of Paris.'

'I'll have to go to Paris then after we've routed the Hun.'

'Can I hold your revolver, Uncle Teddy?' asked Sebastian.

'I don't see why not.'

'I do,' said Rebecca.

Edward smiled apologetically. 'Sorry, Sebastian, you'll have to wait a few years. How about I buy you and your brother something from the little shop instead?'

'Can it be chocolate?'

'It can be whatever you wish. You can help me, Mama.'

'I'm not fighting my way through all those people again,' said Emily. 'I'm sure you can manage without me.'

'And I'm sure Rebecca would care for a few moments alone with Rupert.'

Emily smiled. 'Oh, yes, you're right, you probably do need some help. Come along, children.'

Rupert guided Rebecca away from the masses, although the chatter of others remained loud enough to hear. 'I'll be home soon', every soldier seemed to be saying, as if the threat of death had been removed from their minds. Rebecca stared at Rupert, desperate for him to say the very same words, to give her the same comfort. Instead, she could see tears form in his eyes. She reached to wipe them, but he stopped her hand.

Rupert swallowed. 'Remember, I can't show weakness.'

'You're going to war, Rupert.'

'Which is why weakness or fear can't be shown, not by any of us.'

'I have every right to be fearful.'

'I know, but not here, or in front of the boys, please.'

Rebecca, fighting back her own tears, felt her heart turn suddenly cold with sadness. She reached into her bag and pulled out a small brown envelope. 'This is for you.'

Rupert removed a photograph from the envelope. He saw Rebecca, James and Sebastian sitting on the bench by the pear tree in the garden at Croft House.

'I had it taken last week. I want you to keep it close while you're away.'

'Thank you,' said Rupert, his voice trembling.

'Uncle Teddy bought me two chocolate bars,' said Sebastian, stepping between Rebecca and Rupert.

'And me!' said James.

Rebecca glanced at Edward. 'How generous of him.'

'I'm sorry,' said Edward. 'I was hoping to keep them occupied for a little longer.'

James moved to the platform edge. 'The train's coming.'

Everyone looked down the tracks as the train rolled into the station and came to a halt.

A sergeant moved down the platform, assigning carriages for officers and other ranks.

'How long till you leave?' said Rebecca, raising her voice to be heard.

Rupert hesitated and said, 'I'm afraid we have to leave now.'

'But we've barely talked.'

Soldiers started to step into the carriages.

'We really do have to leave,' said Edward.

Rebecca bit her bottom lip. 'Boys, give your father a hug.'

Rupert drew James and Sebastian closer. 'Promise me you won't quarrel when I'm away.'

'I promise,' they said together.

'You mustn't worry about me, no matter what you hear.'

Sebastian started to cry. Rupert put his hands on his shoulders.

'Watch out for your mother, and you, James. If you ever see her looking sad, you have to do something to make her smile. Agreed?'

The boys nodded.

'Good. Now give your Uncle Teddy a hug too.'

Rupert stood up. He unbuttoned a top pocket and removed crepe paper that was folded into a square. 'Open it later, not here,' he said, passing it to Rebecca.

'Captain Salisbury,' said the sergeant. 'It's time.'

Rebecca stared at Rupert. Her body began to shake as she was embraced. 'We won't stop thinking about you… I love you,' she said.

'Write to me. Tell me everything about your days, I want to know it all, as if you were speaking to me.'

'Goodbye cousin,' said Edward, kissing Rebecca on the cheek. 'Don't you fret about him, I'll be close to him always. We'll be back here before you even miss us, probably with a couple of medals each.'

'Just come home… soon, please.'

Edward kissed Emily on the cheek, said farewell and strode away.

Rupert stepped back, his eyes never leaving Rebecca's. He turned and she lost him again to the army. She felt one hand being taken, and then the other. James and Sebastian forced smiles for her.

The platform soon emptied of soldiers. The long whistle of the locomotive came and the carriages juddered into movement. Caps were being waved out of every window, and though the band played, the cheering of those left behind drowned out the instruments. Rebecca stood motionless, staring at the train as it became more distant from her. It entered the tunnel and everyone fell silent. Instead of moving away, people remained standing, staring down the line as if already waiting for their loved ones to return. Gradually there was movement, though it was at the pace of mourners. Rebecca noticed Jack Clarke with his arm round his wife's shoulders. Guilt rushed at Rebecca for not seeking out Harry.

‘Here, take this,’ said Emily, offering Rebecca a handkerchief.

‘I can’t believe he’s gone… that they’ve both gone.’

Emily breathed out hard and wiped her cheeks dry. ‘You should be proud of them. Their fathers would be. I wish they were still alive, though part of me is glad they’re not. Neither of them were at ease with their emotions.’

Rebecca said nothing. She looked down at the boys instead. Both of them were opening their chocolate bars.

‘You should take tea at my house,’ said Emily.

Rebecca wanted to go home. She watched Emily wipe her cheeks again and nodded.

‘Let’s leave then,’ said Emily. ‘I’ve had enough of being around people crying. They should save it for when the fighting starts.’

When the evening came, and the boys had gone to bed, Rebecca knelt at her bedside and opened Rupert’s gift. It was a silver brooch. She placed it in the palm of her hand, ran her finger over the front and turned it. On the back was an inscription.

My Darling Rebecca, keep me close. All my love, Rupert

Rupert sent his first letter from Southampton where he wrote that the eagerness of his men to cross the channel masked their anxiety of what was to come afterwards. The crossing itself was smooth, he wrote from Boulogne in his second letter, though there was little he could share about his journey ahead as his correspondence was censored for military affairs. Edward failed to write, leaving Rebecca to answer Emily’s questions about the battalion’s progress.

‘And you’re certain they’re not at the front yet?’ she asked one afternoon in Waterloo Square.

'Rupert would have written it if they were, and the newspapers would have reported it.'

'You shouldn't put your trust in newspapers, dear. I've met many a newspaper owner and they're all scoundrels. They'll print whatever suits them, not us.'

'I did read that the United States has declared neutrality.'

'Now that I can believe. Americans are more occupied with making money than helping us with our troubles. Their neutrality is as dishonourable as siding with the Germans. We're all alone in this war, Rebecca.'

'Canada's declared war though, and Australia, and New Zealand. The entire Empire is joining us.'

'I suppose they'll be of some help if they can get here on time. The war could be over before they've even stepped off the boat.'

Rebecca wanted to repeat Rupert's warning that the war would last longer than expected. Instead, she talked of the boys and how they had boasted to friends about their father being in the army.

'And they should continue to boast,' said Emily. 'The fathers who are doing nothing ought to feel guilty. They need to be shaken up.'

'But tens of thousands have volunteered already. I've heard talk of battalions being formed in hours.'

'That'll be Lord Kitchener's doing. I sat next to him once at dinner. As dour and assured a man as I'll ever meet. Perfect qualities, I expect, for a War Secretary.'

The door opened and Charlotte breezed into the room.

'Sorry for being late,' she said. 'The meeting lasted longer than I anticipated.'

'And what new means of disturbance did you discuss today?' said Emily. 'Or do you plan to keep chaining yourselves to railings and setting post boxes alight?'

Charlotte rolled her eyes. 'The Suffrage Society is tomorrow. Today's meeting was held by the Red Cross.'

Rebecca remembered a poster she had seen in town. It proclaimed 'Matters of vital importance' would be considered at a public meeting.

'There were hundreds of people there,' said Charlotte. 'Everyone was getting very excited about what we're going to do.'

'Going to do?' said Emily. 'What do you mean?'

'To help win the war.'

'I wasn't aware the Red Cross had become militant.'

'It hasn't, but there are many ways we can help.'

'We?'

'Yes, *we*, the people at home.'

'My son's gone to France. Why should I make any further sacrifice?'

'Because others will, and because we should.'

'What can we do?' asked Rebecca.

Charlotte smiled at Rebecca. 'You can knit socks for soldiers, or raise money for the Belgian Refugee Distress Fund, or learn how to make bandages. One man suggested we give up our gardens for vegetable planting.'

Emily scoffed. 'I'll knit a pair of socks for a soldier, and I've already made a significant donation to the poor Belgians, but no-one will ever persuade me to turn my garden into a potato patch.'

'Well, I'll gladly give up mine,' said Rebecca. 'Gardens our size could feed dozens of families if used properly.'

Emily sighed. 'Fine, I'll give up a flower bed or two, but that's all. My gardener won't be at all happy about it. He's more attached to the garden than I am.'

'I doubt he'll care so much when he's being shot at,' said Charlotte.

'Shot at? Impossible. The army would never take him. He's too short and his teeth are dreadful.'

'He's clearly tall enough or he wouldn't have looked so happy earlier.'

'Earlier where?'

'Coming out of the enlistment office. I watched a procession of them emerge as I waited for the meeting to start. The queue to get in stretched down the street.'

'Do you mean to say I'm losing the services of my gardener?'

'It appears so.'

'Those blasted Germans! The sooner we get in the fight and bring them down a peg the better. I hope all of their gardens wither and die like mine will. I've a good mind to go to France and starting shooting at the Hun myself.'

'You'd be of more use as a VAD,' said Charlotte.

'A what?'

'A Voluntary Aid Detachment… a nurse.'

'I think I'd prefer to shoot Germans. Besides, I expect I'm too old to join.'

'Not at all, you're the perfect age. A nurse's greatest quality is how to comfort someone in distress.'

'It's my *maturity* that allows me the right to avoid distress if I can. Only fools would go seeking it out.'

'I'm considering applying, as is Elizabeth.'

'You're younger so you're not so foolish, but I can't envisage Cambridge being too happy about Elizabeth joining. They tend to keep a close eye on scholars' interests.'

'Elizabeth won't be attending Cambridge.'

'So she's come to her senses and chosen Oxford?'

'No, she's decided that if she's accepted as a VAD she won't attend university. At least, until the war's over.'

Emily's jaw dropped. 'So she'd prefer to dress soldiers' wounds than read English?'

'Correct.'

'Then Lord help us. I'm all for women in the lower classes helping to defend our civilisation against the barbarians, but if we allow our young ladies to abandon their place then we may as well surrender now and save lives as the Germans would have destroyed our society, as well as our gardens.'

'That's nonsense,' said Rebecca. 'There should be no difference between the contribution someone who lives in Cheapside can make, and that of a person in Waterloo Square, or Croft House for that matter.'

'So you would nurse a Tommy also? Even though you have two boys to care for, and your husband is absent defending your freedom?'

Rebecca felt blood rush to her face. 'If I was allowed to, yes.'

'James and Sebastian should *not* be without both their parents. Having one in France is more than enough for a family.'

'Oh, VADs don't have to go abroad,' said Charlotte. 'They can be close to home in auxiliary hospitals such as Ashgrove.'

'Ashgrove is to become a hospital?' asked Rebecca.

'That's what my brother says. He's on the committee that selects homes for service.'

'I hope they don't have the nerve to include mine on the list,' said Emily, 'because I'll want it removed immediately.'

'Don't worry, your home is too small to be considered.'

Emily frowned. 'It's larger than most people's. And I very much doubt Ashgrove's new owner will comply. He's, well, how can I describe him? A braggart, an arse, is he not, Rebecca?'

'Perhaps, but the house needed to be sold and his was the only offer.'

'He's still unsuitable for it. Charles would never allow such a man into his home, and neither would Rupert.'

'Rupert and Alfred don't own Ashgrove any more, and the owner may well agree to it becoming a hospital.'

'If he does, it'll only be because he's after a knighthood. All these new money people are chasing them. And he'll be after a wife too. You should warn Elizabeth if she's posted there. I'm sure you've heard the rumours about him.'

Every letter Rupert sent included words for James and Sebastian. There was never a mention of Germans, or soldiers, or guns. Instead, he wrote of the differences between Worcestershire and French countryside, the food he enjoyed most, and that he hoped the boys were behaving and thinking only of school and trying to be happy. It was as if he had not gone to war, but was on a tour of France and would return soon. Rebecca would read his message aloud at dinner and then put the letter away. After the boys had gone to bed, she would read it again, studying each sentence for something she might have missed about Rupert's proximity to the fighting, or his pining for her.

She knew that Rupert would also scrutinise her letters and so she produced draft after draft of each until she was certain he would be heartened by what he read. She wrote every other day, as did Rupert, including all that she could remember had happened since her previous letter, always conscious to avoid sharing her fear their separation would run longer than months. One day in late August, she returned from the vicarage and started to write at once.

My Darling Husband,

You must be wondering why you are receiving another letter so swiftly, and you have no reason for worry, but I am compelled to share what I witnessed this afternoon and do so in the hope it emboldens you in our fight against tyranny. The trauma of war that you have witnessed in the faces of refugees lying exhausted on the roadside in France, has now reached our village. Two Belgian children, Christian, aged eight, and Audrey, aged six, have been taken in at the vicarage. I was passing by when they arrived, and was asked to sit with them. I believe Kate must have thought they would warm to a mother, but these dear children could not bring themselves to talk, even when given cake. They did not leave a crumb, but neither did they smile, and every question Kate asked (she is competent at French) was met with a nod or shake of the head. It is as if the terror of what they have witnessed at the hands of the Germans has left them without speech, or for some other awful reason unknown to us, they are in fear of talking. The newspapers keep referring to the 'Rape of Belgium' and that German soldiers have committed atrocities that I do not have the stomach to write or speak of.

Kate says the children are in shock. When I left, she told me what she knew. They are brother and sister and lived in a town which was shelled by the Germans. Their home was hit and their parents were killed, and so were their neighbours. They have an older brother who led them with other refugees towards France, but somehow in the masses they became separated. I can't imagine his agony, or that of the children's. This war is in its infancy and already I detest it, and those responsible, upon whom I wish the same suffering as Christian and Audrey have been dealt.

Rebecca dropped her pen on to the desk, crumpled the letter and threw it at the window. She went to scream, but at the last moment put her fist to her mouth. She would not allow her rage to wake the boys. War had taken Rupert from her, and now it had infected her with hate, just as it had Emily. She placed a clean sheet of paper in front of her, picked up her pen and started again.

NINETEEN

'Can I hold the tin now?' asked James.

'Just so long as you rattle it as people pass by,' said Rebecca.

'I can rattle better,' said Sebastian.

Charlotte passed Sebastian her tin. 'There, you can compete with your brother for who gets the most coins.'

Rebecca and Charlotte took the placards the boys had been holding. Some people stopped and donated, but most continued on to the racecourse.

'We should have stayed on the High Street,' said Rebecca. 'Men will never part with their betting money, even for Belgian refugees.'

'Then we'll have to be confrontational when they leave so they part with their winnings. And next time you should bring those children. The sight of two refugees should stir any decent person into giving.'

'I'll ask, but it may be a while before they're able to be in a crowd again. Kate says the girl won't leave the vicarage and the boy won't go anywhere without her. He asks every day for news of his brother, and every day Kate has to say there isn't any. She's even placed advertisements in *The Times*. No-one's responded and the Red Cross has no record of him.'

Sebastian rattled his tin loudly. 'Mr Clarke! Mr Clarke!'

Jack stopped just as he was about to step through the racecourse gates. He did a double take and made his way over.

Rebecca leaned down and said, 'It's best not to ask for…'

Sebastian held out his tin before Rebecca could finish her sentence. Jack put his hand in his pocket.

'An excellent cause,' he said, releasing a coin.

'That's very generous of you,' said Rebecca.

'Glad to help. Those poor folk certainly need it, and now that we've reached Belgium they've got some hope of returning home.'

Rebecca thought she had misheard. 'Belgium? My husband's last letter was written from France. He made no mention of even being close to Belgium.'

Jack said nothing.

'Mr Clarke?'

'You haven't heard then?'

'Heard what?'

'That the second battalion has engaged the Germans.'

'No, I haven't.'

Jack glanced at the boys. Rebecca took him to one side.

'Tell me what you've heard?' she said.

Jack sighed. 'The Worcesters have had to retreat…the whole lot of them have.'

'What do you mean, the whole lot?'

'The British Army.'

'The entire army? That's impossible.'

'There's a report in the afternoon edition of the *Chronicle*. It didn't say much. Harry will tell me more in his next letter. They'll all write soon, I'm sure.'

Rebecca's heartbeat accelerated. 'Retreat means we're being defeated.'

'Not always. It can be tactical, to prepare for victory.'

'And is this tactical?'

'I don't know. The report was brief.'

Rebecca looked around her. There were no newspaper boys to be seen. 'Wait here,' she told James and Sebastian.

Rebecca pushed her way through the crowd and on to the racecourse terrace, glancing at people's hands and pockets. Catching no glimpse of a newspaper, she made for the grandstand, ignoring the man selling tickets for seats. People were talking to their companions or staring through binoculars. Rebecca reached the halfway point in the grandstand and stopped. In the middle of a row was a woman reading the *Daily Chronicle*, seemingly unaffected by the men talking across her. The seat behind her was empty. Rebecca thanked people as she squeezed past. She considered waiting for the woman to close her newspaper, but instead tapped her on the shoulder. The woman flinched and continued to read. Rebecca tapped her shoulder again, harder this time, and coughed loudly. The woman turned, studied Rebecca for a moment, and said, 'May I help you?'

'Yes, you can actually. I need to read your newspaper.'

The woman frowned. 'And I need to finish it. Once I have, you may borrow it.' She turned back and raised the newspaper higher than before.

Rebecca heard someone behind her say, 'I wish she'd sit down.' She remained standing, convinced the woman was mocking her by turning the page slowly.

'Sit down!' said someone else. 'You're in the way.'

The woman began to turn another page, and hesitated.

'Sit down!'

Rebecca wanted to shout back. Instead, she leaned over the woman's shoulder, snatched the newspaper from her hands and hurried to the aisle.

'Sorry! Sorry!' she said, treading on the feet of those in her row.

'Thief! She stole my newspaper!'

Rebecca continued her escape, shoving the ticket-seller aside as he stepped in front of her. She wove through the groups on the terrace and found a hiding place behind a wall at the back of the grandstand. Catching her breath, she straightened the newspaper and braced herself for a shock. The dominant headline referred to the surge in recruitment of soldiers for the war, and underneath was an article appealing for people to resist stockpiling food as prices escalated. Rebecca wondered if the newspaper was old. She glanced at the top: it was that afternoon's edition. Jack must have been confused, she thought. If the Worcesters had been in a battle, the report would be prominent. She turned the page, irritated by the notices for garden fetes, the requisition of horses from hunts, and the cancellation of the amateur football league.

There were footsteps on gravel. Rebecca raised the newspaper to conceal her face. The person coming her way stopped and turned back. Rebecca continued to stare at the newsprint, reading over and over the lines shoehorned into page four under the headline, *Worcesters engage the enemy*.

A despatch received this morning reports that the 2nd and 3rd battalions of the Worcestershire Regiment have met the enemy's fire at Mons, Belgium. The German assault has brought the order of withdrawal for the British Expeditionary Force which, however, has inflicted greater losses than those received.

Rebecca stared at the final words, terrified at what they might mean. Her terror turned to anger at the newspaper for giving her so very little information. It would have been more responsible, she thought, to have printed nothing at all than provoke fear. She returned to Charlotte and the boys. They were still rattling their tins, though latecomers to the races were striding past them without making a donation.

'I've got the most money,' said Sebastian.

'Only because you're smaller than me,' said James. 'And it's not your money, it's for the Belgians.'

'I've still got more.'

'You found a copy, then?' said Charlotte.

Rebecca glanced at the newspaper. 'Yes. I'm sorry, can the

boys stay with you a little longer? There's somewhere I must go.'

'Right away?'

'Yes.'

'Can I come?' asked James.

'It's best you stay here with your brother. I'll bring you both back a treat, ok?'

The boys nodded. Rebecca went in search of a cab, finding one at the top of the road. The driver dropped her outside the *Chronicle* building. She lingered on the street, watching people file in and out, wondering which ones were reporters. A man accompanied by a photographer emerged from a side door. Rebecca went to approach him, but remembering something Emily had told her, she let him pass by and instead entered the office. Behind a counter were half a dozen desks with a woman sat typing at each. Rebecca could hear people ahead of her place advertisements, while those waiting in line were discussing either the war or food prices.

When she finally reached the front, a woman aged over 50 and with oversized glasses stared back at her.

'Do you wish to place a notice?' she asked.

'No, I wish to speak to Mr Carlton,' said Rebecca.

The woman appeared puzzled. 'I don't believe anyone by that name works here.'

'Oh, I thought he was the editor.'

'The editor's name is Mr Charlton, not Mr Carlton.'

Rebecca restrained a sigh. 'Then I need to speak to Mr Charlton.'

'I'm sorry, he's very busy.'

'As am I, which is why you should inform him right away that I'm here.'

'And does he know of you?'

'Possibly not. But if you say that Mrs Emily Warwick's niece wishes to speak with him I'm sure he'll find the time to do so. And if you don't, then my aunt will find the time to call him at home this evening and report how obstructive you were.'

The woman pouted and said, 'Please take a seat and I'll pass your message to Mr Charlton's secretary.'

The woman reappeared within minutes. She was accompanied by a man who opened a latch on the counter and approached Rebecca. He was wearing a blue-striped suit and his grey fringe needed cutting.

Rebecca stood up. 'Are you the editor?'

'That's correct, James Charlton.'

'Thank you for coming out, and I apologise if I've interrupted you.'

'Your aunt used to help my late wife. It's no bother to me to leave a meeting to talk to her niece.'

'Yes, well, it's about today's paper. I take it you've read this?'

Mr Charlton looked to where Rebecca was pointing on page four. 'I have, yes.'

'Then please tell me why it's lacking in detail. Surely there must have been more you could have printed?'

'There wasn't, but even if there had been we couldn't have. This came in on our deadline and the final page to send to print was this one.'

'So you can't tell me if any officers were killed before the retreat?'

'I'm sorry, that's not something I can answer, Mrs…'

'Salisbury.'

'We may have more in tomorrow's edition.'

'You *may* have more? I'd say you should definitely have more.'

Mr Charlton said nothing.

'Surely you can ask for more information? And particularly about the second battalion.'

'I assure you, Mrs Salisbury, we'll do all we can to publish the latest news for our readers.'

'So you'll have another despatch before the morning?'

'It's possible.'

'Can you call me if you do? I can't wait until the morning. Please, you must understand, I have to know about the officers.'

People in the queue turned their heads, though Mr Charlton kept his attention on Rebecca. His eyes began to fill with sadness.

'Mrs Salisbury, my only son is in the second battalion. I'm as eager as you are to know what is happening, but we both may have to wait days to have our minds put at ease.'

'Days? No person can endure that long.'

'I'm sorry, that's how this war is, and how it may continue to be until it's over. In truth, we're being told very little by the War Office about the fighting in France and Belgium.'

'There has to be some way of discovering what happened?'

'I'm just hoping my son writes as soon as he can, from wherever they are.'

Rebecca calculated she had 16 hours to wait until the next post. She wondered if she had a letter waiting for her. It occurred to her she could call at Jack's home that evening and ask him to check.

'I really am very sorry I can't help you.'

Rebecca tried to smile. 'You *have* helped me.'

'Please pass on my regards to your aunt. Perhaps you might encourage her to accept my next dinner invitation? She always seems to be occupied.'

'I'll certainly mention it. Thank you.'

The following morning, Rebecca sat down on the bottom stair at home and stared at the front door, waiting for the sound of footsteps on the path. They arrived, as always, just after seven o'clock, followed by the creak of the letterbox and the shoving through of a newspaper. Rebecca turned page after page, expecting to read about the Worcesters. There was no mention of casualties, or the army's position. The only mention of the regiment came in a report about hundreds more men enlisting, and a pattern that should be used when knitting socks for soldiers.

'Mama, I've got a nosebleed.'

Rebecca glanced up the staircase. Standing at the top was Sebastian, pinching his nose.

'I'm coming. Tilt your head back.'

She took Sebastian into the bathroom and cleaned his chin and nose of blood. As she finished, she heard the maid speak to Jack on the doorstep and then the door close.

'Stay still, Sebastian. I'll be straight back.'

There was only one letter on the breakfast table. As Rebecca read it a second time, she sensed she was about to cry.

'Has Papa written?' asked James, pulling out a chair.

Rebecca put down the letter. 'I have to go out. Look after your brother until I return.'

She made for the riverbank, striding away from the village until she reached the rope tied to the willow tree. A memory came to her. It was the day she left the Fens. Tilly had told her to say goodbye to George.

'You may never see him again,' Tilly had said. Now she never would. The Germans had killed him.

All of her anger at the war, and the Germans, and the newspaper rose within her and she screamed. She drew in quick breaths and screamed again, caring nothing for the pain it caused her throat.

Five days had passed since Rupert's last letter. Even in retreat he should have written by now, she thought. Others would have found a way, and he would have predicted her anxiety and known he had to write, which could only mean his letter had been misplaced or he was one of the casualties.

'You can't think that,' she said under her breath, as she returned to Croft House. 'Don't think that… don't!' She wiped her cheeks and entered the dining-room. James was sitting at the table.

'What are you doing?' she said, crossing her arms.

James dropped Tilly's letter.

'That's addressed to me, not you.'

'I'm sorry. I thought it might be from Papa.'

'Well, it isn't.'

'When will he write next?'

'Soon.'

'This week?'

Rebecca took back Tilly's letter. 'I don't know. He's at war. Nothing's how it should be.'

'Perhaps I used the wrong address.'

'What do you mean by that?'

'For our letter. Well, it was more my letter. Sebastian didn't write much.'

'You wrote to your father?'

James nodded. He took a bite of toast and began to chew.

'You should have told me you'd written. When did you send it?'

James swallowed. 'Umm… a week or so ago. I used the address on one of Papa's letters. Mr Clarke said it looked accurate.'

Rebecca thought she would be sick. Rupert would never delay his response to a letter from the boys, no matter where he was.

'Where's Sebastian?' she asked.

'He's reading. He said he wasn't hungry.'

'Right. Well, keep an eye on him.'

'Where are you going?'

'Into the village. Don't leave the house.'

Rebecca borrowed the maid's bicycle and set off up

Peachley Lane, wondering if it was wise to ask Jack whether he'd received a letter from Harry. She risked upsetting him if he hadn't, but if he had, it was quite possible it would refer to Rupert.

'What's the hurry?'

Rebecca wanted to carry on. She braked instead and turned back, stopping at Mrs Munn's front gate. 'There's no hurry,' she said.

'Glad to hear it,' said Mrs Munn. 'My brother was in a hurry once riding a bicycle and he fell into a pond.'

'I've no intention of cycling past a pond, but I really must be on my way.'

'How are your sons coping?'

'They're coping fine.'

'That's a relief. Best they don't read the newspapers though, that's my advice.'

Rebecca sighed. 'Even if they did it wouldn't matter as there's never any details in the *Chronicle* about the Worcesters.'

Mrs Munn stared blankly at Rebecca. She went to speak, but hesitated.

'Yes?' said Rebecca.

'I take it you haven't read his morning's *Daily Times*?'

'No.'

'I think you should.'

'What does it say?'

Mrs Munn's expression was one of anguish. 'Wait here.' She went inside, re-emerging from the house within seconds. She passed Rebecca a folded copy of the newspaper and stepped back.

FEROCIOUS ATTACK ON BRITISH TROOPS
GERMANS GAINING GROUND
WORCESTERS IN THE THICK OF IT

Rebecca raced through the report and returned to the start. The shock of it all caught up with her and she reached for the gate to steady herself.

'Do you want to come in and sit down?' asked Mrs Munn. 'A drop of brandy, perhaps?'

Rebecca continued to stare at the newspaper. 'This can't be true.'

'It might not be. Someone could have got confused.'

Sentences attacked Rebecca: *The Worcesters were in the hottest part of the fight and suffered worse than any other… their ranks were cut to pieces by shrapnel… they outnumbered us ten to one… our losses were enormous… one regiment was captured.*

'Rupert's been captured.'

'Now, now, Mrs Salisbury, best not to think like that.'

Rebecca gave back the newspaper. 'I must get to the barracks.'

'On a bicycle? It's a good twelve miles away.'

'Can you tell the boys I'll be a while? Say I've had to go into town.'

'If you wish. Just remember what I said about my brother.'

As Rebecca reached the top of the lane, a car came at her, forcing her to swerve into a hedge. The car came to a quick stop.

'Rebecca?' said Emily, poking her head out of the driver's window.

'You almost hit me!'

'You were in the way.'

'I was not!'

'You were on the road, weren't you? That qualifies as being in my way.'

Rebecca brushed herself down and picked up the bicycle.

'It's a little early for a ride, isn't it?' said Emily. 'I hope you've eaten. You'll become light-headed if you haven't.'

'Rupert may have been captured.'

'Captured? I very much doubt it. Not according to my news.'

'What do you know? Tell me!'

'There's no need to look so worried. I'll tell you in the house. Come along.'

Emily drove off. She was heading into the house when Rebecca caught up with her.

'Tell me what you know about Rupert,' said Rebecca.

'I really would prefer coffee to tea, but I don't wish to be any bother. Are the boys upstairs? James... Sebastian?'

'What do you know about Rupert?'

Emily entered the dining room. 'Rupert? Oh, yes. Apparently he's running short of cigarettes.'

'Pardon?'

'He's running short of cigarettes. Edward told me so in a letter I received this morning. I've been asked to send packets to them both and a fruit cake from Clinton's. I can only presume Rupert doesn't want you to be troubled. I, evidently, can be.'

'So Rupert's not a prisoner of war?'

'I'm sure Edward would have mentioned it if that were the case.'

Rebecca sat down. She closed her eyes and said, 'Bless, you, Edward.'

'I suppose so.'

'What else did he write?'

'That was all, just cigarettes and fruit cake. Mr Charlton managed to tell me more about the fighting.'

'That surprises me. He knew little yesterday.'

'Yes, I gather you went to his work.'

'He called you afterwards then?'

'No, he waited until seven-thirty this morning. It was very important I told my niece, he said.'

'Told me what?'

'About the battalion. Not that he had much news, only that his son had written to him and mentioned that his commanding officer, Captain Salisbury, had recommended him for a medal. Something to do with disarming a German machine gunner, although I may have misheard. It was far too early to be concentrating.'

Another wave of relief came over Rebecca. 'That means Rupert's alive.'

'Of course he is, it's in his blood. His father served for thirty years or more in the army and the only injury he suffered was when he accused a man of cheating at cards. Foolish thing to do as the cheat was the rank above him and struck him straight in the nose.'

After seven days, Rebecca received a letter from Rupert, and an apology for his delay. There was no reference to a retreat, only that he was on the Belgian border and that in war lost ground could always be regained, and gained ground always lost. As with each of his letters he wrote nothing of death. He gave room instead to questions about the boys and home, and though Rebecca answered each in her reply, all she cared to do was share her terror, as if doing so would remove it from her life. Every conversation she was drawn into became dominated by talk of the war, and of what someone had heard, read or feared. Emily became convinced one of her neighbours was a German spy, and threatened to alert the police. He qualified as a spy, Rebecca was told, as he had the look of a German, the arrogance of a German, had mentioned in passing he had once travelled to Berlin, and that Beethoven was often his preference of gramophone record. Emily's conviction grew when the newspapers began to refer to 'the spy peril' and 'the alien enemy', and that these 'aliens' were being rounded up by police.

'I read that two dozen of them were captured during the

weekend,' said Emily, one September afternoon in Waterloo Square.

'Captured? For what crime?'

'For being German. A perfectly adequate reason to me.'

'Having German ancestry doesn't qualify a person as a spy.'

'In your mind perhaps, but not in mine, and thankfully not in the minds of the authorities. The sooner all those with German names are taken off the streets the better.'

'My cousin Alice has a German name.'

'Then she should use her maiden name or she'll be forced to leave the country with all the others. If I was in charge, not a single German would be allowed to return to their homeland. Put them to work for our benefit, and then lock them up at night.'

'Alice's husband has secured a commission. I hardly think she'll be arrested while Ralph prepares to leave for France.'

'Ah, but what use will he be? He may well reach the battlefield and realise he hasn't the stomach for shooting his countrymen.'

'I doubt it.'

'Well, you should. Germans are cowardly like that. Observe my neighbour from afar and you'll soon agree with me.'

'Your neighbour is not a spy.'

'He is, I tell you. It wouldn't surprise me if he's listening to our conversation and plotting how to protect his secret. If I'm found dead with a knife in my back, you'll know who did it.'

'Then maybe you should visit Hallow more often, instead of me always coming here.'

Emily pulled a face. 'Oh, there's no need for that. Anyway, Mr Thomas is hard of hearing so we're perfectly safe here. And besides, you're about to let your maid leave.'

'She wishes to contribute to the war effort. Most girls are.'

'Which is why you should employ someone who's too old to go anywhere, and is no use for the… what is your girl doing?'

'She's joining the First Aid Nursing Yeomanry.'

'That's the group, the FANYs. Charlotte wants me to help raise money for them. I said you'd help too, though you won't have much time for such matters once you're without a maid.'

'I can manage without a maid. And so can you.'

Emily scowled. 'You may be content in the kitchen, but I certainly have no intention of joining the lower classes, even if we are at war. I'd sooner employ a German than sweep the scullery.'

'I'm surprised you know where the scullery is.'

Emily looked to the door, pretending she hadn't heard Rebecca's comment. 'That must be the newspaper. I've taken to ordering the afternoon edition as well. One likes to keep abreast of all that is happening.'

The maid placed the *Daily Times* on the little table between Emily and Rebecca, and asked if more tea was required.

'I don't believe so,' said Emily. 'Rebecca, would you care for another cup?'

Rebecca shook her head. She reached for the newspaper, her attention taken by the STOP PRESS column on the back page. She looked up and down a list, and then again. Rupert and Edward were not included.

'There are so many,' she said faintly.

'So many what, dear?'

'Names. It's a list of the names of the officers killed in the regiment. Sixteen already. There are dozens, even a hundred, wounded or missing. There must only be a handful of officers left.'

Emily's face suddenly lost all colour. 'Edward's not on there, though?'

'No, but I recognise some of the names. Rupert had talked

about them, they were his friends… I don't understand why there are so many dead and he hasn't mentioned any of them to me. He would have been with some of them when they were killed. He might have held them at the end, or carried them, or buried them, and he's said nothing to me about it.'

Emily took the newspaper from Rebecca. 'He's most likely deceiving you, but only to protect you, and the boys too.'

'Protecting us from what?'

'Evidently from what he's seen.'

'Well, evidently he believes I haven't the stomach for it.'

Emily pointed to what had been printed next to the list of officers' names. 'So you have the stomach to read this, do you?'

'What is it?'

'It's an extract of a letter from a private in the third Worcesters to his wife. He writes about the battle Edward and Rupert were in around Mons. This chap clearly doesn't wish to protect his wife from the truth.'

Rebecca hesitated for a moment and said, 'Why don't you read it to me?'

'Very well. I'll ignore the opening lines and begin at the interesting part. Are you ready?'

Rebecca nodded.

'The soldier writes, "Altogether we lost about five thousand of our men on Saturday and Sunday. I had to fight two days with a bullet wound in my leg and then I got another one. We saw some terrible sights, women and children cut up. I shall never forget some of the things I saw until the day I die. It was maddening to see one's fellows shot down right and left, and to be wondering all the time when it would be my turn." Shall I read any more? That seems to be all the colour.'

Rebecca slid her hands down her face. 'No, I've heard enough.'

'So that's what Rupert has kept from you: that he's seen

women and children cut up, and witnessed his friends being shot down around him, all the while expecting his turn to come. Is this what you would prefer he wrote to you? That he was convinced he was about to be killed?'

'No,' said Rebecca in a small voice.

'Then you can understand why he's being deceptive in writing about the countryside, and seemingly nothing to do with war?'

'Of course I can.'

'Good. Then you should follow suit and refrain from ever troubling him with your concerns as they are trifling compared to his. Keep to saying that all is well at home, the boys are studying hard and send a parcel with a fruit cake from time to time.'

'I can't always deceive him though.'

'Until the war's over you can, and you should. It's a wife's duty not to worry her husband, particularly when there's a war on. I'm sure it was in your marriage vows, so you shouldn't be surprised.'

TWENTY

Casualty lists became part of every edition of the newspaper. Rebecca read each list twice, even on days when she had received a letter from Rupert. He continued to protect her, writing nothing of what he had seen or done, or his fears. As grateful as Rebecca was for this compassion, there were moments when she wanted to read the truth, for Rupert's denial of it to end, believing the principles of a strong marriage demanded it. She wanted Rupert to write that he had killed Germans and whether it was from a distance or close quarters, and what he felt when he saw a bullet he'd fired strike his enemy. She wanted him to write that no-one escaped terror, and that when he came under attack all he could think of was her. If he was honest, then so could she be in her reply. Instead of writing of the change of seasons, Sunday School, and village affairs, she could write of her hatred of Germans, her exhaustion brought by not replacing the maid, and the growing anger she felt towards the men who had yet to enlist.

They pass me by on the High Street, some pausing to make a donation, others pressing on with their heads down, or arrogantly high, ignoring the refugees' cause and their duty to help. They look able, of correct age and proud, yet they should carry no pride, only shame. I expect to find myself stopping one of the shirkers soon and asking, 'Your friends must have enlisted, so why not you? What argument for exemption from the war do you have? Cowardice, I suspect. Britain has no place for cowards. Enlist or leave with the Germans as you're as spineless as they are'. I want them to read the names in the newspaper, and do so aloud as I force them towards the recruitment office. And then I halt myself and wonder if one of the names was my target's brother, and that this unfortunate soul is concealing their grief from judgemental others such as myself, and that all they care to do is avenge their brother's death, knowing they risk bringing further grief upon their parents.

Rebecca knew she would never send Rupert such a letter, although her resistance to creating a scene weakened every time she helped Charlotte collect donations for the First Aid Nursing Yeomanry, or Belgians, or when she saw the refugee children holding hands in the village.

Any hope she had of the war being brought to a swift end died as late summer passed into autumn. The number of casualties on both sides reached a quarter of a million. Men continued to enlist in their thousands every week, yet it seemed to Rebecca they were merely replacing the ones killed or wounded, and that if the same replenishment was occurring in Germany the war would last years.

The Worcesters' recruitment campaign expanded from the city. At meetings in village halls, men of fighting age were told it was their duty to volunteer and women were told it was their duty to deride those who did not. Rebecca had heard that at each meeting a table manned by a sergeant was set by the door to ensure embarrassment came to any man who left without stopping and signing up. Posters urging men to join the army were commonplace in public buildings and shops. Charlotte gave Rebecca one to put in a front window at Croft House. It was an image of a young mother with her child at her side, gazing proudly at soldiers marching past her home. In the background was the countryside, and at the top of the poster ran the words, *Women of Britain Say – "Go!"*

The parish newsletter was equally aggressive in rousing patriotism. It included the names of all the men in the parish who had died fighting, were presently serving and those who had volunteered. The column was titled *Our Brave Boys* and was introduced with the sentence, *The names below are those of the men to whom you owe your freedom. Serve your King and Country and enlist today.*

The vicar was listed as the newsletter's author, though Kate had long ago let slip to Rebecca that she gave direction to what was written, just as she did with her husband's sermons which since August had referred consistently to honour and that God's protection would come upon those who had volunteered. The names of men from the parish who had enlisted since the previous Sunday were always read out, and a prayer was said for them and for those who had still to 'find the courage to do their duty'.

One Sunday in late October, the vicar stepped up to the pulpit and announced the deaths of Alfred and John Stanton, both corporals in the second battalion. Rebecca did not recognise the names, though she noticed Mrs Munn wipe a tear from her cheek.

'They're from Lower Broadheath,' she whispered to Rebecca. 'Their father served with my husband in South Africa. He didn't make it home either.'

'Their poor mother.'

'Thankfully she's long departed. There's only a sister left now.'

Later that morning, Rebecca returned home from Sunday School to find the boys playing cricket on Peachley Lane. James was bowling, Sebastian was fielding, and in bat was Alfred. He struck the ball into the air, towards Rebecca. She ran forward and caught the ball in one hand.

'Out!' shouted James. 'Uncle Alfred is out!'

'Clearly it's a fault with the bat,' said Alfred, passing it to James.

Rebecca smiled, questioning if she had forgotten that

Alfred was due to visit. 'Wonderful to see you, Alfred,' she said, embracing him.

'My apologies for the surprise.'

'Don't be silly, you're always welcome. The boys have missed you.'

'Yes, well I'm definitely sorry about that. It's all been so frantic since the war started. Still, it's refreshing to escape London. The black outs for the Zeppelins are infuriating.'

'Are the Zeppelins as terrifying as people say they are?'

'I wouldn't know, I haven't seen one. But then I rarely get to step outside these days.'

James hit the bat against the ground.

'I think that's my cue to bowl,' said Alfred.

'Are you staying the night?'

'Yes, but I'm booked into The Star Hotel in town. Some business over my father's estate has come up. I thought I'd travel a day early and call in.'

'I hope you can be here for a while, for the afternoon at least.'

'Of course. And I'll return again tomorrow if the solicitor doesn't drag his feet.'

James hit the ground again.

'Patience, nephew.'

'I'm going to hit a six!'

'That's the spirit. Rebecca, would you care to field again?'

'You won't catch me out,' said James.

'Is that so?' said Rebecca. 'Then I'll just have to bowl you out. Alfred, pass me the ball. You can field as I'm about to take James's wicket.'

Over lunch, Rebecca was struck by how rapidly Alfred had aged in the months since she had last seen him. His hair was receding, and the hair left behind was grey as much as it was dark. He was ambiguous about his job, revealing only that the War Office had tasked him with work he thought beyond reason.

'They're certainly not short of ideas, but are always short of patience,' he said. 'Nevertheless, I'll have to somehow make the impossible possible, however much I wish I couldn't.'

'Why do you wish you couldn't?'

'Because there are limits to what man can expect to do to one another. The limit will soon be disregarded in this war. What will matter will be who crosses that threshold first. The Germans, or us.'

'Why aren't you a soldier?' asked Sebastian.

Rebecca scowled. 'Sebastian, that's very rude.'

'Please, I don't mind,' said Alfred. 'I understand your curiosity. The reason I'm not in the army like your father is, is that I'm not allowed to be.'

'Are you too old?' asked James.

'Almost, sadly. The reason I'm not fighting, however, is that I'm deemed too important to go anywhere. Rather unfortunate really.'

'I'd argue it's fortunate,' said Rebecca, thinking about the Stantons. 'If one brother is fighting, the other should be excluded.'

'Papa's in France,' said Sebastian. 'He told me he had bread and honey, and he dipped it in hot chocolate.'

'Sounds delicious,' said Alfred. 'Although your father is no longer in France.'

Rebecca dropped her fork on to her plate. 'Where is he then?'

'Back in Belgium, in the part known as Flanders. It's very flat, like the Fens.'

'The Fens flood. In winter they're treacherous.'

'Yes, well, the conditions in Flanders will be…' Alfred glanced at the boys. 'The conditions will be not quite as good as France. It'll be the same for the Germans though.'

'How do you know he's in Flanders?'

'He told me so in a letter. It came yesterday.'

'Can I read it?'

'I left it in London.'

'What did he write?'

'There wasn't much. Just that the battalion was on the move, and asking I call here, which I was planning to do anyway.'

'Have you replied?'

'I shall this evening.'

'Will you write that you called here?'

'Of course.'

'Then can I request you write nothing that might trouble him?'

'I don't believe I could.'

'Tell him about the cricket,' said Sebastian.

'No! Don't!' said James.

'Tell him, Uncle Alfred, tell him!'

Alfred smiled. 'I'm sorry, James. I can't avoid it.'

James sulked. 'It's humiliating.'

'Now, now, every cricketer is bowled first ball at some point in their life.'

'Not by their mother.'

Sebastian laughed. Rebecca followed and then Alfred.

'Sorry, darling,' said Rebecca. 'You have learned a valuable lesson though.'

'Which is?'

'Never underestimate your opponent. And never underestimate a woman, particularly your mother.'

The clatter of the letterbox closing reached the kitchen. Rebecca shut the oven door, hung her apron on a hook in the alcove and glanced at the clock. The boys would return soon from the swing, she thought. No doubt Alfred would pass on a scone and make for the gin bottle instead. It was dusk, after all.

Rebecca stepped into the hall and noticed footprints on the tiles. She tutted, though part of her was pleased the boys had been so excited about playing they'd forgotten the muddy shoes rule. Pausing in front of the mirror, she straightened Rupert's brooch and remembered the letterbox. On the doormat was a brown envelope. Rebecca picked it up and sat down on the staircase, irritated that no-one had knocked. Perhaps I didn't hear them, she thought as she slid her finger along the envelope's seal and removed a piece of buff paper. The thick black letters of Post Office Telegraphs dominated the upper half of the telegram. The balance was divided into ruled sections. On the left, handwritten, was Rebecca's name, after which came two lines of text:

Deeply regret to inform you that Cpt. R.J Salisbury

Died of wounds October 31st. The Army Council express their sympathy.

Rebecca stared at Rupert's name, certain it would change to another's.

'I climbed a tree!' shouted Sebastian, from the back door.

'Only because I helped you,' said James.

'I did, Mama, I did!'

The boys were now at the foot of the staircase. Rebecca bowed her head. Her hands, still holding the telegram, began to tremble.

'He did climb it,' said Alfred, stepping into the hall.

Rebecca did not respond.

'I say he should have first choice of the scones.'

James followed Sebastian towards the kitchen. Alfred watched them as they passed by.

'Sorry,' said Alfred. 'They'll be bickering over the biggest now.'

Rebecca pressed her elbows into her hips, and let the telegram fall on to a step. She looked up and caught Alfred's eyes.

'Are the scones ready?' asked James, walking back towards the staircase.

Alfred stopped James from seeing Rebecca. He produced a coin from his pocket and said, 'Go and buy a pennyworth of biscuits from the shop. Take your brother. Hurry along.'

'Sebastian! We're going to the shop!'

Rebecca sensed Alfred stepping closer to her. She went to speak Rupert's name, but the air had been sucked out of her lungs. Her whole body now began to shake.

'Rebecca, talk to me,' said Alfred.

She stood up sharply and ran up the stairs, making the washstand in her bedroom in time. She vomited, paused, and vomited again. She felt a hand on her back. Her nausea was unforgiving and she retched again, but her stomach had nothing left to give. Her legs gave way. Alfred held her up and guided her on to a chair. He put his arm round her shoulders. She started to wail, saying Rupert's name between her gasps for breath. Minutes passed by without Alfred speaking. He continued to hold Rebecca, swallowing hard to choke his own tears.

Rebecca again repeated Rupert's name, much louder than before, as if trying to reach him.

'Uncle Alfred?' called out James. 'Are you upstairs?'

Rebecca suddenly remembered where she had left the telegram. 'Did you pick…?' Her question was interrupted by the pounding of footsteps up the stairs. They continued along the landing. Rebecca turned her head. James stepped into the doorway. His arms were limp by his sides and his eyes were moist. In his right hand, pinched at a corner as if he shouldn't hold it, was the telegram.

'I don't understand,' he said, his voice cracking.

Sebastian, with his red scarf trailing from his coat pocket, squeezed past. 'Can I have my scone now, please?'

Rebecca looked again at James. His cheeks were now wet with tears.

'Why is James crying?' asked Sebastian.

Rebecca pushed the chair back and fell to her knees. James went to her, followed by Sebastian. She held them, tightening her grip as the waves of grief smashed her. Minutes had passed when James pulled his head away from Rebecca's shoulder. His face was pale and his eyes bloodshot. He swallowed and said, 'Say it's not true.'

TWENTY-ONE

Rebecca pulled the quilt away slowly and climbed down from her bed. Sebastian moved, but remained asleep. There was no noise coming from James's room, though downstairs Rebecca heard the chink of cups being placed on saucers.

Alfred was straightening two envelopes on the table as Rebecca entered the morning-room. 'They're both for you,' he said. 'Can I pour you coffee?'

Rebecca nodded, wondering if Alfred had been awake most of the night as she had. He glanced at her clothes as he moved a cup.

'I've worn black enough in my life,' she said. 'I don't need to announce to strangers that I'm grieving.'

Alfred nodded. Rebecca looked at the letters. The handwriting on one was as familiar to her as her own. She opened the other. The grade of paper was of high quality and at the top there was a coat of arms. Rebecca suddenly felt light headed and reached for a chair to steady herself.

'Who's it from?' asked Alfred.

'Buckingham Palace.'

'What does it say?'

Rebecca passed Alfred the letter. She gave up trying to stop her tears.

After a few seconds of silence, Alfred swallowed and said, 'I'm certain the King could have managed more than just one sentence of gratitude for Rupert's service.'

Rebecca stared at the second letter, seduced by the thought a mistake had been made; that Rupert had written to say he was alive and that any telegrams about him should be ignored.

'Can you make the boys some toast if they come down?' she said.

'Where are you going?'

'Outside. I need to be alone.'

Rebecca went to the bench by the pear tree in the back garden. She shivered, but did not care that she was cold. She slid her finger under the envelope's flap and removed Rupert's letter.

Belgium, October 28, 1914

My Darling Rebecca,

How comforting it was to have a letter from the boys. They are adorable sons of whom I am most proud, and as ever, you. Your confession you had moved our wedding photograph, and asking whether I objected, was blissfully you, and of course there is no protest to be made by me. It soothes me to know that you now have a clear view of our day when you wake.

Alfred hopes to call at Crofty in the coming days. He'll be in Worcester on matters I shan't bore you with, though you shouldn't expect him to stay as his work, whatever it is, will no doubt pull him back to London before he catches his breath. Edward is blundering about nearby. I hope to come across him later, particularly as he is never shy of cigarettes (I'm almost out, please send) and a smile (may I have one from you also).

Please tell Mr Clarke that his son is acquitting himself with distinction, and should Mrs Clarke enquire, it may be reassuring for her to know that I am never too far away from Harry. As for my wife, please avoid all worry. We are 250 yards or more from the German line, so perfectly safe. Tomorrow we shall be relieved and billeted two miles from here in a farmhouse where I understand I shall have my own room! From there we might return to our current position, or move elsewhere. Wherever I shall be, I'll be thinking of you, James and Sebastian.

With all my love, Rupert

'You should put this on,' said Alfred, walking up the path with Rebecca's coat over his arm.

Rebecca wiped her cheeks. 'I should be inside for when the boys wake.'

'James has just come down. He asked about Rupert.'

'What did he ask?'

'Where he's buried.'

'What did you say?'

'That you would want to speak to them.'

It suddenly occurred to Rebecca there would be no coffin or eulogy. There would be no goodbye, or grave to visit and stand at. All she had was a telegram and a mass produced note from the King.

'I can be there with you,' said Albert.

'No. I need to be alone with them.'

She found James lying next to Sebastian. They were both under the quilt, staring at the ceiling in silence. Rebecca knelt by the side of her bed. 'Boys, I need you to come closer to me.'

James pulled back the quilt. Both he and Sebastian perched themselves on the edge of the mattress.

'Look at me, please,' said Rebecca.

The boys raised their heads.

'Uncle Alfred said you wanted to know where your father is buried.'

James nodded.

Rebecca breathed in. 'I'm afraid… I'm afraid, I don't know where he's buried.'

There was a long silence. Sebastian reached out for Rebecca. He came down from the bed, followed by James. Rebecca put her arms round them, pulling them closer to her as their crying intensified.

Sebastian sniffed. Still crying, he said, 'What happened?'

Rebecca tried to form an answer that excluded *died of wounds*. 'I only know that it happened in Belgium.'

'Can we go there?'

'No, not yet.'

'When?'

'When the war's over.'

'When will that be?'

'I hope very soon. Everyone does.'

James wiped his eyes with his sleeve. 'What happens now?'

Rebecca raised the boys' chins. 'We're going to be strong, just as your father would have wanted. Can you do that for him?'

Rebecca looked down the garden, watching Alfred, wondering how she could persuade him to stay a little longer. He lit his pipe and removed a letter from his coat pocket.

'Is it from Rupert?' asked Rebecca, as she stepped closer.

'I forgot I kept it in my coat.'

'What did he write?'

'He told me what he'd seen.'

'Can I read it?'

'It's not, how can I put it, pleasant reading.'

'Please.'

'You may find it distressing.'

'Then you read it to me.'

Alfred hesitated and said, 'very well.' Alfred unfolded the

letter and cleared his throat. 'I saw the corpse of a dead German soldier aged no older than sixteen, and thought nothing, and neither did my men. I stared at this boy, contorted in hawthorn with his stomach and some other organ by his side, and wanted to feel moved, for something inside me to protest at the injustice of it all, but there was just a quiet submission of acceptance. Time did not allow a grave to be dug for the boy and even if it had done, I would not have ordered it. I fear, my dear brother, we have been already been stripped of the humanity we were sent here to fight for. All that remains is survival and clinging to the fading memory of home.'

Rebecca snatched the letter from Alfred's hands and read it to herself.

'Mama, there's a car here,' said James, appearing at the back door.

'It'll be for me,' said Alfred.

Rebecca's heart beat accelerated. 'You're certain you can't stay?'

Alfred nodded reluctantly.

'I understand.'

'If I discover more about what happened I'll write immediately.'

'So shall I.'

Rebecca and Alfred stared at each other in silence.

'He loved you very much,' said Rebecca.

Alfred looked down. 'He was a beautiful man, and a very fine brother.'

A car horn sounded.

'I should say goodbye to the boys.'

'What will you tell them?'

'That I'll return soon.'

'Will you though?'

'Of course. You're all I have.'

'And you definitely won't volunteer?'

'I could apply for a commission in every regiment in the Empire and no-one would take me. I assure you I'll be spending the duration of this war in a laboratory, whether I wish to or not.'

Rebecca counted she had seven hours to endure until the boys returned from school and her life resumed its purpose. You have to find a task, she told herself; you have to keep moving. She picked up her basket and left the house, wondering if Emily had told anyone about Rupert. Even if she had not, the casualty list in the newspaper would inform the village. The vicar and Kate would call, and Mrs Munn, and condolences would be said at church. Some would ask questions. Those damaged by war would know best to ask nothing.

A bell rang as Rebecca pushed open the shop door. Mr Cherry, wearing a white coat, was standing on a ladder behind the counter.

'Good morning, Mrs Salisbury,' he said, half turning. 'I'll be with you shortly.'

Two ladies, both aged around sixty, were sitting on a bench, watching Mr Cherry at work while they talked. Rebecca was on speaking terms with neither woman and waited three steps back from the counter, staring straight ahead.

Mr Cherry moved the wheeled ladder along the shelves. He worked quietly as he selected items from a list written on the back of an envelope. Rebecca tried to repeat her own list in her head, but her concentration was broken by the chatter to her side.

'I never have enough pegs,' said the woman closest to Rebecca. 'I reckon someone's pinching them.'

'You'll have to buy some from the gypsies next time they pass through.'

'I suppose. Money's tight though.'

'Stay that way till the war's all done with.'

'Did you hear about Jack Clarke's lad?'

'No.'

'He's been wounded. Shot somewhere in Belgium. He's in a bad way, Jack said.'

'Poor Harry.'

'Poor his mother too. She's always been a worrier. She'll be in a terrible state.'

Rebecca felt winded, as though she'd been punched in the stomach. She concentrated on Mr Cherry. He tied a paper bag with string and placed it on the counter.

'Is that all Mrs Jones?' he asked.

'It is, can't afford any more with these prices.' She paid Mr Cherry and left the shop with her friend, saying something about bread as she closed the door. Rebecca turned questions over and over in her mind. Had Harry been with Rupert when he was wounded? Who had informed Jack? What did they tell him?

Mr Cherry coughed. 'Mrs Salisbury?'

'Sorry… I…'

'How may I help you?'

Rebecca rattled off her list: a pound of sugar, half a pound of cheese, four ounces of peppermint humbugs, half a pound of butter, and a loaf of bread.

'I'll find you the freshest loaf,' said Mr Cherry, pulling out a drawer. 'Although it won't be fresh today. I don't want to get into trouble.'

Rebecca went into a trance again. *Shot somewhere in Belgium. He's in a bad way.*

'I can't see much sense in only being allowed to sell bread at least a day old,' said Mr Cherry, finishing Rebecca's order. 'Now, shall I put it on your account?'

'Please.'

Rebecca paused outside the shop, convincing herself it would be insensitive to pester Jack for what he knew. She made for home instead, though her desire to ask questions persisted. Standing in her kitchen, dithering about whether to remove her coat, Rebecca could sense her frustration being replaced by rage. She snapped and pushed her basket off the table. The groceries landed on the tiles. All the bags remained intact. Rebecca put them in the pantry, removed her coat and glanced at the clock. She had six hours left.

Rebecca heard a noise in the hall and stood up quickly. Everything suddenly went dark. She closed her eyes, waiting for the faintness to pass. You must eat, she told herself; you can't become weak. She made for the kitchen, though instinctively glanced at the door. On the doormat was a brown card. Rebecca bent down, taking care to rise slowly. The card was titled Field Service Post Card. Edward's signature was on the back. Typed above it were three sentences:

I am quite well

I have been admitted to hospital

Letter follows at first opportunity

'Edward's in hospital,' she said under her breath. 'I must tell Emily.'

She looked at the telephone and then back at the card. The date was 02.11.14. Edward had sent it *after* Rupert's death, she thought. His letter would have details about Rupert; what happened and where he was buried. She stared at the door, thinking. It occurred to her Edward's letter may have arrived at the post office. She looked again at the telephone. Emily could wait for the news about Edward. She had to find Jack.

The post office had closed early when Rebecca reached it. She peered through the window, but there was no sign of Jack or his wife. She knocked on the door, expecting to see a face. She knocked again, harder and with her fist. Still no-one appeared. She struck the door a third time, and then a fourth, and started to pound both fists in tandem.

'Mrs Salisbury?'

Rebecca turned to her left.

'Are you all right?' asked Jack.

Rebecca looked down in embarrassment. 'I'm sorry.'

'How can I help?'

'I… I need to talk to you.'

'You can come inside, if you wish?'

'I'm not intruding?'

'No. Please excuse my wife though. She's resting upstairs.'

Rebecca followed Jack to the back of the post office. She was shown through to the parlour and invited to take a seat.

'Can I make you a cup of tea?'

Rebecca nodded her head. 'You're certain I'm not disturbing you?'

'You're not.'

There was a long silence. Rebecca wondered again if it was insensitive to ask about Harry.

'What did you want to talk about, Mrs Salisbury?'

'I heard about Harry today. A woman in the shop said he'd been wounded. She said he was in a bad way.'

Jack breathed in slowly. 'I don't know much. Until your cousin wrote to me I only knew that Harry had been wounded.'

'Edward wrote to you?'

'Godsend it was. All I had before it was a card to say Harry was in hospital. My wife opened it. She's been in shock since.'

'What did my cousin write?'

'I'll get it for you.' Jack left the room, returning seconds later. 'Here,' he said, passing Rebecca the letter.

Southampton
5 November, 1914

Dear Mr Clarke,

I write to you about your son, Private H.Clarke. In a desperate battle, which occurred in Gheluvelt in Flanders, your son displayed gallantry of the highest order and was critically wounded. He did not flinch when the hour to serve his country came and like many alongside him was prepared to make the greatest sacrifice. He was transported to a hospital in France from where some patients are transported to the coast and taken to England. You should take heart in knowing he is receiving the care a hero warrants.

Capt E.G. Warwick
2nd Worcestershire Regiment
B.E.F

'I'm awaiting a letter from my cousin,' said Rebecca. 'Has it arrived yet?'

'Not yet.'

'I should leave you be then.'

Jack saw Rebecca out. At the door, he hesitated and said, 'I'm sorry about your husband.'

'How did you know?'

'The casualty list in today's newspaper. Your husband probably was in the same battle as Harry.'

Should Mrs Clarke enquire, it may be reassuring for her to know that I am never too far away from Harry.

'Will you tell me if you have any news about Harry?' asked Rebecca.

'Of course.'

'I'd be keen to write to him. He may know what happened to my husband.'

'I understand. Goodbye, Mrs Salisbury.'

The study was so cold that Rebecca could see her breath. She stood in front of her father's books, relieved they remained in categories, and ran her finger along the spines, halting at *Flanders' Position in Belgium: its past and future*. There was only one reference to Gheluvelt in the index. It was on a map that at its centre had a town named Ypres. There was a wood near Gheluvelt and symbols for a chateau and a church, but that was all. Rebecca stared at the name, confused as to why Gheluvelt was of such importance that a battle took place there. What had Edward kept from Jack? She closed the book and returned it to the shelf just as the grandfather clock in the hall struck two. She had three more hours to go.

Jack was cycling up the lane as Rebecca waved the boys off to school. He came to a stop and handed Rebecca a letter.

'This could be what you were waiting for,' he said.

The tremor of his hand and the shadows under his eyes suggested to Rebecca he'd spent the night in the company of a bottle. 'How are you?' she asked.

Jack, avoiding eye contact, said, 'We're holding up.'

Rebecca wanted to ask after Mrs Clarke, but Jack was already cycling away. She returned inside and opened Edward's letter at once. It was written on paper headed 1st Southern General Hospital, Birmingham, and there was only one sheet.

November 6, 1914

Dearest Rebecca,

I am able to write to you because of Rupert's bravery. He passed from us on the afternoon of October 31, giving his life to protect mine. He did not suffer and was buried in the grounds of a chateau in Gheluvelt, Flanders. A Bible passage was read and a cross placed at his grave. Rupert's personal effects were passed to me, including two letters: one for you and one for the boys. I shall keep them until you wish to collect them. I arrived today at this hospital, which has taken over the University of Birmingham, and shall be here for some time, three weeks at a minimum. The visiting hours are 10.30am to noon, and 2.30pm to 4pm. I've been assured the nearest station on the Worcester line is King's Norton, and there's a tram service to here. Please come alone. I would prefer my mother come alone also and shall write to her with this request. You should be forewarned that you'll be disturbed by the appearance of some of the men. They've been through much trauma.

I grieve for you as I grieve for Rupert.

With much love, Edward

Rebecca dismantled every sentence. Edward had given her what she wanted: the knowledge that Rupert had been laid to rest and where. What she could not understand was how he had died of wounds, but had not suffered from them. She checked the visiting times again. If she made the morning hours she could be back in Worcester for the end of the school day and return to Hallow with the boys. She hoisted her skirt and ran up the staircase and into her bedroom. In her writing desk, among cards, paper and booklets, she found the Worcester Railway ABC Guide. Towards the back there was a timetable for the Birmingham train. You can make the next service, she thought; you've got time. She checked the clock. Even if a car was waiting on the lane she would not reach the station in time. She closed the desk drawer and sighed heavily. Edward would have to wait for another day.

TWENTY-TWO

The boys were sat at the table, their hands on their laps.

'Please, begin,' said Rebecca, pulling out her chair.

James and Sebastian began to eat. Rebecca waited until their mouths were full and said, 'I'll be coming with you in the morning. I'll meet you after school and we'll travel home together.'

James swallowed. 'Why will you be in Worcester all day?'

'I'm not, darling. I'll be in Birmingham.'

'Why are you going there?'

'To visit your Uncle Teddy.'

James looked confused. 'Why is he in Birmingham?'

'He's in hospital.'

'Is he poorly?'

'I don't believe so.'

'So why is he there?'

Rebecca hesitated and said, 'I expect he's hurt.'

'From the war?' asked Sebastian.

'Yes.' Rebecca took a sip of wine, hoping the questions would stop. James was soaking a potato in melted butter and Sebastian was chewing on a piece of bread.

'Was Uncle Teddy with Papa?' said James.

Rebecca remembered what Edward had written: *Giving his life to protect mine*. 'He might have been.'

'How do you know he's in hospital?'

'He wrote to me.'

'What did he write?'

Rebecca took a longer sip of wine. 'He told me the hospital he's in and the time I could visit.'

'Can we come?' asked Sebastian.

'No, you need to be at school.'

'Can we go on Saturday then?'

'Perhaps.'

James stabbed another potato with his fork. 'Why didn't he tell you what was wrong with him?'

'I really don't know, James.'

'Can I read his letter?'

'No, you can't.'

'Why not?'

'Because you can't.'

'I don't understand.'

'It was addressed to me, that's why.'

'But…'

'That's the end of it. No more questions.'

James released his cutlery on to his plate.

'James!' snapped Rebecca, banging her fist on the table. 'You will not behave like that.'

James dropped his head. He finished his dinner in silence and was excused from the table, taking Sebastian with him. Rebecca looked at the three empty chairs and reached for the wine bottle. She poured herself a second glass and then a third, and a fourth, not touching her food. The boys had gone to Rupert whenever she had raised her voice. Now they only had each other.

As she climbed the stairs, she listened for James and Sebastian talking. Their bedroom doors were ajar. Rebecca watched the counterpane on James's bed rise and fall with his breathing, and went to check on Sebastian. He was asleep with his back to her. She could make out the collar of his pyjamas touching his ears and saw he had folded his clothes and placed them on a chair. Shame overwhelmed her. Her sons had taken themselves off to bed while she overindulged in wine. She had neglected them. She crept along the landing to her bedroom, put on her nightgown and with the room swaying closed her eyes, desperate for sleep to come.

Rebecca patted beside her, certain Sebastian had climbed into her bed. All she felt was the quilt. She brought her hand back to her chest, irritated she had been awoken by a spasm of the night. A door creaked downstairs. It must be a draught, she thought. She closed her eyes again and rolled over. There was a thud; something had struck the floor. Rebecca sat up and lit the lamp by her bed, now more worried than irritated. She decided to count to thirty. If she made it without another noise she would close her eyes. Ten… twenty… twenty-six… twenty-seven… twenty… there was something wrong about the room. Rebecca lifted the lamp to head height. The room appeared how it should be, but the smell had changed. She climbed out of bed and stood rigid, inhaling until her lungs were full. She was not imagining the smell. There was no question what it was, only it belonged in a dream. The lamp's flame cast light just a few steps in front of her as she descended the staircase and skirted the dining-room. Nothing was out of place and the room smelled as usual. She returned to the hall and paused. The smell had gone; the wine had tricked her senses. The harder she thought about it, the more her head hurt. She moved round the banister and froze. Someone was in the morning-room.

'Who's there?' said Rebecca, opening the door.

There was movement in the corner. Rebecca edged forward and was overcome by Rupert's scent. 'Is that you?' she asked, her voice trembling.

The figure in the corner began to whimper.

'James?'

James began to sob. Rebecca put down the lamp and embraced him. Rupert's smell, attached to his coat James had wrapped around himself, rushed at Rebecca. She held James until he stopped crying. Part of her wanted to encourage him to talk. Fearing she would only extend his suffering, she said, 'Would you like to go back to bed?'

James nodded. Rebecca put Rupert's coat over her arm and returned upstairs with James. She tucked him into bed and told him she loved him. Back in her room, she opened Rupert's wardrobe for the first time since he had left and hung his coat on the rail. His smell, the smell of the life she had lost, would have crushed her had she not been so exhausted. She closed the wardrobe and got under her quilt. Only a few hours separated her from Edward.

The Birmingham train had already pulled into the station when Rebecca arrived. She found an empty compartment and watched a soldier on the platform say goodbye to a young woman. He unlocked her arms from around his back and stepped on to the train. The woman stood rigid, weeping and alone.

Rebecca forced her thoughts to Edward. She hoped he would answer her questions without prompt; that he would reassure her that Rupert had not suffered, and reveal what he had said at the end. It was possible that a hospital ward, even one in a university, could suffocate Edward's instinct to talk. She remembered his forewarning and wondered what conditions awaited her. Would there be men with broken bones and wounds? What could be disturbing about that? Surely, she thought, they would feel lucky to have survived.

The compartment was full by the time they reached King's Norton. Rebecca anticipated being early for visiting hours. She bought a newspaper for herself at the station kiosk and a pack of cigarettes for Edward. A boy shouted where to go for the university tram. Everyone leaving the station made for it, and everyone alighted when the university was reached. They all seemed to be in a hurry and no-one spoke as they passed through wrought-iron gates and on to an avenue that led to a building with a domed glass roof set opposite a red-brick clock tower.

At the top of the avenue was also a courtyard. On one side ambulances were lined up. Orderlies were removing men on stretchers. Every soldier was filthy and had their head or a limb or both covered in bandages. There were no blankets and some men had lost their boots and socks, exposing black toes. One soldier wheezed as he was extracted from a bunk and placed on the ground. Rebecca noticed he had a rifle as a leg splint. More orderlies, accompanied by young women with society faces, were called by a doctor to an ambulance. They emerged moments later with a stretcher that sagged heavily in the middle. The patient raised his neck. His whole head was bandaged with exposed nostrils and lips the only evidence of a human face. Rebecca looked back at the soldier with the rifle splint. He had propped himself on his elbows and was studying the visitors. Slowly, he raised his hand. For a moment Rebecca thought he was waving to her, but then a woman broke from the column and ran to him. She said nothing, as if incapable of speech, and just held his hand as he was carried away. The matron intervened and the woman stood still, watching the stretcher until it was out of sight.

Rebecca had seen enough. She went up some steps and entered a foyer where visitors were fanning left and right of a desk. After a minute or so she reached the front.

'I'm here to visit Edward Warwick of the Worcestershire Regiment,' she said to the man behind the desk.

'Is he an officer or other rank?'

'Officer.'

'Then please take a seat down there. Visiting starts in fifteen minutes.'

A wide corridor was being used as a waiting area. Chairs faced double doors that had curtains drawn across the glass panes. Some of the visitors were knitting socks for soldiers they would never meet, others were watching the clock, and still no-one was speaking. Rebecca found a seat on the back row and opened the newspaper as a distraction. She drifted past the advertisements, stopping at an article that stated there was distress in Germany as the nation's casualties had risen to one million men. Rebecca read the sentence twice, calculating that an average of 83,000 men were being lost every week. The number seemed impossible to her. She began the calculation again, but stalled as a headline caught her eye. It read: *A Glowing Tribute*. Underneath were a few lines of text.

Sir John French in his latest despatch says, 'If any one unit can be singled out for special praise it is the Worcestershires. Just think how proud you will be in years to come if you were able to say "I was there."'

Rebecca felt irritated there was no mention of where people would say they were proud to have been. The editorial continued the applause.

The glorious annals of the army know no more glorious achievement and Worcestershire must be proud indeed of the part which the County Regiment played in it.

Surely, Rebecca thought, this glorious achievement was at Gheluvelt? Surely, Rupert gave his life for this victory? She searched every page for a reference to the village. She failed to find one and crumpled the newspaper in frustration. Heads in front twitched, but the doors opened and a nurse came forward. Rebecca was struck by how tired she appeared. She was young, probably no older than 25, but her cheeks were pale and there were dark rings under her bloodshot eyes.

The nurse cleared her throat and said, 'The patients are exhausted and some find it difficult to talk. To avoid a crush I'll move you in stages. Those at the front can stand and enter the ward.'

Slowly, the rows began to empty. Rebecca stopped at the doors and braced herself for the sight of Edward in a hospital bed. At the far end of a grand hall was a stained glass window with ranks of organ pipes either side and a stage underneath. Beds projected from the walls and were also back to back down the centre of the hall. Rebecca guessed there were about a hundred patients. Those without visitors were watching the doors. Some of them waved. Rebecca took the left aisle, holding her breath for a moment as the rush of chemical smells turned her stomach. She pressed on, hearing one rehearsed greeting after another. Bedsprings squeaked as officers sat up. There were no pips or insignias to be seen, only blue-striped flannel pyjamas. One man had lost his right arm and his eyes were covered by a strip of cloth. Rebecca stepped towards him and hesitated, knowing there was nothing she could say that would bring him comfort. She carried round to the next aisle and found Edward. He was staring at the ceiling, oblivious to the chatter around him. Rebecca sat down and coughed.

Edward turned his head. Rebecca could not tell if he was pleased to see her. She leaned forward and kissed him on the cheek. 'Hello.'

'Hello,' said Edward.

'How are you?'

'Better than others. How are you?'

Rebecca shrugged her shoulders.

'What about the boys?'

'They're being brave. They both wanted to come.'

'Not the best of places for a child.'

'No.'

'Or you.'

'Too late.'

'I'm glad you've come. The conversation isn't the brightest in here.'

Rebecca glanced to her left. The man in the next bed was alone.

'His name is Jean-Luc,' said Edward.

'He's French?'

'Belgian. A convoy of them came in yesterday. They ran out of space in their ward.'

'Has he talked about what's happened to his country?'

'No. A subject I'll avoid.'

'It doesn't bear thinking about.'

'Then don't. There's nothing you can do.'

Rebecca looked Edward up and down. His arms were on top of his blanket.

'It's my right leg,' he said, almost apologetically.

'What's wrong with it?'

'A bullet caused some damage.'

'How much damage?'

'Too early to say apparently.'

'Does it hurt?'

'Dressing it can be unpleasant, though nothing compared to what others go through.'

'Will you be sent back?'

'Probably.'

'When?'

'Two, possibly three months, depending on how it heals.'

'Your mother said you've told her very little.'

'Better to tell her in person. She's visiting this afternoon.'

'She's rather annoyed I've come first.'

'Yes, well, your need for an explanation is greater.' Edward winced as he pushed himself up the pillows.

'Can I help?'

'It'll pass.'

'I can call a nurse.'

'Leave them be. The poor things are exhausted.'

'I feel I should volunteer for something.'

'You've got two boys. You've enough to do.'

'I suppose.'

'Have you got help at home?'

'Just on wash day. Everyone's occupied with war work.'

Rebecca looked across the aisle, wondering how to build up to the question she wanted to ask above all others. She turned back to Edward and said, 'I read the letter you sent to Harry Clarke's parents. His father said it helped him.'

'I'm glad. I'm sorry I didn't write any more to you.'

'You don't need to apologise.'

'I do.' Edward's voice cracked. 'Rupert died because of me.'

Rebecca felt her nerve go. 'Are you able to say what happened?'

Edward reached for the glass of water on his locker. Rebecca noticed a tremor in his hand as he tilted it to his mouth.

'I can wait until another day, if you'd prefer,' she said.

'No, I need to tell you.'

'Just stop if it becomes too difficult.'

'Are you certain you want to hear this?'

Rebecca nodded.

Edward stared ahead. 'We'd been fighting for about two weeks without respite. I was shattered, we all were.'

'You were in Gheluvelt?'

'Nearby, in a wood north-west of the village. The Germans needed Gheluvelt for observation.'

'Why?'

'They had the channel ports in their sights. Without Gheluvelt they would struggle to reach them. They got going early. We could hear the bombardment from the wood. By midday we were told that two of our units in the village were annihilated. I expected an order to retreat.'

'It didn't come?'

'The order was to counter-attack. We had seven officers and about three hundred and fifty other ranks. I told Rupert it was madness, which it was.'

'What did he say?'

Edward smiled slightly. 'He said it was fortunate I was mad. He shook my hand, wished me good luck and went to his company. He showed no fear, none at all.'

'Was he close by?'

Edward drew in a long breath. 'Yes. The first six hundred yards were under cover. The Major divided us into two lines. Rupert was in the front line; I was fifty yards behind. And then we left the wood and we saw what was ahead.'

'Which was?'

Edward looked Rebecca in the eye. 'A thousand yards of grass and mud with no cover. We started to pass stragglers from other regiments. They began to shout at us.'

There was a long pause.

'Shout what?'

'Are you quite sure you want me to continue?'

'I am. What did they shout?'

'That we faced certain death if we didn't retreat. We kept going. The order came to move at the double and the Germans let us have it. It seemed like the sky and earth were exploding at once. Dozens of men were falling around me. I was just waiting for my turn.'

Rebecca paused and asked, 'Had you lost sight of Rupert?'

'Briefly, and then I saw him at the bottom of the hill, by the enclosures of a chateau.'

'So you caught up with him?'

'I had to find cover. I saw a coppice and made for it. Only three of my company survived. Harry Clarke was one of them.'

'He hadn't been wounded yet?'

'No. We made it through the trees to a wall on the edge of

the village square. The gunfire started to move away from the chateau. I couldn't understand how we had the Germans on the retreat.'

'Where was Rupert?'

'He would have been somewhere between the chateau and the square.'

'With his company?'

'Possibly. He was most likely on his own though.'

'Because he was the only survivor?'

'There would have been fighting from house to house. The survivors in his company would have been separated.'

'And then you saw him?'

Edward swallowed. 'There was a church in the square. It was the perfect observation post. The Germans had put a sniper in it.'

'You knew that at the time?'

'I suspected it. To reach the church though we had to cross the square.'

'And there were Germans in it?'

'No. I could see from my position the square was clear.'

'What about the sniper?'

Edward looked away. 'Harry's friend was the first to die… it should have been me. I should have gone first. Harry went right after him, roaring with anger. And then it came.'

'What came?'

'The crack of a rifle. I stared at the final soldier with me. I said nothing. He just went, and then came the next crack.'

'What did you do?'

'I waited, hoping the sniper would think there were no more of us. I was wrong, but lucky. He only got my leg. Somehow Harry had only been wounded and reached the cover of a fountain. He dragged me to it. I don't know how the sniper missed us as he did. I must have passed out soon after. When I came around, Rupert was next to me.'

'And he was wounded too?'

'No. He was shot when we moved.'

'But you were protected where you were. Why move?'

'Because I was losing blood. We made it to a shop, a butcher's.'

'And Rupert returned for Harry?'

Edward swallowed. 'He couldn't. He'd been shot in the back saving me.'

Rebecca gripped Edward's hand, but it did nothing to stop her bottom lip from quivering.

'I think I should stop.'

'Please, if you can continue. I have to hear this.'

Edward looked away. 'Rupert removed his tunic and shirt… his back was red with blood. I didn't know what to do. I heard British soldiers and called out for help. They found a cart and pushed us to the chateau. It was chaos, men were lying everywhere. Rupert was next to me. He just seemed to be asleep.'

Rebecca put her head in her hands. Her palms and cheeks were soon wet with tears.

'He was buried the next day.'

Rebecca looked up. 'Were you there?'

'I wasn't allowed to move. A lieutenant found me before I was transported to hospital. He told me about the funeral.'

'What did he say?'

'That a chaplain read from the Bible and the Lord's Prayer was said.'

'Was the grave marked?'

'Yes.'

It was beyond Rebecca to imagine the cemetery. She passed Edward the newspaper and pointed to the editorial. 'Do you know the place being referred to?'

Edward started to read. 'It's Gheluvelt. There was something in *The Times* yesterday.'

'It says it was a glorious achievement.'

'For some.'

'Like Harry… and you.'

Edward said nothing. There was a long silence.

'When the lieutenant came he brought the items Rupert had on him,' said Edward. 'He thought it only proper I gave them to his next of kin.'

'He would have carried very little, though?'

'What most men have: a wallet, wedding ring, watch, pen, cigarette case. Some have diaries.'

'Rupert never kept one.'

'He did have a photograph of you and the boys. The lieutenant said it was put back in his tunic.'

Rebecca felt winded. 'He was buried with it?'

'Yes. He also had two letters. One for you, and one for the boys.'

'What happened to them?'

Edward glanced at the locker. He closed his eyes, as if allowing Rebecca some privacy. She turned in the chair, wondering if she had the courage to see Rupert's personal effects. Part of her wanted to leave the room, and return home.

'You don't have to take them now,' said Edward faintly. 'His wedding ring is inside the handkerchief.'

Rebecca said nothing. She opened the locker and reached down for Rupert's items. She ran her hand across his wallet, resolving to tell the boys their Christmas present for Rupert was buried with him. It was a necessary lie. She flattened the watch straps. The face had a crack in it and the hands had stopped at quarter to two. She imagined Rupert had knocked it as he fought from house to house or when he had dropped to Edward's side.

She put the blue handkerchief on her palm, too afraid to pull back the cloth and find Rupert's blood on the ring. She slid the handkerchief into her pocket and turned the two envelopes. On the top one, Rupert had written: *In the event of my death, send to Mrs Rupert Salisbury, Croft House, Peachley Lane, Hallow, Worcs.*

Rebecca heard the words in Rupert's voice. It occurred to her he had sat in a trench, or even in the study before he left, and written that sentence knowing that if it was read by anyone other than himself it would mean he had died. She went to open the envelope and then quickly slid it into her bag, out of sight. She would wait until she was alone. Edward would not suffer her weeping.

A nurse at the end of the hall rang a bell.

'The cue to leave,' said Edward, stirring.

'I want to talk more.'

'We can on your next visit.'

'Thank you.'

'Only you must stop worrying about me.'

Rebecca kissed Edward on his forehead. 'I'll stop worrying when the war's over.'

'Say hello to the boys for me.'

'I'll give them your love as well.'

Edward slid down the pillows. Rebecca walked away, avoiding eye contact with the patients. She wanted to turn back and ask Edward to search his memory of Rupert's final hours; for any words he had said that she could hold onto. She kept walking. At the top of the aisle she turned round. Edward was how she had found him: staring at the ceiling. She felt a pain in her chest. Living would seem impossible to him now, she thought. If he was ever sent back he would be reckless. He would believe death to be his salvation from guilt. Rebecca felt maddened by her sense of powerlessness. She needed Edward. The boys needed him. He had to survive.

The nurse rang the bell again. Rebecca touched her coat where the handkerchief was, looked at Edward one more time, and left the hall.

TWENTY-THREE

Rebecca, standing at the gate, watched the car turn away from Peachley Lane. She wished she had accompanied the boys and then called on Emily until the school day had ended. Instead, she had eight hours alone. Her desire to stay at home, to have privacy to read Rupert's letter, began to weaken. Part of Rupert remained alive while his words were unread. It was his final letter, the letter he would have resisted writing, but was now with his personal effects in a suitcase in her wardrobe, hidden from the boys. She regretted not opening the letter at the hospital. The urgency to read it had given way to anxiety during the evening, and that morning she had overslept and so had the boys, but they were now away from the house and there was nothing to distract her.

'You'll catch a chill if you're not careful.'

Rebecca looked over. Mrs Munn was waddling towards her.

'I'll be careful then.'

Mrs Munn said nothing.

'Sorry, that sounded ungrateful,' said Rebecca.

'No, no, I won't be having any apologies.'

Rebecca tried to smile. She glanced at Mrs Munn's basket and asked, 'Have you been baking?'

'I have. Couldn't let Harry think I'd forgotten about him.'

'Harry's home?'

'Almost. He's in a hospital in Birmingham. I thought a couple of rock cakes might cheer him up.'

'You're going to visit?'

'No, Jack is. I'd better hurry. Don't want to miss him.'

Mrs Munn walked off, leaving Rebecca with the memory of the ambulances lined up at the university. Harry could have been one of the patients. He could have seen her and ignored her. She *had* to see him. A visit would be possible tomorrow, she thought, and afterwards she could see Edward. That would occupy her for a day. What remained was how to fill the empty hours ahead this day. Mrs Munn's rock cakes came to mind. She would make scones instead. Edward adored scones and so might the Belgian, Jean-Luc.

The two gossips were at the counter as she entered the shop. They both turned to the door, holding their gaze long enough to make Rebecca uncomfortable.

'Good morning, Mrs Salisbury,' said the woman on the left.

'Lovely to see you,' said the other.

Rebecca could not recall the women ever greeting her in the past. They must have heard the news about Rupert. She stepped to the end of the counter and pretended to examine the shelves.

'Will you be wanting anything else, ladies?' said Mr Cherry.

'No, no,' said the first woman. 'We'll be leaving you to serve Mrs Salisbury.'

Rebecca waited. She heard the bell jangle and moved along.

'Thank you for your patience. What would you like?'

'A pound of butter, a tin loaf and two bars of Cadbury's.'

'Chocolate for the boys?'

'Yes.'

'Then they'll be free.' Mr Cherry placed the items in Rebecca's basket. She opened her purse, waiting for a figure.

Mr Cherry swallowed. 'I'm sorry about your loss. We both are, my wife and me.'

Rebecca felt a desperate need to leave. 'Thank you. Can you put this on my account, please?'

'Of course.'

Rebecca made for the door.

'You must be very proud of what your husband did.'

Rebecca stopped still.

'Of him going into sniper territory to save a wounded man.'

Rebecca turned round. 'Who told you that?'

'No-one. I read it in today's second edition. Someone high up has praised him. Mentioned him in despatches.'

Mr Cherry unfolded the newspaper. 'It's here,' he said, pointing.

Rebecca stepped nervously back to the counter. Rupert's name was printed three times in the account of his charge to the chateau and his rescue of a wounded officer. The commander-in-chief who the day before had eulogised the Worcesters, identified Rupert as an *officer of supreme class, whose gallantry will inspire his regiment to victories as exalted as Gheluvelt.*

Rebecca quickly left the shop, forgetting to say thank you. The two ladies were outside The Crown, talking to the landlord. The three of them looked at her for a moment and resumed their conversation. Rebecca could not help but think they were talking about Rupert. It occurred to her she faced weeks of sympathetic greetings and pitying glances. In the shop, church and behind curtains every mood would be attached to her.

'Poor Mrs Salisbury,' someone would say. 'Never seen her so sad.'

'I saw her earlier. Looked fine to me.'

'Pale and thin is what I thought. Can't be eating because of the grief.'

'She should be grateful her husband got mentioned. What about the others?'

Rebecca felt exposed, as if she had been pushed on to a stage because Rupert had saved Edward's life. She *had* to read his letter. She hurried home, took the letter from her suitcase and left the house again, allowing doubt no room to settle. She passed the lychgate and stepped on to the avenue that led to Hallow Park. The great house remained empty. The once immaculate lawns were overgrown and the cattle long sold, but the bench remained. Rebecca sat down, giving a minute to the view of the Severn and the distant cathedral, and then opened the envelope. Rebecca imagined Rupert hesitating as he folded the letter, wondering if he had written all he wanted to, and whether he should tear it up, believing he would return home. Again, she considered leaving it unread. To hide it though would be to oppose his wishes. She paused for a moment and looked down at her lap.

To My Darling Rebecca,

You are not alone as you read this, and never will you be. The exquisite suffering of our separation is temporary as it belongs to this life and where I am now there is no pain and all is eternal. Death cannot weaken my love for you, for our love is the greater, as is the strength you have to endure this present time. Think of me when you are afraid and I promise your fear will pass just as this war will. Do not grieve for what you have lost, or allow anger to settle in your heart. Do not retreat from hope or exile yourself from community. Be the Rebecca I love. Preserve her as I met her at the lychgate and left at the station. Do not allow grief to damage you or the boys, or the people you meet. Do not allow war to kill us both. Remember these words: I have not died as a hero, merely in the service of those I love.

I love you
Rupert

Rebecca returned the letter to her pocket. She put her fingers over the seat edge, gripped the damp wood and bending forward began to weep. Her stomach felt as if grief was twisting it, and she let out a heavy, deep cry of pain. She tried to say Rupert's name, but could not, and she screamed again.

Later that day, after the boys had arrived home, Rebecca called on the Clarkes. Jack answered the door. His wife was resting, he said. The emotion of seeing Harry had taken its toll on her.

'How is he?' asked Rebecca.

'Better than others. The doctor said he was lucky the bullet didn't hit him any higher in the leg.'

'I was hoping to visit him tomorrow.'

'He'd like that. Just so long as it's not any bother for you.'

'It's not. My cousin is at the same hospital.'

'I wish I'd known, I would have taken Harry's letter to him. I only noticed it on his bed when he'd fallen asleep. I thought I'd ask you where to send it.'

'You have it?'

'Wait a moment.' Jack went and fetched the letter. There was no address written on the envelope, only *Capt. E. Warwick*.

'Harry's quite shaken by what's happened. He was very quiet today. He won't be himself when you visit him.'

'I doubt anyone can be themselves again. Not even when it's all over.'

Jack sucked in his breath. 'Whenever that will be. Be a while yet, Mrs Salisbury.'

Rebecca said nothing to the boys about visiting the hospital, though as she came down the stairs the following morning she heard voices in the kitchen and remembered she had left her basket on the table. The boys would have to be told the scones were not for them.

'Good morning,' said Rebecca, entering the kitchen.

'It wasn't me,' said James. 'Sebastian opened it.'

Rebecca looked at her basket. Harry's letter had been moved. 'Why did you open it?'

Sebastian was silent.

'Answer my question, Sebastian.'

Sebastian dropped his head. 'James read it, not me.'

Rebecca turned to James. He dropped his head too. 'You've no business reading other people's letters.'

'I'm sorry.'

'People's letters are private. You know that.'

'It wasn't finished.'

'Yes it was, Mr Clarke gave it to me.'

'There's only one sentence. It didn't make sense.'

Rebecca uncrossed her arms. 'You didn't understand the words?'

'No, what the person meant. Here, read it.' James passed Rebecca the envelope.

'I'll do no such thing. It's for your uncle and you shouldn't have read it.'

James sniffed. 'Will you tell him?'

Rebecca hesitated and said, 'No, he has enough on his mind.'

James walked off, followed by Sebastian. Rebecca placed the letter underneath the plate of scones. Later on, when she was on the train to Birmingham, intrigue got the better of her and she opened the letter. At first glance it appeared unfinished as James had said. All Harry had written was: *I'll keep my word, but I want no reward for my lie.*

Rebecca repeated the sentence over and over in her mind, disbelieving that Edward had kept something from her. Doubt, nevertheless, attacked her until she reached the university and despair took its place. Ambulances were lined up on the gravel and more were still arriving. The soldiers on stretchers groaned in pain as they were carried inside. Some of the visitors acknowledged them with a hesitant glance; others pressed on towards the steps as if the men did not exist.

Inside the building, boards with lists of patients had been set up. Rebecca found Harry's name and followed the signs to Room Two. Visitors were lined up against the corridor wall. There were no chairs and everyone was staring at the double doors, waiting for them to open. Rebecca noticed the visitors' coats were too thin and their gloves needed mending. She suddenly felt out of place and certain that people were looking at her thick jacket and expensive gloves, wondering why she was not visiting an officer. As she made her way down the line, two women created space for her. They continued to whisper, though as no-one else was talking Rebecca could hear every word.

'Mine's been in here over a week now,' said the woman next to Rebecca.

'And mine.'

'Must have been wounded the same time.'

'Probably the same battle. All his pals were killed in it. The battalion's near destroyed.'

'Good job we've got all these volunteers.'

'Most of them on my street have signed up. There's only the too old ones and boys left.'

'The boys should join the scouts. I've heard they're protecting the reservoirs.'

'From what?'

'From the Germans poisoning us.'

'They wouldn't, would they?'

'They're German, they'll try anything. Their ships even bombed Yarmouth the other night.'

'I'd be moving if I lived on the coast. My dad said the German guns can fire for miles.'

'They didn't hit much, mind. But they'll be back, they've got a taste for it.'

The doors were pushed open. A nurse spotted a heavily pregnant woman in the line and ushered her forward. Everyone else fell in behind her, shuffling into the room. Rebecca stood by the doors and searched for Harry among the rows of patients. Every man was washed clean of the trenches. Some were sitting up, others were flat on their backs, and three of the sixty or so beds had screens around them. The room was warm, but could have been warmer, and while the windows were tall and wide the only light coming through them was as grey as the walls.

Rebecca searched the rows once more. Still, she could not see Harry. 'Excuse me,' she said, stopping a nurse. 'Where's Private Clarke?'

'Which one?'

'Harry.'

'Oh, Harry, bless him. He's on the other side of that screen.'

The nurse pointed down the near aisle. Again, Rebecca sensed that people were watching her. She stood at the top of Harry's bed and watched the blanket rise and fall with his breathing. For a moment she thought not of Harry, but of her sons and that she may well have been staring at them had they been just a few years older. Harry was sound asleep, even though people were talking and a chap opposite was snoring with the noise of two men. Rebecca wondered which of Harry's legs had been shot and what damage had been done. She wanted to cry or scream, or do both. The last time she had seen Harry, at the station after the parade through the city, he had appeared invincible. They all had. Harry still looked too young to shave, and his freckles remained prominent despite the scratches on his face and fading bruises.

Rebecca pulled out the chair by Harry's bed and sat down. The man opposite sprung up and began to thrash his arms about in his bed, as if he were drowning. His visitor grabbed one arm and a nurse the other.

'You're in hospital now, son,' said the man. 'You're safe here.'

The man froze. He ignored his father and instead stared fixedly at Rebecca.

'Lie back now,' said the father. 'Easy does it.'

Two orderlies placed screens around the bed and the man fell silent.

'Mrs Salisbury?'

Rebecca turned to Harry. He opened his eyes fully.

'Hello, Harry.'

Harry pulled the blanket up to his neck, concealing his pyjamas as best he could.

'I thought I'd surprise you,' said Rebecca.

Harry smiled ever so slightly. With a faint voice, he said, 'My parents will be happy.'

'They know I'm here.'

'Oh.'

'I called at your home yesterday after they'd visited you.'

'Was my mother there?'

'She was.'

'How was she?'

'Busy.'

'But was she all right?'

Rebecca hesitated and constructed her lie. 'She was as well as any mother with a son in hospital could be.'

Harry nodded.

'You shouldn't worry about her, or your father,' said Rebecca.

'They worry about me.'

'Because you're their child and you're also a soldier.'

'I feel like a cripple in here.'

'You'll be back on your feet soon.'

'I suppose.'

'Though hopefully not too soon.'

'I'm going back. I want to.'

Rebecca restrained a heavy sigh. Harry reached for a cigarette case and a box of matches on his bedside table.

'You'll need to sit up if you want to smoke.'

Harry pushed his fists into the mattress. Rebecca positioned the pillows and sat down again.

'I heard about your friends,' she said. 'I'm sorry.'

Sadness filled Harry's eyes. 'I'm sorry for you too, and your sons.'

Rebecca touched Harry's arm. She swallowed hard and said, 'Can I ask you about it? About Gheluvelt?'

Harry bit his lip. He wiped a tear from his cheek.

'Perhaps another day?'

Harry nodded slightly. He lit his cigarette and glanced down at Rebecca's basket.

'I've brought you scones.'

'You made them for me?'

'Two for you, and two for my cousin Edward. I'll have to leave soon or I'll miss the visiting hours.'

Harry looked surprised. 'Is his hospital close by?'

'It's this one.'

'Captain Warwick is here?'

'He's in the Great Hall.'

'Does he know I'm here?'

'I'm sure he would have visited you if he did.'

'Will you tell him then?'

Rebecca thought of the letter again: *I'll keep my word, but I want no reward for my lie*. 'Would you prefer I didn't?' she asked.

Harry shrugged his shoulders. Rebecca noticed a slight tremor in his hand as he drew on his cigarette and stubbed it out in the ashtray.

'Your father gave me a letter from you. It's addressed to my cousin.'

Harry's eyes widened. 'You've not delivered it?'

'I thought I'd give it to him after I left you.'

'I don't want you to.'

Rebecca frowned. 'Why not?'

'It's not finished.'

'Your father wouldn't have given it to me if it wasn't.'

'He must have taken it when I was asleep. I'd like it back… please.'

Rebecca pulled the letter out from her coat pocket and passed it to Harry. He snatched it and put it under the blanket. There was a long silence. Rebecca wanted to press Harry to explain what he'd written. He slid down the pillows and began to close his eyes, perhaps deliberately so.

'You won't get any more out of him,' said a nurse, pausing at Harry's bed. 'They've all got weeks of sleep to catch up on.'

Rebecca continued to stare at Harry, sure he would open his eyes any moment and she could ask him again about what happened at Gheluvelt. He has a secret, she thought, and Edward must know what it is. The man opposite roared. Harry's eyes did not even flicker. Rebecca looked at the clock; she still had time to question Edward. Her questions for Harry could wait for another day when his parents were also there. He wouldn't lie to her in their presence.

Rebecca pulled the blanket up a little more, covering Harry's shoulders, and left the room. The soft hum of conversation reached the corridor outside the Great Hall. Rebecca stood on her tiptoes at the doors and looked through the glass. Emily was standing over Edward, adjusting his pillows.

'Why didn't she say she was visiting?' Rebecca said to herself. 'Why didn't she tell me?'

Rebecca dropped down on to her heels. She took a seat and stared at a poster on the opposite wall. A man with a moustache pointed his finger at her and boomed, 'Your Country Needs You!' She had seen the poster before, at the railway station, in the post office, even in Waterloo Square, and now it was in a hospital for wounded soldiers.

'How dare he?' she said, as she stared at the man's horrible little eyes. 'I gave you my husband and you still want more. How dare you!' Resentment rose within Rebecca. She stood up and with her heart beating violently pulled the poster off the wall and ripped it apart. She threw the pieces to the floor and stood on them as if she was standing on the man's very face.

'How dare you!' she shouted. 'How dare you!'

One of the doors opened. Rebecca glanced up at the nurse standing in the doorway and walked away, kicking the paper under the chairs.

'Rebecca?'

Rebecca stopped. She sighed and turned. 'Aunt Emily. Hello.'

'What *are* you doing here?'

Rebecca said nothing.

Emily raised her eyebrows. 'Well?'

Rebecca felt compelled to reveal her suspicions. 'I intended to visit Edward.'

'Then visit him.'

'You're here. I don't want to overwhelm him.'

'Nonsense, it's Edward. It's impossible for him to be overwhelmed.'

Something stirred deep in Rebecca's memory. It was her mother. She was in her bed, lifeless and cold, having used death to guard the truth. Edward can wait, Rebecca thought. 'I need to see Harry. He has no-one.'

'At least travel back with me.'

Rebecca considered saying no. 'If you wish. I'll meet you here at the end of visiting hours. And don't tell Edward I came. It'll upset him.'

Rebecca strode past young nurses and soldiers with crutches, fighting her feeling that it would be wrong to wake

Harry. In the corridor to Room Two a woman was rocking a perambulator back and forth. The child kept crying.

Rebecca observed the woman. She reminded her of Tilly, only a little younger.

'He's just 'ungry,' said the woman. 'It'll pass.'

'Can't you feed him?'

The woman shook her head.

'Have you eaten today?' asked Rebecca.

The woman looked away. 'Not yet. Needed the money to get 'ere, didn't I?'

Rebecca reached for her purse.

'Don't,' said the woman.

'It's no bother.'

'It is to me.'

Rebecca put her purse away. 'I understand.'

The baby stopped crying.

'Is his father resting too?'

The woman swallowed. Rebecca noticed her clothes, plain and black, black as grief, and regretted her question.

'His brother's in there,' said the woman. 'He won't talk about it.'

Rebecca stepped a little closer. 'So you don't know anything? You haven't been told anything?'

'I know a German killed my husband. I don't need to know anything else. He's not coming 'ome. None of 'em are. Only those who are wounded.'

The child started to cry again. The woman just stared at Rebecca, deaf to the noise.

'I'd best go in now,' said Rebecca. 'Take care.'

Rebecca left the woman and entered Room Two. Harry was sitting up, looking away from the doors, holding a mug.

He tricked me, she thought. He lied to me.

Rebecca kept her attention on Harry as she crept down the aisle to his bed. 'You're awake again,' she said.

Harry flinched, spilling his tea on to the blanket. 'I thought you'd gone.'

'I went to see my cousin.'

'Oh. How is he?'

'He's tired.'

'And you didn't say I was here?'

'No. Perhaps next time.'

'Don't,' whispered Harry.

'Pardon?'

'Don't tell him I'm here.'

Rebecca stepped round the bed. 'Why not?'

'Just don't. Please.'

Rebecca did not need to look at Harry's trembling hands to know he was scared. 'Are you worried about your letter?' she asked.

'I can't say.'

'Yes you can. What did you write to him?'

'Nothing.'

'That's not true, is it?'

Harry's cheeks flushed with anger. 'You read my letter?'

'I might have done.'

'Then you did.'

Rebecca clenched her jaw. 'I read it, yes.'

Harry turned on his side, away from Rebecca. 'I don't want to talk anymore.'

'Well I do. Tell what me what you promised to keep your word about.'

'I'm not saying.'

'I'll only ask my cousin instead.'

Harry turned back to face Rebecca. 'No! Don't do that.'

'Then tell me.'

A nurse coughed. 'Please, lower your voices.'

Rebecca barely glanced at the nurse. 'What happened at Gheluvelt, Harry?'

'I'm not saying.'

'You began the day in a wood. Polygon Wood, didn't you?'

Harry nodded.

'And you charged down a slope, correct?'

Harry nodded.

'But you got separated from the others and were taken to a square.'

Harry closed his eyes.

'You were shot and so was my cousin, and my husband dragged him away.'

Harry bit his lip. His eyes remained closed.

'Is that what happened? Is that the truth?'

'You must keep your voices down,' said the nurse.

Harry started to cry.

Rebecca raised her voice a little more. 'I have a right to know, Harry. What were you offered a reward for?'

The matron stepped past the nurse. 'You need to be quiet or I'll have to ask you to leave.'

'Leave us alone!' said Rebecca.

Harry pulled the blanket over his head. Rebecca pulled it back and shouted, 'What happened? What happened to my husband?'

Rebecca felt her arm being tugged.

'It's time you left,' said the matron.

Rebecca lashed out at the woman's arm, striking the bone hard with her fist. 'Leave me alone!'

'Get out!' said the matron. 'Or I'll have you arrested.'

Harry's sobbing became louder. The sight of his body, curled up in fear under the blanket, triggered a rush of shame. Rebecca collapsed to her knees and began to weep too.

The matron gripped Rebecca's arm again and with the nurse pulled her to her feet, escorting her past the row of staring soldiers. She went to protest but her jaw ached. All she could say was 'Tell me… tell me!'

TWENTY-FOUR

Rebecca told Emily she didn't want to talk during the journey home. Emily talked anyway, passing on Edward's concern for her and the boys, and his determination to return to the war.

'He's jealous of the others,' said Emily. 'I don't know why. A hospital may be dull, but at least there are no guns being fired. Will you talk to him? Suggest he draw out his recovery. He seems to dismiss everything I say.'

Rebecca stared out of the window, listening, but unresponsive. All she cared to do was withdraw into herself until her embarrassment had passed. She lied to Emily the following day when invited to visit Edward, and kept out of sight when Jack called with the post. Even Mrs Munn's knock went unanswered. Her torment over what was truth and what was not lingered like an illness of the mind. It was ferocious when she was alone, forcing her to remember what Edward had said and compare it against the newspaper reports and Harry's silence. Surely, she thought, Rupert had died just as she had been told: of his wounds, without suffering, having saved Edward's life.

Sunday arrived and she could hide away no longer. She sat with the boys in their usual place near the front in church, and during Sunday School played the piano as normal, smiled as normal, spoke to Kate as normal, all the while thinking of what to say the next time Emily invited her to the hospital. To say she remained unwell would risk Emily calling for the doctor, and to say the truth, that she feared the temptation of confronting Harry again, would prompt questions for Edward. She would have to accompany Emily and resist asking Edward what she wanted to: *what lie did you offer a reward for*? Perhaps he'd already made his confession to the Belgian, or a nurse, and would repeat it in Emily's presence. Or perhaps Harry was the one with the disease of the mind and he was infecting others with it.

After Sunday School, Rebecca told the boys she had errands to run and they should walk home without her. The graveyard was empty, which suited her. She took one of the grass channels that branched from the gravel path and walked to the end. The grass by her father's grave needed cutting back. Rebecca went to curse the verger and then remembered he'd volunteered for the Worcesters along with his friends. She felt insulted by what she saw. The grass was long because of the war, the war that had killed Rupert and now left her father's grave looking abandoned. In the little shed by the side of the church she found a scythe, which though old had a blade that appeared sharp enough to cut grass. Rebecca carried it back to her father's grave and began to cut down the grass. Within a few minutes she had finished, but looking around her she noticed other graves blighted by the war and so she cut and cut, ignoring the pain in her back and arms. She completed her task and stood at her father's grave a moment, reading the headstone inscription.

JAMES EDWARD LAWRENCE
HUSBAND OF ELIZABETH
FATHER OF REBECCA
WHO DEPARTED THIS LIFE
DECEMBER 4 1905
AGED 54 YEARS
THE END BROUGHT PEACE

Rebecca stared at her father's name. He had protected her from the violence of his grief, and now she had to do the same for James and Sebastian. Someone coughed. Rebecca turned sharply. Standing at the top of the path was Mrs Clarke.

'Were you waiting for me to leave?' asked Rebecca, stepping closer.

'No, no, not waiting.'

'Some other reason then?'

Mrs Clarke raised her head slightly. 'It's my Harry. He won't talk. He won't tell us anything.'

'You shouldn't be surprised. He's been through a lot.'

'But I'm his mother.'

'It's because you're his mother that he won't tell you what he's seen. He's protecting you.'

Mrs Clarke started to rub her hands together nervously. 'I was wondering, if you wouldn't mind, that is, telling me what Harry wrote in his letter to you?'

Rebecca thought she had misheard. 'Sorry, could you repeat that?'

'Harry's letter to you, what was in it?'

'I haven't received a letter from Harry.'

'He gave it to my husband. I saw him do so.'

'When?'

Mrs Clarke stepped back. 'I'm sorry, I must have got confused. Forget what I said.'

She's lying to me, Rebecca thought. 'Wait!'

Mrs Clarke turned and hurried away.

'Stop! Please.'

Mrs Clarke picked up her stride. Rebecca followed her.

'How could you have got confused?' said Rebecca. 'Did Harry write to me?'

Mrs Clarke didn't stop.

'He must have done or you wouldn't have said so.'

Mrs Clarke rushed through the lychgate and on to the path. Rebecca stayed at her shoulder.

'Where's the letter? What did your husband do with it?'

'I told you I was mistaken. I'm sorry.'

'No, you weren't. You saw Harry give your husband a letter for me and he hasn't delivered it.'

'It might have got lost.'

'Your husband wouldn't lose a letter from his son.'

Mrs Clarke had her head down and was walking as fast as she could.

'Tell me where it is!'

'Perhaps one of your boys took it. You should ask them.'

'Perhaps I should ask your husband instead.'

Mrs Clarke stopped suddenly. 'No, don't. Please.'

'Why not?'

'Because.'

'Why, Mrs Clarke?'

She swallowed and almost stuttering, said, 'He'll think I've betrayed him, gone behind his back. He'll get angry with me.'

Rebecca touched Mrs Clarke's hand. 'What do you mean?'

'I have to go. I'm sorry.'

Rebecca stood still, watching Mrs Clarke until she turned up the lane to her home. She would search for Harry's letter, she thought. *She plans to destroy it*. Rebecca hitched up her skirt and ran to the back of the post office. She knocked the door once, and then again, with more effort. Jack opened the door and squinted, as if he had just woken up.

'Afternoon, Mrs Salisbury.'

Rebecca could smell beer on Jack's breath. 'Is this a bad time?'

'No. What can I help you with?'

'I'm here about Harry.'

'Oh, is it about what happened at the hospital?'

'No.'

'Because I won't judge you if it is. Grief can make people act like that, as I said to the nurse this morning after she told me.'

Rebecca sighed quietly. 'I'm sorry if I upset Harry, or you, but I'm not here to talk about that.'

'Fair enough. I won't mention it.'

Rebecca wondered if she should walk away. 'As I said, I am here about Harry though.'

'What about him then?'

Rebecca swallowed. 'Did he write to me?'

'That's a question for him, isn't it?'

'Not if he gave you the letter to deliver to me.'

Jack crossed his arms. 'What are you suggesting?'

'Harry gave you a letter for me, didn't he?'

Jack sucked in his cheeks and glanced down.

'What have you done with it?'

Mrs Clarke appeared behind Jack. She looked at Rebecca and shook her head pleadingly. Rebecca hesitated, and raising her voice, said, 'I want my letter.'

'He shouldn't have written to you,' said Jack. 'He made a mistake.'

'Have you opened it?'

Jack brought his arms higher up his chest.

'You opened his letter? You read his letter?'

'He's my son!' snapped Jack. 'I can read his letters if I choose to.'

'He's not a boy. You've no place reading his letters.'

'I've every right to! He shouldn't have written what he did.'

'What did he write? Was it about Gheluvelt?'

Jack gripped the door. 'It's not your concern.'

Rebecca started to cry in anger. 'You stole from me! You're a thief!'

Jack started to push the door. Rebecca put her hand against

it. 'How dare you tell me it's not my concern. My husband's dead!'

Jack pushed harder. Rebecca fought back, striking his chest.

'Get out!' roared Jack.

'Give it me!'

Jack forced Rebecca backwards. She fell down, hitting her head on the ground. She remained conscious, but groggy. She could hear the door being bolted and voices becoming louder.

'No! I won't!' shouted Mrs Clarke.

The bolt was slid back again and the door opened. Mrs Clarke came forward, spluttering apologies through her tears.

'I can get the doctor,' she said, helping Rebecca to her feet.

'I'll be fine.'

'Jack's not good with his drink.'

Rebecca looked at Mrs Clarke's red eyes and felt a surge of pity for her.

'And seeing Harry in a bad way upsets him.'

Rebecca brushed herself down and made for the path, already planning to confront Jack again the following day. As she reached the green, she sensed she was being followed and glanced over her shoulder. 'Go home, Mrs Clarke.'

She kept walking, aware she was still being followed. She turned quickly. 'What do you want?' she asked firmly.

Mrs Clarke put her hand into her apron pocket. She pulled out an envelope and offered it to Rebecca.

'It's Harry's letter,' she said. 'I found it when you were talking to Jack. I haven't read it. I promise you I haven't.'

Rebecca accepted the letter. 'Does your husband know you've taken it?'

'He'll probably be looking for it at the moment.'

'What will he do?'

Mrs Clarke shrugged her shoulders.

'You can stay at my home if you're scared.'

Mrs Clarke sniffed. 'I'm not scared, I'm disappointed. I didn't think Jack was a thief.'

Rebecca said nothing.

Mrs Clarke glanced at the letter. 'There must be something in there he doesn't want you to know about.'

'Must be.'

There was a long silence. Rebecca guessed Mrs Clarke wanted her to read the letter in front of her.

'I'd best be leaving you to it then, Mrs Salisbury.'

'Remember my offer.'

Mrs Clarke nodded and turned away.

Back in Croft House, Rebecca washed her hands and face and put some food out for the boys. The shock of what had happened with Jack suddenly caught up with her. She poured herself a large gin and emptied the glass in two before escaping to her bedroom. She collapsed to her knees at her bedside and started to punch the mattress, restraining her voice, but not her fury. She kept punching, left, right, left, right, increasing her speed until it was impossible not to scream in rage.

'Mama?'

Rebecca froze. She could not bring herself to look at Sebastian's face, or allow him to see hers.

'Go downstairs,' she said. 'Close the door.'

The door was gently closed. Rebecca heard Sebastian's light footsteps on the stairs and punched the mattress again. The boys' voices drifted from the morning room. Rebecca crept past the door, saying she'd lost her brooch in the church and she'd return soon. She made for the riverbank and the old jetty. The day was cold enough for her to see her breath, but there was no wind and no-one in sight. All was still, menacingly so.

'You've suffered enough,' Rebecca said to herself. 'Throw the letter in the river.' The Severn was high and preparing to burst its banks. Rebecca crumpled the letter in her hand.

'Stop! Harry wanted to you to receive it. He wanted you to read it.' She checked she was alone and decided to do as Harry wanted.

November 20, 1914

Dear Mrs Salisbury,

I can't stop thinking of what you told me when I was a boy and I said I'd practised before my piano lesson, when I hadn't. You didn't like liars, you said. I didn't lie to you ever again. I couldn't. And I can't now.

I saw what happened to your husband, and I saw what Captain Warwick did afterwards. He wouldn't have told you all of it; the parts no man would want to share. Only he and I know.

I got knocked out in Gheluvelt. When I came to I could see all my mates were dead. Captain Warwick wasn't there. He was cowering behind a wall. Captain Salisbury ran over to him and brought him out. He was shot soon after. I don't know how long passed before Captain Warwick found his courage and came to me. I asked him where Captain Salisbury was. He ignored the question and told me to go into the church with him.

All the Germans in it had fled. There was just a sniper, up there on his own in the tower. He looked petrified when he turned round and saw us. He put down his rifle and surrendered, and started saying 'orders' over and over. I reckon he wasn't a day older than sixteen. Captain Warwick didn't care. He started hitting him with his fist, knocking his teeth out. The boy's face was red and broken, and every time he said 'orders' Captain Warwick hit him again. I pulled him back and he broke my nose, and then hit the boy again, telling him to stand up.

'Move,' Captain Warwick said.

Every time the boy stumbled, Captain Warwick kicked him, and then when he reached the final step he pushed his boot hard into his back.

'Find some rope, Clarke,' he said.

I thought he wanted to tie the boy's hands. And then I looked into his eyes and saw hatred and I knew the rope was for another purpose. I went round the church, pretending to search, and told him I couldn't find any rope. He said I was incompetent and made me stand guard. It didn't take him long to find the rope I'd seen.

'You're blind, Clarke,' he said.

I knew that if I looked at the boy his terror would haunt me forever. Keep your head down, I told myself. But I couldn't. I needed to show him I meant no harm, that I was just like him: obeying orders. I should have killed him quickly. Captain Warwick wouldn't have it. He wanted him to suffer. He even told him to tie the noose, only his hands were shaking too much.

'You do it, Clarke,' Captain Warwick said.

I pleaded with him to show mercy.

'Do it, Clarke.'

I couldn't. Captain Warwick shot me in the leg.

'Get up, Clarke, or I'll shoot you again.'

Somehow I got up.

'Make the noose, Clarke.'

The boy wept as we took him outside to a tree. Captain Warwick got annoyed and knocked him out cold. I thought that would be it. I was wrong. Captain Warwick put the noose round his neck and slung the rope over a branch. We pulled the rope until the boy's feet came off the ground. He woke up and started kicking at us. Captain Warwick just pulled harder.

Eventually, the boy's legs stopped moving. We let his body go.

'He can rot,' said Captain Warwick. 'Remove the noose and hide the rope.'

I did as I was ordered. Then he made me his offer. Tell the story he'd give me and he'd recommend me for a medal. Or tell the truth and he'd create a story of insubordination and have me court-martialled.

'My word has more authority than yours does,' he said. 'Make your choice.'

I can't say how Captain Warwick got shot afterwards, but it wasn't by me. I shouldn't be telling you any of this, but I know my Commandments and I'm not going to hell for being a liar. I'll be going there for being a murderer. And so will your cousin.

Harry

The jetty creaked. Rebecca flinched.

'Don't be startled,' said Jack. 'I have to talk to you.'

Rebecca searched the riverbank opposite for someone she might call out to for help. The jetty creaked again.

'Will you not look at me?'

Rebecca stuffed Harry's letter into her coat pocket. She clenched her fists and turned. Jack was at the end of the jetty.

'You followed me here, didn't you?'

'I must talk to you.'

'No, you must apologise to me.'

Jack looked down. 'I didn't intend to push you. I'm sorry.'

'I want another apology.'

'For following you?'

'For opening Harry's letter.'

Jack sighed. 'I don't regret opening it, but I do wish he'd never given it to me.'

Rebecca stepped forward. 'No, what you wish for is that he hadn't written it and you weren't having to consider his suffering. What you wish for is ignorance because you can't comprehend that your son hanged a man.'

'He had no choice! Your cousin forced him to!'

'He still did it. He still pulled the rope!'

'That's not my son!'

'And that's not my cousin! My cousin is *not* a murderer.'

'Well, Harry's not a liar, so yes, your cousin *is* a murderer, and he's a coward too and your husband is dead because of him.'

Rebecca pushed Jack out of the way. He followed her.

'What will you do with the letter?' he asked.

'Leave me alone!'

'You can't tell your cousin. You can't!'

'I'll tell him whatever I want to.'

'But he'll have Harry court-martialled.'

'He wouldn't do that.'

'Yes, *he* would. Please don't say anything, for Harry's sake.'

Rebecca stopped. 'And what about for my sake? I can't ignore what Harry wrote. I can't sit with my cousin and ask him how he's feeling, or how his leg his. I can't sit with him always wondering if Harry is being truthful.'

'Harry wouldn't lie.'

'But what if he did? What if he's lost his mind?'

'So you think he's mad? Because I don't. I know him.'

'And I know my cousin is not a coward.'

Jack looked Rebecca in the eye. 'You're going to ask him, then? Even though it puts Harry in danger?'

Rebecca swallowed. 'I have to.'

Jack went to speak. He hesitated and then said, 'I'd best get home then. My wife will be getting worried.'

'Don't be harsh on her. She gave me the letter because Harry wanted me to have it.'

Jack nodded.

'She hasn't read it.'

'Then at least don't tell her what's in it. Her nerves will get worse if you do.'

Rebecca wanted to refuse. 'If that's want you want.'

'It is.'

'Then I'll lie to her. For her sake, not yours.'

The telephone rang that night. Rebecca stood by it until the noise stopped. It was most likely Emily calling about visiting Edward. The following morning, she arrived early at the station and took the rear third class carriage. She watched Emily step on to the platform and make for the front of the train, and then waited out of sight at King's Norton while the first tram departed. The ambulances were lined up as normal at the university, and inside there were now three boards with lists of names on them. Harry remained in Room Two.

'You have to do this,' Rebecca told herself. 'You have to confront him.'

The doors were open. Visitors were settling into their conversations or sitting in silence. Leaning over Harry, straightening his blanket, was Mrs Clarke. He said something that made her smile.

'Can I help you?' asked a nurse.

Rebecca did not respond.

'Madam?'

Rebecca continued to stare at Mrs Clarke.

'Which patient are you here to visit?'

Rebecca snapped out of her stupor. 'Sorry, I… I shouldn't be in here.' She turned sharply and hurried away, though in her fluster she took a wrong turn and found herself approaching the Great Hall. A woman's voice carried down the corridor. It was Emily's.

'I can't fathom why you, a doctor, would allow him to leave?' she said.

'I assure you he was fit enough to leave.'

'And I assure you that he was not. You've no business sending him to Scarborough. How do you expect me to visit him there?'

'Visiting arrangements are not my concern.'

'They certainly should be! You should have consulted with me first before abandoning him.'

The doctor crossed his arms. 'I'm sorry if you've been inconvenienced, but…'

'It's more than an inconvenience. It is irritating and inconsiderate, and rash of you.'

'As I was about to say, Captain Warwick seemed quite willing to leave.'

'Without talking to me? I doubt that very much.'

'He made no objection yesterday afternoon.'

Rebecca cleared her throat deliberately. Emily and the doctor looked her way.

'They've moved Edward to Scarborough,' said Emily.

'I really must return to the ward,' said the doctor. 'Good day, Mrs Warwick.'

Emily pouted. 'Incompetent man. Edward should have been kept here. Now I'll never see him.'

'Scarborough is not so far away,' said Rebecca.

'It's in Yorkshire. He may as well be abroad.'

'Why send him up there?'

'That's where they go, apparently, before being declared fit again for service.'

'And how long will that take?'

'Evidently not soon enough. Why would he be so eager to leave without saying goodbye?'

For a moment, Rebecca thought to tell Harry's account of what happened at Gheluvelt.

'Did he indicate to you he wanted to be far away from us?' asked Emily.

'No.'

'Then why would he do it?'

Rebecca considered the letter again. 'I can't say. You should write to him, or better still, visit.'

Emily raised her eyebrows. 'I've never been that far north, and for good reason.'

'Well, now you have a good reason to do so.'

'As do you.'

Rebecca swallowed. 'The smell in here is making me feel poorly. Can we leave?'

'Gladly. There'll be nowhere adequate to eat in Birmingham so we'll lunch at my home. Charlotte will call afterwards. She wants to discuss war work, as normal. I'll happily ask acquaintances for money, but how knitting mittens for soldiers will help us defeat the Germans is beyond me. The army needs men, not warm hands.'

Rebecca could not shake the sight of Mrs Clarke at Harry's bedside, acting as any loving mother would. She felt pity for Mrs Clarke for having a son in the war, and then envy that she was protected by ignorance. She would never learn of Harry's claims. He would never dare speak of them, and if they were true, neither would Edward. The only threat was the letter. Rebecca wished it had never been written, or that Jack had kept it to himself. The thought of reading it again turned her stomach.

James said he wanted to visit Edward, as did Sebastian, though neither of them was certain where Scarborough was. They went to sleep late, but Rebecca remained awake. Sitting in the kitchen, warming herself with a hot whiskey, she stared at Harry's letter sitting on the table.

You can read it, she thought; you can pick apart every sentence and prove that Harry was lying, that Edward was not to blame for Rupert's death; that he was courageous, and could never be a…

She reached for the letter. A sudden hatred for it took hold of her and she opened the range door. The coals were still alive with heat. Rebecca tore the letter in two and tossed the pieces on to the coals. She went to reach for them, but quickly withdrew her hand and closed the range door.

'Burn.'

Four years,
five months later.
April 1919.

TWENTY-FIVE

'Oh, there you are. I was beginning to think something had happened to you.'

Emily huffed. 'It has, Rebecca. My maid has just told me she's emigrating.'

'Emigrating? To where?'

'Australia, and she won't be alone. All of her unmarried friends are joining her. Apparently, they each receive free passage for serving in the Land Army.'

'That seems fair to me.'

'Well it doesn't to me! And because of it I now have the inconvenience of finding a new maid. I was happy to part with her during the war, but the war is over now. The colonies have no business taking our servants.'

Others waiting on the platform shuffled forward and looked down the tracks as the locomotive came into view.

'If he's missed the train I'll be damned annoyed,' said Emily.

'He wouldn't do that.'

'The army could have made him.'

'Hardly. Not after all this time.'

'They cancelled his leave after the armistice, didn't they? I wouldn't...'

The locomotive's brakes drowned out Emily's voice. The train came to a gradual stop. Steam rose from underneath the carriages as the doors opened.

'I can't see him,' said Emily. 'Where is he?'

An officer stepped out of a first-class carriage, followed by Edward. The officer shook Edward's hand and approached a woman with a young girl at her side. Edward observed the reunion for a moment and then looked Rebecca's way.

'Come along,' said Emily.

Rebecca kept a step behind. Edward removed his parade cap and embraced Emily. He said only a few words and made for Rebecca.

'Hello, cousin,' he said, kissing her on the cheek.

'Hello, Edward. Welcome home.'

'Thank you.'

Rebecca drew back. The rings under Edward's eyes had darkened heavily in the time that had passed since his previous leave.

'You look as if you've been on lower rations than we have,' said Emily. 'One would have thought normality would have returned after the war, but some still wish our suffering to drag on. Did you know, it's impossible…'

'I'm sure Edward doesn't wish to hear our complaints,' said Rebecca, interrupting. 'Particularly after such a long journey.'

'Don't worry,' he said, 'everyone in the army seems to complain now. Demobbing can't come soon enough for most.'

'Yes, well, let's forget about the army,' said Emily. 'And the sooner you're in civilian clothes the better. I don't want any reminders I've only got you for a week.'

As they left the station, Emily kept up a stream of questions. Edward's answers were brief and his response about his wounded leg the most cursory of all. He said only 'it's fine' and the questions stopped.

During lunch, Emily spoke of her friends and what she had read in the morning newspaper. Edward had little to say and from time to time glanced round the dining room as if he had never seen it before. His return home was toasted, though he took only the slightest of sips. A long silence fell upon the table. Rebecca played with her food, wondering what to say. Edward ate quickly and began to turn his dessert spoon over and over.

'The Mayor was pleased to be told of your return,' said Emily. 'He called yesterday.'

Edward put the spoon down and smiled politely.

'He was disappointed Rebecca wasn't here, particularly as he'd expected her to be.'

'Yes, well, I couldn't be,' said Rebecca.

'I have to say, I was a little embarrassed.'

'I'm sure you were, but something more important came up.'

'More important than entertaining the Mayor? I doubt it.' Emily turned back to Edward. 'He wanted to thank me for my fundraising contribution to the homes for disabled servicemen. He would have thanked Rebecca for her support had she been here.'

'I didn't fundraise so that the Mayor could thank me,' said Rebecca. 'And I spent yesterday afternoon with Mrs Clarke.'

Emily raised her eyebrows. 'And do you have a temperature?'

'No, I do not.'

'You can't be too careful. You must say if you feel at all unwell.'

'Mrs Clarke does *not* have the Spanish Flu.'

'Her husband did, and now he's dead. I pity the woman. Death will be her only comfort now.'

'How is she?' asked Edward.

'Her spirits are low,' said Rebecca.

'I wanted to write to her about Harry.'

'A lieutenant did.'

'What did he write?'

'He praised his courage and sacrifice. It helped.'

'Could you not have called on Mrs Clarke another day?' said Emily.

Rebecca wanted to groan. 'Yesterday would have been Harry's birthday. I didn't want Mrs Clarke to be alone.'

Emily blushed a little. 'I understand… and I'm sorry. Besides, the Mayor can thank you at dinner on Friday. The Mayoress will also be joining us.'

'I shan't be there.'

'Pardon?'

'I'll be away.'

'Away where?'

'London.'

'London? Whatever for?'

'I'll be staying at Alfred's the night before I sail for France.'

Emily looked dumbfounded. 'I must have misheard you. I'm sure you just said you're going to France.'

'You heard correctly.'

Emily frowned. 'And why on earth would you wish to go there?'

'So I can visit Rupert's grave.'

'But that's in Belgium.'

'I know. I'm going to Gheluvelt.'

'Have you lost your senses? France and Belgium are ruined.'

'But not abandoned.'

'Well, you won't find a decent hotel. In fact, you probably won't find any hotel that hasn't been damaged by the Germans.'

'I can manage.'

'Even if you do, it remains madness, and rude also.'

'I can't see how it's rude.'

'It's rude because Edward is here. He's just arrived and has been expecting to spend time with you. Haven't you, darling?'

Edward shuffled a little in his chair. 'Of course.'

'There, you heard him. So you should put this pilgrimage of yours out of your mind.'

'I'll do no such thing,' said Rebecca forcefully. 'The war has ended and I want to visit Rupert's grave.'

'I understand that, but travelling on your own would not be safe.'

'I shan't be on my own.'

'Alfred's accompanying you?'

'No, he'll be caring for the boys. Edward will travel with me, won't you?'

Edward nodded. 'I can't let her travel alone. As you said, Mama, it wouldn't be safe.'

Emily's jaw dropped. 'Then wait until it *is* safe.'

Rebecca sighed from deep in her chest. 'I've been waiting nearly five years and I'm not waiting any longer.'

Emily scowled. 'You coerced him somehow, didn't you?'

'No, she did not!' said Edward, with sudden energy. 'This is my decision and I won't change it. If you wish to accompany us then you're welcome to do so.'

Emily drew a breath. 'You know very well that's out of the question.' She looked at Rebecca. 'You could have at least had the heart to have the boys stay here.'

'It's important Alfred has time with them.'

'I'm surprised he has any time given his importance.'

'He's not so occupied now the war is over.'

'Then let's hope he remains so,' said Edward.

Emily waved a hand dismissively. 'Don't be so hopeful. Someone will find a use for his brain. But if he's not so occupied, he should have stayed at Croft House while you're away.'

'I want the boys to see Uncle Henry too,' said Rebecca.

Emily pouted.

'You should come with us to London.'

Emily reached for her glass and said drily, 'Should I now?'

'Yes, you should.'

'And what do you think, Edward? Or would you prefer not to be inconvenienced by your mother?'

Edward brought his hands up from his lap and made them into fists. 'What I would prefer is to remember what being at peace is. I've spent four years in hell waiting for it, so if you don't mind you'll make no complaint about anything I do until I leave the army. That is what I would prefer.'

Emily shut her mouth tightly and nodded. Edward stood up and looking past Emily, said, 'Excuse me. I need to go for a walk.'

Rebecca told Edward he had no need to apologise. He did anyway, arguing that his weariness was no excuse for what he had said. He remained subdued, speaking to Emily and Rebecca with brevity, exhausting 'I believe so' and 'that's correct', though he tried harder with the boys, as if reserving his limited enthusiasm for them. James and Sebastian asked questions only about the war. Rebecca objected at first, conscious of protecting Edward from re-living his hell, and the boys from thinking of their father. Nevertheless, he satisfied their curiosity. While on the train to London, Sebastian turned from the window and said, 'Uncle Teddy, how many Germans did you kill?'

Edward stared at Sebastian. Rebecca wondered if he was calculating a number. He leaned forward and said, 'I wish I hadn't killed a single one. But I had to, and so I did.'

Sebastian bit his lip and gazed out of the window again.

'Henry has promised to take the boys around Parliament,' said Rebecca.

'Then they should take the opportunity,' said Emily. 'Lord knows what will happen when every woman gets the vote. The Conservatives may win every seat or none at all.'

'Our being over thirty makes our right to the vote no different to that of a woman aged under thirty.'

'Poppycock. A woman of twenty-one has no comprehension of political matters. She barely knows the names of the parties.'

'So you would have it that a woman of twenty-one nurse your son in a field hospital, or harvest crops so that you may eat, but you wouldn't allow her any say in who governs her country?'

'No, I would not. They can all be patient and wait for the vote just as we had to.'

'What did you receive your medal for?' asked Sebastian.

Rebecca touched Sebastian's hand. 'Darling, remember what I said earlier.'

'It's all right,' said Edward. 'I can answer.'

Rebecca nodded reluctantly.

'I was recognised for something I did in a German trench.'

'What did you do?'

Edward smiled painfully. 'I did my duty.'

'Was Papa there?'

Edward glanced at Rebecca and then back at Sebastian. 'No, it was after he died.'

'Who would like a piece of fudge?' said Emily quickly.

James and Sebastian both grinned and chimed, 'Yes, please.'

'I thought you would. You'll have to earn it. Sebastian, you can go first. Are you ready?'

'Yes!'

'What's seventy-two divided by six? Quick now…'

Alfred's home was set in a square in which Emily said 'the very best of English society resides'. It was a fitting home for a person of inherited wealth, though not a bachelor, thought Rebecca. There were four guest bedrooms and a rarely used dining room that could seat a dozen. Alfred said he preferred to eat in the kitchen, even with his cook present, or at his club, at which he often slept during the war because it was only a hundred yards or so from his workplace.

'Remind me,' said Emily, 'what was it that you did?'

Alfred dropped a sugar cube into his tea and stirred. 'I helped devise the means to restrict the enemy's fighting capacity.'

'Oh, so you found more ways to kill Germans, then?'

Alfred hesitated and said, 'I did, yes.'

'And what ways did you find?'

'Just ways.'

'Such as gas?'

'Correct.'

'Though it was the Germans who introduced gas.'

'They did, yes.'

'Pity.'

'Is it?'

'Well, if you had been a little hastier we could have landed the first punch.'

Without looking up, Edward said, 'If you had seen a man dying from gas, Mama, you would not have wanted anyone to land the first punch, English *or* German.'

There was a long uncomfortable silence. Rebecca heard movement on the stairs and wondered if the boys had eavesdropped.

'How is your cousin Alice?' asked Alfred.

Rebecca thought of the previous time she had seen Alice, when she had sat with her every day for a week knowing there was nothing she could say that would stop her from weeping. Almost a year had passed since then. Ralph's body remained lost, buried somewhere in French soil.

'I believe Alice is as well as any widow could expect to be,' she said.

'And her daughter?'

'She remains quiet. She can't understand why there's no grave to visit.'

Everyone raised their cups except for Edward. He was staring across the room.

'I've noticed that Henry has not had any difficulty with talking of late,' said Emily. 'The newspapers seem rather keen to print his opinion. Thankfully, they've also taken to mocking it.'

Rebecca rolled her eyes. 'He's entitled to speak his mind. And as a Member of Parliament he has a duty to do so.'

'I agree. The more he speaks his mind, however, the more I find myself annoyed with him.'

'Then so be it.'

'Surely, you disagree with what he's saying about Germany?'

'No, I don't. As a matter of fact, I agree with him.'

Emily frowned. 'But Germany must be punished. They are responsible for the war, thus they must pay for it. Any patriot would want to bleed Germany dry of all it has.'

Rebecca felt a sudden anger come over her. 'Germany has already been bled dry. Victory grants us no right to inflict any further hardship on her people. They are starving. They need our compassion, not punishment.'

Emily scoffed. 'I'd sooner show the Devil compassion than a German.'

'It is our compassion that took us to war. Should we now be lacking in it we may as well consider ourselves defeated.'

'We were not defeated,' said Edward quietly.

'Of course we weren't,' said Emily. 'Our victory was glorious.'

Edward looked at Emily. There was no warmth in his eyes. 'I felt no glory at the end. Neither should you.'

Another silence fell. Edward rose stiffly and went to the window. Softly, Rebecca said, 'Can you tell us what you did feel?'

Edward kept his back turned. 'I expect most of the men felt relieved it was over. Some of them cheered.'

'But not you?'

'No, not me. I can't say I felt anything.'

'And now?'

Edward bowed gravely. 'I find it best not to. Too many memories.'

Rebecca swallowed. 'Yes, I understand that. Too many memories.'

Emily insisted on giving Edward and Rebecca some money before they left Alfred's.

'You're to buy a first-class passage,' she said. 'If the crossing is rough you'll be glad you're unwell in respectable surroundings. And if the ship is sunk you'll be close to the lifeboats.'

Edward sighed. 'The ship will not sink, Mama.'

'Nevertheless, one must be prepared for the worst. There may still be German submarines in our waters.'

'There are none.'

'You can't be certain of that, Edward. They may not have been told the war is over. The message may not have got through.'

Edward changed back into his uniform. Now, Rebecca thought, there was no liberty for any feelings to surface. They were restrained by the discipline of the greatcoat, tunic, brass buttons and the thick belt that wrapped around the waist and up over the shoulder.

Soldiers and officers were coming and going on the approach to Victoria Station, weaving between civilians just as they had done during the war, only the war had finished and still they were travelling to France, leaving the life they wanted for the life they did not. Rebecca studied them, wondering if any had been involved since the start. How long ago that must seem to them; how impossible to believe they once expected to return home triumphant after just a few months of fighting.

As they entered the station, Edward dropped a coin into a hat which was on the ground by a man's feet. The man was holding a sign. It read: *Four children. No income. Served since 1914.* Rebecca paused and looked left and right. There was another man with a sign and a hat, and then another, and another. People were filing past the men, glancing at them, but not stopping.

'Rebecca,' said Edward, 'we're this way.'

Congregated on the platform were groups of women. Rebecca noticed they were mostly younger than her and from the lower classes. The women boarded the boat train in their groups, though later, as the crossing to Calais began, they stood or sat on the deck in pairs. One pair came and stood next to Rebecca and Edward. The closest was young, twenty at most, and her companion at least twice her age. Rebecca decided they were mother and daughter, or aunt and niece. The younger one blew into a handkerchief and wiped tears from her cheeks. The older woman put her arm round her back. Still, the woman cried. It occurred to Rebecca why. The woman was probably a widow or perhaps had a fiancé or brother killed in the war. She, like the others, was on her own pilgrimage to a grave. Rebecca looked away. She could sense her own deep grief rise within her. Rupert too would have stared at the cliffs of England's coastline believing the next time he saw them he would be only a day's travel from home; just two train journeys from the boys… from her.

Gradually, people made their way inside, escaping sea-spray and a wind that cut through coats. Rebecca joined the trail of passengers, steadying herself as waves buffeted the ship.

'Shall we eat?' asked Edward.

'I want to lie down,' said Rebecca. 'You go.'

Edward headed for the dining room. The thought of eating angered Rebecca's stomach. It seemed to be rocking side to side with the ship, expanding with each step to the cabin. Rebecca started to panic she would not reach the privacy of her room before she was ill. Placing her hand across her mouth, she quickened her stride, pushing past those in front of her in the corridor. She made her cabin in time and rushed into the bathroom. Bending over the washstand, she brought up the Scotch broth she had eaten on the train. She gasped for air and retched again. Whatever remained in her stomach was forced up her throat and into the basin. She wiped her face clean with a towel and slumped to the bathroom floor, catching her breath. Slowly, the nausea began to pass. The cabin door opened and closed.

'I haven't an appetite,' said Edward.

Rebecca said nothing.

'Rebecca?'

'I'm in here,' she answered weakly.

'Are you all right?'

'I'm unwell.'

'Can I come in?'

Rebecca made a faint noise. Edward's polished boots came into view. She dared not raise her head.

'What can I do to help?' asked Edward.

'Water.'

Edward stepped back, returning moments later with a glass of water. Rebecca took a long sip, waited, and sipped again.

'Do you want to stand?'

Rebecca nodded. Edward crouched down and put his hands under her arms. He lifted her up and guided her to the sofa, placing a pillow behind her head and a wastepaper basket at her side. She closed her eyes, willing the English Channel to show kindness and flatten itself. The strain of the journey started to overwhelm her. Edward asked if she wanted another glass. Her eyelids suddenly felt too heavy to remain open and she could murmur only, 'I need to sleep now.'

When Rebecca woke, the boat had stopped moving and Edward was standing over her, holding her hand.

'We've arrived,' he said. 'You're in France.'

Away from the ship, in the port's cold, grey arrivals building, Rebecca noticed the pairs of women had returned to their groups. Each group was gathered round a man calling out instructions. The sight of the war widows huddled together, far from home, maddened Rebecca. The government should have paid their fares, she thought, and the fares of all the others in Britain. The women at the back stood on their tiptoes to catch what their guides were saying. Others disembarking the boat had no need for guidance. They were hurrying into the building. The officials who were employed to inspect documents and ask questions had no interest in such tasks, instead waving passengers through towards the railway station. France, Rebecca decided, was either eager to avoid delaying its visitors, or was indeed as lazy as Emily had often said. She was relieved, nevertheless, to avoid a stranger's questions. She wished to be far away from the ship and the sea, and anything that swayed. Leaving a ramp and entering the station, she discovered why the ship's passengers had raced past her. The train waiting on the platform had only three carriages and all the seats appeared to be occupied.

'Is this our train?' asked Rebecca.

Edward looked up at the platform sign. 'Yes,' he replied.

'Will there be another?'

'Probably not for some time.'

Rebecca sighed. 'Then I suppose we'll just have to stand.'

Edward tipped the porter and took the cases. Emily, Rebecca thought, would have found it incomprehensible there was no first-class carriage. Edward led the way down the first carriage and into the second. No-one seemed willing to give up their seat. Rebecca heard French being spoken and wondered if people were talking about her. The third carriage was as fully occupied as the previous two. Rebecca tried to remember the stages of the journey. She was certain Edward had said the first would take at least two hours. Two hours of standing after being weakened by illness suddenly seemed impossible to bear. The train jolted forward. Rebecca lurched forward with it, reaching out in panic. There was nothing to hold on to except for the closest passenger's shoulder.

'Sorry! Sorry!' said Rebecca.

'Ce n'est pas grave,' said the man, middle-aged and broad-chested.

Rebecca raised her eyebrows in confusion.

The man stood up and pointed to his seat. 'Please.'

Rebecca shook her head. 'No, no. There's no need.'

The man pointed again. 'Please.'

Rebecca sat down. 'Thank you… merci.'

The man smiled and moved past Edward to the end of the carriage. Rebecca wondered if he had been wounded during the war as he had a limp. There were other men of fighting age on the train, though Edward was the only one in uniform. Rebecca caught some of the women stealing glances at him. It occurred to her that strangers would assume they were married. For a moment, she wanted to correct any such assumption and have people know that she too was a widow who looked with envy at husbands and wives going about their days. She looked over at Edward. He was standing straight and tall, and staring out of the window. Rebecca was overcome by a new sense of gratitude that he was alive, and that she was not travelling to visit his grave as well as Rupert's. By some miracle he had survived his hell and was now using his leave to escort her to the village where his dearest friend had died. Perhaps he was seeking redemption, she thought, or perhaps Harry had lied and there was nothing to seek redemption for.

The woman sitting opposite Rebecca opened a round tin and said with a French accent, 'Would you like one?'

Rebecca inspected the tin's contents. There were only three boiled sweets remaining. She shook her head and smiled. The woman kept her arm outstretched. 'They'll help your recovery,' she said.

It occurred to Rebecca she was probably still pale from being ill. She took a sweet and put it in her mouth. The taste of ginger burst on her tongue.

'Keep them,' said the woman, placing the tin on Rebecca's lap. Rebecca went to pass it back, but the woman raised her hand as if anticipating the response. Rebecca noticed she was wearing a wedding ring and was about her age.

'That's very kind of you. Thank you.'

The woman shrugged her shoulders and started to speak in French to the lady next to her. Edward looked Rebecca's way. His expression gave no hint of his thoughts and he returned his attention to the window. Rebecca swallowed the remains of the sweet and opened the tin for another.

The woman left the train after two stops. No-one else came on board, so Edward took her place. His rest lasted half an hour at most as the train reached the end of the line. It was dark and the day's drizzle was deteriorating into heavy rain. There were no taxis outside the station, the name of which was the same as the town it served: Ghyvelle.

'Are we in Belgium?' asked Rebecca, staring down a long, dark road that led from the station.

'Nearly. The border is only a mile or so from here.'

Rebecca felt her stomach rumble. What she cared for most was a hot meal and a bed.

'We can wait until the rain eases,' said Edward. 'The town is at the end of the road.'

'And the hotel?'

'Not far.'

Passengers were heading into the gloom. None of them had umbrellas.

'We should go now before the hotel closes,' said Rebecca. 'Agreed?'

The hotel was dimly lit. In the ancient lobby was a fireplace that had no coal or wood, only ash, and if there were any guests they were either in their rooms or out as no noise was coming from the bar. Rebecca swept her wet hair away from her forehead and used her sleeve to wipe rain from her cheeks. She instinctively stepped closer to the fireplace, even though the fire had long gone out, and hoped that a hot bath awaited her. Edward rang a bell. A man, thin and dressed in undertaker black, came through the open doorway at the back of the reception desk. Edward said a few words in French, introducing himself and 'Mrs Rebecca Salisbury'. The man looked puzzled. He asked Edward one question after another, and as the exchange intensified, so did the volume of Edward's voice. The man cut in, and removing his glasses pointed to the front door. In a flash, Edward banged his fist down on the counter and spoke at a speed that allowed no interruption. Rebecca could understand nothing of what Edward was saying other than he kept repeating something that sounded like 'la gare' or 'la guerre'. He stopped abruptly and turned to Rebecca. The man studied her for a moment and opened a cupboard on the wall. He passed Edward a key, straightened his tie as flustered people do, and sat down.

'Merci, monsieur,' said Edward, a little less harshly.

The man did not look up and went about some task on his desk. Edward stepped back.

'Sorry about that,' he said to Rebecca. 'We're on the third floor. We'll be carrying our own cases.'

Rebecca waited until they were out of earshot and asked, 'What just happened?'

'There was some confusion and only one room had been booked. All the others are occupied.'

'Surely he should have apologised to us?'

'That's what I said.'

'And he didn't agree?'

'Correct. In his view, only one of us can take the room as we have different surnames. When I gave him a piece of my mind, he told us to leave.'

'But you said something after that and he gave you the key.'

'I told him that your husband died in the war and that if it wasn't for him and the British Army he'd be accommodating Germans, not us. He could hardly argue.'

Rebecca paused on the stairs. 'Oh. Well done. Sorry, are we sharing a room?'

'I'll sleep on the floor.'

'Won't that be uncomfortable?'

'Compared to a trench dugout it'll be luxury. And don't worry, unless I have a drink there's no chance of me snoring.'

'Will you?'

'Will I what?'

'Have a drink?'

Edward clenched his jaw. 'No, I don't seem to have a taste for it these days.'

TWENTY-SIX

It was eight o'clock when Rebecca awoke. She lay still, staring at the ceiling. Worries crept up on her; the same worries she'd had in London, of Sebastian's nightmares and his crying, and James's stubbornness when sad. They're coping, she told herself. Alfred will be keeping their minds occupied; there's no need for concern. She listened for shuffling on the floor and concluded Edward had gone down for breakfast. She sat up and stretched. Her back ached from the discomfort of an old mattress and the demands of the previous day. The journey ahead would not be as arduous, she thought. They were close to the border and Gheluvelt was only another seventy miles or so from there. If they left soon, they could reach the village by lunchtime.

She dressed quickly as the room was cold. Edward was nowhere to be seen downstairs. There were other hotel guests in the dining-room, though all was silent except for the mechanics of people selecting their food and using their cutlery. Rebecca took a table in the corner, certain that people were looking at her, perhaps pitying her as she was alone. The waiter poured her a cup of coffee that was stronger than she was accustomed to, and muttering something in French he pointed to the breakfast table. Rebecca surveyed the options and wondered if rationing remained in place. The only meat was cold, and there was no toast or any means of making it. She took two slices of bread and spread plum jam over them, scraping clean the serving dish to get her money's worth. She kept her head down as she ate, and paused only briefly between finishing her first slice and starting her second. As she considered going up for a third, Edward appeared beside her.

'Good morning,' he said, pulling out a chair.

'There's no bacon, or eggs. Just bread and some meat that looks a little tough.'

'It's horse.'

'What?'

'That's what some of them eat here.'

'How could they?'

'Because they're hungry.'

'Well, I'm certainly not eating it. And I hope you didn't.'

Edward said nothing.

'Edward!'

'We've a long drive ahead of us. I wasn't going to be fussy about what I ate.'

'Drive? I thought we'd travel mostly by train?'

'The railways have all been mined from here. Horse or car are the only options for transportation, unless you care to walk, which I don't.'

Rebecca noticed guests were turning their heads. She leaned closer to Edward and lowering her voice, said, 'As all the horses seem to be in people's stomachs, we don't have much of a choice. I don't know how we'll find a car though, so we may well be forced to walk.'

'Our car is outside. I acquired it while you were asleep.'

'You bought a car?'

'No, not exactly. We have it for two days at most. Any later and I'll be in trouble.'

'Oh, we'd better leave now then.'

'If you don't mind. Finish your coffee. You'll need to be alert for what's to come.'

The car was like none Rebecca had seen in England. It had a canvas roof and canvas sides instead of windows. The wheels would have been more fitting on a tractor, and the exterior was covered with mud, so much so it was more brown than the intended green.

'Where's it from?'

'America,' said Edward. 'The British have it now.'

'It's kind of someone to let us use it.'

A guilty look came over Edward's face.

'Edward?'

'Just make yourself comfortable. Or at least try to.'

The road away from the hotel was smooth, but as the town was left behind the road turned into craters that could only be navigated by driving on to neighbouring fields, which meant driving at half the speed required to reach Gheluvelt by lunchtime.

'So it wasn't just the railways that were mined then?' said Rebecca.

'No, the roads as well.'

'Will it get any easier?'

'I'm afraid not.'

'Surely it won't get any worse?'

Edward drew on his cigarette and exhaled. 'I could tell you to imagine what ruin looks like, but there would be no point.'

'Why not?'

'Because you're about to see it.'

They crossed the border into Belgium and approached a town, or what remained of one. There was not even a sign to identify it and the rubble of destroyed buildings looked too high and wide to ever be cleared. The streets were deserted. It was not inconceivable, Rebecca thought, that Edward and she were the only people in the town. It was all theirs, though it was worthless. There were homes with the back half missing, homes that looked like giant dolls houses in that walls had been removed, exposing bedrooms and bathrooms, and homes so weakened from shellfire it seemed a strong wind could topple them. The church had lost its steeple and stained glass, and the people had lost their lives. Edward was correct. The Germans had been defeated, but no glory could be felt in victory.

Edward found a way through the shattered town and headed south. If war had not touched Flanders the view would have reminded Rebecca of the Fens in that the fields were flat and landscaped with drainage trenches. But the war had reduced the windbreak trees to stumps decaying among wire entanglements and blackened tanks, and there were so many holes filled with water that the fields resembled marshes, not farmland. Crops would never be harvested in these fields again, Rebecca thought. The fields had died and were now cemeteries. Thousands of crosses, all cheap timber and identical, as if assembled in a factory, were erect in the mud with barely space to stand between graves.

The road deteriorated the farther south they went. People began to appear. Some were pushing carts weighed down by furniture, others had mules to take the strain, but none could be helped, Edward said.

'We can't be delayed,' he said. 'They'll be at their homes soon enough.'

What homes? Rebecca wanted to say. *There are no homes.* She considered trying to persuade Edward they had to help someone, but she was aware that dusk was nearly upon them and they had to find somewhere to sleep and eat. They passed a milestone. One of the names was familiar to Rebecca.

'Will there be a hotel in Ypres?' she asked.

'There's nothing in Ypres. The town is flattened. We'll be avoiding it.'

'And staying where?'

'On the other side of Ypres, at a farm I was billeted at once.'

'And what if the farm has been destroyed?'

Edward took a hand off the wheel and opening his cigarette case, said, 'Then you'll be waking with a sore neck from sleeping in here.'

It was nearly dark when they turned off the road and on to a track that led to the farm. The outbuildings had collapsed, yet the farmhouse had not been hit by any of the war's instruments. Edward brought the car to a stop in front of the house. There was a light coming from inside.

'Best you wait here,' said Edward. 'The farmer may be none too pleased at being disturbed by a soldier.'

'What if we're not allowed to stay? What then?'

'Don't worry about that. So long as the farmer is hungry we'll be staying here tonight.'

Edward removed a small box from the back seat and took it with him to the front door. He knocked twice and stepped back as the door opened. A woman came into view. Edward said a few words and held up the box. The woman peeked into it, glanced towards the car and showed Edward inside. He re-emerged alone and empty handed.

'We can stay,' he said.

'What was in the box?'

'Tins of bully beef. I told her it was delicious.'

'But it isn't.'

'It is if meat is in short supply.'

'And it just happened to be in the car when you borrowed it?'

'Something like that.'

The woman introduced herself to Rebecca as Elise Dumont. She guided them to the kitchen and prepared a meal of bread, hard-boiled eggs and bully beef. Rebecca put her age at close to fifty-five, and though she had never been to England, her English was adequate enough for a conversation. She asked Rebecca why she was in Flanders. Hearing her answer, she shared that her son was killed in the first week of the war, and her husband had died soon after. Elise, it occurred to Rebecca, remained a prisoner of war for she was surrounded by its reminders: the destroyed barn and fields, cemeteries and trenches, refugees on the road and the long silence of her own company. There was no escape from what had been taken from her. It was permanent, eased only if she moved far away.

'Would you sell the farm?' asked Rebecca.

Elise looked as if she might cry. 'I can't. No-one has money. No-one has anything.'

After dinner, Elise showed Rebecca and Edward their rooms. As Rebecca went to say good night to Edward, a question came into her mind.

'When were you billeted here?'

'1914.'

'After Gheluvelt?'

'No, before it.'

'So did Rupert stay here?'

Edward nodded solemnly.

'In which room?'

'Don't do this.'

'In which room, Edward?'

Edward hesitated and then pointed down the landing. 'That one.'

Rebecca sucked in her breath and stepped towards the door.

'It could be her son's, Rebecca.'

Rebecca stopped. She continued to face the closed door.

'Don't go in there. It's not right.'

Rebecca turned away. She said nothing to Edward and went to her room. She was too tired and cold to undress, and removed only her boots before climbing into bed. She pulled the blanket up high and closed her eyes, thinking of what was to come at Gheluvelt.

'Rupert,' she said, under her breath. 'Help me… please.'

An engine came to life. The sound of crunching gravel followed and then the acceleration of a car. Rebecca jumped out of bed and pulled back the curtain. Edward was driving away from the farm. She hurried down the stairs and out of the house, waving and calling out, but Edward was too far down the track to hear her. He reached the end and turned on to the road.

'Where is he going?' asked Elise, approaching Rebecca.

'I don't know. Where does that road lead to?'

'To the village.'

'Gheluvelt?'

'Yes.'

Why would Edward go without me? Rebecca thought. What is he hiding?

'Come inside,' said Elise. 'I'll make breakfast.'

'Do you have a horse? I need to get to Gheluvelt.'

'My horses were taken by the British. You should walk.'

'It's ten miles!'

Elise raised her eyebrows. 'Ten? No, it's two.'

'Edward told me last night it was ten.'

'No, it's two.'

The car went out of sight, taking with it Rebecca's hopes that she could catch up.

'I have a bicycle,' said Elise. 'If you know how to ride one.'

Rebecca had not ridden a bicycle in years. She wobbled down the track, convinced she would fall into a ditch. She made it to the road and found her balance, avoiding the rubble and holes, all the while expecting to see the car coming the other way and Edward ready to explain why he had taken off. But no car approached and she reached Gheluvelt as suspicious as when she had left the farm. Other than the surrounding woodland, the village appeared no different to the others they had passed through since crossing the border. Roofs had collapsed, shutters had been burnt and people were hiding or had left. It was a village for ghosts; one that Rupert had died defending, and now seemed ignored. Rebecca wanted to cry out, to tell people not to hide away, to be grateful for what they had, to show her gratitude for what she had lost. But she held back. Her task was to find Edward. There was only one place he could be.

She headed down a narrow street and began to knock on the doors of the homes that were intact. No-one answered and she emerged into a square. Ahead of her was what remained of a fountain and beyond that a church.

This is where Rupert was shot… where he came to Edward's aid… where Harry's friends had run from the wall… where they were all killed.

An image of Rupert, lifeless and cold, drained of blood and placed among the dead, flashed at Rebecca.

'Madame?'

Rebecca turned slowly. A man, grey and frail, came forward.

'Chateau?' said Rebecca. 'Where is it?'

The man looked confused.

'Chateau?'

The man pointed and said something Rebecca did not understand. She nodded in appreciation and the man returned to his home. It was humble and sloping, but was untouched by the war, unlike his neighbour's house which had been gutted by fire. How is it that the man was protected, Rebecca thought, but his neighbour was not? How is it that he survived and others did not? The image of Rupert flashed at her again, only now he was alive and choking, but no-one was coming to help. He took his hand away from his throat and his head fell back. Life left his eyes.

Rebecca suddenly felt very faint. She leaned the bicycle against a house and sat down on a wall, staring at the abandoned square, waiting for her tears. The church door opened. Edward stepped away from it.

You fool, Rebecca told herself. Edward just wanted to go to church. She went to shout, but her voice cracked. Edward kept his head down and went to the side of the church. The car must be round there, Rebecca thought. She stood up and walked quickly along the edge of the square, trying not to look across at the fountain, and the wall, and the tower where the sniper had been. On reaching the church, Rebecca stood still, listening for the sound of an engine. None came so she followed Edward's path. She saw him and froze. He was in front of her, some fifty yards away, with his back turned. He was standing in front of a tree, and by the trunk was a wooden cross. Edward sank to his knees in front of it, unaware he was being watched. He leaned forward and began to weep, punching the earth with his fists.

'I'm sorry,' he said loudly. 'I'm sorry.'

Rebecca went to scream, but clamped her mouth shut.

Harry didn't lie to me... Edward hanged the sniper... Rupert died because of Edward's cowardice.

Rage took hold of Rebecca and she began to tremble. Something made her pause and look at the cross. It occurred to her that the sniper's family would never come and mourn here; that they would never know the truth. Don't bring anger to this place, she told herself. Don't become like Edward. She retreated without being seen. Her instinct was to break down just as Edward had, but instead she ran, trying to remember where the man had pointed to. She went through the gap in the wall and stopped. Beyond a paddock, at the end of a long, wide lawn, was the chateau. Rebecca walked towards the boundary, recovering her breath, waiting for the grief of what she had just witnessed to confront and overwhelm her. The fence at the top of the lawn was broken in parts and the trees on the perimeter had been shelled or chopped down, but the chateau was untouched, as if everyone had agreed to protect it. Rebecca searched for the cemetery as she made her way down the lawn. The grounds were vast, but not so vast that graves could be hidden. She went to the side of the chateau, expecting to be confronted by the owner or servants. Perhaps they're all dead, she thought, and the house is empty. There was nothing growing in the shattered glasshouse or the flowerbeds, and no voices drifting on the breeze. There was nothing to suggest that life was nearby. The whole estate was a graveyard and the chateau a preserved corpse.

Rebecca walked across a terrace and on to a path that took her into a walled garden. She could hear only her own footsteps on the gravel, yet she felt she was being followed. She closed the gate and glanced over her shoulder. There was no-one there. She exhaled in relief and turned around again. The cemetery was in front of her. Grand headstones of marble with chiselled names and epitaphs were arranged within a square patch of land bordered by a low wall. The soldiers' graves were behind, marked by wooden crosses of different heights set among grass. There was no inscription about the deceased, just a name written in white paint. Rebecca stared at the crosses, all two dozen or so, wondering where the others were. She began to panic. Edward could have lied about Rupert's grave too, she thought. He could have been buried elsewhere and his grave not even identified.

Rebecca wanted to leave at once. She knew she would find it impossible to cope if Rupert's grave was not before her. Instead, she swallowed and stepped forward to the first row of graves.

G.Crawford… C. Hadley… E. Burton… W. Morris… H.Simmons

She moved up to the second row.

A.C Smith… J Turley… G.F Poole…

Rebecca stopped. Her hands started to shake and then her legs. Slowly, she knelt down and stared at the name on the cross: R.J.Salisbury

Rebecca ran her finger over the letters as if she needed convincing of where she was. The paint should have faded by now, she thought; someone must have inscribed Rupert's name again. She glanced at the next grave. The name was also legible and the grass had been recently cut. Perhaps the chateau *is* occupied, she thought. Perhaps someone in the village does care. She tried to remember what she had intended to say to Rupert. Her mind emptied. She could not get past the reality that Rupert's body was just beneath the ground she was resting on. Hours after his death he had been covered with earth at this place, and she had endured a wait of nearly five years for this moment. She wiped her cheeks. Some of what she had intended to say returned to her.

'It's me… I came. I'm sorry you've been alone so long.' She swallowed hard. 'I should have brought the boys. They wanted to come… they need to. It'll help them.' She paused and looked down. 'They miss you… they talk about you, remember things that you've said, and your birthday, and holidays.' She drew in her breath. 'James reminds me of you. He's a wonderful son. So is Sebastian. They've been so strong… you'd be so proud of them.' She swallowed repeatedly to clear her throat. 'You shouldn't have died… you shouldn't be here… you should be at home with us.' She bit her lip. 'I know what happened. I know what you did… I know Edward is to blame… you shouldn't have…' She bit her lip again. Her whole body was shaking. 'I can't do this, Rupert. I can't be without you.'

She rocked back and forth on her knees, unable to control her weeping. Rain began to fall. She realised she had left her coat at the farm. She did not care. The rain became heavier. Rebecca stared at the raindrops hitting the earth and wailed as if she had just learned Rupert had died.

'Come back to me… come back to me… please.'

Rain seeped through her clothes to her skin. She shivered and swept back her hair.

'Rebecca?'

She twisted sharply. Edward was at the gate. Rebecca expected him to approach her, but he stayed where he was. She turned back to the cross and stood up.

'I love you, Rupert,' she said. 'I love you. Wait for me.'

TWENTY-SEVEN

Four months later

'Will you sell the house?' asked Tilly.

'No, I don't wish to,' said Rebecca.

'You'll need to find another tenant soon then. It doesn't seem right being empty. John Thomas needs a home, you could ask him.'

'Who's John Thomas?'

Tilly leaned forward and whispered, 'He's the one over there in the corner on his own.'

Rebecca glanced across the lounge of The Three Tuns. John Thomas, bearded and gaunt, was staring down at his tankard.

'His son died at the Somme.'

'Eric Thomas?'

Tilly nodded solemnly. 'Died the same day as George.'

Rebecca could remember George Turner's face, but not Eric's. For a moment, she wondered if she should re-consider her decision. John Thomas looked as if he needed help, perhaps more so than Tilly.

'I can tell him about River Cottage, if you like,' said Tilly.

Rebecca took a sip of her drink. The brandy's warmth felt good on her chest. 'There's no need. I'm not seeking a tenant.'

Tilly's eyes lit up. 'You're moving back? Oh, please say you are. Please!'

Rebecca shook her head slowly. 'I'm sorry, I'm not. It wouldn't be fair to my aunt.'

Tilly looked confused. 'So if you're not selling the house, and you don't want a tenant, and you're never going to live in it, what are you going to do?'

'I'm giving it to you.'

Tilly raised her eyebrows. 'To me?'

'Correct.'

'I can't take your house.'

'Yes, you can.'

'But it was left to you.'

'Which means I can do whatever I wish with it.'

Tilly still looked confused. 'This… this doesn't make any sense. I already have a home.'

'One you pay for, not one you own. And I suspect, not one you can afford to keep on a widow's pension.'

Tilly swallowed. 'I manage.'

Rebecca reached for Tilly's hand. 'I know you do. But you're my dearest friend and I can't have you just managing, not when you have a family.'

Tilly's eyes began to fill with tears.

'I know what you go through. I know how much it's hurt since Tom died, and I can't ease that. I can ensure you don't worry about money though, and give you a home that will be yours, not mine. I want River Cottage to go to you. I want you to live a life in it. It's what my parents would have wanted.'

Tilly wiped her cheeks.

'They loved you, Tilly.'

Tilly closed her eyes and breathed in. She went to speak, but her tears choked her words.

'Please say you'll accept this,' said Rebecca.

'What about your boys? It should be left to them.'

'Rupert's father was wealthy and I've inherited his share of that wealth. The boys have no need of River Cottage.'

Tilly looked down.

'Don't be embarrassed.'

'It's just so generous of you. I don't know how to thank you.'

'You're not meant to. All I ask is that you accept and your children come to love the house as much as I did growing up.'

Tilly bit her lip. Tears were now streaming down her cheeks.

'You can move in tomorrow if you wish. All you have to say is yes. Will you? For me?'

Tilly smiled. She nodded and said, 'Thank you… thank you.'

'You're very welcome.'

'Promise me you'll visit. Promise me you won't leave it so long again.'

Rebecca held Tilly's hands tighter. 'I promise.'

'This is still your home.'

Rebecca thought of her afternoon, of how she had ridden across the Fens and stared at the distant cathedral and fields of lavender, and said, 'I know it is. It'll always be my home.'

Rebecca left Tilly to go and speak to her children. It was late, but not so late to put off her walk along the riverbank till the morning. She paused outside The Three Tuns and peered into her bag. Nothing had fallen out since she'd last checked it. She breathed in and set off on the path she had walked a thousand times or more, telling herself there was no reason to be anxious. Her anxiety remained, nevertheless. She increased her pace, head down even though there was no wind to brace against. And then she came to it and stopped. The garden gate needed painting, but it had not changed in all these years. Rebecca put her hand on it and with her heart beating faster, raised her head. River Cottage, her home, was asleep. She waited on the front step, half-expecting to hear a voice, or some noise.

Only silence followed and she unlocked the door. The hall was empty of furniture, as was the kitchen. At the parlour door, Rebecca hesitated, dreading what her memory would force upon her. She turned away. She knew she hadn't the strength on any day to remember sitting in the parlour, next to a coffin, staring at her mother's white face as people came and left their sympathy. At the foot of the stairs she paused. Don't go up there, she told herself. You don't have to do this. She closed her eyes for a moment and gripped the banister. All of her conviction about stepping into her parents' bedroom left her and she retreated to the back garden. There was no coal in the bunker, but there was firewood in the outbuilding. Rebecca filled a basket and returned inside, making for the morning room. She arranged the wood in the fireplace, and taking a newspaper and a box of matches from her bag, she started a fire. She sat down on the floorboards and watched it take hold, listening to the cracking of twigs, questioning what she intended to do; whether she was in the right, or if she was just being cowardly.

Time passed. Darkness fell upon the Fens. Rebecca fetched more firewood, refusing to let the flames go out. She sat still, just staring, still questioning, and still believing she was a coward.

'It's gone if you do this. It's over.'

She reached into her bag and pulled out her mother's diary. She ran her hand over the leather, thinking of how the diary was now back where it was begun, where it concealed deceit and shame, and pain. She wished she had never read it. It should have remained hidden. Its truth should never have escaped. And yet it was where her mother retreated in her suffering, because she could never tell the truth. It was what she rested upon, what she used for a relief.

Rebecca flicked her thumb through the pages and began to weep at the sight of her mother's handwriting. She wanted to start again, to read every page, to find something she had missed. Perhaps she had misread what her mother had written; perhaps her father had not helped her to die; perhaps she had imagined it all. She slid her finger into the back pages and opened the diary to the entry for December 2. She swallowed hard and began to read.

I shall no longer be a burden. James has agreed to release me from this slow death. The date will be my choice. May God bless James with the strength needed to support our daughter.

Rebecca slammed the diary shut and tossed it into the fire. It rested between two logs. Fire took hold of its edges. But there was still time to grab it. Some of the pages could be saved. Rebecca stretched out her hand and quickly drew it back. The flames were now turning inwards; the pages were being lost. Rebecca edged backwards, taking temptation with her. The paper was giving new life to the fire. The diary was now past being retrieved. Its truth was destroyed. Rebecca stood up and turned her back on it. She glanced up the darkened staircase, and back down the hall, and left the house. It was Tilly's now.

ACKNOWLEDGEMENTS

I wish to thank the following people for their guidance and encouragement:

Anna Harrison, Tim Wilson, Amanda Clinton, Amy Baker, Natalia Deyr, Sally Connor, Hannah Bartlett, Sarah Clark, Anja Bornman, and my wife, Alexandra.